A Rokian's Curse

Krista Jain

This is a work of fiction. Names, characters, places, and incidents either are the product of the author's imagination or are used fictitiously. Any resemblance to actual persons, living or dead, events, or locales is entirely coincidental.

Copyright © 2019 by Krista Jain

All rights reserved. No part of this book may be reproduced or used in any manner without written permission of the copyright owner except for the use of quotations in a book review. For more information, address: krista@kristajain.com

First Edition: August 2020

Editing by glow_writer
Cover design by Mousam Banerjee
Map by najlakay

ISBN 978-1-7348768-0-2 (hardcover)
ISBN 978-1-7348768-1-9 (ebook)

www.kristajain.com

To all of my readers and supporters.
I would not have made it this far without you.

Contents

1. Stranger on Yon Hill 1
2. Ignorance is Bliss 7
3. Love at First Sight? 14
4. Dreams and Reality 25
5. A Cold Dawn 32
6. Rokians and Vayen Aray 47
7. Fool Me Twice 67
8. The Scholar 86
9. Setting Sail on a Winter Sea 98
10. Stranded 113
11. Red Ivory 128
12. A Selkie's Tide 145
13. A Friend in Need 160
14. Lonely Streets 171
15. Reflection 180
16. A Bandit to Be 199
17. Standing before Power 220
18. Queriven's Phantom 234
19. Alone in Spirit 252
20. Rescue Mission 264
21. Against the Tick of Time 276
22. A Dangerous Goal 292
23. Lost in the Eastern Forest 301
24. Seelie Versus Unseelie 312
25. A Ghost from the Past 322
26. Sylinna's Once Trusted Knight 337
27. Tears and Vengeance 351

28. Lord of the Forest 367
29. The Starlight Festival 374
30. Bittersweet Emotions 392
31. The Calm before the Storm 400
32. Tricking the Trickster 408
33. True Power.. 424
34. All for Nothing 438
35. The Cursed Opal 453
36. Unchanged Lands 464
37. The Rokian's Last Spell 471
38. Second Chances... 487

Glossary 493

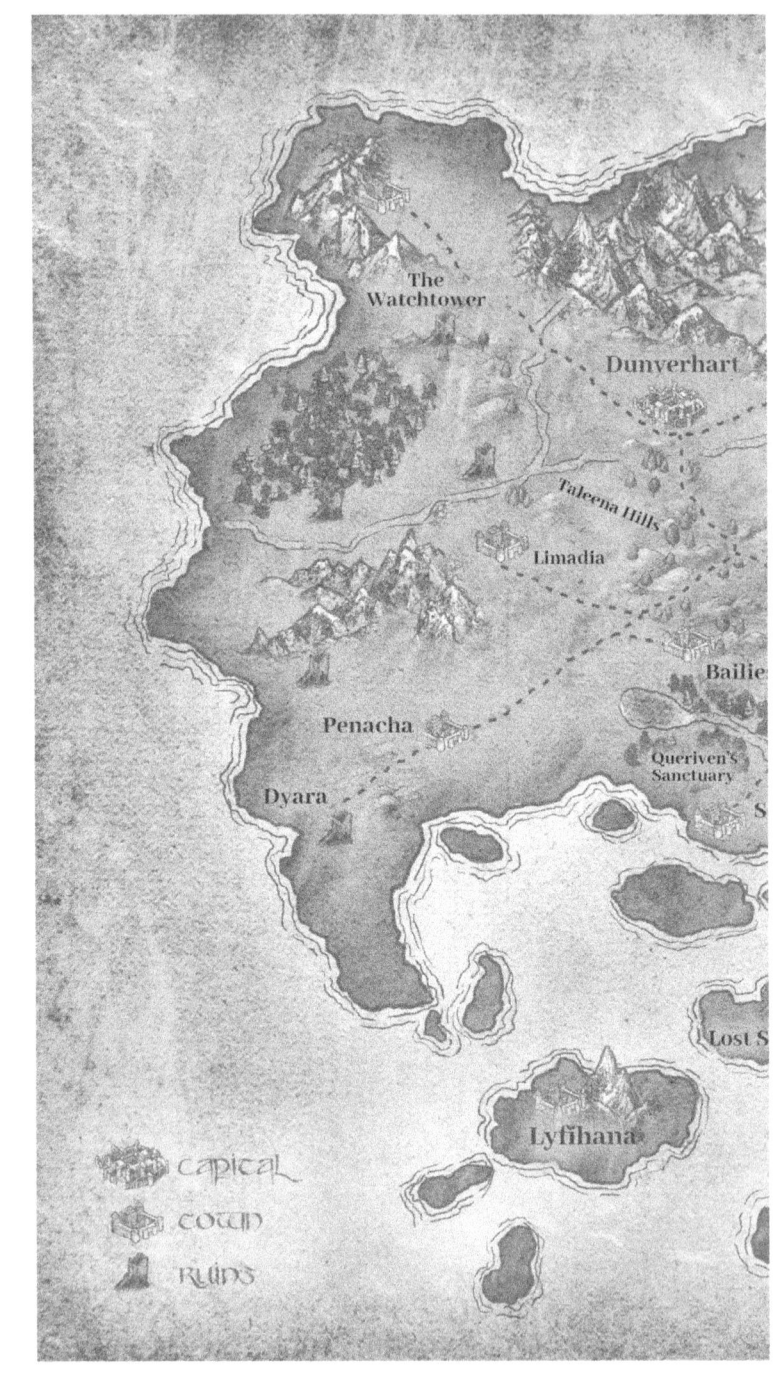

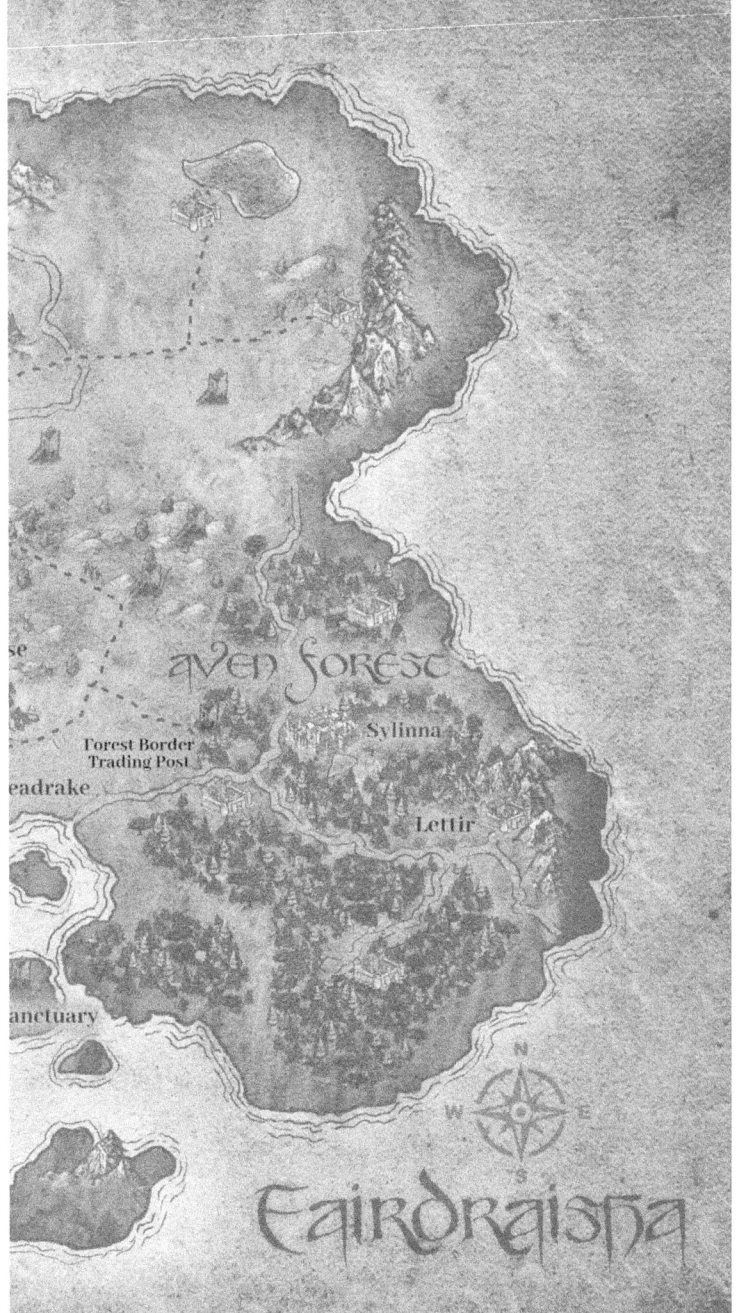

CHAPTER ONE
STRANGER ON YON HILL

Bailiese was over the next hill. The foreign man could already see the smoke billowing up into the air. For late summer, it was already growing chillier by each passing day, especially in the mornings and evenings. The elf's heart began to race as he reached the peak of the last hill. A wide grin spread over his face as he saw the little secluded village huddled in the valley below him. It was just a small town filled with simple families.

The stranger leaned forward and watched the humans walking by, unaware of his presence. The houses were simple, but not poor. They were sturdy and made of strong stone. The tall chimneys' were already puffing out the smoke he saw earlier despite the lingering warm sun. There were small gardens to and fro around the town, but the village specialized in its herd of goats kept beyond wooden fences on the edge of town.

None of that mattered to the elf. He wasn't here for the goats, nor was he here for the town. He's been searching for a long time for something else, and he's finally found it. All that he had to do now was figure out which one of these humans was going to help him. His slender fingers tip-tapped against the ancient horn hanging from his hip. The time was now, and he couldn't wait any longer.

◊ ◊ ◊

Blair Tripps leaned against the fence of the goat pen as she sat on a large box, her face buried in one of her many favorite books. Her work for today was finally done, and now she was winding down in the lovely weather. She didn't even have a jacket on, but that didn't bother her. The braying and calls from the fluffy gray and black goats behind her didn't distract her or move her from her position. Her mind was buried in an unfamiliar world, one filled with frightening giants, magical dragons, and charming elves.

She didn't even stir when someone stopped in front of her. The young man bowed his head, trying to catch a glimpse of the title on the cover. "'The Magical and the Bizarre', huh? You like those kinds of stories?"

Blair blinked and slowly lifted her eyes, the world of her book disappearing like the shine of the hazel colors in her gaze. She recognized the speaker to be Hector, a goat herder only a few years older than her. "Yeah," she replied, tossing back a handful of dark golden hair behind her shoulder. "They're very interesting."

He raised a friendly eyebrow. He wanted to know why she was so intrigued, and it took a while for her to catch on. Blair laughed and slid a dried leaf between the pages of her book and closed it with a light thud. "Who wouldn't dream of seeing something so mysterious? Don't you ever think about going on an adventure? How about seeing something new, something that lives only in memory?"

Hector shrugged, but he understood. Personally, he was very content here in Bailiese working with the other herders, despite him growing up in the big city of Dunverhart for most of his life. Blair, on the other hand, was born and raised here. The Tripps raised goats for many generations. Blair was truly a small-town girl. In a world filled with such mystery and magic beyond their doorsteps, it was only natural for her to be so intrigued with it.

Then Hector realized her innocent eyes were staring up at him now, the many freckles on her face moving with every change of expression. "Is your master doing any better this morning?"

There was a pause, and the young man looked away for a second as he gathered his thoughts. He breathed in a chilly breeze wafting over the still, green grass. His copper hair danced to the side. Finally, he answered as he straightened the locks of hair. "Not much, but I do have high hopes for him."

Blair's pink lips ceased smiling and she regarded him a little more seriously. "You always say that, and he's been sick for a very long time. Aren't you concerned he might not build his strength back again?"

"A little," Hector admitted with no hesitance, "but I'm doing everything I can. I can't stress myself further by trying to do the impossible." The young man was an apprentice of a master blacksmith. But ever since he fell sick, Hector brought him out here, where he could recover in the fresh air. Sadly, it didn't seem to help much.

Hector shifted a boot in the grass and folded his arms. Blair didn't reply, and he gazed at the sun setting on the horizon. "It's getting late. I should go home before it gets dark."

Blair agreed and stood up. She hugged her book tight and shivered. "I should as well. My parents will be wondering where I am." She was already walking before she finished, and Hector waved.

"Give your father my condolences, and I'll see you tomorrow morning!" he called to her. Blair didn't stop, but she looked over her shoulder and smiled.

With each step down the hill, it seemed a little colder, but she wasn't sure. With the shortened days and the approaching change in season, it wouldn't take time at all for the trees to change. Blair lifted her head; she could already smell the crisp leaves and spices.

She had just entered the streets when a sudden sound like a steady siren stole her attention. She froze and cast her gaze to the south where the sound was coming from. It was a low but powerful tone. It broke through the air and increased slightly before it held out a single note for too long. It was a horn of some kind. Blair panicked and looked around at the few people lingering outside, wondering if she was going crazy. They heard it too and dropped what they were doing to listen. The song of the single tune danced over the top of the town, booming in Blair's bones despite it not being very loud. It didn't seem like a distress call; at least, it wasn't from the people of Bailiese. The sound was coming from the hills near the woods, not from the goat pens behind her. It bellowed like the memory of a giant beast, but nothing followed it. It certainly wasn't a war horn because no terrible army rolled down the hills.

Before she could react, the first responders took up shabby swords and tools and headed up to investigate. Blair suddenly turned to the southeast again. Something else grabbed her attention then, but this time, it was more like an emotional tie. It was the horn. She swore it was asking for her in particular. It was asking for help and she had to answer it.

Blair followed the men heading for the southern hills, propelled by the summoning of the horn.

Her legs were on fire, and each cold breath of air froze her lungs. The men charged ahead of her as she stopped and looked back. The village of Bailiese was so small now. Blair could reach down and pluck it from the ground if she wanted to. She looked back up the hill. It was very high up, but she was near the top. That wasn't the main reason she stopped though. The song of the horn disappeared a few minutes ago, but she couldn't explain the feeling that it moved. The caller was closer to the woods now than he was before. How did she know that? If she was wrong, what would cause her to think such a thing in the first place?

Blair decided she wanted to take the chance and seek out her own answers; besides, the men had this area covered. Without a second thought for personal safety, she turned and ran up for the trees.

The voices behind her grew distant and she finally reached flat ground again. Her heart was leaping up to her throat and she almost collapsed. Beyond the physical shock, she was surprised to see she wasn't alone up here. "Dad?!" she yelled at the man facing the trees.

The burly, bearded man turned and regarded her with a curious stare. "Blair," he returned. Duncan Tripps knitted his heavy brows together. "You came too?"

A growing worry was spreading through her now. "What's going on?"

Duncan shrugged and shushed her. "The caller has to be here. I can feel it." Without saying anything more, the bushy man turned toward the trees and took a step forward, but that's when the figure hidden there decided to show himself. The elf allowed the plants around him to ruffle as he came out of the shadows. Duncan staggered back, but the stranger didn't make a move against him. "You... found me. Well done."

Blair studied the man before her. He was tall and slender, his face angular and handsome. Indeed, he was not from here. Blair couldn't believe her eyes when she realized his ears were poking long and tall from his long brown hair.

"An...an elf?!" Duncan cried with horror. He backed up to protect his daughter. "On our land? What do you want from us?!"

The stranger wasn't even fazed. He said nothing else as the humans scrambled back in amazement. Blair wasn't sure what was more astonishing: the fact that an elf, the people who were nothing but a mix of rumors and stories in Fairdraisha, was standing right in front of her, or that she wasn't nearly as scared as her father was. There was a sense of dangerous intrigue and curiosity. She wanted to know more about this strange man.

Before any more questions could be asked, a few villagers started heading their way. They must have seen the company standing by the woods and wanted to see what was going on. There were too many witnesses now. The elf had to leave, but this wasn't for nothing. He knew who he was looking for now. He would be back.

Duncan didn't chase after him as he turned and disappeared in the trees again. The pounding footsteps of the villagers stopped behind Blair and they asked him what he saw, to which Blair's father only bumbled about the presence of the elf. A few of the braver men charged forward in the woods, while the rest stayed behind.

"Was he the one with the horn?" a man asked.

Duncan answered loud and out of fear, "I'm sure that was him! I didn't see him use it, but I just know."

A thousand questions roared out at once. Blair heard someone announce the importance of sending this notice to King Brenmor — that an elf roamed their lands. Then the voices gathered and became nothing but a mix of murmurs. She backed up quietly.

"Blair!" a voice beside her called. It was Hector. His dark eyes were wide with alarm. "I saw you coming this way. What happened? Did you see the elf?"

She nodded, not sure what her response should be.

Hector's worry increased and he held out his arms on either side. "What did he want?"

"I...I don't know..." Blair breathed. Hector didn't press her for information but stood by her side as the people, including Blair's father, continued to bark and argue.

Blair thought about all the tales she had read about the elves. They were considered dangerous people. They aligned forces only with animals and magic. They were untrustworthy and angry. One wrong word and they'll drag you under their powerful magic, then they can do what they wish. They were said to be undeniably beautiful though... Despite the rumors, Blair wanted the truth for herself. However, if she would have known the reason for the elf's appearance, she would have stayed well away from the beginning.

CHAPTER TWO
IGNORANCE IS BLISS

She dreamed about him that night. She walked with him through the winding Aven Forest. Once she stood between the tall whispering trees, the air was thick with the aroma of herbs and flowers. The elf showed her a display of magic that sent lights and sparkles to his fingers. The culture of his city was beyond that of Fairdraisha. It was rich and earthy, and just as mysterious as the stranger himself.

Blair awoke in her familiar bedroom. The light of the early morning sun was poking through her window. She was already cold before she slung off the blankets and goat pelts. She changed clothes and grabbed her jacket, tossing a quick glance at her collection of books. With a skip of her heart, it reminded her that she really saw one of the elf folk with her own eyes. Then she continued out of her room.

Her mother, Isabelle, was already setting breakfast on the table. Blair took a seat and ate as her father continued to rant about the elf they saw yesterday. As it turns out, a messenger set out immediately the night before to alert the king. Blair frowned in thought. The elf didn't do anything. He didn't hurt them or even threaten them. Still, no one had seen an elf in these parts for a long time. Blair couldn't help but think her father and the village were overreacting because of fear. She said none of these things out loud.

Neither one of her parents bothered her, but she crossed their minds. Blair didn't seem very worried and it reminded them of her love for stories about mysterious races and monsters. Both prayed she didn't daydream too much about her encounter with the elf. Much to their dismay, it turned out she was spending a lot of time in her fantasy world.

Even so, she left with her father immediately after eating to help herd the goats. The activities played out as normal and Hector was there as well. Blair tried to engage them with her full attention, but she was often pulled off into her own mind. This made her become more quiet than normal. Hector caught on, thinking she was uncomfortable and tried to cheer her up. She smiled, played along, and continued working like always.

Duncan hoped to distract Blair from her thoughts by suggesting she help her mother with her flower garden after work. He was happy to see her excited about that. Blair loved helping her mother just as much as she liked to help him with the goats, though that didn't stop her from reading her book afterward.

Her father decided he wanted to talk with her about it. After all, they were always pretty open to each other. She was found sitting outside their door with her beloved book in her arms. He approached her, stroking his dark-gold beard, and wondered if he should bother her or not.

Too late. Blair looked up from her open book and smiled. Duncan had his choice made before him. He sat down next to her and sighed. Birds chirped and flew over their heads, and he soon caught a whiff of baking bread. He took in his senses and surroundings, trying to find inspiration to talk to his daughter. Neither said anything for the longest time, and Blair returned to her book. Duncan scanned the pages she read, not surprised to see it was about elves. On the page, tucked away from the words, was a simple drawing of such creatures. It depicted what looked like a young man with a smooth, handsome face. The tall ears were on either side of his head. It didn't look too different from the stranger who visited them on the hill. "...Can I talk to you about something?" Duncan asked with lingering hesitance.

She sensed the seriousness in his tone and rested the book in her lap. Her eyes glittered as she turned to him with respect. Again, the hesitance, but Blair waited patiently. Duncan pressed his lips together and frowned. "I want to understand what you are thinking, particularly in regard to that elf we saw yesterday."

He had thought it would be easier once he started talking, but it ended up being no different. Blair blinked and didn't retaliate, though she looked confused. He continued, "Seeing that... thing... was frightening and dangerous. We're lucky he didn't try to pull us in with that wicked magic of theirs." He paused to study her reaction. She was slowly beginning to catch on what this was about, though she didn't regard him much differently. Those eyes held no fear, like she doubted the elf had meant any harm. That worried Duncan. "Your mother and I are a little concerned you may think differently about this outsider based on your reading."

Blair exclaimed with realization and moved the book from her lap to the side of her chair. "I see!" she answered. Her father was pleased she didn't seem upset. "You have nothing to worry about then. You know I'm interested in tales of magic and other kinds of people, but I also know what I'm doing. There's a strong difference between stories and reality."

Duncan nodded. Her words were correct, but there was something still remaining he wished to say. "There is, but I don't want you to try and predict this stranger's moves based on what you read."

Unfortunately, that didn't sink as much as he'd like. "But isn't it odd? What was with that horn he carried and why did he use it? I can't find anything about a horn like that in any of my books. The one he had is magical. I'm sure of it!" She was beaming with excitement again.

Duncan's heart began to pound. They were right about her. "What does it matter?" he asked. "They're dangerous people. Let the king handle this elf. You don't have to research him yourself."

Blair's eyes dropped and her sudden energy faded. "I'm just... curious. The horn called my name. You said it called yours too. That has to be important, as we were the only ones that know exactly where he was hiding."

"Blair," he repeated, looking her right in the eye. He held her there for a moment. "I don't want to hear any more about it. You'll stay safe as long as you stay home. Understand?"

She sighed and looked away, bringing her book back up in her arms. She ran a finger over the leather binding, tracing the indentation of the title. "Fine," she replied. When her eyes lifted, Duncan saw the life and playfulness coming back to her freckled face. "I'll go back to my stories of knights and dragons. They were more entertaining anyway."

Duncan smiled, causing wrinkles to appear around his eyes. Satisfied, he patted his girl on the head and went into the house.

Blair opened her book back to the page she read last. Immediately, her heart skipped a beat when she stared into the image of the handsome elf. He was stunning and far from her ordinary lifestyle. If the elf on the page could speak, what would he say to her, she wondered. She had no idea, but she imagined it with that soft and melodic accent of his. Do all elves talk like that or was it just him?

There was no way she could find the answer, as that sort of thing wasn't found on paper. Blair hugged the book close and finally went inside.

Blair went to bed hours ago — that or she lost track of time. Either way, the memory of sitting with her family at the supper table seemed so long ago. She growled and threw an arm over her eyes. She wished she would fall asleep already! It was bad enough that her parents were telling her what to read. She didn't want her father to be suspicious of her lack of energy while herding the goats.

Seconds ticked by in a soundless rhythm. She was still awake. Blair tossed her long hair behind her and buried her face into her pillows. She was nearly choked by the smell of goat leather and feather-packed fabric. Her wide eyes blinked back the darkness again. The elf occupied her mind. He was all there was when she closed her eyes.

Finally giving in, she sat up and looked around the room. Or at least she tried to, as she could only make out the slightest outlines of her shelves and desk. She tuned in to the silence and thought she heard her parents snoring in the other room, but she wasn't sure if it was her imagination or not. The whistle of an autumn wind was one thing she knew was real. If her window was open, it would be sweeping her soft curtains on either side of the frame.

She almost stood at the call of a wolf, but let it go. There was no need to wake her father for this one, as it was too far away to be a concern. Blair sank back into the warmth of her bed, closing her eyes one more time. Her shoulders were more relaxed than they had been and she listened for the ruffling leaves outside.

With her focus on the calming sounds out the window, she almost fell asleep. Almost. Instead, there came another sound; one that started low and played on like a song. Blair's sleepy mind didn't recognize it at first. Then she jolted upright. It was calling her name again.

Her breath came quickly, her blood pumping with adrenaline. The elf was back! She flung her legs over the side of her bed and stood. What should she do after that? Should she alert her father? Did he already hear it? She couldn't stand around and do nothing, so she changed clothes and pulled on her boots.

It was then she realized her parents were still sleeping. Her first step out the door was to wake them, but then she stopped. This may be her only chance to see the stranger again. Already, she knew she could find him. She already knew where he was.

Was this a dangerous thought? Yes, it was, but it was also a bold chance to escape her peasant lifestyle. She may never see anything like him again. Her beloved stories will always remain that; just stories of epic splendor she'll never see for herself.

She grabbed her jacket, a lone candle, and answered the call.

No one came out to stop her as she left the house. Her town looked so different in the dead of night. It was now drenched in deep blue. The light of the moon and twinkling silver was the only thing distinguishable between the profound sky and solid hills.

Blair wrapped her arms tight, wishing she carried with her the warmth and comfort of her bed. Her breath was already appearing as puffs of steam.

She was almost out of the streets before common sense snagged her. Blair was about to face a potential danger. She shouldn't go unarmed. She turned around at a little fenced-in garden she passed and saw a hoe leaning against the wood. It was better than nothing, and she wanted to find him before he disappeared again. Blair took it with her and headed again for the southern woods.

Her lungs were lining with frost with every breath. Finally, she reached the top of the hills. The woods were just ahead. She swallowed her rising fear. She made it so far already and the morning would be arriving soon, but the silhouette of the tall, concealing trees intimidated her. The stranger was dangerous enough, but she may encounter other beasts in there. She looked down at her sleepy town. It was far too late to turn around. The elf was still here, and he was close.

Blair crept up to the trees with a shaky step.

The elf's presence was starting to fade. The cry of the horn hadn't sounded for ages. A wolf cry tore her focus. It sounded closer. She spun, holding the hoe before her as her gaze spilled desperately around the trees. Even with her candle, she could barely see anything in here. It was at this point that she regretted leaving her bed. She wished to turn around and head home, but which way did she come from? She was already lost. The realization had her shaking with fear.

Then a dark form, moving too quick for the candle to recognize it, rushed before her eyes and ruffled the plant life behind her. She turned and lost her breath again. He stared at her with a shimmer of deep emerald, frozen with his head turned behind his shoulder. Long, light brown hair wafted around his lithe shoulders and neck. His features were sharp and handsome, and his lips were thin and tan. She'd bet his eyes could track a skilled assassin to the ends of the earth. And most of all, she noted the ears that pointed out from his hair. Time slowed to a stop. It was him, the elf!

His expressionless face turned away and he marched ahead. "Wait for a second!" Blair called, stumbling forward a little. "You're just leaving me here?" But he didn't flinch and he didn't turn around. She had no choice but to follow him.

CHAPTER THREE
LOVE AT FIRST SIGHT?

The form ahead of her moved through the trees and fallen branches like he was at home with the rougher terrain. The night didn't shorten his vision. Blair had little luck. She tripped, struggled, and lost the stranger in every turn. It didn't help that he wore a dark cloak. Yet, she'd catch a tiny trace of him, an outline, a boot lifting off the ground, something that kept her on his trail. He also didn't seem to mind her following him. She was sure he could have lost her if he wanted to, but his movements didn't change.

Finally, she lost him one final time. Then she burst free of the woods. She didn't know she was this close to the lake and the sight of it shocked her. It was like it ran up to meet her from nowhere and she was lucky she didn't fall in the cold waters. Now that she was free from the thick dark trees, the moon shone again, sparkling in a wavy image in the water. The starlight twinkled and danced, and hovering insects dipped on the surface. The water was rich and lively, and it offered a light smell of fish that mixed with the stronger leaves and wood from the trees. She drank in the different scents, almost tasting the ripe texture.

She glanced up at the sky. It must have been a few hours after midnight. When her gaze fell again, she realized yet again she wasn't alone. The stranger was by the lake edge, watching the rippling reflections, As soon as she looked at him, he returned her gaze. "Beautiful night, is it not?" he asked.

There it was, the one thing she recognized the most from him, his sweet foreign accent. It flowed to her ears exactly as she remembered it. No doubt, this was the same stranger she was looking for. He sounded like he was the true essence of the forest, breathing life with every word he spoke.

Blair had never seen an elf before; only very few people had. They lived within the thick Aven Forest far to the southeast of the continent, but either side of the borders minded their own business. Back in many generations past, the kingdoms used to trade with each other. The elves and humans met on the borderline and exchanged goods, but mutual disagreements broke them apart.

And because of those disagreements between the two rulers, they began to show hostility to each other, not wanting the other to cross the border. King Brenmor would not be happy to know this stranger was here. So why was he here?

Blair leaned forward, trying to find her voice and respond to the stranger, but too many questions ran through her head and she remained silent. "Don't worry," said the stranger, turning his gaze back to the lake. "I know why you followed me. I would have done the same if I were in your shoes. The only question I have is, what will you do now?"

But Blair's confused mind didn't have room to take in and digest his message. "You...You're an elf, aren't you?"

He sighed. "That I am. I came all the way from the forest itself."

Blair continued to edge closer. "So, why are you here? And why did you use that horn earlier? I'd figure someone of your heritage would want to stay quiet."

The stranger didn't move for a second. Blair marveled at his rich green eyes he rolled to the side before he turned and came to her. "So many questions, but you're right, again. Truth is, I was... looking for someone. Yes, someone I had lost within these woods. I was growing desperate. I hoped they would hear me."

"So... Did you find them?"

The stranger shook his head. "No, unfortunately. And it looks as if consequence caught up with me. I've been found out."

"What now?"

"That's a good question. What will we do now? The outcome lies with you, I'm afraid."

Blair blinked and scrunched her face in further confusion. "With me? Why am I to decide?"

The stranger shrugged. "Well, I believe you know I'm not supposed to be here. Either you allow me to continue my mission here or you turn me in to your people. I won't fight you, if that's what you choose."

She stared at him for a while, considering what he was suggesting. Was this even happening? Maybe she fell asleep after all and this was nothing but a weird dream. Nothing this extraordinary can happen to her small town. And even if it did, she wouldn't be the one involved in it. It was more than unlikely. She looked back behind her and saw only the faint outline of the trees, then she looked to the lake. One by one, she listened to her senses. All were there, and even though the situation still seemed odd to her, it was unlikely she was asleep.

She met the face of the foreigner. He was waiting patiently for an answer. He seemed so calm, as if he was sincere with letting her decide. She was sure he wouldn't break away if she tried to bring him back to town. Though his eyes, sparkling with the moonlight around them, searched hers curiously. For a second, she held her breath. He could have hurt her already if he wanted to, she realized. Could it be so hard to believe his story? If what he said was true...if there was another within those woods, she couldn't tear him away and leave them behind. "You're sure they're in those woods? Are you telling the truth?"

His slender but muscular chest puffed as he inhaled his answer. "Every word I said is true, and he was in those woods last I saw a trace of him."

"Then we need to make sure he's safe."

The stranger breathed a sigh of relief she didn't know he was holding. "Thank you...thank you so much. We owe you our lives."

His selfless plea tugged on Blair's heartstrings. Those eyes weren't lying. Driven to his mission, she blurted the next part out without thinking about the consequences. "And I want to help you."

The stranger's eyes lifted and a smile spread over his face. "That's a great idea. I'm sure that with the two of us, we could find him. The name is Queriven by the way."

She bowed her head, holding the hoe out by the side. "I'm Blair Tripps. I work with my father to herd the goats of the village."

He bowed further, "Miss Tripps, it's an honor to meet you, truly. So when shall we meet again?"

She thought for a second. Blair would be helping with the goats in the morning, but she doesn't really want to after her uncomfortable talk with her father. Then she thought of something else. She'll need to sneak away without anyone knowing she's coming here. It might be difficult at times, but she was sure she could manage. "How about I meet you here tomorrow before supper? I think I can slip by unnoticed then."

"Great! I'll meet you then," he replied, glancing out to the east. "But it's too dark for a young human to be wandering about. Allow me to walk you back to your village."

Blair wished she could explain to her family what she just witnessed and how the elf really wasn't as bad as people thought! His eyes revealed a green canopy of leaf-filtered light in the heart of summer, his voice as sweet as golden honey.

As it turns out, the town of Bailiese was awake again, though the people didn't go far in the hills. It was just too dangerous to go searching around the woods at night. There wasn't an outright panic, but a few people heard the horn and woke others up.

Her father and mother were among them, unfortunately. And they were on the edge of panic after they found their daughter's room empty. Blair told them nothing of the stranger; just that she woke and stepped outside in curiosity. She lied when she said she didn't leave the town. That didn't stop her father from complaining about her choice of books again.

She chose to ignore him and retreated to her room. There, she finally slept the last few hours before morning. She was already excited to return to the lake again.

But by the time she rose from bed again, both her mother and father wanted to speak with her. They thought her choice of books was an unhealthy obsession of hers. They wished she was more focused and stopped living in a daydream. Finally, Blair retaliated against them. Her books were never a problem in the past! They were only pestering her now because of one creature she read about that came to their little village.

Her parents weren't convinced and told her to lay off the stories for a good long while at least. Duncan hated the expression she returned them. Her normally cheerful smile was gone and her eyes were now filled with hurt and betrayal. He didn't back away, no matter how sad it made him.

The father and daughter had a unique relationship together. Now it was hard to work in the fields. There was an uncomfortable silence between them. There were no jokes or chit-chat. Even Hector caught on to the family difficulties, and he left Blair alone when he noted how annoyed she was.

Perhaps, going back to bed would have been the smarter idea. That way, she wouldn't have to argue with her parents over and over, and she would be more rested when she left to see Queriven.

Her disagreements with her family only made her more excited to see the exotic elf again. She still couldn't believe that she spoke with him and that he wasn't nearly as evil as they say.

With work done for today, Blair allowed her father to leave without her. At first, he protested, but she lied and said she wanted to spend time with the goats for a while. Well, it wasn't totally a lie, as she certainly didn't want to head home yet. Still, she's already told more lies than she ever had in her entire life. Guilt was already creeping into her mind. But between her parents and the elf, she thought it was worth it. She shouldn't have been so blinded by the elf's tricks. Her life was fixing to change forever.

◊ ◊ ◊

"Miss Tripps, you came!" Queriven yelled as she came into view. Blair marched at a quick and steady pace, rounding the edge of the woods where the trees thinned and the lake could be clearly seen.

"I hope I didn't keep you here for long," she replied, rushing to stand by his side. She was already more joyful. She didn't show any of her problems from home.

"No, you're fine."

She huffed, trying to catch her breath from her long walk. Queriven regarded her for a moment. "I hoped to have found a fresh clue or something in the woods, but I'm afraid I haven't found anything. Looks like we'll be searching blindly today."

Blair placed her hands on her hips for a second before a question came to her mind. Then, she smoothed the folds of her simple blue dress and asked. "Before we start, can I ask you something?"

Queriven blinked, his eyebrows lowering. "Of course, go ahead."

Blair thought back for a second and shifted her weight to her other foot. "It's about that horn. Whenever I hear it call, it's like it speaks to me directly. Even if I didn't know where it was coming from, I knew exactly where you were. It only worked on my father and me; no one else. Why is that?"

Queriven merely laughed. "That's certainly an interesting question, Miss Tripps, though I don't think I have a good answer for that one. I was using it to call for my missing friend, but I haven't heard from him. I found evidence of an attack right at the forest border. I chased them down and found two dead humans. I assumed those were his kidnappers. I'm thinking he's injured as well, and I tracked him here. I don't know why he didn't return, but I fear for his safety." He fell into seriousness again and looked at her. "Turns out you heard the horn calling for you. Why do you think it happened like that?"

She sighed. "I have no idea."

Again, he responded with a laugh, then he pondered seriously for a moment. "Maybe even some humans can sense a bit of magic when it's around them."

"Magic?" she whispered, a falter in her step. "Do you mean yourself or the horn?"

"Both, I guess."

She frowned and tilted her head. "You mean the horn is magical?"

"I haven't told you about it, have I?" Queriven reached for the horn strapped on his waist and held it close, studying the wondrous design. It must be ivory from some rare monster, judging from the tint of deep red. "This horn has been passed down, even in a few elven generations, through my family. It was originally given to us by a long-forgotten people." He seemed to pause when the last part left his lips, as if he tasted the words before it echoed. Queriven turned it over in his hands and Blair could barely make out the sketches in the ivory. It must have been really old. "It was already enchanted and they told us to call using the horn, and no matter where we may be, they'll find us."

"So... If they can hear it, they'll know exactly where it's coming from, whether it's hidden somewhere or it stops?"

He thought about it for a moment, then dropped the horn back to his waist. "For a time before the magic fades away, yes."

Blair frowned and repeated her earlier question. "But for some reason, it worked on me and my father and no one else?"

She still didn't find her answer through him. He turned to her, his foreign gaze speaking a mysterious language. "Yes, it would appear so." The elf offered her nothing else and glanced up at the sky. Clouds were creeping under the colors of sunset. "It'll be growing dark soon. We should look for a trail before it's too late." And he started for the woods with Blair at his heels.

Blair was only human. She couldn't see every snapped twig, every impression in the soil, but she marveled at how the elf could. He picked up everything as easily as Blair could tell how her goats were feeling. In the end, she wished she was of more help to him. And when she wasn't struck with awe by what he was doing, she spent most of her time trying to cover more ground and fanning out around him.

Queriven was quiet most of the time they were in there. He was focusing on every little detail, though once in a while he would show her and explain something about the soil and tracks.

Night closed in, and he stood up from his position over the ground. "Well," he lamented, "I'm beginning to wonder if he's still here. I don't know if I'll ever find him again."

There was a genuine pain in his voice. Sympathy took her and she dearly wished he wasn't so upset. "I'm sure if anyone can find him it'll be you," she replied shyly.

Queriven began walking back, taking the two of them back out of the woods. His shoulders slumped and he didn't respond to her words of encouragement. Once they were by the water's edge again, he sat down, watching as a light evening breeze rippled the water.

She stood quietly by him, taking in her surroundings again. Her parents would be wondering where she was. They would be finishing up supper without her by now, but she couldn't bring herself to leave, not with Queriven like this.

So after a short while, she plopped down with him. Together, they sat in silence and watched the last rays of the sun. She looked at him several times, like she was searching for something to say, but changed her mind each time.

He, on the other hand, remained still and quiet, never looking away from his stare at the water's surface. It seemed he'd given up on all hope. She could see it in his eyes. It was like the crisp breeze stopped, leaving the trees in a stagnant air.

Finally, Blair gathered the courage to speak. "What is his name?"

Queriven was still for a long moment before half-turning to

look at her. "Aswren," he replied and then turned back to the water. "He always had my back even when I was wrong."

She nodded, not knowing how to reply him. She thought about asking more of him, but by then, her built-up courage was gone and she looked away. It was Queriven who spoke next. "It's about time you headed back. Your family will be wondering where you are."

She hesitated. "I suppose you're right, but..."

"Don't worry, it'll be fine."

She hugged her knees and looked to him again. "What are you going to do now? Will I see you again?"

For the first time since they left the woods, he matched her stare. She watched him curiously. There was a pause for a moment before he shrugged and tossed long strands of hair from his shoulders to his back. "I don't know," he admitted. "I made a vow that I wouldn't return without Aswren, but I'm not finding any answers here."

"Can I help you tomorrow?"

It was Queriven's turn to regard her curiously. "Why do you care so much? I have nothing to return."

She already asked herself that question. Perhaps, it was an excuse to escape her own troubled life and help someone with their own. Or maybe, he was the exact thing she was looking for; that magical creature she's never had in her life before, and it was too soon to let him disappear in the fog.

She was unable to express those feelings in words. "I just... I don't know. I've never had the chance to help someone from the outside before. And I always thought the elves were more like people than monsters."

A short smile eased on his face. "Thank you. I really do appreciate all you've done." And he stood up, moving a bit more freely than he did a while ago. "If you wish to meet me tomorrow, I'll be here."

Blair rose up with him. "I'll see you tomorrow then."

He turned, nodding toward Bailiese. "I'll walk you back again. I don't want to be responsible if something should happen to you."

She thanked him and followed him away from the lake.

"Queriven, I have something else I wanted to say."

"Yes?" he asked without turning or stopping.

"The villagers were very upset you were here the other day. They've already sent for help. A search party will start soon."

At first, he said nothing, then his pace slowly came to a stop. He looked at her intently.

Blair squirmed shyly under his foreign gaze. "They believe your kind is evil. Did you know about that? What do they say about humans in the forest?"

If he was worried about the soldiers coming toward Bailiese or the viewpoints of humans, he didn't show anything. "The humans," the elf began, taking in the autumn air and running his hands over his cold arms, "believe in a lot of silly rumors. I'm sure you know about that by now. Sadly, the time between our people was a long one on the humans, and so they began making up stories because of their fears. The elves remember your kind better, as some of us were still alive back in the day of trade." He sighed and embraced the cold, seeing he couldn't help it now. "But it's too late to change their mind. I'm sure a search party is coming and there's nothing I can do about it."

Blair slumped. She wished once again she could help. If Queriven's captured, he may never find Aswren. The beautiful mystery that was the elf gave her a reassuring smile. The sight of it changed his entire looks, those eyes brightening like emeralds, his curved lips warm enough to melt ice. "Don't worry about it. I'll be fine. I'll even hide for a while if I need to. Thanks for telling me." He bowed gracefully before her and held out his arms to the village in the valley. "This is as far as I'll go. Have a good night, Miss Tripps."

Blair returned his smile and wished him farewell before she descended down the hill. Queriven watched her depart until she blended in with the dark ground. The chill came back over him and he breathed a puff of white air at his fingers. The girl was gullible. She believed every lie so easily. Just a little more and she'll be his. He could hardly wait, and it may take longer for him to convince her to follow him away from here. If only there was a way…

Humans were foolish. He's seen her type before. This one

had her head in the clouds, where she spends too much time in stories away from her own duties. Perhaps, he could use this to his advantage somehow. She seemed so enamored by him. Maybe she could even fall for him if he played right. That would speed up her demise. The elf smirked and retreated back to the trees.

CHAPTER FOUR
DREAMS AND REALITY

Several weeks later.

Autumn finally arrived. Its cold breath whisked every morning, carrying with it the scent of old, fire-colored leaves. Blair had to wear her warm jacket almost every day now, and though she helped her father with the goats most of the time, she always kept her promises to meet Queriven by the lake.

They've never been able to find any sign of Aswren, though she still continued to try and help regardless. She was with Queriven every moment she could until the search party eventually came and Queriven disappeared for a while. No one was able to find a trace of him and the party left after a long week. Then, she retreated back to the lake and was glad to see he returned.

At first, her father justified her frequent disappearances, saying that she needed extra space in this hard time where they did little but argue with her. Now, of course, they were growing a little more suspicious, and it was becoming harder and harder for her to reason with them.

It sent Blair running to visit with Queriven even more. He had Blair head over heels already. He could see it in how she looked at him. The two would sit by the water and talk about their lives until sunset. Blair wasn't sure what part of their talks she liked best — those where he listened to her troubles without judgment or those where he spoke of the forest to the east.

He talked of his homeland with passion, describing it as a place unique to the rest of the world. A place you would have to see to believe it exists. He said the trees there were taller than castles, and everything was pure and natural, the way things should be. He said the people only used what they needed, and whatever they took had to be repaid.

Blair would close her eyes and cast herself into his memories like she was there to take in every moment. She used his forest-grown accent as her guide as she walked through the tight trees. The wilderness was aflutter with mysterious glowing lights of magical origin and the cities were like hers in ways they were not. When she was at home, her heart was still bursting with fluffiness and her mind lingered with him every minute, longing to be a part of him.

She made a mistake by daydreaming too much again. Her mother confronted her one day. "You're reading that book again," Isabelle remarked more than asked.

Blair lowered the book on the kitchen table and raised dangerous eyes. "Just for fun" was her only answer.

"Your father and I are concerned those books have been too unhealthy for you."

Blair growled. Her mom ignored it as she picked the empty glasses from the table. The chinking only enraged her further. "We've been down this before. I'm not researching that elf anymore. The king's men found nothing. The elf has gone away."

Isabelle's tone was rich with anger. "Maybe, but his appearance has changed you. We've decided it might be best for you to leave off the stories in general."

Blair's jaw fell agape. "You can't be serious! I'm grown up now. You can't just declare I'm going to stop reading!"

She couldn't tell if her mother was still full of rage or if she was simply pleading now. She stopped her chore of cleaning the table and faced her daughter. "Please, Blair, won't you listen? Just walk on the ground for a while. We're worried you might get hurt. Bailiese is the only place where you'll ever be safe."

Blair's content face disappeared and she flinched, jerking away from the table. "You're the ones who won't listen! I'm not planning to leave home! Why can't you hear that? This is only a hobby."

Isabelle came up to the table and held out her hand, hoping to hold her attention. "A life in the clouds doesn't work in this village. I don't know where you got it."

Angry tears stirred in Blair's eyes as she stared at her mother. Finally, Blair turned for the door without another word.

Upset, Blair broke away and ran for the lake only to find Queriven upset as well. He was standing silently by the water as usual, but this time, he didn't turn and greet her. All the hurt from home forgotten, she sidestepped around him to see his face.

A solemn, broken gaze dropped on her for just a second before staring off in the distance again. "Queriven," she called out quietly. "What happened?"

He sighed, his breath cracked and uneven. "I found Aswren last night." Silence crept in and she didn't know what he meant until he didn't elaborate.

A wave of nausea fell over her and she gripped his arm, giving him a light squeeze. "I'm sorry," she whispered, drawing closer to him. "Where was he?"

"Several hours up the road," he answered. "He'd suffered from a terrible wound, probably from that fight where I found the kidnappers. Aswren took shelter in one of the old forts and..." He trailed off but remained steady. He looked down at Blair where she still hugged his arm. "My mission here is done. I will return him to the forest where he can finally rest."

Worried eyes glanced up to him, but she said nothing. What will she do now? Her home was falling apart and the one person who helped to take the pain away was leaving. He didn't belong here; she always knew that and she always knew he would have to return to the forest one day, but now her heart hurt.

Gently, Queriven took his arm from her grasp and wrapped her tight with it. "You've risked everything to help me. You gave it so freely and I could never begin to repay your kindness. I never imagined I could find someone out here who'd treat me like a friend." Still gripping her tight, he turned her around so he could look at her eye to eye. "And that's why I'd thought to ask you to come with me."

The words echoed in her mind before she finally understood what he asked of her. "Come with you?" The idea fell into her gut, weighing everything down.

"Yes," he answered. "So you could see the forest with your own eyes! All the days we've spent together out here you've been wanting to see it. You could leave all your worries behind here and start anew."

Time stopped. Nothing moved for a long while and Blair fidgeted, looking from Queriven's determined expression to the border of Bailiese just around the distant hill. This was her chance. This was her lifelong dream. She'd spent her whole life reading and listening to stories of magical places and countries. She never dreamed of fame and fortune. All that she wanted was a memory to last her a lifetime. If it was even half as magical as he described, it would be everything she could ever ask for.

So why was she hesitating? Her heart was pounding at her to scream "yes!" and her head was already dizzy from racing thoughts, but still, she couldn't give him an answer. She instead stared at the village behind Queriven's shoulder.

This was the exact prediction from her mother. All this would prove that she, Blair Tripps, was just like they thought her to be, daydreaming and reading stories until she ran off on her own. And despite their arguments and troubles, she dearly loved her home and family. They may argue; her mother may have wrongly accused her, but she couldn't leave home. Memories of the good times with her parents floated in her mind. There was still a chance for them to learn and grow even closer as a family. "Well..."

Queriven was growing excited. "It's the least I could do.

Please."

She met his gaze again, which was now growing desperate. "Our time together means the world to me and always will," she answered calmly, "but..."

"I know," he interrupted and shook his head. "And Blair, I've never felt this way for another person before. I feel like I can't live apart from you. The forest would be too far if you don't come with me."

"I..."

He continued, "We could raise goats on our own! And if you're still homesick, I can even bring you back here if you wish." Queriven was growing more and more anxious by the minute when she didn't answer him, and his movements turned for the rougher. With each word, he shook her more and his grip became tighter, falling from her shoulders to her arms.

Blair's heart began to pound for a different reason then. She tried to pull him off, but his grip didn't weaken. "I can't go with you! Not now, please!" she begged. "Let go. You're hurting me!"

Queriven still held on but was lowering his tone. "Blair, don't fight." But she never stopped thrashing. He tried to hold her still. "I need you."

But the longer he held on, the more she kicked and pushed. Finally, he let go. Blair nearly threw herself down to the ground as he did. "There...See?" he whispered. "I didn't mean to hurt you. I'm sorry."

But Blair didn't reply. Tears were forming in her eyes and she held her wrists close to her chest. Queriven slowly approached her like she was an agitated tiger. With each step, she took one back as well. "I wanted to come with you," Blair began, her voice breaking and quivering with each syllable, "but now's not the right time."

"Why is now different from any other? There's always going to be something keeping you here! Do you want to grow old and gray here?" He nodded towards Bailiese. "You need to make a decision. If you don't leave now, you'll be trapped here forever." He brought his hands toward his own chest. "Or you could have everything you wanted with me. You could have freedom."

"I've already made a decision!" she yelled, stopping him in his tracks. He watched her quietly as she took a second to breathe and calm herself. "I'm staying here in Bailiese."

Slowly, Queriven's expression dropped and a fit of sinister anger flashed in his once beautiful eyes. Then suddenly, he lunged at her again, grabbing her wrist and pulling her arm forward. "I didn't want to do this."

"What are you doing?!" she yelled and tried to break free from him again, screaming all the while for someone who couldn't hear her. No matter her struggles and calls, Queriven barely seemed to notice or even care. Instead, he closed his eyes and fell into a low chant.

Blair's fight for freedom only intensified when she heard the words she didn't recognize. He was using magic on her. She didn't know what kind, but she needed to free herself and now. Adrenaline pumped through her veins, making her blind with strength, but still, she was unable to break loose.

The spell took only a moment. When the words stopped, angry eyes popped open and he pushed her back. "This is your fault, you know?" he said in a different voice, one free of the melodic accent; one deeper and rougher, like a dry cliffside. He turned around. "It didn't have to end like this. You've forced my hand."

Blair held her wrist tight and slowly fell to the grass as she watched the man she once loved leave her like a pile of garbage. But it was his last words to her that stained her precious memory of him. Words she would remember until her final breath of life.

"Now you have only a year. When the trees catch the colors of fire again, you'll no longer be a part of this world."

She collapsed on the ground and buried her arm under her, whimpering and crying to herself. For the hours she remained there, she was too terrified to look at the wrist he held. She couldn't even imagine what might be there now, but she didn't want to see it. She didn't want to know.

When she finally decided she needed to see the damage left behind, she held it up right before her eyes, trembling all the more when she saw it. It was like three strands of thin wire, entwining and spinning around her wrist completely like a binding. He cursed her.

CHAPTER FIVE
A COLD DAWN

The cold began to bite like a viper as the sun faded, but she barely noticed it. Blair's mind was too much in a turmoil to notice much of anything. It'd been several hours since Queriven left, but still, she remained the same where he'd left her, curled in the first fallen leaves, whimpering and clutching her marked wrist.

You'll no longer be a part of this world. She heard him saying over and over again in her mind. She was dying, like the bind on her skin was sucking her very life force. The worst part was that she had a year before it finishes her off and there was nothing she could do about it. It would have been better if he had killed her there and then. This was a fate worse than death. *You'll no longer be a part of this world.* Regret filled her stomach. She shouldn't have listened to him. It was just too unreal. Everything they said about the elves was right after all.

Why did she trust him? He was an outsider, and obsession took control of her. She should have known better. The thought made her burst into another series of sobs. She was a complete fool. Why didn't she listen to her parents when they told her to leave it alone? They already knew this would happen, and they've been telling her from the start.

Finally, she lifted her reddened, swollen eyes to see the last few lights still lit in Bailiese. What will she tell her parents? She froze, pondering the question seriously, but she didn't have an answer. She needed to tell them something, right? The thought of explaining her visits with the stranger made her sick. But she can't afford not to share her visits, she lamented. She'll be gone in a year. She couldn't do it. This was her mistake and she could only hate herself for it.

The grass quaked under her hands as she pushed herself up from the ground, though she didn't know if it was from the disbelief or the pounding headache she now had. She held a hand to her head, swaying back and forth as she took a few steps toward town.

She didn't cry for help, and she didn't wave for anyone's attention when she was back in the village again. Desperately, she wanted to feel the safety and comfort of her little home, but nothing penetrated her cold fear.

So she stayed quiet, tried to keep straight, and wiped her wet face before she stepped back into the house. Duncan rose from his spot by the hearth when she did. "Your mother told me you were out," he remarked. "We just finished with supper, but if you still want something, you can head to the kitchen."

But Blair couldn't speak. She was fighting too hard to not make a sound before him. Duncan's welcoming smile melted away then and he came to comfort her. "Are you all right?" he asked, placing a calm hand on her shoulder. Blair twitched at his touch but didn't push him away. "Isabelle told me you two had a pretty bad argument earlier. I'm so sorry it became so ugly. She wanted to apologize to you."

"I'm fine," Blair lied, hoping he didn't notice the new mark on her right arm. She kept it down and by the folds of her dress. "Just needed some fresh air; that's all." She then gently brushed him off and slowly came to the kitchen where her mother was wiping down the dining table.

At the sight of her, Isabelle froze mid-wipe and met her eyes. "Sweetie, I am so sorry," she said after a moment of hesitation. "I've said some things I shouldn't have. I was mean and controlling, and I've hurt the two of us because of it. I was wrong and foolish to treat you like a young child. I can't keep you from your books and neither can I change who you are."

Blair came around her side of the table and wrapped her arms around her. "I'm sorry too," she whispered, cracking up again. "I want to work out something between us; I really do."

Isabelle hugged her tighter. "I'll try to be more understanding and patient from now on, darling. It'll be all right."

No, it won't. The voice in Blair's head screamed, but she didn't say anything.

Isabelle suddenly released her tight embrace of Blair, looking a bit livelier. "Now, the food has gone cold but I can still fix you a plate. What do you want?"

Blair was anything but hungry, even though she hadn't eaten anything for a long time. It'll just give her a stomach ache anyway. "Actually, I think I'd rather go to bed."

Isabelle turned her head to the side. "Are you sure?" she asked. "You're not looking very well. Maybe a spot of food will fill those cheeks back up."

But Blair still waved her off. "I'm sure, Mother."

Isabelle lovingly brushed back a dark blonde strand of hair as Blair went past her. "Well then, come get me if you need anything."

She'd thought that if she could fall asleep, then maybe she could wake up without the mark Queriven left on her. If anything, sleep would have been a blissful escape from the tragic event earlier. But her mind fought against her, always screaming to remind her that she was doomed.

So once again, she found herself lying in the quiet of her room. It was dark; so dark she could barely make out where her bed ended and where it began, but she was still focusing on the cursed mark. She could see a little bit of the first, dark curving line and she was pinching at it with her nails. It didn't feel any different than her own skin; it was almost like it was a tattoo or birthmark. Every time she dug her nail in it, there was just a normal prick of pain. It was still thicker than paint, and there was no texture of the skin masked underneath it.

The more she picked at it, the angrier she grew with it. She'd almost wished to cut it off and be done with it, but she knew that wouldn't get rid of the curse itself. The answer was too simple.

As the hours went by, she could only see the outcome of two actions she could take. Either she lives out this year in silence and endures the disaster herself or she tells her parents the truth and the whole village will panic hopelessly with her. Either way, she couldn't avoid the curse. It was too late.

It was impossible to break. There were few peasants skilled in magic, and the few who were wouldn't be powerful enough to help her. If someone could break it, it would have to be a wiser man, and one wealthier. Few men like that would stoop low enough to help a lowly peasant girl with a powerful curse.

And so, all options led her to a dead end. There was nothing more she could do. The only thing she had left was a meager hope that it was all a dream. But the more time passed in her lonely room, the more she believed it was too good to be true.

What if she chooses neither of these options? The last thing she wanted to do was to sit like a duck and allow this spell to take her. And while she couldn't do anything else about it, at least, she didn't have to accept her fate.

But the curse happened because she didn't want to leave her village. What will she prove if she had to stand up and leave it anyway? Glistened with worry and stress, she glanced about the room, staring at outlines of her shelves and trinkets. It would be too painful, she realized, to live like normal while this countdown was ticking over her head.

Better to live in the unfamiliar, even if she still dies with it.

Slowly, she stood back up and felt for a candle sitting on her nightstand. Once it was lit, she changed back into her day clothes and dug in her dresser for an old piece of parchment. Then she carefully came into the living room. If she was serious about leaving home, she was going to leave something behind for her parents. She sat down and placed the paper on the low table in front of her. Then she stared down in silence for a moment before pressing a quill to the discolored paper.

Mother and Father,

Nothing hurts me more than to say that I've gone against what we all wanted and left town in the night. And by the time you read this, it'll be best if you didn't search for me. I don't know where I'll be going and I don't know when I'll be back. But please understand that this was not your fault. I left for a reason I didn't share with anyone, and one day, I hope to return and explain it to you myself, but that is not for now.

And Mother, I'm very sorry. I meant every word when I said I wanted to work things out... Father, I hope you'll take care of the goats while I'm gone because we have a history we should be proud of; those of our family traditions and our teamwork.

Please don't dwell too hard on my disappearance. I'll be back one day and explain everything. I'll miss you and Bailiese very dearly.

With love,
Your Dear Blair.

Tears bubbled back up in her eyes when she finished and she smothered herself in the sleeves of her jacket to muffle her cries. It wasn't too late to do this, she thought. She could take the note and hide it in her room and return to her warm bed. But the mark of the curse peeking out a little before her eyes reminded her of why she couldn't retreat.

So she left the tear-stained note where it was and headed back to the kitchen where she took bread, meat, and water for her trip. She even ransacked her savings from her room before she finally stepped out of the door.

Leaving her home was easier than she first thought, but it was when she came to the town's border that she hesitated. This was real. No extreme emotion like this could possibly come from a dream. With every step, she longed to turn and run back for the safety of her room. Her heart was pounding faster and faster and she struggled to breathe, but she had made up her mind that she wasn't going back. She had no choice but to continue forward.

She walked, huddled in the little bit of warmth that was in her jacket until Bailiese was long out of sight. The nightlife called out around her and she thought she heard wolves out in the distance. Maybe leaving in the middle of the night wasn't the best of plans, but she had little choice. If she wanted to make sure no one knew she left, she had to go now. But that also meant she couldn't camp until she was well away from the town.

Which way should she go? The question resurfaced when she came to the trade roads. The packed dirt roads stretched on either side before her feet. Blair hasn't been to the trade roads very often, and so she didn't know much about where they led. She knew there was a town, Penacha, just a little bigger than her own to the west, all the way to the coastline. And the northern road ran all the way to the capital city of Dunverhart. When she was little, her father took her to the city when he was selling a few of their goats. She had fond memories of the trip, though that was a long time ago and she didn't remember much of the city itself.

For a long while, she stood in the cold considering her options. If she wanted a chance to seek help, Dunverhart would be the best answer, though she still doubted there would be anyone there willing. It was the best start. She didn't have anywhere else to turn to.

◊ ◊ ◊

Hours later, her senses finally came back to her as her upset head and stomach cleared. She was both hungry and exhausted. Blair took out a loaf of bread as she pushed her sore feet forward. As tired as she was, she still refused to rest until she was sure no one from Bailiese could find her.

The first rays of the breaking sun were edging through the night sky, and as the nocturnal creatures retreated to wait for dusk again, Blair noted a flare of activity about her. Little rodents scurried about the dry leaves looking for anything they could salvage for the upcoming snows, and the birds that chose to stay in the region were already waking up and going about their usual mornings.

For a brief while, Blair entertained herself by wishing to be like one of the animals. She'd never have to worry about curses or family troubles. Life would be simpler. Make a shelter fit for a modest home, spend the day gathering food, and find love. Maybe there'll be a dangerous situation or two, but it still sounded better than her own life.

A tinge of regret passed her mind. Perhaps, she should have brought something for defense. In her rushed and terror-struck mind, she had forgotten of the dangers out here in the wild. It would be a wonder to find a dangerous creature on the roads, but she knew she had to be careful. She knew there were monsters out here in the wild and that brings to mind the highwaymen who may be watching for a weary traveler with valuable goods.

Blair slowed her pace. Was it time for her to move away from the road? She was shy about meeting a trade wagon or another wayward traveler. She didn't want the attention. But on the other side, perhaps, she'll meet someone heading to the capital and she could ride along. Yes, that would be a good thing indeed.

The sun was well over the horizon. Blair had walked all night and through the early morning hours. She was strong and stubborn and had pressed on through her exhaustion, but the consequences were starting to catch up with her. Her eyes burned, blisters formed on her feet, and everything was hazy like she was seeing things.

She must be seeing things now. There was no way a fox made entirely of crystal stepped out from the bush just ahead of her. Though if it was just her imagination, why did her step falter and why did it stay there staring at her? Could it really be there?

This fox, which could either be a figment of her imagination or not, had a body made of a deep blue crystal. The sun was glistening through purple tips on the ears and it watched her curiously with sparkling baby blue gems. It moved its legs slowly, mimicking the exact movements of a live animal. Blair swore she could almost see the tufts of fur on its tail ruffle in the breeze.

But then a call from a nearby wagon sent the mystical creature dashing back where it came from. Blair took a single stride, thinking for a second to run after it. That's when she realized a wagon was coming straight toward her! It was a small wooden wagon and the two horses pulling it were running at full gallop!

The three young men driving them were whooping and hollering as the wagon rocked and tipped, threatening to roll over. Then they saw the lone girl holding her arms before her face. The boy sitting in the middle of the seat cried out and stole the reins from the man to the side, bringing the horses to a quick stop.

The horses reared up in protest but obeyed. The animals huffed and swung their mighty heads around, seemingly upset with the sudden commands. Blair lowered her arms and met the faces of the three men. "Sorry 'bout that, Missy!" the boy in the middle called. "Craig was just having a bit of fun with the reins."

Blair moved to the side of the road, watching the wagon suspiciously. They were lucky it didn't fall apart. No seasoned driver would taunt and drive their horses like that. Those boys could have been killed! "Hey, uh..." the one known as Craig started. "What're you doing out here on your own?"

Blair didn't answer; she only met his gaze.

"Do ya need a ride anywhere?" Craig asked, speaking each word slowly like Blair was too dumb to understand him.

She shook her head. "I'm fine, thank you." And she turned again to the road, ignoring a stench of alcohol on the wagon.

"You sure are a pretty gal," the third boy called and Blair prayed he wasn't talking about her, but, of course, he was.

Craig laughed. "Yeah, you know what happens to pretty girls walking on the roads by herself?" he called to the still walking Blair. "They get captured by thieves and eaten by monsters and such, or worse. Who thinks we should lend her a hand?"

The other boys cheered and Craig hopped off from his seat. Blair couldn't help but look back from the sound of the disturbed dirt. He was swinging his arm low, bowing with swaying balance. "By my honor," he said with a mock accent, "we shall escort the pretty lady to her destination and protect her from slimy creatures and stinking monsters."

Blair took a few steps back. This wasn't good. "I can make it on my own."

He was standing up now and had his hand against his chest. "But dear maiden, I'm hurt. Let me help you."

She tried to hide the uneasiness in her eyes as she turned again and jogged down the path. Again, she was regretting how she didn't have anything to protect her!

"I'll insist," Craig repeated quietly, pulling himself back to his seat where he snagged back the reins.

"Hey hey hey, Craig!" the middle boy protested. "She's going the wrong way. We don't need to be backtracking!"

He snapped the lead and turned the wagon around. "It'll only take a minute," he said with a sudden change from teasing to determination.

Blair could hear the wagon racing behind her again. Why did she have to be in trouble now? She was only minding her own business and she already had a wagon chasing her. These men must have a death wish!

The horses were catching up with her and they weren't

slowing down. She had to think of something else quick. Her first instinct was to panic, and she was busy trying not to look behind her. She feared for her life. Was it possible for her to die already?

Adrenaline fogged her mind, making it hard for her to come up with an answer, but then, something did occur to her. The men were driving the wagon recklessly again that it would be hard to control at that speed on uneven ground.

Immediately, Blair broke to the right and the wagon went ahead on the road before it turned for her again. She could hear the two other men still riding crying out as the wagon left the road. She half expected it to crash there and then, but it was still going. Blair had to coax it further.

So, she raced for the ground worse for travel. The wagon bounced, tilted, and jolted, but Craig continued to push the horses at full speed. Blair charged ahead for the ground sloping up, the burning ache in her feet moving up to her legs as well.

She raced under a few, tightly packed trees, and the men followed her through, sending a jolt down her sore legs. Twigs and leaves slapped and scratched the faces of the three men, pushing the driver further into rage. No woman was going to evade him this far.

The wagon was now racing up much slower and the horses were straining to follow the driver's commands. Craig was so focused on catching his prey that the signs of impending disaster didn't cross in front of his face. She had pushed him too far.

Suddenly, she stopped and a wide grin crossed over the driver. He slapped the reins several times, already tasting the sweet victory. Then, Blair picked up again, though this time, she ran around the side and headed back downhill.

Craig gave a final jerk on the reins, trying to turn around, but the horses were going too fast and they whinnied and tumbled, bringing the wagon down with them. In a loud smash, the wagon splintered underneath the riders, falling apart in a million pieces.

Blair caught a glimpse of the wagon pieces, horses, and men, all rolling down before she continued jogging. A part of her wanted to check to see if they were hurt in the disaster, but she wasn't ready to risk her life again. If Craig was somehow still in a drunken uproar, she wanted to be out of sight as soon as possible.

Her breath came hard and unsteady, her mind still hazed from a restless night. Blair was pushing herself beyond the point of exhaustion now. And when the road finally came back in her view shortly later, she tripped and collapsed to the cold ground. Anxious, she begged her legs to lift her up again, but they were too heavy to move and darkness overtook her.

There was a sound of rolling wheels, and it was coming steadily closer. She could almost feel the heavy wagon dig deep in the dirt. Blair stirred, confused and hazy. Then she noted the grass pricking at her face. *What happened? Did I fall?*

Finally, the wagon came to a stop and a voice cried out. Like a trigger to an old nightmare, Blair remembered the men who were chasing her earlier. They were back. They found her! She didn't even remember the wagon breaking like glass at first. There was no way they were back. Her eyes popped open and her heart began to pound. But before she could react, she heard the voice again. It didn't belong to any of the men from earlier. It was gruffer and older.

She lifted her eyes just above the grass where she heard it ruffle under someone's boot. Someone was coming to her. She could see the legs and the wagon behind them. "Is she injured?" a different voice called by the wagon, this one a woman's. Blair noted how different this wagon was from the last. It was not a wooden peasant's wagon. This was an open carriage, and a fine one too! Maybe it wasn't fit for a king, but Blair's family would never have enough money for something like that.

A rough and calloused hand planted softly on her back. "Are you awake?" the voice from before asked her. He was bending over her now and she lifted her head to see his face. He was a man a little older than her father, and he was peering down curiously at her. Time and wrinkles lined his face, though his hair was still thick and mainly free from grays. Thick eyebrows dropped over his eyes as he questioned her. "My dear!" he exclaimed. "What are you doing lying in the grass like that? You had us worried."

Blair had no response. She didn't know the answer herself. The man tossed his head back without waiting for an answer and shouted back at the wagon, declaring the girl was fine. Then he reached down and began pulling on her arms.

Immediately, Blair's feet returned to the old ache and she remembered why she fell in the first place. She scoured the sky for the sun. *How long have I been asleep?* she asked, but she didn't find her answer. The earth flipped upside down once she stood on her feet again and she nearly fell with it, but the man with the rough but gentle hands held her up. "What happened to you? Is there anything I can do to help?"

"No, I..." Blair lightly brushed his hands off and nearly fell over again. The man extended his arms, but she steadied her balance in time. "I was just making my way for Dunverhart, but I tripped."

"You tripped?" he repeated.

She shook her head, trying to clear her surroundings further. "Yes, I was being chased and...and well, I guess I didn't know how exhausted I really was."

His eyes popped up in shock. "Chased? My goodness! Well, we were just going to the capital city ourselves." He pointed to the carriage and Blair counted three people riding and one driving. "You're welcome to come with us. It's still quite far."

At first, she waved him off without a second thought. Then she stared down the empty road; her feet screamed for a rest. She already ran into danger and she still had a long way to go. She narrowed her eyes at the man. *Can I trust these people?* she asked herself honestly. It seemed she ran into all the wrong people lately...

"It's no problem," the man said.

Blair took a second longer before coming to a decision. She

smiled softly. "I suppose... I could use a little help."

"Wonderful! Come then, I'll introduce you," he replied happily, beckoning to the carriage.

Blair followed, still nervous and thinking twice about her decision. She hesitated shortly after he climbed up first. Again, she stared at the road ahead, but it still looked just as empty as she first looked at it. If these were good people, she thought, she should reach the city way sooner anyways. Both options were dangerous, but this one had better potential.

As soon as she pulled herself up, there were greetings all around her. On the bench to her left were two men. One had a round figure with big eyes to match, cropped hair, and a short beard around his neck, and the other was much younger, barely middle age.

The older man from earlier seated himself on the other side next to a woman with blazing red hair. Blair looked at either bench before sitting next to the round man. Almost immediately, the driver kicked the reins and the carriage started on the road at a healthy pace.

"So, I'm Kain," the man sitting on the other side began. He nodded to the younger man across from Blair. "That there is my son, Connell, and the one next to you is Lynny." They responded with a kind hello as he introduced each person. "The driver is Fergus," Kain pointed and Fergus raised his hand without turning back. "And this is my lovely wife, Anita." He patted her hands gently and she smiled.

Blair greeted each in kind, but the introductions were quick and she was already struggling to remember who was who. Despite the kind faces, she was a little uncomfortable. These were all people of a finer lifestyle. They all had decent clothing, a nice carriage, and she noted a stack of various musical instruments lining the floor just behind the driver. Blair, on the other hand, was nothing more than a peasant. It also didn't help that her rest on the grass left her dirty.

"Now it's your turn," Kain said. "Tell us about yourself. What's your business in the capital city?"

Good question. She couldn't tell them she was looking for

help with her curse. Instinctively, she pulled her sleeves down tighter, keeping the mark buried. She'll have to come up with something else, and quick. "My name is Blair and I come from Bailiese. My family specializes in raising goats."

"Interesting," Anita spoke. "Were you on the way to sell them then?"

"No..." she hesitated. "I left to find...to find something to..."

Kain must have seen her unease because he waved her off. "You don't have to give us all the details if you don't want to, you know."

At that, she breathed a sigh of relief. "Thank you, Sir."

"For us," Anita went with the change of subject, "we're heading to the city to perform our music in various locations, popular and otherwise."

Lynny nodded enthusiastically. "She's talking about all of us. You see, we're a group of traveling performers — bards."

Connell leaned over so he could look the newcomer in the face. "It doesn't pay well sometimes, but it's all worth it in the end."

"We've been in so many towns and cities..." Lynny continued. "Rich ones and poorer ones and we've even sung before the king himself!"

"Though I prefer any other place than his company," Anita was quick to add, "personally, he creeps me out. I don't think he's the right man for this wondrous land."

Bold words, Blair mused. Such thinking could have her in trouble before the royal court. And there was something about Anita herself that was throwing Blair for a spin as well. She never met her eyes when she spoke. As a matter of fact, she didn't meet with any of the speaker's.

"He even asked us to become his personal bards of the castle," she continued, "but we feel more freedom out here in the wilds, singing for the more common folk."

"Was that a hard decision to make?" Blair asked, growing curious. "Those kinds of opportunities don't come around for everybody."

A short silence, then heads and shoulders began to shake

around her. "A life within fine castle walls would have been great," Lynny answered, "but I agree with Anita. There's much more freedom out here and more inspiration to move us."

"Yes, I don't feel much regret for our choice," Anita finished and leaned back on the bench sighing past the refreshing yet cool air. "Anyway, we'll be very glad to have you join us, Miss Blair."

Blair smiled. After Queriven left her in his dust, she was afraid to trust again, but she wanted to trust these people. There were still good people in the world somewhere.

CHAPTER SIX
ROKIANS AND VAYEN ARAY

The ride to the capital city brought Blair much enjoyment. The bardic group showed genuine excitement as they neared their destination, and even showed off their instruments proudly. She listened to a few catchy tunes and interesting myths.

But even though Blair tried her hardest to take in the tunes of the joyous band, a lingering fear still pinched her every now and then. It was growing later in the afternoon. It's now been over a day since the curse was set on her and the carriage pulled by several trees that now the hot colors of autumn. The sight sat on her mind like an evil grin, though the bards barely seemed to notice it beyond their beauty.

By this time next year, she would cease to exist in this world.

She struggled to contain her disappointment when the group stopped to make camp. Fergus pulled the carriage off the edge of the road and immediately jumped off, helping the others with fire. They worked briskly like they've done this same thing thousands of times before under a veil of sunset.

Anita was last to leave the carriage. She reached for a long walking stick Blair didn't think about before and carefully made her way to the edge where her husband lovingly helped her down.

It all made sense then. That was why Anita never made eye contact with anyone. "You're blind!" Blair gasped when she realized. Then, after a moment set over her, she suddenly regretted her exclamation. Blair stepped down from the carriage, dropping her eyes and kicking at a blade of long grass. "Sorry, I didn't mean..."

Anita laughed. "You're fine. You can't offend me easily." She walked toward the smoldering flame. "When I first lost my sight, I struggled with adapting to it. But it doesn't bother me anymore. I can still hear and play music, and that's what's important to me."

Blair, secluded from the rest of the world in her little village, has never met someone like Anita, who lost the ability to see. She's heard about people who struggled with situations like that before, of course, but this was new to her. Her curiosity grew, but she was nervous. The last thing she wanted to do was respond inappropriately. "May I ask how...?"

"How it happened?" Anita finished. "My eyesight wasn't always great, to begin with. I've had problems with it ever since I was a baby, but as I grew older, my sight steadily continued to become worse. By the time I was a young woman like yourself, I could barely see at all, and now there's nothing left."

Blair watched her carefully, but Anita was so confident. She couldn't imagine going through those struggles, but at the same time, Anita moved just as well as a person without the problem.

The two stopped before a fresh fire and Anita turned toward her. "We all have our own challenges, Blair. At times, they seem impossible to overcome. Believe me, I struggled at times, but I learned how to make the best of it. We can find an answer when we need one. We can learn to keep perspectives in the positive however hard it may seem."

Blair wanted to take the words to heart, but very few people ever had to fight with curses like the one she had. The best she could do is pray she could have that sort of confidence one day. "There's quite a bit of wisdom there," she said solemnly.

Anita laughed again. "Thanks. I learned it from experience.

It's true though." Then she turned and sat down on a rock next to the fire.

"Do you want to help us bring the cooking supplies out?" Connell asked, handing Blair a giant pot. She accepted it and set it by the fire.

That night, the group ate a delicious meal and played cheerful music around the warmth of the fire well into the night. As it turns out, the band of musicians enjoyed Blair's company as much as she enjoyed them and they laughed as they told her stories about each other, both hilarious and serious.

Anyone passing through that cold autumn night would have seen the camp as inviting as a sunbeam seeping through on a cloudy day, and the music played was sweeter than a songbird's. It wasn't hard to believe their story, where the king requested their company. There were fiddles, drums, flutes, and pipes, and they exchanged them after each song easily. Many of them could sing too. The harmony flitted in perfect tone, and each beat was captivating and soul-stirring.

Blair was so tired. She fell asleep as soon as her head hit the ground. A sense of thinning time made her sleep restless. There wasn't a particular dream she could remember, but she was uncomfortable most of the night. And when she awoke the next morning, she didn't know where she was and who was around her at first. The bards were already waking up and Fergus started a fresh breakfast before they set on the road again.

She couldn't wait to see Dunverhart, though it was another day away. The caravan finally made it into town the next afternoon.

Blair couldn't remember the last time she saw so many people in one place! People from all over the kingdom crowded the streets. There was the rich and the poor, the young and the old, those making business at the marketplaces and those enjoying a cool autumn day. The clip clap of the horses' hooves was peaceful against the bubbling river they just crossed over, and chattering voices filled the air around them, surrounding the carriage. All at once, the crisp breeze mingled with the warm baked bread and the hay from the livestock on sale.

The city was vague and distant from Blair's mind. She could sense the familiarity, but the sights were smaller and newer than she remembered from when she was a little girl. The memory tugged sadly on her heartstrings. She came here with her dear father then. What was he doing now, she wondered? No doubt, they would have found her letter by now and were heartbroken. Blair could only pray she could live to see them again one day.

Fergus slowed the carriage to a stop next to a few other wagons. None of them were finer than their own carriage. One by one, the band of bards climbed out from the seats and jumped down on the wide stone plaza. Blair followed the group and scanned the sights of the city all around her as they talked about their plans.

"We'll be playing for the Tied Cambric tonight since that's where we'll be staying anyway," Kain began once the others were present.

"Do we have a lot of locations here?" Lynny asked. "How many days will this take us?"

Kain ruffled through some parchment he kept in his pocket. "We have a few. Let's see..." He found the one he was looking for and held it before him. "Tomorrow, we have a feast at the royal court, a dance in the town square, and since we're here, I'd figure we'll sing for some other places if they'll have us as well. Maybe... Two days unless something else comes up."

At that, the others nodded excitedly. "A fair schedule. I'm ready," Anita exclaimed. "Let's go to work." And they all began at once for the tall stone buildings further into town.

They parted around Blair like water and she stayed in place. This was her destination. Here, she'll look for help, whatever that may mean. But where should she look first? Insecurity crept up within her like she was a lost child.

"Hey, are you coming?" a voice called out to her. Blair looked up. The musicians were still on their way, but Connell stopped and looked back at her. "You're still our guest unless, of course, you have something else calling you at the moment."

Blair hesitated for only a second. The search for help was important, but she didn't know where to look. It wouldn't hurt for her to follow them to the tavern. She jogged to catch up with the group.

The Tied Cambric wasn't too far away. She could see the sign above the door before she even knew which building the others were heading in. Fergus was the first one to reach the door, and he held it open, allowing all the others to enter the warm light first.

Blair wasn't sure what she was expecting, but the tavern impressed her. It was tidy and clean, and by this hour, it wasn't too full either. There were only a few people talking quietly by the tables. This tavern must be one of the more popular ones, she gathered. There were a lot of chairs and the building was in a convenient place in town. It was also more professional than any building she's been in.

The bartender was standing before the polished counter, wiping the already perfect surface down. When he saw the group approaching, he stopped and greeted them. It was Fergus and Kain who came to the counter to speak. The rest stood back and waited.

"Miss," Lynny asked, turning to Blair, "do you sing?"

She shook her head immediately. She never did like it when people heard her sing. "Sorry, but even if I could, I wouldn't want to ruin your show. Peasants don't carry much knowledge of music."

"If you wanted to stay," Anita said next, "we'll be honored for you to listen. We even want to help you rent a room if you let us."

"You are very kind," Blair answered, holding her hands in front of her, "but I can take care of myself from here. You don't have to help me much further than you already have."

"You're a young girl and a peasant at that. Trust me, even if you have enough money to live on for a while, you'll still need every bit of help you can find."

Again, Blair was uncomfortable by the offer, but she said nothing.

After the band settled in their rooms, Blair went out through the city for answers. She first found the city library. When that didn't work, she tried speaking with locals, but those who answered her questions about elves and curses didn't know enough to help her. She heard many statements about elves, even though many of them were contradictory to others.

They told her elves were immortal, but she also heard a rumor that they were once humans infused with magic. They were able to speak the language of plants and animals, but others said they merely understood them without language. Some said they were beautiful people and could perform no evil, and others said they were the essence of evil itself. They protected the forest or it protected them, and so forth...

Defeated and not knowing any more than when she first set out, Blair returned to the Tied Cambric and found the band of musicians together with their instruments. The quiet and mainly empty room was no more. Now almost every seat was occupied. The sun was setting, which meant drinks all around.

"She made it!" Lynny cried above the crowd, holding his hand up so Blair could see.

She was too frustrated to smile back, but seeing the group brought her a little peace as she walked through the crowds and found a seat at the counter.

The band started with a gentle tune before Anita's flute began to lead the rest sweetly. The two fiddles followed slowly behind the flute, dancing through the air across the tavern, and bringing a sweet, soul-tugging tune to each ear. The main melody started, coming up high and swerving back down, teasing the ear with an unfinished sequence. Then it came back around again. The patrons in the tavern hushed their whispering and focused on the musicians. They closed their eyes or swayed slowly with the music. It even compelled Blair to move along despite her worry and stress.

   The fiddles slowed down behind the flute this time, playing like an echo. When the flute took a break and the fiddles carried on, there was a second tease, this time in the form of the pipes playing quietly in the flute's place before it returned for the chorus again. Finally, the song relented to the teasing finale. People clapped and whistled, and the group prepared for their next song. Blair leaned back against the counter and allowed the music to soothe her stressed mind.

Another song began, but this time, the fiddles started first and it started with a slight dissonance. Both Kain and Lynny were holding drums this time, and Anita had dropped the flute and was swaying with the beat of the drums.

A long interval passed, and Blair relished each beat and stroke of the strings. The fiddles and drums played a long time together. When Anita suddenly began to sing, a beautiful voice broke out among the instruments and stunned the audience.

"A long time ago,
When green hills ran aflame,
Perilous raids rode through night and day,

In homes, on fields, the fiends came,
They stole, and cursed, those tricks were
played,

Foreign rogues from land away they be,
Scouting and looting for new territory,

They shall not have what we've fought for!
Those wicked tribes will be no more!

Charming tricksters and thieves they were,
The people were powerless, though
together,"
Something within Blair's mind caught hold of the lyrics. Charming tricksters, foreign rogues, and curses! It was all so

familiar. Could Anita be singing about the elf who cursed her? Before she knew it, she was standing up from her seat, watching the band as the fiddles played another interval.

Of course, these were bards! She should have known. Blair's mind was spinning with questions and anxiety, and she did all she could to remain still and not run up on stage. It was important for her not to interrupt. Instead, she made a mental note to ask them about the subject later.

By the time Blair was tuning into the song again, Anita finished another chorus and was singing the final verse.

"Lucky, help arrived on wings,
They fought these people for centuries,

'Worry not, we know these fiends,
And a spell will rid them quite surely,'

The spell banished the foreign rogues,
Though there was not without cost,

And the winged heroes,
Followed the banished lot,
Into the spell they go!"

Once the song and the instruments came to a stop, Anita bowed gracefully and a few more instruments changed hands before the next one began. Blair sat down in her seat again, fiddling with the sleeve that hid her mark.

Anita's song lingered in her mind during the rest of the performance. It didn't reveal too much information about the foreign people or the tricks they played, so what happened to those with such curses? Was there hope for them or did this banishment merely saved those who weren't under magic? The question stirred in her mind and made her innards sick. Her hands were trembling now. She didn't want to know the answer anymore.

Sometime later, Blair tried not to think too hard about Anita's song. Instead, she tried to relax and listen to the music peacefully. But during the show, she still hardly let go of her sleeve.

By the time the music was slowing and members were breaking up, it was later into the night. The crowds had thinned considerably. Now was her chance. She stood back up with a skipped beat of her heart as she approached Anita, the closest member.

"What a night," she sighed, lowering herself at a table. Closer to the stage, Blair could hear the men of the group cheering happily, patting each other on the back for a job well done.

"That was wonderful music," Blair remarked, sitting opposite her. "And you have a beautiful voice too."

"Thank you," Anita laughed.

Blair's hand jumped from her sleeve to her fingertips as she rested them on the table. "So about that song you were singing... I couldn't help but wonder who the rogues were. Were they elves?"

"No. Actually, they were called rokians. They were a tribe of people who came from a large jungle far to the south, or so they say."

So who cursed her wasn't the same as these people. Blair sank in her seat, suddenly disappointed. Anita continued. "That song was a translated, simpler version of the original, but I like this one a lot better. It's actually pretty gruesome, those acts. The rokians were smart and terribly cunning. It didn't help that they were masters at different kinds of spells, from enhancing their abilities to horrible curses. They could shapeshift too."

That last one stabbed Blair like a needle. "They what? What could they turn into?"

She shrugged. "Anything, depending on their personal power, though there were some conditions they had to follow." Anita held her hand up, listing those conditions. "The person they disguise into has to be alive in the world and they need to carry some kind of item or article that links them to that person."

Blair leaned forward again. "So they could disguise themselves as anybody? What kind of curses did they cast?"

Anita sucked in a breath. "I didn't know you found this so

interesting!" She smiled, happy to share the story. "They cast all kinds of curses. Poison, insanity, and more complicated things, such as spells that gave poor fortune or broke families from being together. The simple ones were immediate and the stronger ones took time before it began to work, sometimes even years later. But it always left a mark, like a tattoo on the body."

Blair nearly tumbled off her seat and she caught the chair just in time before it collapsed on the floor. There was no doubt. She was under one of these exact curses! "What happened to them?"

"History says they were unhappy with their own land and they wanted more. They were always moving territory because they always wanted what they didn't have. This brought them to our land of Fairdraisha. Our people fought them for many years, but the rokians were winning over time. This is why old ruins and forts cover the kingdom. We had to set up defenses and watchtowers.

"Anyway, the winged people in the song were the vayen aray. They lived on the islands just off our mainland. The rokians were their enemy, as the song states, and they've been butting heads since the dawn of time, many said.

"The legend states that the vayen aray had a plan to defeat the rokians, but the humans were growing impatient and they tried to ambush the tribe themselves and a large battle broke out. The vayen aray had to act fast if they were to save those people. So they, despite being unprepared, joined the battle and cast that spell to banish the rokians in a different dimension." Anita sighed and shook her head sadly. "It was all the humans' fault really. Because the vayen aray weren't ready, the spell took them in as well. No one has seen either race since that day."

Blair meant to ask about the cursed people, but her rushed words confused Anita. She took a breath. "About the curses again. Was there a way to break them?"

Anita shrugged. "The stories never said much about the cursed. But if they could be broken, the vayen aray would have been the best people to counter it, I guess..."

But the vayen aray were gone. Was there no help for Blair's curse? She slumped back yet again and said nothing. A moment of dreadful silence passed before Anita decided to break it. "Are you all right?"

For a while, she didn't speak a word. Then she found her voice again. "I came to this city for that very story. You probably won't believe me, but I'm sure one of these people you describe left a curse on me." She pulled back her sleeve, revealing the three strands weaving around her wrist. Only then did she remember Anita wouldn't be able to see it anyway.

Anita tilted her head in further confusion, her red hair bouncing from her shoulder and drooping down in front of her. "But that can't be. These events happened thousands of years ago. How were you cursed?"

Again, no response.

"I'm curious. What happened? I won't shun you. Did you meet with a rokian?"

"I...I don't fully know," Blair answered. "If I did, he was in disguise as an elf."

When Anita didn't reply, Blair told her the truth of the story, starting from her hometown in Bailiese. She told her the story of how she met Queriven, how he cursed her that day, and how she ran away all the way until Kain picked her up near the road.

But Anita's questions only grew. "So you knew him several weeks before he chose to leave you with that curse. Why, I wonder? I'd think the village would be of more importance, but you make it sound like his target was you."

Blair had no more answers and she shrugged.

"That seems unlikely. How and why is he here now? Perhaps, it wasn't a rokian. Maybe it was a wizard from Aven Forest?"

"Maybe, but what about the mark?"

"It does seem like you might have a rokian's mark..." Anita sat up and pondered. "And this fox you saw on the edge of the road is interesting too."

"The crystal fox? What about it? There are tons of interesting creatures in the fields."

"True," she answered, playing with strands of fiery hair. "But there are legends centering on these crystal beasts. Very few people have ever seen them. It's a good thing the wagon scared it away."

Blair shrugged her shoulders. "Why? What does this mean?"

"Well, the beasts made from crystal are said to appear to...to..."

A frown covered Blair's face and she leaned forward, curious.

Anita's face dropped. "To people with an upcoming important responsibility, usually those with a... doomed fate."

"Doomed fate?!" Blair cried, her voice cracking.

"But not always. It just means you have a tough fight in front of you." She tossed her hands up, trying to settle Blair from leaving the chair. "They appear and offer help to these people by often leading them away from their destiny. But it turns out for the worse. Their help is nothing but a trick to get them lost and leave them behind. They're a bad omen, no matter how peaceful they seem."

Despite Anita's efforts, Blair jumped up from the table, holding a hand to the side of her face. "What am I supposed to do?! Is that it then? Am I just doomed?"

Anita remained calm and at the table, listening to Blair's shaking cries of disbelief before she spoke again. "I don't know how to break that curse, but there might be help for you yet."

Blair stopped her pacing and looked at her.

"There were people, humans, who studied the spells cast by the rokians since they were so different from our magic. They didn't learn to cast them or to counter them, but they learned how to read them. I know of a scholar. He's a rich man by the name of Aen Vidwal. He lives in the Limadia Estate in the Taleena hills of the west. He can help you."

Blair returned to her panic, muttering to herself and taking up her supplies on the table. Anita stood up and begged for her silence again. Gently, she reached and took hold of her arm. "Listen, I know you feel pressed for time, but you need to take it easy. Those hills are dangerous. There are reports of ambushing highwaymen there. That's no place for a lady to go there alone. You'll need help, and it's best if you fight the hills instead of traveling the roads. Stay here for the night, gather supplies, and find help."

Blair was shaking underneath her grasp as she thought about the words before Anita spoke again. "You need to stay wise. You'll only make things worse on yourself if you don't rest or think this thought. It's just one night."

"Anita," Blair managed, speaking slowly as to calm her shakiness. "I'm only a lowly peasant girl. Who's going to help me?"

She thought for a second, then answered as she released Blair's arm. "You'll be surprised. There are a lot of kind people out there willing to help. All you have to do is ask. In the morning, you can try the guild. They're open to helping citizens, or you can try a few more taverns. Some people who'd like to be hired for such a job linger in the seats, but be careful." Anita started to leave, but then stopped after a step. "I'll be sending a prayer for your safety tonight." Then she continued, heading for the stairs past the counter where the rooms were.

Blair mouthed a silent thanks and stood in the now empty room before she too retreated upstairs to her own room.

Blair's sleep wasn't much different from last night's, but at least the room was warmer and more comfortable than the cold hard ground. It was rather a fine place to stay, for sure. It was clean, organized, and fresh. By the time she woke up the next morning, she gathered her supplies and went downstairs. There, she found the band of five eating a wonderful breakfast.

They made room for her at the table and their faces dropped when they heard she was leaving that morning, but they wished her luck anyway. Blair embraced their company like a shelter in a dangerous wood, knowing her trials were only beginning once she left them behind.

It had rained in the night. Puddles of many sizes have formed on the stone pathways. And the darkened clouds above promised more sometime later. Either the air has gotten colder too or the room she stayed in was just well cut off from the nighttime chill.

Blair stood by the tavern's door just below the sign that read Tied Cambric. She scanned the tall buildings around her in either direction before she left for the plaza they were in the day before. The streets were already crowded and she found herself thankful for her little village where such crowds were rare. Insecurity crept back up in her and she began to tug on her sleeve again.

Feet clicked on the stone around her. Chatters and broken conversations deafened through her head, and strangers brushed by with a fixed destination. She was near the marketplace again, and each stall she passed had people calling her to try their homegrown fruits or a new fuzzy sweater for the season.

She ignored them. Her mind was only set on the guild. Would she be able to see it from here? She lifted her eyes above the head of the crowd but found no answer. Was she at least nearby? Eventually, she had to stop and ask for directions and found it soon after.

She was still unconvinced they would help her and she hesitated to go in. She had to try. Unluckily for her, Blair had no idea what to say when she sat down before the desk. When the man asked, she only said she needed an escort to the Limadia Estate. It was only after that left her mouth that she realized she should have come up with a better excuse. The man didn't even take an offer of money.

Now angry at herself, she got up and left. Once outside again, she didn't linger on the streets but kept moving, watching for more taverns as she did. She found many inns and bars, but she didn't find much help. The men for hire wanted either too much money or had an attitude she couldn't trust. *If I can't find someone for the job,* she decided, *I'm still leaving today, even if I'm alone.*

She was ready to give up when she found herself by the Tied Cambric again. Perhaps, it was hopeless, but she went in anyway. This was her last stop. She might as well ask here.

Like the first time she entered with the bards the day before, it was clean, quiet, and empty, save for a few occupied tables. Anita and her group were long gone by now, and Blair approached the familiar bartender behind the counter.

"What can I get you?" he asked, stacking plates and cups neatly to the side.

"I was looking for someone who might help me reach the Limadia Estate?"

Glass chinked softly as he added another plate to the stack. "Have you tried the guild?" he asked with no hesitation.

Blair nodded and rolled her eyes. "That, and I've tried other taverns."

He shrugged, but his eyes looked off to the ceiling as he continued to think. "Well, beyond the taverns and the guild..."

"Have you tried the lodge just by the roads before the river?" a different voice asked. Blair turned where one of the men sitting at the table snuck up by her, now leaning against the counter. He was a tiny, scrawny man, his breath smelling of a rancid liquor.

The bartender growled, disgusted as he exclaimed. "Not now, Cam! For kingdom's sake man, you're drunk and it's not even noon yet! Have some respect."

But the man leaning against the counter ignored his comment. "There's a knight staying there, you know?"

Blair watched the man carefully. Was he playing her? "Why would a knight be staying there away from the main parts of the city?"

He leaned closer and hushed his voice. Blair winced as his breath whisked into her face. "Because he's an outsider. He doesn't belong here."

Nervous, Blair met with the bartender's disapproving gaze for help. He shrugged and shook his head. "I've never heard of such a thing. Are you sure you even know what you're talking about?" he asked.

"Of course, I do. How dare you test my judgment?! These eyes have seen him; they have!" he barked, then cooled as he returned to Blair. "He keeps a cowl up, but I've seen the buried spear on his back and a bow in his hand. Nothing short of a knight's quality." A light smile touched his lips and he sidled closer, scanning Blair's dusty blonde hair down to her stained boots. "I'd be happy to show you there myself."

"Not another word or I'll throw you out!" yelled the bartender. He was growing red in the face.

Cam's smile weakened and he returned to his spot by the counter. "If you...want me to, that is."

Blair nearly fell back; she was leaning away from him so far and she sucked back her breath. "I can handle it on my own, but thank you." Before he could insist much further, Blair nodded thanks to the bartender and quickly jogged outside.

She'd passed the city's walls and crossed the bridge over the wide river. Should she even bother with the lodge? At this point, she might as well go on her own. She was careful to give the incoming wagons and carriages plenty of room around her. Once she reached the grass again, she turned her head to the west. Suppose she was going alone after all...

And then she met the road again. She could almost see that lodge Cam was talking about in the distance. It wasn't too far. Blair asked herself again if she should try it. More than likely, Cam was just drunk and trying to catch her attention, but what if he was right? What if there was a knight there willing to help her? Blair stood by the roads, glancing from the far hills and slopes to the little lodge. It was a little out of her way, and she was growing anxious as time continued to tick by. But if those hills were as dangerous as Anita said, she would appreciate the help.

I'm already out of the main streets of Dunverhart. I can afford to check the lodge really quickly. She kept a tight pace, her hair and jacket bouncing with each step.

Blair was out of breath by the time she got to the lodge. It was a lot further than it looked, she lamented. This lodge, despite the rest of the city, was much poorer than the tavern she stayed in. It was wooden rather than stone, and the planks were slightly lopsided. Perhaps, this was here to offer visitors a more affordable place to stay. What did that tell her of this knight who was staying here? Was he poor? Cam said the man didn't belong here. Or maybe he chose this place for another reason.

The door creaked as she stepped in. A single candle sat on the otherwise empty table before her and a light mustiness hung in the air. "I'll be with you in a moment!" a light voice called and, seconds later, a little old lady in a stained apron came marching in from a hidden back door. She brushed dirt down her dress and pulled back yellow and gray hair behind her petite ears.

"Can you help me?" Blair began after a polite greeting. "I heard there was a man staying here; maybe an outcast or a soldier."

The lady's eyes glanced away and Blair thought for a moment she had no clue how to answer the question. Then she spoke up, "I suppose... We might have someone by that description. Why do you ask?"

Blair shrugged. She wished yet again she had a better excuse. "I need help. If he's willing, he may be my last hope."

The woman stared at her again. Either she wasn't sure if she really had a knight at the lodge or she wasn't pleased with Blair asking to speak with him. Finally, the woman put on a fake smile and pointed down a short hallway. "He's staying at the door all the way at the end. Go and ask him."

Blair thanked her and started for it. Her boots stomped heavily on the floor even though she tried to stay light. The mustiness in the air increased as she passed by the other doors. A few were open, and she could see messy rooms, tables, and beds pushed against the far walls. Dust floated in a cloud above the old floors. The old lady must be in the process of cleaning.

Finally, Blair stood in front of the last door. She swallowed the rise of anxiety and knocked. The wooden frame stared down on her, intimidating shy Blair as she considered just walking away. Still, she knocked a few times more.

Nothing happened. All Blair could hear was the set of footsteps behind her as the old lady continued with her work. Perhaps, she knocked on the wrong door? Surely not. There was only one door at the far end. She turned her eyes behind her, but she didn't know how many of these rooms were occupied. It would be rude to knock on the wrong one.

Then, she heard another set of steps, this pair from inside the room she knocked at. She held her breath. It was coming closer. Finally, the door clicked and Blair's heart pounded as it swung inward. It revealed a curious face peering down at her from underneath a dark hood. "Hello," she greeted. Her planned speech was already forgotten. "My name is Blair and I was hoping to…"

But those eyes were too green, that face too angular. Blair stopped and forgot how to breathe. Images of a lake crossed her mind, the colors of the moon were shining through those deep eyes. And then there was hostility, those neat hands gripping her wrists too tight as she begged for him to let go.

"Queriven," she broke through in a pained whisper.

But there was no smile and no tease came from his lips. Instead, his handsome brown eyebrows dropped down in an expression of confusion at the mention of his name. He said nothing.

Uncontrollable tears spilled from Blair's eyes and she backed away. "Why?" she cried at him, but he remained still. "Why are you following me!?" she yelled, her desperation growing louder and louder with each word. She wanted him to answer then. His unbroken, still curiosity bothered her, but he was still silent, though he was visibly growing uncomfortable. "You've already cursed me. What else do you want? Why do you continue to haunt me!?" Upset as he still gave her no answer, she turned and fled. Queriven did not pursue, but his mouth twisted as to ask her what was going on, but she was already gone.

Tears bubbled and spilled down her face as she rushed by the little old lady and went out the door. Out in the chilled open again, she stopped and looked behind her at the door. She hasn't even left town yet and she was already lost. A breath choked down her throat and her heart pounded painfully like a claw that was raking her chest open.

She wanted to fall on her knees. She wanted to give her whole quest up, but she remained standing with the door to the lodge behind her. Enough minutes passed when the old lady opened the door to shake down a dusty rug.

Blair wanted to keep quiet, but the lady caught Blair standing a few feet away. "My dear, what happened?" the lady asked, holding onto the rug but no longer shaking it.

Blair turned back to face her. Red swollen eyes met hers, then dropped to her boots. A second passed, and Blair gripped against the end of her dress, slightly swaying the folds side to side. Then she wiped her eyes and once the lodge owner closed the door, she spoke. "I need to know the easiest way to reach the Limadia Estate without taking the road," she asked almost in a hushed whisper, glancing every now and again at the shut door.

The woman stood baffled for a moment, but then she answered, "If you don't want to take the road, then I guess you can follow the river west. Keep it in your view at least."

She thanked her and turned her back again. The lodge owner still made no move to continue her work. "Are you sure you'll be all right?"

"It should be fine" was her only answer as Blair picked up her pace again. Her voice was empty.

On the other side of the wall, Queriven stood listening through the cracks in the wood. A human man would have only caught the old lady's response, but he was an elf and his sharp ears even heard Blair's hushed tone. Curiosity continued to rack his mind. Why did she act that way toward him? He didn't understand her accusations. It was true that many humans didn't take Queriven's heritage with a warm welcome, but they usually didn't blame him for cursing them nor did they usually know his name before he was introduced.

He let the odd encounter go, but it resurfaced in his mind later in the day. It continued to bother him until he wanted answers. Somehow, it concerned him. He was sure of it. This can't be a mistake. No one could confuse him with someone else, and she even used his name.

The girl was heading toward Taleena hills. Those were dangerous hills for anyone, let alone a young human girl. She may find herself in terrible danger. Queriven couldn't leave it alone, especially now that he knew she was going there. Early the next morning, Queriven checked out of the lodge. He already had a new destination in mind.

CHAPTER SEVEN
FOOL ME TWICE...

The Taleena Hills were mountainous. Blair's legs burned with each mountain she had to climb. And as evening fell, the clouds became heavy with a cold shower. The cold mist dampened through to her skin. One glance at the deep gray sky revealed it wasn't stopping anytime soon. It was still several hours until dark. She was stubborn enough to keep going.

There were many critters taking shelter from the cold and the rain. Tiny birds took rest in the crooks of trees, rabbits huddled in the low bushes, and insects were long gone in hiding. If Blair kept going on like this, she could catch a cold. There was no shelter for her here anyway. She kept going.

The steady droplets encouraged the rush of the river further down the hills, and colored leaves were dropping one by one off the trees. The colors won't last beyond a few weeks and the boughs would be empty like naked veins. There just wasn't enough time for Blair to act. She wasted too much time already.

A lone raven sat on a high branch and called to her. Blair lifted her eyes further to the cold mist and was angry once more when there was another crystal body shining past the dew. "Go away!" she called back at the thing, waving her arms over her head. "I'm not going to follow you!"

It tilted its sharp beak and regarded her in silence as droplets slid off and left the raven with a crisp white sparkle. The pinkish purple beak opened and released another caw. Then it lifted perfect feathers and took flight. The raven soared over Blair's head and continued south. She watched it until it was just a lonely twinkle against the dark sky.

Blair huffed at its quick retreat and continued once again. She held her arms tight in front of her to try and keep a little bit of warmth, but it was little help. The air was perfectly crisp and clean, but she still wished it was more comfortable for her. The lovely freshness chilled her lungs with each breath, making her wish she didn't have the need to continue to breathe. The ground was a mix of frozen grass and dirt, crunching and slipping underneath her feet.

She walked past the burning aches until she slipped and slid. It was amazing she didn't fall. The hills were quite a thing to hike without the chilly rain, and she ended up relying on a thick tall stick she found near a collection of brushes and trees. Slowly but carefully, she hiked the edge of a firm hill with an almost sudden ascent.

Little did Blair know she was very close to a small encampment. Thieves and bandits occupied those tents and their campsite was several miles away from the wealthy trade roads. The men, despite the cold drizzle, were setting out for a good meal, and a slide of boots on the nearby hill had caught their attention.

Blair had no idea she was being followed.

The men chuckled to themselves. "She doesn't seem to have a lot of riches on her, but that doesn't mean she won't be valuable." And they split up, nearly surrounding the unsuspecting young woman in every angle downhill, just waiting for a clear view to strike. These were not average thieves. These were experienced highwaymen and their footfalls never slipped and never revealed their positions.

It wasn't until Blair climbed the height off the side of the mountain that her hair stood on end, and not from the cold.

She paused, scanning the ground. She had a clear view of shriveling grass except for the trees she left behind her. The ground here was unsteady and she had a slope on either side of her. One hill reached up into the higher mountain and one fell further down toward the river. She didn't see anything ruffle. Not a single trig snapped, and no critter ran from disturbed nests or perches. Then, a breath caught on the wind with ill intents brushing close against her neck. Seconds past as she stood poised like a concerned doe weary of a hunter. Then, she dared to think it was nothing and carried on.

The men carried on as well, beating the flat of knives on their palms as they came closer and closer. Finally, one burly figure took his last step out in the open and grabbed Blair from behind. At least, that was his intention, but Blair was turning again and he grabbed onto one arm instead. A shriek escaped from Blair's mouth and she tumbled to the ground. The bandit didn't have a fair grip, to begin with, and she slid from his grasp. Already, more of the men were coming up behind him.

Blair leaned against her hiking stick and scrambled back to her feet. Her eyes, now wide and filled with fear, moved over each rough face before her. Her breath caught in her throat and she took a step back, holding the stick close.

The men said nothing but continued to draw closer until one lunged. Blair ducked and dashed out to the side where the others jumped for her. She spun, trying to avoid them and whacked one in the face. The man held his hand against his skin. Blood was dripping from his nose.

Now they were angry. They fell into her as a big heap. Blair tried to defend herself with her only weapon. She swung the hiking stick at the nearest bandit. She was lucky with her first hit and the strike fazed the burly man for only a moment before he gripped the weapon and tore it from her hands.

Now she was weak and vulnerable. She turned to run, but only went a few feet before they took hold of her again. The man holding her stopped her meager struggle with a blade against her neck. "You're coming with us," he whispered, his breath hot and the knife cold. She cried and begged, but the group ignored her as they started for the trees she thought she left behind. The sharp point retracted and stuck to her back, reminding her not to make a fatal mistake of breaking free.

The last thing Blair remembered was a whistle past her ear, followed by a loud groan behind her. The knife tip disappeared from her back and the hand gripping her shoulder let go. She turned her head and saw blood pouring from the man's neck where an arrow had hit.

"What the...?" the bandit on the right asked, glancing for the source. At first, they saw nothing, then another arrow whistled by, the tip sparkling like a star. This one struck the man in the hip.

There's the shooter! Blair spotted a cloaked figure further down the hill right before some tall bushes. He was already holding another arrow, pulling back on the string. The stranger didn't say anything, but he held the arrow like he was giving the other bandits a choice to flee.

"Leave us!" the next rogue called to the newcomer. "This doesn't involve you." To back up his threat, his buddy threw a knife at the figure. It sliced through clean air for the cloaked figure's shoulder, but the figure ducked just in time and the weapon landed uselessly in the brush behind him. He stood straight again and released the arrow. The thief barely avoided it. "Now I've had it!" he yelled in rage and left his captive behind to race and fight the stranger.

The stranger tucked his bow away and brought a spear in his hands, where he raced to duel his attacker. The tip was unlike any other metal. It sparkled the purest white Blair has ever seen, and it even hinted a few colors and sheens within. He spun it so easily like the weapon was a part of him. The stranger kept it leveled and perfectly balanced, dancing and moving with each swing. His grace and speed left the experienced highwayman looking clumsy.

Blair didn't notice it until a few minutes later, but that was the same cloak he wore earlier. He even had a bow and spear. The stranger was none other than Queriven!

The shock was no more welcoming than the last time she

saw him. Fear pierced her mind. Whatever his reason for being here was, she was sure it wasn't good. She glanced around her. The bandits were distracted. If she ran now, she could escape both them and Queriven. She turned and ran for the hill again.

But one bandit had glanced back and seen his prize taking the advantage. He broke from his group to chase her down. She heard him coming, but only ran faster. However, this man had muscles fit for his job of crime, and he caught up with her before the descent. He took hold of Blair's dress and pulled her back, but she didn't easily fall in his arms this time. She was turning and before he could wrap his arms around her, she pushed off from him.

But she lost her balance and the bandit didn't have a grip on her. Blair fell away from him and tumbled down the descent of the hill toward the river. She couldn't recover and the decent rolled her faster. Her vision sickened her and she wasn't able to make out anything but a blurred quick view of the grass and the sky. She tumbled off the prickly grass where she crushed her arm. Finally, her tumble down the hill ended when she crashed her head against a tree. Her vision blurred further and the rest of her senses quickly followed.

A rumbling sound came to Blair's ears. It was constant and it dug through her mind. Slowly, she began to awaken. There was a white flash beyond her closed eyes, and a loud roar followed it. It took her a while to realize it was a rough storm. Her conclusion supported the few cold sprinkles that splashed on her skin.

Then the pain kicked in. Her head ached and pounded harder than it ever has before. Her arm was in slight pain as well. Come to think of it, there was soreness and ache that ravished her entire body. What happened exactly? She remembered the bandits and the cloaked stranger. She was running away from one of the thieves when she fell... Then what?

She balled her fist when she couldn't remember and opened her eyes. The view of the dark and tightly packed leaves around her made her head hurt worse. Her vision was still blurred and fuzzy. She didn't even notice the darkened figure sitting away on the grass.

When she fell down the hill, did she hurt her head? Why then is this ground flat? This wasn't near the hill she tumbled down from. She was sure of this. She lifted her better arm to support her still pounding head, then she discovered an old blanket over her.

"You're awake. How are you feeling?" It was that sickly sweet voice. Suddenly, she was even sicker and filled with panic. Blair prayed she merely misheard it. The figure was growing closer. She lifted her head.

His hood was still up, but there was no denying the long bracken hair that spilled over his shoulders. Blair saw a hint of green in those shadows under the cloth. "It's better if you don't lift your head," he whispered.

Blair gasped. It was him! She crawled away from the blankets. A sick shiver raced through her spine and she gasped from the cold alone, but she continued until her back pressed against a tree bark. "What are you doing?!" she cried, her voice cracked.

Queriven stopped and regarded her curiously like he did back at the lodge. He sighed, bent over, and picked up a soaked cloth that fell from Blair's head when she moved away. "Please come back," he asked gently. There was no malice forming in his voice. "You're scared. I can see that, but you're also hurt. You're in no condition to be crawling around on the cold ground."

He took another careful step forward and lifted his arm. Blair shrunk back further, pushing against the bark and sitting up. "Don't come closer!" she begged.

Queriven obeyed and held his slender hands before him. "All right. I'll stay away, but don't push yourself into standing.

You're not ready."

Despite his warning, Blair was already doing just that. But as soon as she released the tree she leaned on, she nearly collapsed again. Queriven rushed forward, catching her before she fell and drew her back to the wrap on the ground.

Blair recovered before he could and pushed forcefully against him, but not before losing her balance a second time. She sank to the ground where she sat on top of the blanket. Queriven backed away from her.

Blair pressed a hand to her head and found it wrapped in cloth. "What happened?" she asked.

"You hit your head against a tree. You're lucky that fall didn't kill you." Silence cut in before more lightning struck. "I did the best I could to help. You'll live, but you need to rest."

"Why?" she asked, still holding onto her wrapped head.

Queriven scoffed. "Because that was a serious fall, and on your head no less. You lost a lot of blood."

She returned his scoff and a smile, not one of joy, but one of anger. "No, I meant why did you come all this way to help me?"

His eyes broke away from her. "I was confused. You knew my name and accused me of some kind of curse. I didn't know what was going on."

Now it was Blair's turn to be confused. Her gaze widened. "What?" she breathed, her mouth agape.

"So I listened to your conversation outside. You're going to the Limadia Estate. I understand your choice in not taking the road, but the hills are still dangerous, as you well know by now. I was right when I thought you'll be in terrible danger once I caught up with you."

"You mean you don't know why I was so angry?" she asked, her voice rising above the rain.

Queriven shook his head. "I wondered if it was because my heritage was found out, but then you mentioned a curse."

"Are you kidding with me? Is this another one of your tricks?" The rage in her tone was only growing stronger. "You cursed me. You left me behind saying I had a year before I'm not a part of this world. You're telling me you don't know any of this?"

"I didn't do these things!" he replied, more shocked than angry. "What are you talking about?"

"I don't know what you're playing at, but you won't fool me again."

"What does that mean, *you won't be a part of this world?* What's the curse doing to you?"

Blair looked away, afraid his elvish eyes would catch the tears building up. "You already know the answer. I'm not stupid."

He shrugged and held his arms helplessly before him. "I wouldn't be able to cast a curse if my life depended on it. Magic was never one of my better skills."

"I'm not talking about it anymore."

Queriven merely shook his head and lingered to the end of the trees. "Get some rest. The more you sleep, the better you'll feel tomorrow."

"Where are you going?"

"Obviously, my presence disturbs you and you need to sleep. I'll see you in the morning." Then he rounded the trees out of her view.

Blair was beginning to shiver, and once he was gone, she slipped back under the wrap and closed her eyes. Her head was still pounding. She considered running away while she had the chance, but the world was moving too fast. He trapped her again. Exhaustion took her shortly later and she drifted back to sleep.

The birds were chirping and flickers of light wavered through the red and yellow leaves. Blair was still in pain, but she was a little better than last night. She remained in the blanket though, huddled as tight as she could make it. She turned on her side and watched the light touching the grass before her eyes.

What happened the night before came back in snippets of

memory. It made her wonder; where was Queriven now? She brought her arms out from the comfort of the wrap and pushed herself up. She scanned the trees. Nothing but birds and insects disturbed them. She sighed and tucked herself back in the wrap. That was all right with her. She didn't ask for his help anyway. Weariness drew her to close her eyes again.

Minutes passed as she listened to the calm song of nature playing around her. The day was chilly, for sure, but the sun was up and warmed the ground a little at least. What time was it now? She wouldn't be able to tell unless she threw off the covers and walked where she could see the sky, and she was too weak to try moving again.

A disturbance came to her ears. Someone was picking things from the leaves opposite her. She drew her gaze to the source. Queriven was leaning over some brush. This time, his hood was down, showing the tips of his ears poking out from his hair. The hood was useless now that she already knew what he was.

He was picking at some plant buried within. Then he stood and brought it up to his nose. That's when he noticed she was awake. "Finally. I worried you'd sleep for the whole day!"

Her brow narrowed. "The day?" she repeated. "How long have I been asleep?"

He turned back to the plant in his hands. "It's well past afternoon."

"Afternoon?" She whined and sat up. Her head grew dizzy again. "I need to reach the estate!"

"Please don't worry yourself," Queriven answered as he came closer. "It'll only make you sick. Here," he held before her some kind of canteen, but the canister seemed different from the ones she's seen before. It wasn't made from leather but seemed to be woven tightly by some kind of thick plant material. "It's only water," he said when she squirmed away. Blair stared at him for another interval before taking it.

"Are you hungry?" he asked as she sipped cautiously. "I wanted to fix you a proper human breakfast, but I'm afraid I just have to offer you what I have."

Blair couldn't focus much because of her stinging body. But now that the mention of food was brought up, she realized just how empty her stomach was. "And what's that?"

He showed her some kind of pear in one hand and a collection of leafy stems in the other. She took it from him, now hungry enough to not care where her breakfast was coming from.

Queriven hugged his arms as a cold shiver jolted through him. He tugged at the edges of his cloak and sat on the grass where he began eating another pear. "It was a frigid morning," he lamented quietly. "It's not long now when the first snows will start."

Blair ignored him. She didn't care to give him small talk. A dead silence parted through them instead. Blair didn't even say anything when their eyes met for a moment. Something felt different to her then. There was something wrong with those eyes. When she met him before at the lake, his eyes were full of life, like a forest flourishing in the summer. She remembered the reflections of the moon in that emerald gaze. How his eyes shone through it like a mirror!

But these eyes were nothing like she remembered. They were like a green canopy, but the wind refused to blow. No life flickered in his gaze. Those orbs carried a solemn sadness. Blair's observation led her to notice other things about him. His skin was dull and tired, and he looked like he hasn't had a good night's sleep in ages. *Something's wrong,* Blair thought. Perhaps, he was telling the truth...? She remembered Anita then. It could be possible the Queriven she met was a rokian under the disguise of an elf. There was a good amount of evidence he may be innocent. No, she decided, casting off the thought immediately. He was a good liar and he wanted her to think exactly that. There was one thing she was sure about; she couldn't trust him, no matter the odds before her.

"When you're finished," he spoke, breaking her focus, "I'll like your permission to redress your wraps. We need to keep that wound clean."

Blair hesitated for the longest time. Finally, Queriven repeated his request. She still didn't want him anywhere near her, but he was probably right. She couldn't treat it herself either. Blair gave him a short nod.

Queriven thanked her and strode behind her, taking a seat in the grass. "I'll try to be careful." His thin hands reached up and untied the wrap on her head gently and removed it. Blair's dark golden brown hair covered the bloody wound. Queriven parted the strands to the sides. Old, dried crimson stuck to her head, but the injury was better than the night before. "You're a quick healer," Queriven remarked.

His hands disappeared from her head and Blair couldn't help but turn back to him. He was bringing out a small wooden bowl from his belongings. Then he sorted through a collection of herbs. Blair didn't know most of them, but he had many different kinds. He picked a few from his stash and added a few leaves and stems into the bowl. "If you don't mind," he said, "this is a paste that will protect you from infection by keeping out dirt and helping close the wound." Nervousness returned, but Blair allowed it and turned away again.

A few minutes passed and Blair listened to him sort and mix the contents of the bowl. Then he dipped his fingers in and brought it up to her head. "This may sting a bit," he warned, and Blair closed her eyes. A coat was added and Queriven prepared another wrap. "So what did you say your name was?"

She nearly laughed at him. "You already know what my name is."

"I don't... At the lodge, you introduced yourself as..."

"Blair," she growled, wincing as he pulled the wrap over her head.

"I'm sorry," Queriven replied to her angry tone. "It's hard to get these things to stick sometimes." When he had it where he wanted it, he worked on tying a knot in the back. "You're done." And he quickly gathered his supplies and stood up. Finally free from risking her temper, Queriven worked on sorting his tools. "Why are you going to the Limadia Estate?"

Blair didn't answer. Even if she wanted to, she could find nothing to say. She was trying to find out if she could break the curse, his curse. Her business there was going to remain secret from him.

Queriven caught the rage in her eyes and his face dropped back to his work. Blair thought she caught a tinge of hurt in his expression for only a moment before he blinked it away. He exhaled. "I swear I'm not trying to offend you. All this time, I've only been trying to help. I fought back the bandits, treated your wounds, offered my only bed wrap for you to use... I don't understand the hostility. Could it be something else you saw that cursed you?"

Of course, she considered that too. It would make sense, but Blair looked away. Her breath was coming a bit forced and she cleared her voice as to set her mind straight again. She'll continue to dodge him. "I highly doubt that. You're just trying to convince me to trust you again."

He shook his head and finished with his work. "Fine then. I'll just take every bit of blame you have." And without waiting for a response, he stormed past the trees.

A little guilt crossed her mind. She was giving him no space for gratitude or emotional safety after everything he had done for her since she fell. But like everything else, Blair shook her guilt away. She couldn't afford to trust him. She couldn't afford to trust anyone. Out here in the wilderness, she had few friends and many enemies, and she needed to take control of herself from now on.

But a seed of doubt lingered. Queriven, as tricky as he was, gave her no opening to exploit. He denied every jab of accusation and grew upset with her unrelenting stubbornness. He went as far to hide a moment of hurt. Why would even the greatest liar do that?

Blair rested her head again and listened to the soothing sounds of peace around her and tried not to think anymore about the issue.

Queriven did return later in the evening, this time carrying a good stock of wood. He piled it away from the trees sheltering Blair. "Now that the wood has dried, we can build a proper fire tonight."

Blair regarded him curiously, looking for an opening of any

kind where she could attack him. "I didn't think elves built fires. It's disrespectful to the trees or something." She remembered reading that in her books.

An ironic laugh pierced his lips. "We don't usually, but sometimes you have to do what you have to do." He gathered a few of the sticks in a tight huddle. "In order to survive cold nights, I had to build fires or freeze to death. I chose the former." Small lines of smoke were already wafting between his hands as he worked the fire. "And it's not because it's disrespectful to the trees; we just never really needed to do it." The embers followed before the fire took over. Queriven stood back to his full height. "Besides the point, don't be surprised if I follow along with what humans do. I've been out here long enough."

"Why did you leave Aven Forest?" she asked, watching carefully for his answer.

He shrank back from answering. "It's complicated." His voice was dull like she hit a buried topic he wasn't ready to bring up. "Are you coming to the fire to warm up or not?" he barked, taking Blair by surprise with his rough tone this time.

Carefully, she stood up and sat down by the fire where Queriven sat a few feet away. He tugged against his cloak again and huddled a little too close to the flames. He avoided Blair entirely.

She watched his quiet hesitance. There was something about him she just couldn't catch on to. Blair noticed every time he thought to look at her before he chose not to. Once again, silence filled in. The fire crackled and flickered the cold grass floor in an orange-red light that stretched by the trees. There was now a thick shadow behind them. The first early crickets began their song before the sun disappeared under the hills.

The smell of hot embers and puffy smoke brought her eyes to the dancing fire. Instantly, she thought of the words that he left behind, and those fiery colored trees came with it. It reminded her of a doomed sense of dread left by the man sitting quietly by the fire with her. The seed of doubt continued to grow and suddenly, she thought of something interesting.

"Whatever happened to that horn you carried?"

With his legs tucked in tight, Queriven watched something at the other end of the fire. She wasn't sure if he spotted something of interest or if he was still avoiding her. A heartbeat brought his gaze up to her. "Horn?" he asked.

She nodded, but his thoughts merely wandered nowhere. Blair explained. "I heard it calling to me. You had it when we met by the lake near Bailiese."

"I never had a horn," he stated, his expression and tone not changing.

She was going to push him on this one. "But there was one and you told me it used to belong to an ancient people."

His eyes sparkled. "An ancient people?"

Blair saw it and continued to elaborate. "Yes. You said the ancient people gave it to the elves of your family, and if you ever needed help, you could call and they would sense exactly where it was coming from, though for some reason, I was sure it took its effect on me and my father."

"Really?" he asked, his gaze a long distance away. He pushed to his feet and fell into thought.

His silent pondering was beginning to unnerve her. "What's wrong? Why does this mean something to you now?"

He didn't seem to give her any notice and began to pace. Blair could only imagine the hurricane going on in his mind. His pace became more desperate, his eyes scanning the ground for something invisible. "What is it?" Blair couldn't begin to understand what was causing him to pace like he was now. "What's going on?"

Suddenly, he stopped, though he was still lost within the chamber that was his mind. For just a second, he looked at her before losing himself again. "What did the horn look like?"

Blair stuttered, though she was not sure how to answer. She saw enough of it to give him a good response, but hesitation took over. He was beginning to scare her. "Why do you ask this? None of it makes sense. You should know exactly..."

He turned and threw his arms up in rage. He screamed at her. "*What did the horn look like?!*" His voice split the air and the flutter of wings followed when birds scattered from the nearby trees. Blair flinched and lifted her hands to her face. She watched him, her heart threatening to break from her chest and flee.

Queriven held his angry pose, and she decided she best answer him before he attacks her next. Blair's eyes dropped to the ground as she tried to remember how to speak. "The...the horn... It was...it was red. And there were engraved patterns. They looked like... They were like wings caught in the wind!"

Queriven murmured something she didn't understand then; something in a different language. He looked like he was going to be sick and he started to sway like he was caught in an earthquake. His hands went up to his head right before he broke away, dashing out of sight. He didn't even hear Blair calling behind him.

He was long gone and Blair decided against chasing him down. It was growing dark and she hasn't tried walking or running a long distance since she injured her head. She was sure Queriven would easily outrun her even if she wasn't hurt. So Blair remained by the fire. Would she even see him again after this? She wasn't sure.

This was too good for even the master of lies. She didn't want to think he was innocent, but she was beginning to suspect it. Even if he was, it would be hard to trust him, but she knew she was treating him horribly for no good reason. Her guilt returned tenfold.

He knew something about the horn though. She didn't know what he knew or why the topic sent him spiraling into terror, but he left without any answers. She wasn't even sure if he would ever give her a chance to understand. One thing was for sure; Queriven was gone and she wasn't going to catch up with him tonight.

Blair sat huddled by the warm embers for an hour until her mind tired out from her unanswered questions. She brought the wrap closer to the fire and quickly fell asleep.

But sleep never came for Queriven. He was sitting still in the grass just past the trees overlooking the river that flowed calmly despite his horror-struck mind. He thought that the horn was lost for good, and maybe it should have stayed that way. He tucked his knees in closer and wrapped the cloak around him. Each breath showed a visible mist in the air. A complete image of the horn unburied from his mind, but with it came the screams of a losing battle. He could almost see the blood spilling down onto the innocent grass. He closed his eyes tightly shut, as if that would blind him from the scene in his head. It was no one's fault but his own, and now it has come back yet again to haunt him.

Queriven understood now why Blair remembered seeing him at the village. Once again, it was all his fault. The carnage would only continue from this point, and he was powerless to stop it.

Because of him, more victims would fall.

Blair woke up earlier than she did the day before. The sun was rising several yards off the hills, telling her it wasn't early morning, but still early enough. Thanks to the fire and Queriven's wrap, Blair had fallen into a more comfortable and warm sleep. She felt new; the aches and drowsiness were long forgotten.

She sat up and stretched, embracing the no-longer taut muscles of her previously sore shoulders. Then in mid-stretch, she froze. The campfire had simmered down to nothing but cooling embers, but it was Queriven hunched over and sitting by it. Once again, his gaze drifted past the camp into something she couldn't see.

Surprise almost drew a shout from Blair. She didn't think she would see him again after what happened last night. Not wanting to startle him, she quietly spoke his name. Her voice turned his head and brought him to sit straighter. "Are you all right?" Blair asked him, curious at how he will respond.

He didn't, but he was trying to shake free of his thoughts. He slowly stood up, tossing a stick he was holding into the charred pile. "I'm really sorry about last night." Blair continued. "I didn't mean to upset you."

Queriven, still silent, drew closer and gave her another pear. She took it, though she didn't bring it to her lips. "You didn't do anything wrong," he finally said as he turned away from her again. His voice was dull, like pleasant music gone sour. He traced back to the smoldering wood. "But I was wondering if I could ask you something."

"Sure," she whispered, slowly dropping the pear to the side of her leg.

"I was wondering if you would tell me the story of how you came here." He turned toward her, but he refused to meet her face. "Of how you said you met with..." He trailed off before finding his voice again. "With me."

Her gaze drifted away from the grass and into the trees as she wondered how she could begin. "You... He..." She struggled, but Queriven remained patient. "He called from the edge of town..." The memory was like a persistent nightmare, always replaying in her head over a thousand times before leaving her empty and exhausted. But Blair pushed on, sharing with him the truth of the tale.

Though the truth contained the fact that she fell for this stranger. Between her dream of seeing something from another world besides her own, his sweet tone and sharp handsome features, she grew to love him. And before that day where he cursed her, he showed to her the same feelings. Blair lost her voice for that part of the story. This man was different from the one she met, but he looked just like him. A red blush crept through her cheeks as she shied away from telling him she thought she loved him.

"He told me he found Aswren's body in the old ruins up the road and he wanted help to gather him for a proper burial." Her thoughts scattered and her eyes betrayed her withheld information, but Queriven wasn't watching her at the moment to notice. "I told him I had business at home and that's when he cursed me," Blair finished, her heart beating loudly in her chest as she watched for a response.

Queriven's stance shifted as he remained by the piled wood. There was something else that stirred him from her tale, but she couldn't tell what it was. "Obviously, there was more to it than just wanting help to move a deceased friend."

Her breath caught in her throat. He knew there was something missing from her story, but then he continued. "He wouldn't have cursed you because of that, though I don't know why he would have gone through the trouble."

Blair exhaled the caught breath. "That's why I'm going to the Limadia Estate. Someone told me there was a scholar there who could read the meaning behind my curse. The only thing I know about it is that I have until next autumn before it takes me."

"Then I wish you all the luck in the world."

"Queriven, for some reason, this man disguised himself as you. Don't you find that a little odd? Out of all people, it was you. This is important somehow and we need to find the answer."

He nodded and turned where he took a few steps away from the charred wood. "And I'm sure you will, but I regret I can't be of more help to you."

Blair cocked her head in confusion. "You're not coming with me? Don't you think this concerns both of us?"

But he shook his head before she was done. "I can't. I'm sorry." A slender finger came up and pointed to the pear still sitting against Blair's leg. "You should eat. You need all your strength to reach the estate."

Her eyes darted down to the pear and she closed her hand back around it. "You're leaving now, aren't you?"

"You've been resting for a few days now. Though I advise you to be careful, listen to your body and rest when it's tired."

Slowly, she came to her feet, the edges of the wrap falling away from her as she did. "I know you recognized that horn last night. There is something more to this. What do you know that you're not telling me?"

A jolt raced through him and brought him anger, but he didn't yell at her. "No, look! I can't help you anymore, and I'm sorry. Now, if you could please..." Queriven came closer and reached for the wrap. Blair stepped back onto the cold ground, allowing him to pick it up. He thanked her and began to fold it tight. "I wish I had a weapon I could leave with you for defense in these hills." Once, he met her gaze for the last time. "May we meet again one day."

He picked up his pace before she could speak, leaving her in the old camp they occupied for the last three nights. She held her hand out for him, asking him to stop, but he either didn't hear her or his mind was made up.

Blair remained still in the very spot he left her. Awkwardly, she glanced back to the cooling wood where the fire was. Queriven was hiding something; something he didn't want anyone to know about.

CHAPTER EIGHT
THE SCHOLAR

Blair, with a walking stick in hand, climbed the side of the hill. Once she was on level ground, she stopped and took in the view.

This was where she tumbled down and smashed her head in the tree. And looking at it now made her dizzy. The ground slopped incredibly, racing down through trees and then turned flat just before the river. Queriven was right; she was lucky that fall didn't kill her. She shook off the uncomfortable tingles running down her shoulders and pressed on.

The hills were climbing higher and higher, and Blair grew tired quickly. The more tired she became, the more balance she lost. Heeding the elf's advice, she rested often. She still had a sense of urgency to reach the estate as quickly as possible, but this time, she approached those emotions with more wisdom. It would do her no good to reach the place injured or sick.

The day passed through slowly and the nights were cold as soon as the sun left the sky. Blair, after failing to build a fire herself, huddled in a group of rough, brown weeds to keep warm. She missed Queriven's warm bed wrap... Sorely, Blair regretted that she didn't make herself more ready for such a journey as this.

Where was Queriven now? Was he also settling in for the

night or was he still moving? The thought of him made her wish he was here to give her some much-needed advice on what to do when you fail to build a fire. A violent shiver ran through her and each breath became a white cloud before dispersing in the air.

The next morning brought the first flurries of the long winter season. Chilled to her bone and not feeling more rested than the night before, Blair continued. The light dustiness of white littered her hair. Her lips were nearly blue with frost and her fingers were so cold they threatened to chip and fall off. Just before she started to lose her mind and think she'll never make it, finally, the roof belonging to the Limadia Estate crested just under the last mountainous hill. Blair leaned over the stick, huffing and nearly collapsing from the welcomed sight after a long cold day. Nearly every house had a string of smoke rising from it. The workers below endured the frosted morning as they tended to flocks of animals or chopped wood for fires. Blair had to stem her excitement lest she risked diving off the hill. But at least seeing the fine estate at the edge of the valley brought her a bit of relief and warmth.

Eagerly, she kept an even pace once she reached the ground. Eyes from nearby workers glanced her way as she moved past them. With a swing to her self-esteem and preparedness, she realized that everyone wore gloves, scarves, and heavier coats than what she had with her. Blair made a mental note to buy some better supplies after she meets with the scholar. As for the moment, the unsettled instinct in her gut pushed her to the estate first.

The Limadia Estate perched high, overlooking the rest of the valley and homes. It was made from a finely carved white stone. Each level had maybe twenty windows, and the ends of the green-tinted roof tipped up into spires, giving it a look like a castle.

With each step closer, Blair found it harder to breathe, and only part of it was because of her reason for coming here. She's never been this close to such a huge building before. Of course, she noticed the castle back at Dunverhart, but that one was so far away still. With the finances of her entire life and family combined, she could never live in a house even a little smaller than this.

The grounds near the Limadia Estate had neat hedges and ferns lining the pathway and walls. Two men were standing together at the edge of it, looking out into the community. One was a stern elderly man dressed in a dark jacket. He was bundled from head to toe from the cold, but his image remained a wealthy one. The other wore a finer suit, one of silver and blue satin. But beyond that, he wasn't dressed for the weather. He didn't seem bothered by it either. He was cleanly shaven with a skinny face and a long nose.

Awkward and shy, Blair wasn't sure if she should talk to these men or not. She was beginning to reach the conclusion that it might be better than entering the mansion on her own. Now was a good chance for her to ask about the scholar living here. Before she could, however, the older one suffering the cold spoke to her first. "You!" he cried, pointing at her. "Where exactly do you think you're going? The Limadia Estate is off limits to peasants without permission."

The gruffness in his voice drew attention to the one next to him, but instead of anger, he regarded Blair's presence with curiosity. Her step faltered and she shrunk under the first man's harsh glare. "Sorry," she apologized quietly. "I just wanted to ask a question."

His wrinkles cut deeper, as he only grew in rage. But before he could snap further, a blue sleeve jutted in his way. "Don't worry, I've got this," the younger man said in a light tone. He pulled the first one aside and smiled, his cheeks pushing up the ends of his face, making it seem a little wider. "We don't want to scare away our community, now do we?"

He received a tired growl in return, but there was no further protest. The old man nodded and went on his way, heading for the warmth of the manor. "That was my steward, but don't mind him. He's always in a bad mood," the younger one stated once he was out of earshot. "Now, what's going on? Something the matter with work?" he asked, concern showing in his eyes.

THE SCHOLAR

Blair opened her mouth to speak but he interrupted, leaning forward and scrunching his thin brown eyebrows. "Wait... You're not one of my workers. Who are you?"

"I'm looking for a scholar. Does a man named Aen Vidwal live here?"

He straightened then and brought his hand up to stroke his chin like he had a beard. "Aen Vidwal? That happens to be me. What do you want?"

"You're... Vidwal? My apologies," she said first with shock, then formal politeness. "I'm Blair Tripps. I came here because I heard you studied the old curses performed by the rokians."

His eyes popped wide then. "I do sometimes, I suppose... But what does that matter?"

Vidwal's sudden lack of interest disheartened Blair, but she continued. "This may sound mistaken, but I carry one of these curses."

Any wider and he would have lost his eyes. Vidwal stood there for a long while, frozen in place until he closed his eyes and shook his head. Blair noted how he tried to stifle a sarcastic chuckle in his response. "That's not possible though. That was thousands of years ago. Perhaps, you were cursed by some other wizard or creature or whatever."

She tried to snuff the desperation creeping up within her, and instead of telling someone whose rank overthrows her he was wrong, she pulled up her sleeve and held out the mark before him. He nearly jumped out of his skin and scared her when he grasped her wrist for a better look. He turned her wrist to either side, running his fingertips over the mark. Blair tried to keep it steady and not pull away as he gave it a rough scratch. "It looks real," he said.

"So can you help me?" Blair asked.

"I don't know. You see, my family has been studying these curses for many generations, but there has not been any use for it since the rokians were banished so long ago. Other than what's in my practices, I've never had the chance to use any of it," he replied, dropping her wrist. "To be honest, I haven't taken too much care in my studying anyway. I've never seen the purpose for it. I would rather be out here..." he said, holding his arms out around him. "Among something real; something that's moving, this is where I can learn more important skills that I can actually use."

Blair answered after breathing warm air onto her frozen fingers. "But this study has passed through your family for generations. Don't you think you should continue to pass it down so that it doesn't disappear?"

He shook his head. "There's no need for it anymore. I understand there was in those times when people first studied it, but we live in a new time now."

Blair cocked her head to the side. She always valued the practices of the past and she couldn't understand why he was willing to drop such an old subject without much of a thought. "Please," she begged, "I don't know what to do. I'll do anything for you to help me."

"Anything? Hmm," he turned, thinking with his hand to his chin again. "I suppose it wouldn't be much trouble for me to try." His face turned in her direction before he was lost in thought. "But what could a peasant offer me? She wouldn't be carrying much money and I already have enough workers..." His face, with harsh glare of judgment, snapped her way again. "I already have everything I need for a pleasant lifestyle. I'm not convinced you can offer me anything."

"What?" Blair scoured the air for hidden inspiration. "I know I don't have much money, but I can pay you back over time." But Vidwal's expression didn't change. "You must help. You already said it wouldn't be too much trouble."

He looked away again, but her desperation continued to climb. She was losing him. "Anita sent me here to find you. She told me you would help." The raised eyebrow begged her to elaborate. "Anita with the traveling bards?"

"Really?" He looked at her once again. "Anita and Kain sent you? Why didn't you tell me? They're good friends of mine, you know, and easily the best musicians in the land." Suddenly, a finger flew up and his jaw dropped. "I got it!" he cried. "How about you bring them back for a few shows, yeah?"

Blair considered that as a rather odd request, but it was the easiest one so far. With a turn of a brow, she agreed and Vidwal took her cursed wrist and led her to the door of the estate. The whole way there, Vidwal jumbled about how much he liked Anita's group of musicians. He mentioned how he had them over for parties and the like before, but he hasn't seen them for several months. Only continuing to grow with excitement, he spoke aloud ideas on what to do with having them for some more shows.

He barged through the door with short hesitation and led Blair through a carpeted room with soft couches and a fireplace. Blair felt the soothing warmth coming off the fire as soon as she stepped in the room, and if it wasn't for Vidwal's sudden excitement to try out the practices he's been studying his whole life, she might have stopped to warm her hands.

Vidwal led her past the cushioned chairs and down a hallway where he opened another door. Lines of books took up the walls and stole Blair's breath away. They raced all the way up to the ceiling and higher past the candelabra. Blair nearly shrieked. She's never seen so many books in one place! There were too many of them for her to read in a lifetime! Vidwal led her by rows and shelves as normal, not giving them a second look. There's got to be many here that he's never even looked at, she thought.

He stopped before a large round table and beckoned for Blair to have a seat. She did so and Vidwal stood by a shelf looking at the books. "Usually, I don't bring in peasants for anything if they're not on the job, and I most certainly don't offer them a seat." He finally chose a book; this one was large and thick. Vidwal held it with both arms and it thudded loudly on the table when he set it down. Giving his finger a light lick, he went through some of the pages. "My steward, Doulan, assures me that we don't offer those treatments, lest everybody will want a chance for a stay in my manor." He stopped suddenly and leaned in, a mischievous look in his eye. "But if it bothers Doulan, then I usually disobey just to spite him, you see." Then he returned to the book, turning its pages.

Blair leaned back in her chair, trying to steady her discomfort. "So what will this require?"

Vidwal, still glued to flipping through the oversized book, only muttered to himself. "Ah, it won't require much... If this first one works, that's it. Let's see..." Finally, the flipping stopped and he slapped his finger to the words Blair couldn't see from the other end of the table. "Yes, rokian curses!" After a moment of reading, he stood up, muttering again how he needed a few more things. From the shelf, he retrieved a jar of water along with a bowl and a few candlesticks.

He placed down the bowl to the side and uncapped the jar, pouring the contents into it. "I've never actually done this, so I want to make sure I'm doing it right," he said, capping the jar and putting it away. Next, he lit the candles, moving them one for either end, but the third one he kept nearby. Then, he sat in front of the book again, running through the steps in his mind. Blair remained quiet, but her eyes were wide with worry as he picked at his hairless chin again.

"I have it now," he said, closing the book and dropping it to the floor. When he came back up, he held his hand before him, wanting to see the curse. "Whatever happens, I need complete silence so I can focus. All right?"

Blair nodded and exhaled before she gave her exposed wrist to him. Vidwal took it and laid it out on the table, palm up. He also took a nervous breath and closed his eyes.

Silence fell and Vidwal remained perfectly still. Blair wasn't sure when he started, but she noticed he was humming quietly to himself. Steadily, as his thin shoulders relaxed, his humming grew a little louder and began to form words of an unknown language. They were long and strewn out but kept a constant rhythm.

Then, his eyes opened and slowly traced invisible sigils in the air. Despite his intense glare on both the mark and the sigils. His unsteady arrogance was gone, and a personality of surety and knowledge took over. It was like Vidwal fell into a deep trance and someone else awoke in his place. Those focused eyes had a blue spark to them that Blair didn't see before.

His fingers twirled the last symbol and he reached for the mark of the curse. Still humming, he traced the pattern all the way around Blair's wrist. His fingers left a smooth blue light on the mark where he touched it.

After the tracing, the light was fading until it disappeared completely. Slowly, he reached for the candle by his side. He picked it up and held it over Blair's wrist. Allowing it to drip from his fingers, a drop of hot wax fell on the mark. The burning rolling wax made Blair want to cry out, but she bit her lip. The move was no accident, and Vidwal set the candle down. Then he took his finger to the wax, closing his eyes again as he twirled it and moved it around her skin.

Finally, the humming stopped and he opened his eyes. He leaned closer, examining the wax on the curse, as if it was a page from his book. "I see it," he stated after a moment of silence. Vidwal was back, though those eyes still carried that tint of blue. He turned her wrist over. The wax was quickly hardening.

"This is interesting... You have until next autumn before the curse pulls you away from our world, but it won't kill you." He turned his head, watching the wax. "It's tied to you like an anchor. Currently, it's doing nothing, but it's waiting to slide you away into another realm."

"Another realm?" Blair echoed. "What does that mean, another realm?"

He shook his head and turned her wrist to the side again. "All that I can see is it's a 'realm of banishment'. It looks like a desolate place where only a few different species live."

A realm of banishment? As in the one from Anita's song? Blair took a few breaths, unsure what her next words should be. "So I'm going into banishment?" Her eyes glanced around her surroundings. "Do you see any way to stop it?"

"This magic allows me to see how long you have and what it does. I can't see more than that." Then Vidwal dropped her wrist and pushed the bowl of water before her. Those eyes were returning to their old hue. Blair picked the wax clumps from her skin and cleansed the residue in the bowl. "I know both of the ancient races have been gone for so long, but the ones who understood the rokians' tricks the best were the vayen aray."

Blair looked up at him, flicking droplets from her fingers. "So there's nothing to do then? I'm just stuck?"

Vidwal snagged a towel from his shelf and handed it to her. "I don't know much about that. I might have said 'good luck' and rushed you along, but this is making me think." He planted his elbow on the table and held his head up. "No doubt, it was a rokian who cursed you, but I'm wondering how and why is he free from the spell the vayen aray played on him? If the rokians are out, then maybe the vayen aray are too."

"But how can we be sure?"

"That's a good question. None of them have shown themselves or gave us a notice or anything." He watched the towel absently as Blair pushed it to the side. "But if they're here, then you might find a clue at their old home."

That last bit snagged Blair's attention. "Whose old home?"

His eyes met hers and answered like she should have known. "The old home of the vayen aray, of course. You do know about the island, don't you?" But Blair was unsure and slightly shook her head. Vidwal sat back with a scoff. "I'm talking about Lyfíhana! The people lived in a tall mountain alone in the center of an island. They had beautiful feathered wings, so living on a mountain in the middle of a wide span of water didn't bother them." He studied her for a second before he continued. "If there's an answer for your curse, and if the vayen aray are here on this world as well, then you should find something in Lyfíhana. It's the biggest island in the southern cluster, due south of here."

Frustration welled up in Blair's head. *Great! It wasn't enough for me to come all the way out here. Now I have to figure out how to reach a distant island?*

Vidwal shrugged, scrunched his face, and looked to the side. "I'd suggest... The harbor town of Seadrake. You'll have to look for help."

Blair's first response was a roll of her eyes. That bit of advice *really* helped her the last time. When she focused again on Vidwal, he was watching her curiously. Despite the grim news that her search for a cure continued to push her along boundaries she'd never crossed, she should be grateful the scholar went out of his way to help her. She tried to offer a smile, though it appeared more like a grimace. She stood up and pushed the chair against the table.

Seeing her stand brought Vidwal to his feet. "It might be hard to find someone who'll take you for a low price though. Sailors can be fickle when it comes to who is on their ship."

"Yes, it's that I'm worried about." *Especially when it comes to women,* Blair finished silently in her mind. She sighed and bowed before him. "But I'll do my best to figure it out. You've done your part. Thank you for that."

He nodded, a knowing smile spreading on his face. "Just don't forget our deal. And if it doesn't work out, then I'll have to come up with something else. I may not need workers now, but that doesn't mean one of them won't become sick and will need a replacement."

Blair accepted the charge without a verbal answer. She made a quick mental note to talk with the band of musicians as soon as possible, but she knew she wasn't going to actively look for them now. Vidwal stepped out in front of her and escorted her past the rows of books and back through the rooms of luxury. Blair was not excited to be a part of the cold outdoors again, but she knew that Vidwal wouldn't appreciate her staying longer than needed.

As soon as the entry door swung open again, a cold draft blew in, leaving Blair to shiver. Not backing down from its harsh weather, she gave Aen Vidwal a final look and stepped out. The door swung shut behind her.

The cold only seemed to increase as the day went on. She pressed her bare hands against her chest. The chill was racing through her skin and bones without even slowing. A breath caught of unsteadiness and white mist raced past her lips. She was going to need every coin she had, if not more, to find a ship to take her to Lyfíhana, but she also needed supplies before leaving.

A part of her wanted to forget about them and begin anyway, but the unforgiving wind reminded her the weather was only turning for the worse. She needed to stop for supplies. Giving the door of the estate another look, she sighed yet again and descended down the path.

Miles away and at the same time Blair was leaving the Limadia Estate's land, Queriven was sitting in the room of another lodge, avoiding the dreaded frost outdoors. The thick walls blocked out the whistling gusts, keeping the inside warm and peaceful.

But despite this, Queriven was neither of these. If someone was watching him then, they would have seen a solemn and quiet figure sitting still on a chair. He turned his head to the window, slightly looking down. Long brown hair fell dangling on either side of his face, but those eyes were not focusing on the disastrous weather outside. It wasn't hard to tell that.

And if one watched long enough, they would notice something was wrong. The elf was too still, almost like his body was empty of spirit. Shutters thudded loudly on the outside wall with each strong burst of frigid wind. The hearth popped and cackled, but the figure on the chair never moved.

Inside him lay a tormented soul, but something recent had pushed him further into withdrawal. His tired mind fed him falsehoods until he gave in to believing them. Blair was right; Queriven recognized that horn. He wanted to deny his own knowledge; even more, he wished he never followed Blair into the hills.

But he couldn't run, and he couldn't act. That horn was gone now, and ever since it disappeared, Queriven hoped that he will never run into it again. Alas, there was no doubt this involved him. Blair was the target now. It was already his fault so many lives died in his hands. Could he live knowing he had doomed another victim, if not more? She was nothing more than a human girl after all.

No, her image will continue to haunt him regardless. This was his doing, and now because of guilt and greed, he will choose to sit back and allow the worst to befall her. But was it really too late? Blair was not doomed yet and she would have better chances at survival if she had help...

Queriven shook his head in frustration and panic. The chair underneath him squeaked when he rose from it. His mind yelled at him, making him sick and angry. There was no help he could give. Finding her again would mean he would have to face his buried past, and that was not going to happen.

But Blair still had a chance! The voices continued to argue and contradict. Which was better? For him to sit back and allow his bloodied history to engulf another helpless, innocent life? Or should he stand up, despite the pain, and do everything he can to fight it?

His pace slowed when he came to the window. Weak from internal arguments, he watched the flakes whisk and cling to the corner of the glass. He never came to a decision.

That is, he remained at war with himself all through the night. Finally, sleep pulled him into a daze toward early morning. But before it could pull him deeper, he shot out of it, the picture of his hated memories fresh in his mind. He couldn't go through it again. He wanted the nightmares to stop.

CHAPTER NINE
SETTING SAIL ON A WINTER SEA

Yusen Nashögan was a man of great stature. One look at his fine coat and confident stride brought either fear or pride. Firm, trained muscles bulged under the fabric of his coat and thick leather boots crunched the frozen grass mercilessly. His wide face and narrowed eyes focused on an important duty.

Further north, near a cold taiga, Yusen edged ever closer to an old, unnamed watchtower. The door was crooked and rotted but still pushed open. Here, the wind became nothing more than a whistle. The door slammed shut behind him.

The watchtower wasn't the best shelter, as parts of the walls and ceiling were missing, but it was still protected from most weather. Yusen paused, but his posture never grew tense from the suspicious air. The parts that were still together cast a dark shadow and the light from outside revealed disturbed dust that reminded him of its age. The man never turned his nose from the mustiness. If anything, it was familiar and reminded him of home.

He kept his weathered hands in his deep pockets as he glanced over to the thickest shadow patiently. He already knew he wasn't alone. "About time," the dark shifted and Yusen caught the faint outline of a man stepping forward. The first feature revealed eyes of amber and a face cut with sharp angles and chin. The dust hasn't settled much on his skin, but even in the light, it was a dusty bluish grey. The tone of his skin only made his eyes stand out even more. "I was growing impatient," the man stated simply, blinking and turning his face to the side.

Yusen Nashögan bowed his head politely. "Apologizes," he said with a thick accent born of a far continent. "I started my trek late."

Without small talk or proceedings, the other man asked, "What did you find?"

"I was told the girl left her village. Recently, they tracked her at the Limadia Estate."

That brought a sigh from the man from the shadows. "Of course, she has to make my job difficult." He glanced over to the broken walls. A better ray of light leaked through from the clouds, lining the man's face and showing scraggy black hairs on his chin.

Yusen regarded him curiously. "Darkadus, Sir?" he asked. "Does that even mean anything? The scholar is a fool. He doesn't care about anything besides the state of his manor. Even if he wanted to, those practices have lost their touch. He wouldn't be able to read anything."

"No. That one can, and he did." Darkadus pushed off the wall and focused again on Yusen. "And the only place he can send her to is Lyfíhana?"

"Lyfíhana?" Yusen echoed. "Isn't that where..."

"The vayen aray lived. Yes, it is."

"But that place is empty. You told me you were the only one who came out."

Amber flashed as Darkadus frowned from the constant questioning, but still, he answered, "Yes and no. That place isn't quite empty." Without another look, he stepped around Yusen, who merely pondered in further confusion. He opened his mouth to dare and ask a question about it, but Darkadus spoke first. "I will help you where I can, but I need her to be stopped before she reaches her destination."

Yusen turned to see Darkadus watching him, almost like his

gaze alone could place the responsibility on the man's shoulder. Then he shifted to the wall where he kept his silver-toned hand. "I've already used too much magic as it is. Too much more and both of us will be seeing consequences."

"She'll be looking for a ship at the harbor then. Don't worry, Sir, that's my greatest area of expertise," Yusen replied with eyes gleaming, and he bowed his head again before stepping back outside.

Darkadus remained where he was. He didn't even move from the sudden snap back of the heavy door. His magic was, and remained, the most powerful in all the world. He just couldn't wait for the time when he could prove it. In the meantime, he would just have to trust the pirate to do the job well.

Blair covered herself head to toe in tight and warm winter clothing, though she still shivered. The little bit of her face one could see beyond the scarf around her neck and cheeks blushed with hot blood. Strands of golden brown hair flew free in the misty cold air.

The way past the Taleena Hills was long as snowfalls left layers of sticky white at her feet. It was even harder for her to find places to make camp where she could rest. Luckily, that gave her time to improve on her fire setting skills and she had a decent ember-filled camp for one night at least.

In the end, Blair was thankful she went for the extra supplies. She would have been dead already without them. Still, she was losing a lot of time to the hills.

Seadrake was in the far southeastern part of her kingdom, nearly opposite to where she was now, and she gave in to the caravans who offered her a ride for a few coins. That took her to see the harbor town faster than she would have on her own. But on the way there, her heart dropped as she sat in the back seat of a caravan. She barely had any money left in hopes of catching onto a ship. She prayed someone would be generous.

Over a week after she left the Limadia Estate, Blair finally arrived in Seadrake. Busy and hurried people crowded the streets. The sea mist that burned her nostrils and the cry of working men and seagulls only added to the chaos. The city was nearly as full as Dunverhart was, though she considered it might be an illusion as the people here were even busier.

But what a big city it was! There were already many ships lining the long wooden wharf and spacing for a few more. Between glimmers of nearby conversations, Blair swore she could hear them creaking with the waves.

"There we go, Miss Tripps!" the rounded man at the front called as the caravan came to a stop before hitting the bumbling cobble. Blair descended from her seat, calling a cry of gratitude to him.

A sense of familiarity came to her then and it left her with the same sense of broken direction when she jumped from the musicians' carriage at Dunverhart, though this time, a new sight was lying before her eyes; the ocean lining the horizon.

True, she had been lucky enough to stand before the cliffsides that dropped to the seawater, but she's never seen a harbor before it. The ocean itself was so different from how she remembered it. She was near its level now, and it was like the waters lied just beneath her feet, ready to swallow her up.

The ships towered over her like mountains with every step closer to the wharf. Nervous, she tried to avoid those patrolling the docks. But now that she was here among the ships and busy crew, she had no idea what she was doing here. She asked herself what she needed to do now. Blair needed to reach Lyfíhana, but how many ships were going near there? She needed to find a place to ask.

That task took her all day, from looking for a map so she knew where the island was, to seeking an office where she could inquire about a ship. But in the end, an official told her to try a tavern, as that's where most of the crews and captains would be after work.

The thought of a fully crazed tavern filled with drunk

seamen didn't sound like a comfortable place for a young woman to be in, but Blair held tight to her mission. At sunset, she entered the first tavern near the docks, and true to her visions, the room was already full of yelling, dancing drunk sailors.

Timid and avoiding the grasps and stares from men, Blair sneaked further in and choked on the smells of dirty bodies mixed with the tang of alcohol. It made the reek of the perfume worn from the bar ladies even worse. Blair wrinkled her nose, suddenly hoping she wouldn't carry the smell on her when she leaves. When she was near the counter, she picked out a man befitting for the image of a captain and dared to approach him.

The process nearly took all night, and the tavern stayed as busy as it was. Many of the men she talked with were already done for the season. Those few who weren't didn't take her on because she either didn't have enough money or refused because "women aboard a ship is bad luck." Blair was lucky to even find men sober enough to talk to.

Her stinging eyes watered as she yawned, and she scanned the room for another candidate. She found one sitting at the table with the rest of a group. Blair took hope in that he seemed calmer than the rest of the ones she had asked so far. He was content where he was, drawing in the smoke from a thick pipe. The man was leaning back in the seat with his leg up on the other. The edges of his blue coat dipped for the floor.

"Excuse me?" Blair asked.

Dark eyes popped open and he slowly sat up, taking the pipe from his lips. "Yes?" he answered in a higher-pitched tone. She didn't recognize his accent.

"You have a ship, right? Any chance you'll be passing by Lyfíhana any time soon?"

He considered her question for a moment. "We're heading for the island just south of it. 'Won't take us far from those shores."

Blair's heart skipped a beat and she hurried to snag the opportunity. "I very much need to reach it. How much would it be for me to ride with you?"

"You, a woman, want to sail with us?" he asked, bewildered at first. But before she could speak, he wove his arm to those at the table. "Well, this is my crew, and the crew of the Sapphire Reef." Then he leaned into her closer. "Now they say a woman aboard a ship is bad luck for reasons, but I believe you have what it takes to convince me."

"I... I don't have much, but I'll give you the rest of the gold I have," she answered awkwardly, suddenly doubtful she could convince him. From her bag, she produced seven gold coins and held it out for him to see.

But he sat back after just one glance. "That ain't much, Miss." He took a long drag from his pipe, leaving Blair standing with her few coins and wondering what to do next. "But we could always use another hand on the ship. Ever been on one?"

Blair thought about the odd question. Of course, she hasn't. He just told her women usually aren't allowed, but she just shook her head.

His eyes sparkled. "It be the best in all the world, Girl." He sat for a while, shaking his head in the awe and beauty of a ship casting over the sea spray. Behind them, a table of drunkards fell into a rowdy argument, unashamed for everybody to hear. Blair tried her hardest not to become distracted. The man she spoke to, however, didn't even flinch at the sound of a fist slamming against wood. "I tell you what; I know you're short on experience, but we could let you pay with work while aboard."

For a second, her eyes brightened. He was really letting her on board! But then, her face scrunched down in judgment. "What kind of work?" she asked as she crossed her arms over her chest.

The sailor was in the middle of a draw and he took the chance to study what she meant. Finally, he caught the meaning and wove the pipe in front of him. "No, no, no, there be nothing you should worry about. Take the promise of ol' Nekene here." Still holding out the pipe like he was pushing away the notion Blair gave him, he placed the other hand against his heart. Then, he pushed up for a better seating posture. "We'll be leaving at dawn, and when I say dawn, I mean the dark sky right before dawn! See you there at the Sapphire Reef then?"

Blair considered her options again. She didn't want to place her trust in another suspicious person. These people may not be safe. She swallowed her fear. This may be her only chance. If she couldn't reach Lyfíhana, then she's as good as gone.

"Yes, Sir, and thank you," Blair decided. She gave the table behind them one last look before coming back to Nekene again. He was already back in the seating position as when she first saw him. Quickly, Blair broke away, walking a quick march for the exit before the yelling back there turns into a loaded brawl.

The dawn came quicker than what Blair was ready for. The morning was below freezing temperatures and it was hard to fight her tired mind. Surely, the rest of the crew were just as exhausted as well. Who knows how long they stayed at the bar? Perhaps, they haven't even slept at all yet. Whatever the case, when Blair finally found the Sapphire Reef among all the other ships and climbed aboard, the crew was already working hard with little distractions.

Nekene was there to greet her as well, and already, she barely recognized the man. There were details about him she didn't notice in the smoky darkness of the bar. His skin was dark and weathered, his frame was thin and skinny despite his trained arm muscles, and his worn hands showed old rope burns in many angles. He assured her there will be work for her as well, but beyond a few errands now, there wasn't much for her to do until they leave port.

Surprisingly, she wasn't bothered by the men. She had few stares and they kept their work to themselves. Blair counted herself lucky she kept meeting with the right people. She did what she was told and otherwise tried to stay out of the way. Her eyes were so heavy that she sat on a stair for just a minute and fell asleep.

Blair woke up shortly after that to pounding feet near her. The stairs suddenly became heavy with traffic. She barely even heard one man excuse himself as he carefully went around her. As soon as she got the chance, she stood up and backed away, only to find Nekene was behind her. It was that moment when she realized the open ocean surrounded them. The port of Seadrake was creeping further and further away. Perhaps, she was asleep longer than she thought?

"Look alive, men!" Nekene yelled, glancing at the working crew. "None of us should be slacking when the captain comes out! I don't care if you've already done the work you set out to do. Start something else. Keep yourselves busy!"

Blair regarded him and turned her head as his eyes fell on her. "The captain? You mean, you're not the captain?"

Nekene exploded in laughter at that and the men nearby followed suit. The laughter continued on and on. Blair remained still despite it piercing her like a sharp knife. "She thought he was the captain!" Men cried around her.

"Why wasn't he at the tavern last night?" she asked, unchanged by the joking comments.

Nekene's shoulders were still bobbing as he chuckled, but he calmed again under her serious glare. "The captain is a solitary man. He likes to drink by himself most of the time. But I'm not him. No, I'm the first mate."

Blair may not know much about the ways of a ship, but she was not stupid. She squinted, judging him once more. "Then why did you bring me on the ship without talking with him first?"

But Nekene didn't hesitate. "I hold a lot of authority, Miss. Once he comes out of that cabin, you'll learn for yourself." After that, he didn't hesitate further and the group disbanded with the remaining chuckles.

Blair let the conversation go, but curiosity remained for the longest time. She continued to ponder about the captain even after someone gave her a scrub and bucket of water. True to Nekene's words, they kept her busy running errands on the ship, and she did all of it with no complaints.

The crew was kind to her despite them laughing every time she spoke a term wrong or asked what they perceived as a stupid question. Blair didn't have the time to talk with a lot of them, but she could tell from watching that not only did they have a lot of experience with the ship, but they've known each other for a long time. Constantly, they would boss the others around with inside jokes or bluntness. And the few newer to the crew were treated like young cabin boys. They had to obey with no objections or they were made fun of in front of the crew.

The whole trip was so new for Blair. She wasn't very comfortable, but she was glad they took her on. Finally, as she was on the errand of retrieving a net from below deck, she was passing by the door to the captain's cabin when it suddenly opened.

Surprised, Blair jumped back and stood in awe as the captain of the Sapphire Reef stepped out onto the open deck. No one flinched but her. Hardly a person turned to look at him except for Nekene who gave a short greeting.

Blair didn't know what to think, but she knew he was a figure of awesome power and wisdom. He was tall, dark, and strong, and his wide face was weathered and scarred from a hard-working life. Nothing deterred him as he kept his confident stride, and he wasn't afraid to let his boots fall heavy on the wooden deck. His beard was short but thick and black. His hair was nicely trimmed and groomed. His clothes, in particular, caught her attention. They were odd and clearly not found in her land of Fairdraisha. A red pointed hat was set on his head, and it had wide brims that turned almost vertical at the edge. His coat was also just as fancy. It was fit for a formal meeting and consisted of many colors, though it was mainly red and black with spaced buttons and pockets.

Without much of a glance at her or any of the workers, he walked past, heading toward the man by the helm. Blair was stiff in place with her mouth agape, all thoughts of the net forgotten as she watched him. That was a man of importance, and he knew it. Blair was thankful he didn't turn to her. She wouldn't know how to respond to such a man like that. Even when the captain was all the way up the stairs and by the helm where she couldn't see him well, Blair remained stuck for a while longer until she remembered the net with a jolt. Not wanting to be laughed at again, she turned, nearly falling all the way down the hull of the ship.

Below deck was not even close to being as clean as the main deck above her was. It was even worse than the bar! She caught unwashed bodies, lingering tobacco, and livestock, along with more unpleasant smells that told of a long history. She waved it off, trying not to be sick by the old cots and messy belongings of the crew. Permanent stains marred the wood along with sticky stuff of an unknown source.

She found the net shoved in a tight place between heavy crates, almost like whoever was here dropped the net on accident and, not caring a bit, left it there and shoved the crates against it. Blair gripped it with both hands, grunting as she pulled back. It stretched, but slowly pulled bit by bit free from its prison. After Blair recovered from the recoil of falling on her behind, she took it up. The rope was entangled badly, and she wondered if she should risk more time to fix it, but instead decided it would be best if she didn't take too long.

Blair was back on the deck in no time and moved with unsteady feet up the stairs with the net in hand. "...in a day," the member at the helm said as he spoke with the captain. "And then we'll turn back and report our progress."

The captain nodded. "Wonderful," he stated, his voice richly accented and cracked. He opened his mouth as if to say something more, but another voice broke it up.

"Captain Nashögan!" a man on the main deck called. The captain responded and marched down the stairs to speak to him.

More comfortable now, Blair focused again on the job at hand. She held the net out to the worker who asked her to collect it, to begin with. He scoffed at the tight knots but thanked her anyway.

Sometime later, Blair spotted the captain on board again, and she was trying to ignore or deny the fact that Captain Nashōgan was walking his way closer. His destination seemed to be herself, but surely not. Surely, he had more important things to worry about. But indeed, he stopped before her and Blair drew her eyes up to his narrowed gaze.

"Miss Tripps," he greeted, and she held her breath. "Tonight, I'll prepare a place in my cabin where you can sleep. The cots below deck are no place for a woman. I'm sure you already noted that when you went down there."

Fright took hold of her. Were his intentions genuine? "Thank you," she bowed, "but you won't need to go through the trouble."

The captain raised an eyebrow at her but otherwise didn't move. He stood perfectly straight with his arms formally held behind him. He chuckled and nodded to the setting sun on the water-filled horizon. "You have no need to worry. None of the men, myself included, are going to hurt you. No, we're grateful you helped with as much as you have despite the new uncomfortable surroundings."

Blair turned back to the setting sun, still unsure. The captain widened his eyes again. "That is unless you would rather sleep down there with the rest of the crew. You have to rest sometime tonight."

Finally convinced, Blair agreed to his offer. Captain Nashōgan nodded and went on his way. But still, something invisible pricked her skin. It wasn't about the offer from the captain, but something was wrong. She didn't know what it was for sure, but this group of men was too friendly. But as of late, they've been eyeing her more, like she was the center of attention for some reason. Their attitude toward her was changing and she had no idea why.

It was early morning. None of the crew bothered to wake her, not even the captain, though clearly, he was already gone from the cabin. Blair stretched, still lying under a mountain of blankets. To give her enough space to feel secure, the captain made her a place to sleep outside of his bedroom. He layered cushions after cushions on the floor near a window next to a table filled with charts and maps.

The surroundings were hard to become familiar with, but the gentle sway of the sea under the ship, along with the warm moonlight shining through the window and on the wooden walls and floors quickly became a comfort during the last handful of days. The motion didn't bother her much once she lied down to sleep.

Blair tossed the blankets to the side, seeking escape from entanglement. The air was still freezing cold once she was free, but a voice brought her away from the shivers under her skin. Even behind the walls of the neat and colorful cabin, she could hear the call clearly, and intrigue drew her to investigate. "Land Ho!"

There was a sharp wind today and it cut through Blair's face and hair. It threatened to knock her down. Already, a lot of the crew were along the port side of the ship, staring out into the distance.

Blair joined them and saw the island of interest. It was still far in the distance, but it was in the way of travel. The sun was sitting almost directly behind it, making it nothing more than a dark silhouette. Blair could see the island was rocky, full of uneven ground and cliffs. There were even forms of what looked like old ruins and broken buildings, much like the ones on the mainland.

But there was no mountain soaring to the top, and it had to be too soon to have arrived at their destination yet. There was no way this was Lyfíhana. "What is this place?" Blair asked out loud.

She didn't aim the question to anyone in particular, but it was the captain who answered. He was standing just a few meters from her, aiming at the small island with an old telescope. "They call this place 'Lost Sanctuary'. It was once a sacred place reserved for God's holiness, a place where he could reach down to the souls below who needed him the most." Satisfied, he pushed in the telescope and let it rest at his side. "Now it's nothing more than any other ancient building that fell victim to the powerful rokians."

Blair looked from him and back to the island. It was growing closer inch by inch. "We're not stopping here, are we? What purpose could we have?"

Captain Nashögan only growled and yelled directions to the helmsman before backing off from the railing. Growing concerned, Blair also backed away and faced him. "But we're still going to Lyfihana, right? That was the reason I boarded the ship. Nekene told me the Sapphire Reef was passing by it."

"Nekene was only doing as he was told to get you aboard the ship, and now that you're here, we have no intention of going near the place."

She forgot how to breathe as time itself came to a stop. "What?" she asked, eyeing the captain with a wide gaze. "But why would any of you lie to me?"

Growling with impatience again, he answered, "Because my employer knows you're trying to break the curse he cast over you." He leaned a little closer and said, "I can tell you now that you're not going to make it in time, so you can feel free to stop trying."

Blair's voice was nothing more than a broken whisper as she stood before the man involved with her fate. "You know about the curse?"

He laughed over her lost expression and turned away. "You should have known not to board a pirate's ship anyway. Tie her up, men. The last thing we need is to have her running about the ship, even if she has nowhere to run now."

Knowing what he said is true, Blair didn't even move to escape as the crew approached her with rope in hand. Nekene stood on watch as the group pulled the rope around her and tightened her hands together. Not a scream came from her lips. She didn't even shed a tear despite her betrayed look. Blair only accepted the failure and hopelessness. She watched Nekene as he stood there. "You're pirates?" she asked him after a while. The fact that he didn't bother to answer told her they were. She shook her dark blonde hair. "But why would Seadrake allow a pirate ship in? They're supposed to be watching for any sign of crime."

This time, Nekene did speak. "Let's just say the guards are a little corrupt. They're working for your king, so, of course, they're just as blind as he is."

Blair lowered her head but didn't argue. The crew backed away. Only a few remained as the rest returned to their work. The island known as Lost Sanctuary was still growing closer. She could make out the colors of it now. "Who is your employer?" Blair asked in a flat voice.

Nekene laughed and shrugged. "My employer is Captain Yusen Nashōgan. I've never met this employer he speaks of, but I know his goals."

Blair thought about his response, then came to one of her own. "Why do you support this captain? He works his crew toward goals you don't care about. What are you gaining from his decision to take orders from someone you don't follow?"

He shot his answer in quickly. "Listen," he poked a dirty finger her way, "sometimes you don't choose a life of crime; sometimes it chooses you. When it does, you have to understand that your fellow workers won't always do the right thing or support your ways of thinking. But there is always honor among thieves, among pirates."

Nekene's retort was a ridiculous one, but Blair knew he didn't change his mind. He was serious. "Nekene!" the captain called, coming back to face his first mate. Nekene responded by standing straight with a formal response. "When we maroon the girl, I want you to go with her."

The pride that was shining in his eyes faded and he wasn't sure how to respond. "What?" he asked. "But Sir..."

"We have an important mission here. Trust me, I'm not marooning you because I don't need you on the crew anymore. I'm sending you with her because you're the best man I have, and I want you to make sure we succeed. Keep her on the island, and remember, she needs to survive. We'll come back and pick you up near the end of summer."

Without waiting for another response, the captain left him dazed and confused. Blair lifted her head, a smirk on her lips. "What were you saying about honor among pirates? Are you sure you want to continue to follow him?"

Nekene glared at her with the most disgusted face he could muster, which just looked pathetic to Blair, before stomping out of her sight. Shortly after that, two of the men came up behind her and pushed her forward, leading her to the railing. She didn't fight their grip and she buried the rising fear in her gut. All was hopeless. No one could help her now.

CHAPTER TEN
STRANDED

The whole crew stood by the port side of Sapphire Reef. The small boat was already waiting at the bottom for Nekene and Blair. The two were to be marooned on the small island ahead.

The captain shook the hand of his first mate with a promise that he wouldn't forget him, and Nekene, despite still looking upset, climbed down into the boat below. The men by Blair helped to bring her down. Then, they also sat in the boat and began to row.

If the ocean looked big before, then it was ginormous down here in the small boat. Given any other circumstance, Blair would have marveled at how tiny she was before the wide open sea, but her mind was too filled with betrayal. Still, she refused to show any of it to the men. She didn't cry and she didn't beg. None of it would have helped her anyway. For the trip to the island, she didn't meet their faces but tried to allow her mind to draw a blank. She couldn't bear to consider what may happen to her now.

The gulls cried above, echoing her internal sorrows. Blair noted how much the rope around her was beginning to hurt. It also smelled rancid, as if it soaked on a sticky floor of tar for longer than it should. It was so strong Blair couldn't smell the saltwater past it. She slouched, trying both to move the rope to a different area of her shoulders and to burrow down from the cold.

Blair was trying so hard to focus on the things around her, which she barely noticed when they arrived on the shore of Lost Sanctuary. It happened quicker than she thought it would. Nekene was the first to stand and he reached and took hold of the rope over Blair and dragged her to her feet before leading her to the sand. Nekene left the boat but didn't slow and Blair tripped as she was leaving it. Nekene wasn't concerned; he roughly pulled her up and away from the shore. The men left in the boat didn't even offer a goodbye. They just sat down again, rowing back to the ship.

Both Nekene and Blair watched them push back the tide and waves crashing against them. They were free to sail with the Sapphire Reef wherever she pleases. Blair sighed. "Looks like we're stuck now. You can feel free to untie me. It's growing pretty uncomfortable."

He didn't respond.

She gave another sigh, this one rougher and born of annoyance. "You can't ignore me the entire time we're here. We need to be gathering resources. Don't you want me to help with that or not?"

Finally, he snapped. "You're not getting into my head, Wrench! This was all your doing! And now you have me wrapped up into this as well."

He continued to rant his frustrations and put the blame on Blair before she stopped him. "Hold on! This wasn't my idea. I wasn't planning on being marooned."

"No," he agreed as he raised his voice all the louder. The crashes of the waves muffled the focus of the argument. "But if you hadn't tried so hard to break this curse when you got it, we wouldn't be in this mess!"

Still wrapped up in the dirty ropes, the best she could do was flick her hair behind her head. "What would you want me to do then? Give up? What if you were in my shoes? Would you just accept it without a fight?"

Nekene's face, pale before from the crew's betrayal, was now glowing red. Those dark eyes pierced through her and he started to yell. Blair was no longer listening. Just then, something on the far horizon caught her attention. Perhaps, her head was playing tricks or maybe the water was casting an illusion on the clouds. But desperately, she tried to imagine the form far in the distance to be the light of sails.

But back on the Sapphire Reef, the captain saw it too. Indeed, it was as it seemed. Captain Yusen Nashōgan unfolded the telescope in his pocket and glared toward the newcomer. A low growl escaped his throat. The Lost Sanctuary wasn't too far from the harbor of Seadrake, but they were coming this way. It was intentional; it wasn't a mere passing ship. Why was it coming closer? There was nothing here but old ruins.

It could only mean one thing, and Captain Nashōgan had to prepare for the worst. With a strong authority, he sucked the air through his lungs and used it to bellow to the crew. Instantly and without question, they obeyed, rushing for weapons and cannon ammo.

"Is that what I think it is?" Nekene asked. His complaints to keep the argument alive were forgotten. Blair had shown him the form on the horizon after she confirmed it to be a ship. "But why are they over here?"

Blair shook her head. Both of them were staring over the open waters. "I don't know, but maybe they've come to help us."

Nekene scoffed and stepped away, marching for the old church on the rocks behind them. Blair turned. "Wait! What are you doing? Isn't this a good thing for both of us?"

"No," he answered, turning around to her again. "You don't get it, do you? The only reason that ship is here is because it knows us. We're pirates, and that means we face trial if we're caught. We may even be killed. This is not good. And despite this, I'm still under the orders of Captain Nashōgan. My loyalty has not and will never change."

"Wha..." Blair began to ask before he turned away again. Nekene must have gone mad! This wasn't a matter of loyalty. This was straight up betrayal. No one with a right mind should be all right with this end of the deal.

Suddenly, a ripple shook through the air, stopping both of them in their tracks. Sure enough, that boom was from one of the ships' cannons. They were in battle. Nekene turned back to the tides. The smoke was rising from both the ships. "Captain!" Nekene cried uselessly.

But there was nothing any of them could do but watch.

Back on board the ship of the Sapphire Reef, the battle was quickly growing out of control. Already, blood stained the wood of both ships, and swords and spells quickly flashed by at every encounter. The newcomer with the name Enchantress came prepared. It was almost like they knew who owned the Sapphire Reef and where it was.

And in the midst of screams, smoke, and flying blood, a figure stood on the Sapphire Reef, shining spear in hand. Queriven twisted and spun the pole in perfect grace and balance. His set face never showed a grimace in the confrontations, not even once. His focus was set on finding Blair, no matter how many pirates he had to drop.

The captain of the Enchantress had bigger goals. These pirates of the Sapphire Reef have been wanted for a terribly long time. It is high time they were caught and brought in to justice. His crew brought in any and all who surrendered, and those who refused joined the carnage on the wooden decks. Most of the pirates chose the latter, of course, as they knew they faced death either way.

Captain Nashögan never showed pain, either in physical wound or emotion. For the moral of the fight, he had to stay strong, though these men were more than workers. He knew them personally and they were the only family he had.

With each wound and pirate who fell mortally on the floor, it was like a hole sliced in Yusen's heart. He didn't sign up for this. If he would have known the deaths of his crew this day, he wouldn't have joined Darkadus' side, not for all the treasures in the world.

But now it was too late. Adrenaline forced his arm through the gut of a nearby opponent, and he quickly surveyed the scene. That is, he quickly glanced through the battlefield, but it was like time stopped for him. Familiar voices cried their last, and the skins and limbs were ripped from his crew before his eyes. The reek of carnage was wafting through his brain.

The Enchantress won the battle today. He accepted it as he found himself surrounded by her crew approaching him. He winced. The scars lining his upper jaw were appearing deeper than they were. This was personal, and no matter what involvement Darkadus had for this peasant girl, he swore he would take revenge on the people who hurt his family — that he vowed.

Serious damage overtook the Sapphire Reef and she began to sink. Anguished, but silent, Nekene did the only thing he could do; fall helplessly to his knees. Blair, also silent and still tied, watched him sob quietly. She stiffened; he was only falling deeper and deeper into despair and she feared what he might do to her after this.

Whoever came and defeated the pirates, please come ashore. Don't leave me here with this madman. Almost too afraid to move, she glanced at the ruins behind her. Should she leave and hide from Nekene? If someone aboard the other ship thought to come ashore, she would want to remain in eyesight, but she was also worried about being killed by Yusen's first mate, even if he told him not to hurt her.

Deciding survival was best confirmed first, Blair stepped back quietly, turning for the old church. Her pace quickened with each step. She was eager to be far away from Nekene. But despite his blinding sorrows, he looked back and saw her attempt at escape. Driven with fury past the mind's limitations, he picked up a dash for his prey.

Blair was not a slow runner, but the tight rope was hard to carry fast enough, and he easily caught up with her. She screamed a blood-letting curl when his hands took her by the rope and spun her violently around. With the scrape of a white shining knife, he stuck the blade to her throat. His eyes were wide and bloodshot. He spoke with bared broken teeth, but Blair hardly heard the words he said through her churning fear and the prick of a sharp edge on her neck.

With a firm and shaking hand, he grasped her face and turned it to the direction of the sinking ship. "Look there!" he growled. "That was my home. Don't you see that?! How would you feel if you saw your home burst in flames knowing everything you had was still in there?" The tears Blair kept in all this time was now burning on her cheeks. Nekene released her face to grasp the rope again. "It doesn't matter to you, but I'll make sure this affects you as much as it does me."

But with a jolt, he took notice of three forms off the shore. They were leaving a boat and coming right for them. They were already spotted. Nekene had to act quickly. He turned Blair around again, pushing her for the security of the old ruins.

Not much remained of the holy sanctuary, but it still stood tall. Not only was it an important refuge for the poor and needy, but it was still breathtaking in every way. The stained glass shards were dull and dark. It was now impossible to make out the pictures, as the colors lost their shine. Broken stepping stones and pavement jutted up in odd angles. The lovely fountain in the square would never again pour sparkling and clear water.

Inside the church, past the no-longer-existing front doors, there remained not much of a room. Scattered pews and altars littered the weed-filled floors. Sorrowful sunlight shone down on the wreckage like God mourned the loss of the precious sanctuary.

But Blair never made it inside.

A voice cried, bringing Nekene to a stop. It wasn't from behind them, but ahead. "Let her go." There he was, by the wreck that was the remaining rightmost wall. Queriven emerged from the corner of the church, arrow already drawn and pointing at Nekene. The tip sparkled with a beauty no metal could possibly show, no matter how polished. The elf's hand was also perfectly steady and calm. There was no way he could miss.

Blair's eyes continued to spill, but she didn't cry out the

name of her rescuer. She was afraid to graze the knife's edge any closer than she already has. Nekene froze, his expression unchanged and unreadable. Another call came from behind. The three from the small boat finally caught up.

Nekene glanced at the three behind them and hugged Blair closer. He was using her as a shield. He turned back to Queriven again, looking back and forth at his opponents. Finally, the elf repeated his order. "It doesn't have to end this way. Let the girl go and we'll take you peacefully." Light sparkled in Nekene's dark eyes and a grimace of sorrow showed. Queriven already had his answer.

When his attention turned again to the three men behind him, Queriven saw the grip on the knife tightened. Faster than light, he released the sparkling arrow. Mercilessly, it drove into Nekene's side just above the left hip. He yelled, dropping the knife as he was forced to drop to the broken pavement.

Blair broke free, crying hysterical and out of control. She darted for the entrance to the church where she stood. The three men rushed to access Nekene's wounds. Queriven, however, stayed and placed a soft hand on the rope still binding her.

Without speaking a word, he cut the twine from her hands and shoulders. Now free, but blind with fear, Blair grasped Queriven's arms. Weeping, she clung to him like a kitten just rescued from a cold lake. A thousand questions ran through Blair's mind, but none of that mattered now. Queriven came just in time and now she was safe.

Impatience pounded the mind of Darkadus yet again. He was standing on the mainland of Fairdraisha, but overlooking the southern cliffsides. It was a sudden straight drop just under his feet, all the way down the rocks and into the crashing sea.

The air was cold and it seemed much colder with each breath as it entered his lungs. Darkadus wasn't too bothered. He embraced the temperature changes in this realm as there was little where he came from.

He had other matters on his mind anyhow. He needed to make sure the pirate captain succeeded in his task. And so, he spent some of his precious magic on scrying a vision. The Lost Sanctuary was many miles away, yet Darkadus watched them like an invisible spirit.

He watched the whole scene unfold. Everything from when they led Blair and Nekene to the island, to watching the ship sink into the cold winter ocean. Yusen Nashōgan failed, but that wasn't the only interesting point to him. The Enchantress didn't reach the island on her own. Her captain didn't know about the location of the Sapphire Reef. Someone led her there. Darkadus observed the battle, flew back and forth over both ships and found what he was looking for. There was one among the crew of the Enchantress; one who didn't belong there.

"Queriven," Darkadus whispered aloud to the billowing gust. Why did that elf lead them to the Sapphire Reef? He thought that the knight gave up a long time ago. What could possibly change his mind now? Darkadus broke the vision, allowing it to shatter into nothing more than fading sparkles. The image surprised him. He was sure he's seen the last of that Queriven. "It's too late to fix your mistakes. I thought you knew that by now."

Whatever the cause of the elf's course of action, Darkadus' plan of marooning the girl on the island failed. Now he had to take the task into his own hands. Captain Nashōgan was still alive. They took him prisoner on the surviving ship. He'll need help if he's to continue Darkadus' will.

He stepped closer to the cliff, his toes only an inch away. Darkadus didn't sway; he breathed in, taking in the icy air and filling his chest. He exhaled a second later and drew his muscled arms horizontally to either side. His legs braced his weight on the edge, drawing a trace of magic he wished he didn't have to spend.

Then he dove over the side.

◊ ◊ ◊

When the uproar settled and the few by the church started back for the Enchantress, the three hands tried to bandage Nekene's wounds and take him back with the rest of what remained of the Sapphire Reef, but he didn't even make it to the shore.

The arrow had sunk in too deep and he lost too much blood. The last move he made on Blair was a death wish for sure. He knew then he was a dead man.

But the sight bothered the heartstrings in Blair's chest. Maybe it was true that he betrayed her, but Nekene was so nice back where she met him at the bar. It was hard to look at him now and see him as the same man; the man who offered her passage to Lyfíhana.

A piece of her mind told her to look away and spare her innocence, but she couldn't. It was like her eyes were automatically drawn to the horrible figure of the body and the blood. The crew and Queriven tried their best to wrap the form and let him sink in the water, but the image was already burned in her forever.

Absentminded, she followed them in the boat and they pushed it free from the sand. Blair no longer had the tears to cry, but her eyes still burned and her face was as red as the crimson that stained the pavement before the church.

Queriven recognized the look in her dying eyes. He was once a knight of Aven Forest. A knight of pride and honor of the elvish military. This was the exact image of a young girl who saw and carried too much. Seeing that struggle brought too many memories to his mind. He desperately wished he could break it. Quietly, he called her name, watching her like he watched a bound lion.

She responded on the third call. Deep gold locks fell straight. Her kind features were in full despair. Finally, she spoke in a calm but raspy tone. "How did you find me?"

Queriven knew upon finding her again that she would have questions he didn't want to answer, and he still wasn't ready. He took in her voice. The question repeated in his head until he answered. "I knew you were going to Limadia, so I traced you from there," he stated simply, holding his arms limp over his legs. "When I came to Seadrake, I knew you were in danger after you left with the pirates."

Grief returned to her and Blair looked away. She pressed a finger to her lips. "I didn't know they were pirates. I've hardly ever left that little village all my life." *It would have been better if I didn't board a ship at all.* She knew there was a chance they weren't good people. She made a terrible mistake.

Queriven lightened his tone to draw her attention. "Blair, this was not your fault. You're not an idiot."

She only sighed, dipping her hair back down and shifting away. "I don't know. I guess I should have done more research before going aboard."

Those suspicions he had of her was correct. She was diving further into regret and guilt. "Don't do this. You'll only drive yourself in circles. However this happened, you're safe now."

That last part echoed and she tried to embrace the feeling of safety, but it never came. Still, his intentions were honest. She gave him a broken smile. "Why did you come back? I thought you said you couldn't help me the last time we met."

Now it was Queriven's turn to shift away. He stumbled. "I shouldn't have said that."

Blair regarded him curiously, but she let the answer slide for now. The boat just arrived at the ship and she was eager to be away from Lost Sanctuary. The stress left an ache on her bones and she noticed it as she climbed onto the deck. But her weariness only increased once she came up. Finally up close, she took in the full damage from the battle with the pirate ship.

Boards and railings were in splinters, and pools of crimson marred the wood. She could hear the moans of injured men even from here, and those who were healthy enough to be on their feet had their hands full. The whole ship was in a state of chaos, from the damage and the cleanup in progress to the smoke still lingering in the air.

Queriven winced as he came up beside her. "I have to check

up on the captain." And without waiting for a response, he tugged tighter on his raised hood and marched ahead for the door leading below decks. Blair waited, nervous and sick with weariness.

The elf rushed past the busy hands running up and down the stairs. The hull stank of medicine and bloody gashes. The wounded took up almost every surface there was. "Captain Tallin!" Queriven cried to the man standing by the doctor.

The man returned a tired greeting. "Did you find the girl?"

"Yes sir," he huffed, stopping beside him. "She's unharmed. What are the damages?"

Captain Tallin shook his gray head. "Those were some formidable foes, for sure; we were lucky to make it out alive. We have seventeen injured, four are mortally so. The starboard side of the ship is in shambles. We have leaks down the far side," he sighed. "We have work to do before we can sail out of here. I'm not going to rush it, or we'll end up marooned on that island."

Queriven agreed. "We'll do what we have to. I'll have you know I'm quite knowledgeable when it comes to medicine. I can help the wounded if you'll have me."

The captain shook his head at first, but he reconsidered shortly after. A lot of the men were dying anyway. "I'm in no state to refuse that offer. Do what you can."

Blair came down the stairs then, having followed Queriven down. She was like a weed among a garden, as if she didn't belong here on the ship. The captain exclaimed at the sight of her and gave her a polite greeting. "You must be Blair. I'm sorry we couldn't meet in any better situation. I'm Captain Tallin. Your mysterious friend there hired my ship to help capture the pirates."

Blair bowed before him. "Thank you so much for this, Sir. I owe you my life."

He chuckled despite the terror weighing him down. "You owe me nothing. You should be thanking your friend." He cleared his throat, "Anyway, you must be tired. Feel free to stay in my cabin. Don't worry about us. And just so you know," he glanced behind him at the crew, "we'll be staying here by Lost Sanctuary for a while, and then if we can, we'll sail on by Lyfíhana."

Blair's eyes brightened. Queriven knew of her quest to the mountain and was trying to help her as he said. She smiled.

Blair had rested for a long time, but her sleep was hardly peaceful. The time spent with the pirates left her scarred, but at least most of the tense aches have left her by now. She yawned in the scent of the burning candle on the table. It was growing dark outside.

How were the crew doing now? Was it still the same day Nekene had tried to kill her? She stepped outside onto the open deck. However long it's been, they were still stuck here by Lost Sanctuary. Blair leaned out over the railing. It looked so different from this angle against the darkening sky.

She wished her long rest would allow her to see the island with a clear head, but it was already veiled in a dark memory. "You're awake," a voice spoke from behind. Startled, she turned her head. It was Queriven. "I thought you'll be out all night." He approached her, but Blair didn't run or flinch from him. "Do you feel any better?"

Blair met his eyes as he joined her at the railing. "A little." She turned again to the island. The evening was releasing a cold mist over the ocean. "But I'll feel even better if I could forget this ever happened."

Queriven shook his head. "You can't forget something like this. You just have to move on. If you don't; it'll control your life."

Blair remained silent. The thought disturbed her. She suddenly wished she had her father to vent to. How were they doing now? Probably not very well. She only hoped they weren't giving up everything they had to look for her. Blair turned to face Queriven. He was just as lost in thought as she was. Those dull eyes were locked beyond space and time. The cold breeze chased brown strains of hair into his angled face. He was as still as a statue. For the first time since he joined her, Blair noticed tiny droplets of blood staining his fingertips. He must have stayed with the wounded crew for a long time. How does he stay so calm when in these circumstances?

"Queriven," she started, waiting for him to return her gaze, "why do you want to help me?"

He studied her for a while, then pushed up from the railing. "Because... I guess I know what it's like to be in your situation. You're lost in a quest by yourself and no one's willing to help. You're stuck in your lack of experience of the outside world. I can't help but feel responsible for that when I told you I had nothing to offer." It was the half-truth he knew, but it was a better answer than none. "Besides, you were right when you said I recognized that horn."

His focus dropped to the wood under their feet. Blair watched him curiously. "What connection do you have with it?"

He groaned and returned to his spot at the rail. "It was mine once, but it was stolen from me. I don't know why, and I don't know who has it. That was a long time ago, but it must have been enchanted if you said it worked on you and your father. I don't know anything about that." Another half-truth.

Blair didn't suspect him. "I didn't have the chance to say this earlier, but I'm glad you came back. Thank you."

He accepted her gratitude with a nod. Queriven sincerely hoped he wouldn't regret this in the end, though he knew he probably will, one way or another. He stepped back from his perch against the edge. Blair turned to watch him. "I picked something up for you on the way here," he said suddenly, reaching for the back of his cloak and producing a short spear. It wasn't nearly as nice as his, nor did the tip carry that impossible shine those arrows had, but it was a sturdy and modest weapon.

Blair tilted her head to the side. "A spear?" she asked.

She was fixing to explain her lack of using weapons, but he stopped her. "If you're serious about staying safe on this quest, then you need to learn how to defend yourself. No worries," he assured her, holding it out before him. "I've trained with spears since I was a boy. I'll show you how to use this. Catch!"

Blair bent low, reaching for the shaft as it flew horizontally, but it still landed right before her feet. Blair regarded it for a minute and, tucking her hair behind her ear, picked it up. Queriven was already wielding his own staff when she looked up. He held it with a steady and confident hand and in a completely different way than how Blair held onto her own weapon.

Then, he asked if she was ready, and before a response, he approached her. Queriven started with a few easy swings, but Blair stepped out of the way instead of blocking. Her balance was clumsy and the spear in her hands tilted back and forth. Then she decided to try and return a swing. The attack was wide and left too many openings, which Queriven took advantage of. His spear locked with hers and quickly threw her attack to the side, sending the weapon flying away.

He stepped back, allowing Blair to retrieve the spear. "You're leaving yourself defenseless. Treat that spear as a barrier between you and your opponent," he stated as Blair returned with the weapon in hand. She sighed in frustration, but Queriven continued. "Remember, the spear has a longer range than a sword does. Use this to keep your enemies away from you, especially if they also carry a long-range weapon."

"I've never touched a weapon in all my life," Blair growled. "I'm not cut out for this."

Queriven withdrew his prepared stance. "I know this, but that doesn't mean you can't learn. It'll just take practice." Seconds passed, but Blair didn't move. He took the silence to speak up again. "Like I said, you need to learn how to defend yourself on this quest. There may be times still where I won't be around to help you. I don't expect you to learn overnight, but I do have confidence you have what it takes." He held the spear before him again and took another readied stance. "Your first step is to grow familiar with the spear. Hold it firmly like it's a part of you. I'll let you make the first move when you're ready."

She came forward this time, trying to follow his advice.

Even with him going easy on her, Queriven still won every round. He never boasted and he never grew impatient. He only told her to keep trying.

The training lesson played on well through the night, and when Blair finally tucked into the warmth of her blankets, she noted her muscles were sore and tired. She still lacked the confidence Queriven certainly had, but she knew he was right. Blair had to leave her comfort for the sake of her goal. She needed to grow beyond her present self and become stronger. She only hoped she had the potential.

CHAPTER ELEVEN
RED IVORY

The Enchantress didn't stay by Lost Sanctuary for long; only for a few days, which was a much-needed relief as the place was beginning to make Blair sick. Queriven's medicine and treatments were doing wonders on the crew, and many of them returned to work shortly after healing. Captain Tallin was impressed enough with the state of the ship too, and he approved the trip to Lyfíhana.

They gave Blair enough work on the ship, so she was hardly bored. Queriven made sure they trained every single day, and he would lift her spirits by letting her know of her improvements. Every day, Blair grew with more and more respect for the elf. As it turns out, Queriven went through a lot of work to trace her whereabouts. Not just that, but he spent a lot of money to board the Enchantress and convince the captain about the pirates.

Captain Tallin was a good man too. He sought rightful justice on the pirates and yet was in no way connected to the royal government. The only thing the captain really complained about was the weather. There were many harsh, frozen days. He said it would be nice to stay on the island for a while and allow the crew to rest from working in the cold. Then he followed that by saying there will be no rush to leave

Lyfíhana. At least that would give Blair and Queriven plenty of time to find any answers there.

Thankfully, there was plenty of sunshine on the way and only a few storms and clouds to be had. Blair never took it for granted. Fairdraisha was known for harsh winters. It was a blessing to have so much sun.

The call for their destination came without warning one day. At the voice from the crow's nest, Blair dropped the book she picked up in the captain's cabin and ran up on deck. Queriven joined her as they looked out to the small mound of land in the distance.

Even from here, Blair could make out the silhouette reaching for the snow heavy clouds. This is where the vayen aray used to live before they drove themselves into banishment with the rokians. That was in ancient times; many generations before her grandfather were even born. But despite this, she tried to imagine little forms flying on heavy wings around the single mountain. After a while of pretending, she just about swore they were really there. Then Queriven spoke and broke her trance. "So, do you know what exactly we're looking for here?"

Blair turned to meet him and then shook her head. Then before speaking, she silently made a note to continue her daydream later. "No idea for sure. The rokian who cursed me somehow escaped that spell of banishment. If he can do it, then maybe the vayen aray did too. This is the only lead I have."

Queriven stared hard at the island. Silent again, Blair wondered if he was also daydreaming about the race of legend. "That's not much to go on, but we have to make it work."

"How much do you know of Lyfíhana?"

He shrugged, taking the rail in one hand. "Honestly, not a lot of people know about it. Legends and rumors shroud this place. I don't believe in many of them, but I've never been here to prove they were false either. They say the vayen aray built a large capital right in the heart of the mountain. Now, of course, it's empty, though many have said they tried to explore the place and found it haunted by angry spirits. If you remember, the humans betrayed them by ruining their plan. They believe the vayen aray protect their old home from them, never forgiving them for their sins." He leaned his back against the rail, folding his arms against his chest. "But I think that's nonsense. They were sucked into another realm of existence. It's not like they're dead."

Blair pulled back a strand of hair blowing before her colorful eyes. "Maybe they don't know what they saw?"

"I'm confused about it too. I do know one thing for sure though. If they really did see something, then more than likely we will too."

◊ ◊ ◊

The deep gray clouds were expanding overhead. The thought of snow sent shivers through Queriven's shoulders. The elf always hated snow, even as a small child. It always made traveling difficult and uncomfortable. He stared up at the rocky spire standing so tall before them. Did they seriously have to climb up there in bad weather? Could it be that the vayen aray thought of building a set of stairs at the bottom to allow wingless visitors to enter their home? Queriven didn't know for sure, but he prayed the winter storm would start after they were already inside. He turned, meeting the captain as he approached the two. Feeling the early chill, Queriven tucked his slender hands under his arms.

"I know you two have important business, so you run along. It'll be a while before any of us can follow," Captain Tallin said.

Blair only looked back at Queriven, who simply nodded his consent. Together, they packed only the most important of supplies, including Blair's new weapon, which she slung on her back and they left the Enchantress and came to solid land.

The shore of Lyfíhana was long, sandy, and beautiful, and the mountain in the center of the island was so tall. It offered almost complete shadow over the ground. Yet, the vegetation here was plentiful even in winter.

Queriven, without a word, took the lead, rushing by the wooded area quickly. Blair allowed him, but secretly wished she had time to stop and look around first. She respected his leap into action. After all, she had a deadline to beat, but the wilderness brought intrigue and Blair wanted to explore it.

No flowers bloomed in the lush wilderness, but so many forested scents filled the air around them. Even from all the way over here, Blair could still hear the distant crashing of the waves against rocks. Also, many different kinds of birds cried overhead and in trees. There must be so many animals and plants here Blair didn't know existed!

Queriven hardly even blinked an eye at the sounds and smells. Instead, he was so drawn to the mountain itself. His quick pace and quiet grumbling suggested he was trying to find a place good enough to start for the way up. Because of the thick overhang of clouds, Blair could look up the rocks without having to shield her eyes, but she still couldn't see anything that might suggest there was a home up there.

The air was growing colder and the clouds darker. And still, Queriven led her around the base of the mountain. Perhaps, there wasn't an easy way up after all? Maybe the best they could do is just to try and climb it straight up. Blair swallowed, staring up at the spire again. She couldn't even see the peak... How far up do they need to climb anyway? Still, she refused to complain. She was just thankful she had Queriven's help in this.

So as Blair followed the elf quietly behind, her mind began to drift on her surroundings. Suddenly without much warning, a familiar sense of suspense edged into her mind. She thought back to the road heading to Dunverhart. Her mind was too clouded, her future too uncertain. But that wasn't the only familiar thing that came to her. Nearby, a bush rustled at the leaves, and a sparkle shown through the parting. It was a young hare that gazed back at her. A crystal hare.

Blair's step faltered and she forgot how to breathe.

Without looking back, Queriven sensed something was amiss. He slowed, turning back behind him. Blair didn't even acknowledge that he stopped for her. She was stiff as a statue, staring with her jaw to the ground at the third crystal beast she'd encountered. Blair had almost forgotten about them. They haven't bothered her in longer than a month.

And yet, here it was. Its attention was fully drawn on her. Queriven took a hesitant stride forward. The action sent the creature darting away back where they came from. Speechless, Queriven watched it run, then turned to Blair as if he wasn't sure if it was real. But her wide eyes confirmed his unspoken question.

He made a quick call for her and darted for it, only for her to grab his arm and pull him back. "What are you doing?!" Blair cried, almost delirious. "Don't follow it. It'll only lead us into danger! I've heard the stories!"

Queriven took a second to regard her. "What stories have you heard exactly? I thought the rare sighting of a beast wrapped in a crystal was to help the hopeless and lost."

Blair tilted her head to the side and returned his frowning stare. "No," she rebounded crossly, "they appear to people with doomed fates and lead them in circles until they're good as dead and then leave them there."

Queriven shook his head, looking back at where the beast disappeared. "I've never heard that back in the forest. I take it humans always tend to see mythical sights as a bad omen?"

He didn't need to say a thing for Blair to know he still planned on chasing the shiny hare. "So? If we're right, then following that thing will only doom us."

But it was too late to convince him. Apparently what humans thought as nothing but bad luck was the exact opposite to the elves. Queriven broke free from her and dashed back the way the hare ran. Blair shrugged and turned ahead. She almost considered going on without him, but she knew she couldn't. Now frustrated, she took up a running pace and followed. What are the chances the beast waited for them anyway? It's probably long gone by now.

But, of course, it wasn't simply minding its own business. It was hoping they followed. And so after running through the dry brush, Queriven found it waiting for them. At the sight of the two stalkers, the hare turned back again.

The chill was already uncomfortable enough, but running through it was even more so. It made Blair's lungs sore and her cheeks hot red, but she refused to fall behind. Queriven was quick and he was already a good distance ahead of her. Calling for him was useless.

Finally, the hare appeared to him one last time before ducking under a wide collection of stringy moss and spiny thorns. Queriven stopped and inspected the spot where the creature disappeared. Blair breathed a sigh of relief. Thank goodness she was able to reach him! She fell at his side without another word about how bad of an idea this whole thing was.

Queriven was careful to pull back the thorns and sticks, and he did so without drawing a drop of blood. They were right up against the rocky base of the mountain now, and yet the hare was nowhere to be found. After a moment of quiet inspection, however, Queriven saw why. Deep in a crook was a hidden hole. The entrance to the home of the vayen aray.

He looked back with a face that seemed to say, "Told ya," and he crouched down so he could fit inside. If it wasn't for the crystal beast, then they wouldn't have found the entrance anytime soon. It was already far enough behind them by the time they saw the hare. Could it be that Queriven was right? Have they been trying to help her?

The thorns snagged the ends of her dress as she drew past. She ignored them, only giving them a hiss as they bounced back. An overwhelming set of dust tickled her nose, and Blair tried her best not to sneeze. It was so thick she could barely breathe.

Queriven didn't seem to even notice her or have the same problem, though she could hear his breath quicken, perhaps struggling past the dust, but she wasn't sure. In front of them, carved directly in the stone, was a set of stairs going up and up.

"It's so dark," Blair said to no one in particular, though it was the truth. She could barely see the first few steps in front of her, let alone how far it went up. To Queriven, it wasn't nearly as dark as it was to her. He could see a good distance up, and there was a lot of it. The thought of climbing that far didn't bother him too much. The mountain itself, however, caused his shoulders to tense up. It was like the walls were pressing closely together and he feared he would suffocate from the lack of moving air. Still, he pressed on, ignoring the disturbance, and Blair kept him close, using him as her eyes.

She had no idea how long they've been climbing, but it was growing to be quite a routine. With Blair's limited eyesight, she nearly lost her footing several times. She felt sorry about that truly, because Queriven never tripped, and every time she did, she was close enough to bump into him. He never said anything about it other than she was fine and he wasn't mad with her.

Most of the time, she watched his feet touch on one stair after another. She tried to pace him precisely. Only a few occurrences did she look up. There was a bit of dark cloud showing through a small opening like a glimmer of hope. "Queriven!" she cried, pointing at the light even though he wasn't looking back at her. "That's the top. We're nearly there!"

A tone of relief came to his voice, but what he said under his breath was in a language Blair was not familiar with. With more of gray lighting filling this space, Blair was able to speed herself beyond Queriven's pacing. She noted the forms of old web-filled sconces on the wall. Those would have certainly been useful all this time up, but she didn't need them anymore. Excitement filled her head. What will she see next? Will she actually be able to see any of the living corridors? This was like an experience she never even dreamed she would have!

Blair wanted to run off and look around, but she waited patiently for Queriven. The light Blair had seen earlier was, in fact, the open sky. At the top of the stairs, the wall opened up into a series of large archways made still from the very stone of the mountain. A cold wind was blowing stronger now. She shivered.

When the elf finally joined her at the top, she went to inspect the chamber. This was a large space. The ceiling was very high and this looked to be a hallway of sorts, though it was wide enough to have a large crowd passing through it at once.

That wasn't all. There was even a wide floor past the archways, almost like a big balcony. But it was cold enough in here Blair decided against going back there. The only thing in these corridors that she could tell wasn't made of the stone from the mountain was a selection of furniture. Lining the far wall out of the way of the walkway were a few cabinets, dressers, benches and even a few end tables. This would have been a lovely place to sit on a warm summer day.

So far, the pieces of old furniture seemed like a good place to start exploring the answers she was looking for. There was a complete set. They had the same materials and style; dark chocolate wood and golden trimmings and handles. To her dismay, the wood was rotten and fragile, almost like it was made of soft mush and paper. If any of Lyfíhana's people were still here, then they haven't replaced any of the dirty, rotting pieces of their home.

Disappointed but not giving up just yet, Blair carefully opened the drawers. A lot of them were empty, but those that weren't held precious trinkets inside. She examined trophies, knives, scraps of gold, and other materials. She became giddy with each one, but she didn't take a thing.

With Blair over at the walls by the objects and furniture, Queriven was checking elsewhere. Tight rock encased the stairs, allowing no fresh air, light, or windows. It was much easier to breathe up here.

When Blair left to check the furniture, she walked by a tall, open door leading into a dark room of some kind. It didn't look like anyone was in there, but that was as good a place as any to start. Right away, Queriven found it to be a large dining room. There were long tables in the center, making a line that went all the way down. This could easily have seated all of Dunverhart!

Surprisingly, most of the tables were still up, but even Queriven with his slender and light form didn't dare to try any of the chairs. Instead, he walked further down the room. It didn't take his sixth sense to realize that this was the first time anyone walked down this floor in such a long time, even before his time. He turned back and saw the silhouette of Blair coming through the door. A wave of grief fell on him. It was unlikely they would find any help here, but then what do they do? This was her only lead. They had nowhere else to go to after this. *I'm doing everything I can. I just have to believe in that.*

Blair's golden hair flicked back and she saw him looking at her. She called, "Come look at this!"

He did so, his human-made leather boots not even making a sound against the stone floor. Blair was focused on a tall shelf by the entryway. There was a dusty glass door in front of it. Webs and smudges marked the glass, making it difficult to see behind it. Yet Blair saw something that caught her interest. As Queriven came closer, she reached the latch and gently released it. The doors swung open, spilling a cloud of musk. Then she retrieved a single item from the shelf to show him.

He took it from her and turned it around in his hands. It was a small carving of a dragon standing on the tip of a mountain, spreading open its wings. The trinket was made not from stone or gold but from ivory. Blair spoke next. "It's made from the same bone the horn was made of. I recognize that rusty color."

Then, he understood what she meant. Indeed, he can see the red tint of the scrimshaw even in the dim lighting. "You're right. It is the same." His eyes glanced at her before dropping back down. "But it's hardly surprising. The vayen aray made that horn themselves."

So the fake elf Blair spoke to back in Bailiese was not entirely lying. She pondered for a moment. "It was passed through your family, right?"

He gave a light scoff, handing the scrimshaw back to her. "If by family you mean the elven guard, then sure."

"Oh," she sighed, giving the dragon a final look before setting it back where she found it. So the rokian told her a little truth, but not very much. "So you got it when you became a knight?"

Queriven exhaled, slowing down by a table. He brushed the frame of a nearby chair with his fingers and didn't meet her gaze. "Yeah, it's entrusted to the first knight of the guard. The original use of the horn is gone, which was to call the vayen aray for help, but we still used it for our own group. The days when I used to carry it is long gone though."

She watched him. Her curiosity about his life in the forest was returning to her again. "So is that why you're here? To find who stole that horn from you?" *And is that why you're helping me?* She kept the last one to herself.

When he looked at her again, a frown marked his face. If it wasn't for the terrible lighting, or if Blair had half the eyesight he had, she would have spotted the hurt in his gaze. "The sooner we find whatever we need to find here, the better," he turned again, walking away from her. "We can make time for small talk later!"

Well, that was hardly small talk. Whatever. If Queriven wishes to keep his personal life so much of a secret, then fine. It shouldn't matter to her anyway. Blair returned to the open shelf, carefully examining each piece of scrimshaw and trophy.

Something sparkled in the corner of her vision. At first, she thought it was a glimmer of light through the glass. But when she realized it was in a different color than the clear glass, she looked.

It was yet another crystal being. This one was in the form of a small mouse. It met her eyes for a second before it scurried down the cabinet and crossed the floor. Startled, she spun and watched it run for a while. This time, she was the first to take a step to follow. She cried to catch Queriven's attention.

"Another one!?" he exclaimed as he fell beside her. "Maybe we're close to finding something after all." *Or was it the same one from before?* Blair pondered, thinking about how Anita explained they can shapeshift into different animals.

The mouse wasn't near as fast as the hare and kept a decent pace as it led the two through the dark dining room and into another dark chamber. As soon as they left the dining room, the air became heavier with musk. This was another chamber hall, and like the one before out by the open archways, it was wide enough to hold an entire crowd. But unlike it, there was no light and no windows. For a while yet again, Blair relied on watching Queriven walk ahead of her until she found a candle lying about. The light helped a bunch, but the air was still thick and dusty.

The little shiny mouse skittered down halls and broken rooms and even took them up several stairways. After that, other crystal beasts joined the run. A fox and what appeared to be some type of badger joined the mouse and they all ran ahead. They seemed excited, probably because this was their chance to help out the stubborn peasant girl who denied them before.

Finally, they waited for Queriven to open an old wooden door where they ran in at once. This chamber, rather than being long, was wide and spacious. There was a single table that sat in the center, but it was large and round, almost taking up the entire room. A good dozen of people could stand on the platform at once. A lot of people lived here in the mountain before they were forced to leave. It was some sort of meeting room where the vayen aray gathered for the most important of situations. Blair wasn't sure how many stairs and floors they climbed up so far, but they were considerably higher up the mountain. More archways to the outside world lined the far walls. The wind that blew in was chilly and lonely, but she went back to imagining the hall on a warm summer day with crowds of people flying by and sitting at the meeting table.

More crystal animals were waiting inside, and they were all gathered on the table. All were staring at the two followers with gleaming shiny eyes. Slowly, they backed away, and a bit of light escaped the clouds glowing softly on a single object in the middle of the table.

At first glance, Queriven had no idea what it was. It was small and sitting upright in an iron base. Then, his heart skipped a beat. It was a horn made from red-tinted ivory. For a while, he was paralyzed. It looked so much like the one he used to have. Queriven hesitated long enough he thought Blair would reach it before he did, but she also stopped from moving; she was instead looking at him for guidance.

Queriven had none, but when he recovered, he decided to

take a closer look. It's not like it could be his anyway. He knew Blair didn't lie. She saw it for herself in the hands of someone else. He knew the rokian had it, so why was this one here?

He was almost afraid to take it, but he was too intrigued not to. Queriven nearly had to crawl on top of the unsteady wooden surface of the table to reach it. The horn was tight in its base and Queriven knocked it over when he took the horn from it. Carefully and ignoring the creak that came from the table, he pulled it back where both he and Blair could see it. After he had a closer look, he was able to confirm it was not his, but a look-alike. It was the same size and shape, made from the same ivory as his, yet the engravings were different. A language long-forgotten was written all over the edges, and symbols were scrawled near it. The engravings alone looked more formal than the decorative ones on the horn Queriven owned. The animals never left though. They just remained where they were, staring up at the horn with intelligent eyes.

"Now what do we do?" the elf asked, looking at them for an answer, but they still didn't respond.

Blair tried not to be disappointed. As interesting as the horn was, it gave her no answer for her curse. She had to look away. There was no one here who could counter it. It was hopeless.

A moment of silence ripped through them. Queriven still held onto the instrument. It was like it was pulling on his consciousness, drawing him in a world of buried hurt and fear. He remembered the last time he had the horn he lost those years ago. When he came back to the real world, he winced, handing the horn to Blair. She took it from him before he turned and stared through the open archway. Her gaze dropped to the item, and even though her sleeves were thick, she imagined the mark of the curse laughing at her helplessness.

But then, the crystal beasts dispersed at the sound of a low booming voice. Birds flew out on shining wings, and the land creatures either ran back through the room, climbed out over the edge, or transformed into something more feasible. Their change of form was quick — from something as simple as a rat to a full bird of prey in a single flash. But Blair quickly lost attention on the beasts. She was drawn now to the voice.

It spoke again. "Someone found one of the horns of the vayen aray. Who would step into the forgotten ruins of Lyfíhana after all this time?" The tone was curious and soft, but strong and confident. At first, it started as a distant echo, but gently centered in one corner, almost like whoever spoke was in the very room. Neither Blair nor Queriven saw him.

"Not just someone," he said again, "but two someones. Why did you come here?" Then Blair located the speaker near the wall by the first archway. Slowly and seemingly more confused than they were, he came closer to the intruders. He was small and simple at first, but a second showed how different he was compared to a human of Fairdraisha. His nose and chin were long and angled, and his eyes were as sharp as a bird's. Fluffy brown hair was slightly spiked at the top of his head, and dark stripes covered the sides of his face down. It was unlikely he would wear them as tattoos, but Blair wasn't really sure what they were from.

Then, as he stepped further in the light, she realized he had large wings folded on his back. They were bright white but became dark further down. His features were soft. He didn't look to be very old either, but those eyes were wise and told a different story. It was like he held on the knowledge of the world. A little louder, he repeated his question. Blair thought some part of him faded for just a moment.

"Please accept our apologies," Queriven finally answered. "We didn't think anyone was here."

But the newcomer's stare didn't change. "Who are you?"

The elf bowed. "My name is Queriven and this is my companion, Blair. We came searching for any trace of the vayen aray. We need your help."

The man revealed as one of the vayen aray stood straighter. His question was answered. A gleam shone in his worldly gaze. "So we weren't completely forgotten. I'm pleased to hear from you, my two friends," he returned a bow, the dark tips of his wings brushing the floor as he did. "Among my people, I am called Rocanu. You are the first people outside of my kin and the rokians I've spoken to in over a thousand years." He looked at his surroundings, from the open archways to the rotting table in the center of the room. "I'm sorry I couldn't give you a proper welcome. When cared for, the kingdom of Lyfíhana was lively and warm. You'll just have to take my word on this."

Blair watched his every move. The legend was true; every bit of it! She wished to know more about him. Rocanu seemed to recognize this place and he greeted them personally, even though he stated that they were the first two he's spoken to in all this time. How old was he exactly?

"I understand," Queriven answered. He glanced Blair's way before he continued. "A rokian set a curse over my friend. Only vayen aray magic can undo it. Can you help us?"

Rocanu sighed and shook his head in disbelief. "So the rokian follows in the path of his ancestors." He lifted his sharp eyes back to Blair. She shivered, suddenly nervous. "It's true we can undo their curses, but I'm in no position to help you now."

The last bit shocked Blair so bad she barely heard them. Against all odds, they found one of the vayen aray right here in Lyfíhana and he had no help to offer?

But before they could argue his response, Rocanu continued. "I'm not sure if you noticed this, but I'm actually not here. I'm nothing more than an illusion you see after you picked up the horn. My magic can't reach you from this realm."

Queriven growled. So this is how the myth of seeing ghosts here started. "So you're saying there's nothing to do about this curse? Her deadline is the changing of autumn."

Rocanu solemnly shook his head, those eyes dropping to the floor. "I'm sorry. I really do wish I could offer something more..."

Blair said nothing. She was afraid of disturbing the lump in her throat. She tried not to cry. This whole quest was pointless. She regretted ever leaving home. If she would have given up, at least she would be with her dear parents.

"The only way my magic could reach you is if there was

some kind of link," Rocanu pondered. He turned his head and looked to the side. "A magical link supporting the bridge between dimensions. Something like the one we have now. I think that can work."

Queriven focused ahead. "What can? Did you find something?"

"Maybe, but I'm unsure."

Blair gripped onto the last tidbits of hope and listened in.

"You can see me because of the magic in that horn," Rocanu explained, pointing at the object in Blair's hands. "It has some of the strongest magic we own. I believe it can call me closer to you for the same reasons it can call my kin for help. However, it can't draw me out of this world I now live in." He went silent for a moment. He brought a fist to his chin and pondered further.

Queriven regarded his answer in confusion. "None of this is making sense to me. What do we have to do exactly?"

"We need a bond formed in magic," Rocanu recovered, but he didn't repeat what he just explained. "The cursed one is human, correct?"

Blair nodded and he continued, now aiming the conversation at her. "This horn is one of the few we made. We gave one to the humans once as an offering of friendship. Find the horn we gave away and take it to the location of the bond. If you, a human, use it there, the bond in the magic might be strong enough to pull me through to you. Then, I'll cast a blessing and take away the curse."

Blair moved to accept. She was desperate for any kind of answer to push her further, but it was Queriven who spoke next. He was looking down at the horn. "Why can't we do this now then? We have a horn already."

Rocanu saw his point. "Yes, and this one is strong, but it has no bonds tied to it. The only way I can join your realm is if you find the one we gave as an offering to the humans. Then, only a human may use it at the site. You'll be recreating a time of old; a time where the vayen aray and the humans were among each other as allies."

Blair, for the first time since Rocanu's arrival, spoke up. "So where is this horn then?"

But Rocanu shrugged. "I have no idea. We've given it away over a thousand years ago, and worse yet, we're here in this alternate world. I don't know what they did with it or who has it now, but we gave it to the villagers of what was then the ruins of Dyara."

Queriven nodded, familiar with the area he spoke of. "The old village also known as 'End of the Road'? It was once like a part of Penacha, the town next to it, but instead of building it back up, they focused on expanding Penacha instead. It's still in ruins."

"Like I said, I now know very little about Fairdraisha, but you seem to know what I'm talking about. Retrieve the horn and use it there. I'll be waiting for you."

Rocanu grew more transparent until he was hardly visible. Blair thought to call on him one last time. The pressure of another task was weighing heavy on her mind, but by then, he was already gone.

As Queriven and Blair spoke with Rocanu, Darkadus was on his own mission. He was spending a lot of magic for this too. The pirate captain better make this worth it in the end. Worse yet, the winter ocean was reaching his mind, bringing back the realization of cold ice against his skin through the spell. The magic was nearly exhausted, but he was also near his target; the Enchantress.

He had been swimming nonstop for several nights. His goal was to reach it before Queriven and Blair set foot on Lyfíhana. Darkadus was too late for that, but it wasn't too late to take their only way off the island.

Finally, the hull of the ship came into view. A deep growl came from his throat. It was just in time. Slowly, he lifted a cold and wet arm out of the water and pulled himself up. He needed to do this quietly or he'll need to use even more magic to save himself from the crew still on board.

Now up against the railing, Darkadus looked from either

side, making sure he wouldn't be spotted. He ducked for a while, then when the men were past him, he swung onto the deck. Water splashed down onto the wood and he shook off the droplets. He wore a neat collection of furs and pelts to fight the harsh winters of this land, but even with all his talents and trophies, nothing but magic could save him from the ocean. He tried not to shiver too much. The spell was fading away, leaving him drenched and frozen.

Keeping low, he nearly propelled himself on all fours. He needed to find the brig.

CHAPTER TWELVE
A SELKIE'S TIDE

Blair thought several times they'd gotten lost, but Queriven kept going. The darkness and closed walls seemed to tighten around them again. But either Queriven was lucky with his choices of halls, or he remembered the way they came in. It didn't take them long to leave the musty halls. They were back in the old dining room.

Once they were back by the archways, Blair shivered. She was suddenly not sharing Queriven's excitement of leaving the mountain. It was snowing pretty harshly and it was only growing stronger. The rate threatened of a terrible blizzard.

But there was a lot of work to do, and they needed to find that other horn before the end of summer. As much as Blair wanted to wait the storm out, it was best to leave now before they might become trapped in the snow. There was a good chance their exit was already blocked.

Queriven dashed for the long stairway down. He was nearly hopping a few steps at a time. Luckily, the entrance was still wide open, though a few inches of snow was already covering the grass. "We need to return to Seadrake," Queriven explained over his shoulder as they headed back for the ship. "And once there, we need to find where that horn went."

"That information is really old," Blair returned, now jogging to keep up with him. "Can we still find it?"

"It has to be around Fairdraisha somewhere. That I do know."

Then suddenly, he came to a stop. Blair nearly barked aloud when she crashed into him. "What's wrong?" she asked.

"The ship!" he cried, scanning the moving tide before the shore. "It's gone. Where is it?"

Blair peered over the waves. Queriven was right; the Enchantress was nowhere to be seen. Then with a jolt, she pointed far in the distance where a single shine of a white sail was just barely visible in the snowfall. "There it is! But where are they going? They couldn't have forgotten about us."

Queriven cried out, bringing his arms up to either side of his head. "No, the captain wouldn't leave us, not after coming this far. This is bad. It has to be the pirate's doing."

Blair looked from him to where she first saw the ship. "Wh...what can we do now?" Terrified, she imagined the pirates breaking free and slaughtering the good crew.

There was no answer. Queriven shrugged and Blair hugged her arms. A moment of unease passed and Queriven turned to look at her. He squinted and yelled over the blowing wind. "We need to look for shelter. There's nothing else we can do here."

Blair remained silent and followed behind him, though she had no clue where they could take shelter. An icy wind blew through her cheeks and her face turned bright pink. Uncomfortable, Blair buried her face as deep in her scarf as she could.

Queriven, however, blocked the storm with a strong arm as he scanned the region around them. He pushed through the snow with a quick pace, leading Blair with no destination in mind.

The vayen aray made their homes only in the rock of the single mountain. Never once did they build something below. They left the ground to nature. There was no chance of finding a solid enough ruin to hide behind. Queriven cursed against the wind. The best they can do is a sizable rock or tree, but would that really be enough? In all the times Queriven survived in the wilderness, at least there was always some kind of shelter in the thick forest.

Sore and teetering on the edge of frostbite, the two of them were about to give up when Queriven's elvish eyes caught a sign of relief. At first, he didn't even believe his eyes it was there, but then he looked again. There was a group of simple houses. There was help.

◊ ◊ ◊

"So they just left you here then?" the man asked.

"Not exactly," Blair replied before Queriven could answer. She was sitting on a simple bench made of natural wood. She was a complete mess. Her hair was whipped and wet into massive curls, her skin still tingling with a chill, and she tried her hardest not to drop her cup of hot tea from her numb fingers. Trying to hide her pathetic shivers, she tugged the edges of the wool blanket and leaned further toward the fire pit. "We're thinking the pirates freed themselves somehow and took over. That is the only explanation."

Beside her, Queriven sighed and lowered his head. He didn't look any better than Blair did. The man they spoke to, a barrel-chested but soft-hearted man and the village leader, was standing before them on the other side of the fire pit. The villagers lived here for several generations and were hardly ever hosts to visitors. His family and those before him lived simple, quiet lives on the island. They made everything from scratch, from their homes to their clothing.

The leader, who introduced himself as Gal, stared ahead. He was beginning to pace back and forth around the little hut. Fur boots lined up his heavy legs, and the puffs lit up every time he passed the embers. "I'm still a little confused," he admitted. "Why did the captain agree to ship out? I thought ships didn't sail in the harshness of winter."

This time, it was Queriven who raised his head. "I told him it was urgent. I knew Blair was in danger. There was no time to wait. Captain Tallin is a good man and I gave him a good amount of gold to make this trip."

Gal still seemed bewildered like he had more questions, but he only returned to his pacing instead. "Well, whatever the cause or reason, I do believe you're stuck here with us for a while. Not a lot of ships pass by this island, and you definitely won't see any until spring."

Blair shook her head, her darkened damp hair flinging back. "No, we need to return to the mainland. It's important."

Gal shrugged. "I don't know what to tell you. There's not much I can do to help."

Her shoulders slumped. Blair retreated into depression. Queriven turned and looked at her. "We'll do what we can," he stated, trying to bring her a hint of hope. "It's not too late to act in spring."

She met his gaze, but her dying eyes remained unchanged. "We'll lose valuable time. We don't know how long it'll take us to find that horn." They weren't even sure if they would be able to escape in the spring.

Now speaking quietly in a language he didn't understand, Gal interrupted, "I can offer you two a house to stay in for now, and we'll make sure you're fed and cared for as long as you can help us with the work. I'll prepare a place for you and return."

Queriven bowed his head politely as Gal left. Blair returned to her thoughts and stared at her steaming tea. Queriven watched her for a moment with nothing more to say. The fire lit up the mix of greens and browns in her eyes, but she didn't shed a tear. She didn't even complain about the situation they were trapped in, but Queriven saw the pain in her like she was nothing but thin wax. With a jolt, he saw himself sitting in her place. She was hopeless and insecure, the same way he was when he left home in Aven Forest. Just like him, Blair was now nothing but a lost creature, her heart aching for a home she knew she couldn't turn back to.

He hated that as much as he hated the reminder of what he once was. Queriven searched his mind, desperately wanting to offer her another silver lining, one that would at least bring brighter eyes up to him, but he had nothing. He couldn't comfort her, so instead, he stood up and walked away, not wanting to bear the sight of it anymore.

◊ ◊ ◊

The blizzard grew severe that night, causing a blind flow of white outside. The little house rocked and creaked with the gusts of violent snow. At the dawn of morning, it took Queriven a good several hours to crack the front door open. It was surprising the door held up at all that night.

The white flakes were floating gently now, piling up on the already snow-packed ground. A soft growl came from the elf. This was just another harsh winter he had to trudge through. It was going to be a long day.

Blair hardly said anything that morning. She came up behind him in the small living area from her small bedroom in the back. She wrapped herself tightly in the blankets from her bed, and it was like she was under a hundred layers and was still cold.

"We should see what we can do to help Gal with the village," Queriven greeted.

She groaned. Her eyes were still dark with sleep. "I suppose we should find out if they made it out of their houses all right."

Indeed, there was a lot of work to do. The two helped with repairs, firewood, and hunting. Blair, in particular, was more helpful with the repair work while Queriven foraged for what he could in the wild.

Many of the villagers worked on rebuilding warped homes or broken walls where trees fell. They were glad to have some extra help in the village, though an unusual face brought many stares. Blair pretended not to notice as it didn't really bother her much and they kept to themselves, save for the leader, of course. "Thank you so much for doing this!" Gal praised, coming before Blair as she helped carry a log before a ruined house. "We really appreciate this."

"It's fine," Blair replied with a final huff as the log fell in the snow with the others. "I should be thanking you for letting us stay."

Gal grinned, his smile reaching to the ends of his face and beyond. Then, he left again and Blair took a second to stretch her muscles. The clouds were beginning to thin, allowing the sun to peek out just a little. It was cold but manageable. Blair herself was a little quieter than usual. She was still disturbed about being stranded on the island. Therefore, she didn't think too much about the people surrounding her, but something did catch her attention later. She was being watched that day. Whenever she took a break or turned around, one of the helpers, a girl barely in her teen years, was looking at her. Unlike the stare of unfamiliarity like the others had, this one had one of sadness, almost like she wished she had something to offer to this stranger of the village.

At first, Blair continued to ignore it, but the looks were persistent. Finally, curiosity took the best of her. She waited for a second to pass, finishing with a patch in the wall. Then she turned and saw the girl looking over her shoulder at her from a different house.

"Hello," Blair chimed and approached her. The girl's eyes widened like she didn't want to be caught staring. Her hammer dropped to the snow and she backed a few steps away. "I'm Blair. I thought it would be nice to introduce myself. I've been seeing you around all day though we haven't spoken."

The girl stumbled for a moment before reaching down to pick up her hammer. Her arms, though short and young, had incredible muscles. It occurred to Blair that she helps with the village often. "I'm Kerna," she returned. Her voice was light and shy. "Gal already told me about you and your friend. I'm sorry about the ship."

"Thank you," Blair returned. She gazed from her to the workers on the house behind her. "Have you...seen very many visitors?"

Kerna shook her head. Braided brown locks bounced like crazy over her head. "There hasn't been a stranger who stayed with us here in my lifetime."

Blair gasped, though she knew she shouldn't be surprised. *I must look very odd here indeed*, she thought. This girl was even more of a small-town girl than she was!

"Lyfíhana's pretty much forgotten now," Kerna said. "But that's another reason why it's so peaceful and clean," she shrugged. "At least, that's what Gal says."

Blair turned her head, studying the notion. "Gal's been on other lands before? Why did he settle here?"

"Not really Gal," Kerna was quick to answer, "but his grandmother and the original settlers. They came here to research the disappearance of the vayen aray. It took them several years. They didn't find much, and they were haunted by the forms of the beings themselves. Finally, they gave up looking for answers and returned to Fairdraisha. By then, however, any of the members didn't feel like a part of society anymore. A lot of them had a connection to the island. They were building their lives around this place. Some of the researchers were falling in love and already building families. In the end, they decided this was their home."

"Your family has been here for a long time then. Have you ever been anywhere else?"

"No, we never needed to leave," Kerna smiled lightly. "We have everything we need here." She turned her head, giving the workers a quick glance. "I should probably return back to work."

Then she turned, hammer tight in hand, and marched back to her post. Blair took the chance to do the same. Despite talking to the girl, Kerna still seemed strange to Blair, but what did she really know? Blair and Queriven could easily look even stranger to these people. They were a curious sort, but they have been friendly enough so far.

When the day was done, she and Queriven returned to the house. The work exhausted both of them, and Blair rested in the living room next to the fire pit. She was on the edge of sleep. Queriven knelt before the pit, starting the fire. "There's still time you know," he said, breaking the silence of the room.

Blair blinked, attention only half drawn. She lifted her head and refocused. "Time for what?"

A new fire licked at the wood and Queriven sat on the seat next to her. "Time to break your curse. We haven't lost yet."

"I know. You don't have to tell me."

Queriven paused for a moment. "Then why are you on the brink of giving up?"

Deep gold brows furrowed and Blair regarded him with confusion. "What? I'm not..."

"I've seen that look before. You're losing strength." Queriven shook himself away from her, taking the time to look again at the fire. "I'm not the one to be saying this, but you can't give up hope. You never know what the future will bring. It could be that the Enchantress will fight back for their ship and they're returning for us. There's still a chance we can make it out before spring. And even if we don't, it wouldn't be the end of the world. There's still time." Another pause and Blair didn't respond, so he spoke again. His voice grew quieter and more serious. "I may be wrong, but when I look at you, I see a girl fighting against an impossible obstacle. You're giving everything you have, but I don't want you to hurt yourself in the process. You need to think wisely about this situation."

She sighed. "I'm trying, but I have a deadline. I need answers as soon as I can get to them."

"I know," Queriven returned. "But we're doing everything we can right now. Nothing more can change that, but you're not doing this alone."

Blair blinked again, though her eyes narrowed at him this time. For a while, she searched him for words and he waited. "Queriven, why are you helping me?"

His eyes widened, as he was somewhat surprised to hear that question again. "I already told you the reason."

But she shook her head. "There's more to it. There has to be. This is a serious commitment you're giving, and because of what? Because you remembered the horn that was stolen from you? That isn't much of a reason."

He slowly came to his feet. "It's late. You should be in bed." His boots stomped noiselessly on the floor around the fire pit as he headed for his own room. For a second, he froze and turned back to her. "Just remember what I told you."

The door to his room swung to a soft close and Blair remained at the fire with her thoughts. How did he know her thoughts? On many occasions, the elf often gave her interesting wisdom and somehow knew exactly how she was feeling. Blair knew there was more to him than what meets the eye, but she wasn't sure she would ever figure it out.

The feelings he picked from her were mutual though, or at least, they once were. He was familiar with her struggles. Blair could only imagine what happened that made him so wise like that.

◊ ◊ ◊

Nearly four weeks and many snowstorms later, Blair and Queriven were still trapped on Lyfíhana. They grew accustomed to many of the natives and worked with them every day. Blair was still worried about their questionable future. Can they leave the island at all? In the end, Blair tried to keep a better attitude. She continued to visit with Kerna, who warmed up to her little bits at a time.

Oddly, Kerna would apologize whenever the subject of their being stranded on the island came up. Blair was always surprised to hear her tone of voice change, but she wasn't the only one. Queriven was suspicious as well. He even went as far as to investigate the issue.

He never came up with an answer until one ordinary day. Blair was in the wilds just outside the settlement, picking up a rather thin rabbit she found when Queriven spotted her. "Blair!" he cried, rushing up beside her. "I figured it out. I know what Kerna is hiding."

Blair froze, shocked to see him suddenly from nowhere. A moment passed and Queriven glanced uncomfortably at the limp rabbit. "You might want to drop that off first. Meet me by the span where the brush meets the beach and you'll see what I mean."

Before she could respond, he left. After a moment to recover, Blair sighed and headed back for the village. She was slightly embarrassed he caught her with the rabbit. Not only were her hunting skills lacking, but Queriven was unfamiliar with the preparation of meat. Elves didn't eat meat; they couldn't even digest it. And for one reason or another, that made Blair shy of being caught with it. As always, she merely shrugged it off and headed back to the village.

After dropping off the little food she found that day, she wandered off to the shoreline. It didn't take her long to find Queriven. Blair wasn't expecting to find him crouched down and blending with nature, marking the start of the sand. His hood was up and he stayed low, barely lifting his head over a bush.

Knowing him, he probably didn't even make a noise settling there, but Blair certainly did. The crunching of tough snow beneath her feet caught his attention and he gestured her to join him and quickly.

She did so and fell to the ground beside him. She was now just inches away. She could hear his breath beside her. He smelled of nature, even more so considering the overpowering winter around them. "What is this about?" Blair asked suddenly.

Queriven pressed a finger to his lips and shushed her. "Just wait and you'll see."

Blair turned her head and watched the beach. The icy wave crashed against the shore, running over the sand before retreating, and then it happened all over again. The air was chilly, but not uncomfortable. Even a few winter birds chirped overhead. For a long while, she waited and listened for anything amiss. Queriven never moved. His focus remained on point even after Blair thought again that there was nothing here.

Finally, a crunch of snow followed and the two ducked behind their cover. It was Kerna, and she was alone. The girl was still shy, almost like she knew she was being watched. However, she didn't see anyone. Slowly, she came to the sand in front of them and stared out into the ocean. The ends of her long brown hair fluttered toward the water and she became like a statue. She had a hide she twirled around her arms and held across her chest.

At first, she stayed there, and Blair didn't think anything of it. But the hide she kept was important, and she suddenly brought it to her feet. Blair sucked in a breath. She couldn't believe what happened next! The girl, Kerna, was climbing in the skin and drawing it over her face. When she was inside, her form morphed. Her human features and limbs distorted into something unknown. But then, the unknown became recognizable again. Now in the body of a young gray seal, Kerna flopped on her belly into the cold ocean where she disappeared in the waves.

Queriven stood up. They were no longer in danger of being seen as the girl was long gone. Blair slowly followed him, her hands going to her head in wonder. She knew what that was. She's read about it before in her books. Kerna is a selkie, a human who could transform into a seal, thanks to the skin she kept with her. Selkies were rare creatures, often counted as being only in myth. "She's a selkie?!" Blair said, more in bewilderment than in question.

"That's right," Queriven answered anyway, staring off where she disappeared.

Blair looked from him to the beach and stuttered. The elf remained quiet and fixated on the roaring waves, though it only vexed her further when he didn't seem as interested or surprised. Finally, she responded with words. "But why didn't she tell us? Why did she look so suspicious?"

Queriven breathed in and held it like he tried to piece his thoughts together. "Humans tend to over hunt seals. My guess is that she keeps it a secret to protect herself." Then his eyes broke from the water and turned to her. "But don't you see? She can leave the island. That's why she feels so guilty about us staying here. Kerna can help us escape if she's willing. She can get help."

But would it be too much to ask for? If Kerna's worried they might discover her secret, how wrong would it be for Blair to ask her to give up everything to help her, a stranger who doesn't belong in this village?

"You wanted a way out, remember? We might convince her to help," Queriven stated like he read her mind on paper.

Blair let out a heavy sigh, though she relented. "All right. I'll try." Never once did she think Kerna to be anything else but a human, and yet she was a creature of magic.

◊ ◊ ◊

Sometime closer to dusk, Blair saw Kerna in the village again with the sealskin wrapped around her shoulders. There was also a sudden abundance of fish in the village. No one thanked her or gave any credit, but Blair knew Kerna brought that back. Blair sighed sadly. She didn't want to scare the girl. They were becoming pretty good friends. For a while, Blair even thought about not bothering her at all. Why should Kerna expose her true identity for Blair's selfish rush to break her own curse?

But in the end, she decided to try anyway. She wasn't going to hurt her, and she wasn't going to tell Kerna's secret to anyone, so what's wrong with asking her about it?

Blair found the perfect time the next day as they gathered firewood together. The silence was thick in the air, but Kerna worked with a smile on her face as she dug past several feet of snow for suitable wood. Blair fought against her mind. She didn't know how to start, though she planned it out in her head several hours earlier. She decided she just had to go with it. "Can I talk with you for a moment, Kerna?" Without hesitating, Kerna responded positively. Blair thought for a second again. "This may be a bit unnerving, but I need to ask you... If you could help us escape the island."

Not catching on right away, Kerna slowly rose up and turned her head. "I'm confused. I don't know what you want me to do."

"Is it true you keep it a secret because of dangerous humans?"

Kerna, for a second more, still didn't understand. But then realization spread before her eyes and her face dropped. "How do you know about that?"

Blair bit her lip and took a step closer to her. She had to keep her voice light. "You kept it well, but I saw you at the beach yesterday."

"You were watching me?" she asked. Her expression broke

Blair's heart. Perhaps, this was a bad idea after all. Kerna hid her face. She looked scared, almost like she wanted to run away. "So many of my kind were killed by humans. My parents told me to never tell anyone I was a selkie."

"So the villagers don't know?" Blair asked.

Still in the same position, Kerna answered. "They know, but they're the only ones. They know about my family too. They live here when they're in human form. All the other villagers are humans though. I've never met very many strangers before, so I was a little nervous when you came along."

"Kerna, you don't have to be afraid. I'm not going to hurt you nor will I tell any others about your secret. You can swim. You can leave the island. We need help getting back."

She thought her words would cheer her up, but Kerna only withdrew, looking more hurt. Did she not trust Blair enough? "Do you have any idea how much I risk when I'm in the form of a seal? Humans still hunt us. I might be seen when transforming. This island is my safe haven."

Blair said nothing. About the time they were trapped here, she was desperate to do anything possible to escape, but now? How can she beg a friend to risk her life? This time, Kerna spoke next. "Is it really that important for you to leave us so soon? By spring or summer, you might see a few ships on the horizon. It'll be easier for us to reach them then."

The spoken word of summer especially brought a shiver of fear to Blair. She held onto the unease and considered her options. Finally, she decided on her best choice. "There's a part of my story I haven't shared with you yet, and seeing as how you revealed to me your thoughts and secrets, I should do the same." Blair paused and pulled back the sleeve from her wrist, exposing her mark to her. "This is the mark of a curse. I only have until the changing colors of autumn to break it or I'll disappear. I'm running out of time."

Kerna's face was one of bewilderment. Blair continued. "But it gets worse. The man who did this is a rokian. I know this now. I don't know why he did it, but he's not up to any good. Maybe this is bigger than me. Maybe he'll hurt others?"

For a second, Kerna was still as stone. "A rokian? You mean

the enemy of the vayen aray? That kind of rokian?"

"I'm not going to ask this of you again, but I needed to tell you the truth. It's important for you to stay safe. We'll find a way off the island and we'll break the curse."

Kerna shied away and allowed Blair to return to her work. She didn't speak the rest of the time they were in the wilderness nor did Blair.

But Blair was not upset. She wasn't even disappointed. She knew she made the right decision and was even pleased with Kerna's response. She didn't run away, and they remained friends. Blair wouldn't have it any other way. All that Blair needed was a bit of faith. Queriven has led her in the right way so far. She needed to trust he was right and that they would do everything they could.

As evening approached, the two headed back for supper. After dropping off the wood to the central supply house, Blair turned to Kerna with a genuine smile on her face. "I'm going to find Queriven and bring him back for supper. He should be just out of the village. He likes his space."

"Blair, wait," Kerna spoke up. Nervous yet again, she played with a loose strand of hair. "I'm going to do some thinking on our talk earlier. It is dangerous, but I want to help. You have my promise; I'm going to do everything I can."

Blair sighed. "That means a lot to me. Any kind of help is much more than I can ask for at this time, but don't do anything too rash."

"You got it," Kerna answered. "I'll see you two at supper then."

The next morning, it was Kerna who came to the house of Blair and Queriven. She had thought of a plan the last evening.

"She decided she would help us," Blair explained to Queriven and they listened to her idea. Kerna will leave the island and retreat to Seadrake where she'll hire a ship to pick them up if she can.

"Stay away from anything under the royal government seal

if you can," Queriven told her. "We'll have more luck from someone with an independent mind. I'll give you all the money we have left, which isn't much. I spent most of what I had on the last ship. But if they need more, tell them there's a great reward for them once they arrive."

Kerna took the pouch from him. "I'll be as quick as I can, but it'll take me a while to find one. It'll probably be even longer for it to come back here."

"Please stay safe," Blair implored her, giving the girl a quick hug. "And thank you."

"It's the best I can give you guys, my new friends," she responded. "This is the biggest responsibility anyone's ever trusted me with, but I'll do it if it means ruining a rokian's plan." Now free, she took the skin from her shoulders and hugged it against her chest. Then, she gave a last farewell before stepping out of the house.

Now that Kerna's gone, Blair sent a quick prayer for her safety. Finally, she turned to Queriven who was now at the fire pit, cleaning the ashes that blew on the outside edges of the fencing. "Queriven?" Blair asked, "What reward were you talking about? We have no way of making more money right now."

"That's true, but we still have things of value. I have elven medicine I can sell, which was always a strong demand with humans back in the day of trading," he paused, almost like he was considering how he might sell such a thing. "It is hard to sell without sharing my heritage... What about the vayen aray treasures of Lyfihana? There's still plenty there, and anything belonging to the old race would be high value, like that scrimshaw or the horn. We'll give them anything for us to reach Seadrake again."

Then, he took the ashes he swept up and dropped them outside. He was beginning to see more hope from Blair again. But their quest was just beginning, and it'll be harder once they reach the land again. Queriven hoped they'll find the horn in time.

CHAPTER THIRTEEN
A FRIEND IN NEED

Blair prayed for Kerna often as the days flew, as there was no possible way for them to know how she was doing. But one day, they spotted a tall mast on the horizon. There was still no sign of Kerna. Blair sighed; she wished she knew she was safe. There was no waiting now that the ship was here.

The captain and crew were a merchant ship from another kingdom, so, with some herbs, concoctions, and trinkets from Lyfíhana's mountain, Queriven had enough for them to accept the offer. Blair scanned the gathered crowd as they said their goodbyes to the village. She still didn't see the young selkie girl. She wasn't sure if she would see her again. She'll just have to trust she'll make it back home soon.

As predicted, the seas were rough and the work harder in this time of year. If they had favorable wind and calmer waters, they would reach Seadrake much faster. But the weather was worse than the first time they came to the island, so the sail back to the mainland took more than twice that long.

After long days of frustration and grueling hours of work, they finally came to their destination. "What do we look for first?" Blair asked as the men began bringing in the ship at the port.

"We look for records on the vayen aray's relationship with the humans of Fairdraisha. We might be able to trace the horn they passed on from there, then we follow up on it." He paused and studied the quiet wharf below them. "We can start with Dyara as well and read its history. It was a small town, so something involving the vayen aray would stand out from its records."

Blair sighed and tossed back a long strand of hair from her eyes. "You make it sound so easy. We're looking for something that happened over a thousand years ago. Did they even keep records back then?"

Queriven placed a calming hand on her shoulder. "The horn has to be somewhere. I'm just sure there has to be some kind of record made of it. It was, after all, the symbol of joining allies between the two races. That has to mean something to the humans back then."

Blair took some comfort in his words, though she tried to bury her feelings of worry. Spring was just a little ways away. Her deadline was drawing closer. Even if they find a trace of the horn, will they still reach it in time? Was the horn even in Fairdraisha anymore? There was only a thread of hope for Blair to cling to, so she held onto Queriven and trusted he knew where he was going, though he wasn't completely sure himself.

The first day in Seadrake was hard for Blair and Queriven. Both of the two wanted to jump right into chasing down the horn but were instead looking for a place they could stay and afford. They eventually found a place where the tavern keeper was nice enough for Queriven to pay for their rooms later when he could afford it.

Blair was finally free to check into the library while Queriven quietly sold the rest of his supplies in medicine for money. The library was huge! There were rows and rows of books stacked up to the ceiling all the way down the aisles. It wasn't messy either. Every shelf was free of dust and the room smelled like leather and old pages. It took Blair at least an hour to even find the row she was looking for.

There wasn't a lot of scripts about the vayen aray, or even the rokians. Even when she found a few books, there was nothing important. She did learn how destructive rokians were though. They were selfish, power-seeking people who were always pushing to expand their territory. The vayen aray battled them for many centuries even before the tribes moved into Fairdraisha. No one knows how the battles started, but it was easy to see they were enemies for a very long time.

The closest information Blair could find on the horn was when the book spoke lightly about an alliance with the humans and there was an exchange of treasures, including a horn that calls the people to their side. Nothing more was said.

With few answers and even more frustration, Blair left the library after dark and came back to the inn with a goal to head back to the library in the morning. Queriven greeted her there and assured her he will be able to help the next day.

This created a routine, though answers were coming hard. Over the next few days, they still didn't have anything more than when they first started. It was like they were still trapped on the island. They were wasting time with nothing to do. Then one day, all that changed with a knock on the door, though it had nothing to do with the research they were carrying out.

"Kerna!" Blair cried upon seeing the girl. She wrapped her in a tight hug, though the girl only gave her a weak smile.

Kerna looked the same as she usually did, with long braids of brown hair, and dressed in furs and leather of her home island. She seemed very out of place here. Fresh tears dripped from her eyes. "They told me you were staying here. I'm so glad to see you."

Then concern took Blair back a step. "Why are you still here? I thought you were heading back home."

The girl used her sleeve to wipe the wet from her face just as Queriven joined Blair's side. He listened in on what the girl had to say. "I was going to, but I didn't want to ride back on the ship. I was worried about being too close to strangers. It was growing dark outside, and I left the tavern where I spoke with that captain, but my sealskin was stolen before I even left the city road." More tears bubbled up again and her voice raised into a whine. "Now I can't turn back anymore. It's like a lost a piece of my life. I need that skin!"

Queriven held his hands before him, patting the air for her to calm down. "We'll do everything we can. Tell me, what do you remember? Who stole it?"

She sniffed. Her voice was still shaky but focused again. "I left the tavern and was making for the sea. The skin was around my shoulders tight. It was the safest place I had for it. It was unbelievable! There was an older man walking by me. I had a pretty good look at his face even in the dark. His skin was pale, his face long with wrinkles and scars. His eyes were droopy, exposing pink flesh, and he just took the skin from me as he walked by. I turned and gave chase, but he disappeared in a dark alleyway." Her eyes dropped to the pavement. "I couldn't find him again after that." For a second, she glared up at the sky with a desperate expression on her face. "Why would anyone just snatch it from my shoulders? To the untrained eye, it's just an old skin and nothing valuable."

"Unless if he knew what it was," Queriven answered with a low voice, looking over at Blair to further his meaning.

She understood and turned back to Kerna. "We'll look for it, I promise. Until we find it, why don't you stay with us? We'll make room for you."

"Thank you," Kerna chirped as they showed her inside.

This was stressful enough already with the ongoing research for the horn. This was just another distraction to throw them off track, but the feelings only left her guilty. Kerna, Queriven, the crew of the Enchantress, and so many other people were giving up everything to help Blair with her curse. Instead of thanking them, she only continued to press them harder into finding answers. Now, it was her turn to help someone else, and though she only wanted to put it off and continue with the research at the library, she decided to take this as a lesson. People were reaching out to her, and she'll never take that for granted again. Blair will reach back out to them despite the costs.

"So what are you thinking we'll do?" Queriven asked once Kerna was gone. Concern lined his face and he looked as if he was reading her mind again. "This man she describes could be anywhere by now. We need to find a trace of that horn."

Blair didn't try to hide from him. "I know both are important, but if that man is still somewhere here, I'll find him. He wasn't too far from a bar and he disappeared quickly in a dark alley. That tells me he knows his way around the city and that he likes to drink. I'll stop by a few taverns and see if anybody there knows him."

Queriven froze for a second. He wasn't sure which shocked him the most — how she put off their research for this new crisis or that she already had a straight forward plan. He didn't fight for their research. "So you want to help Kerna first? Very well then. How can I help?"

Blair had been in maybe a dozen taverns, and most of them knew the man well. He went by a common nickname of "Mr. Nose," as he often landed himself in places where he didn't belong. He often hopped taverns getting drunk and involved himself in unwelcome conversations with patrons and bar women alike. As for his current location, no one knew where he was currently as he seemed to come from nowhere.

It seems as if answers were just hard to come by these days, Blair growled. The best she could do is wait until nightfall when he might show up again. She shared the news with Queriven, who was busy checking other locations besides bars he might have been to. It could be that the man, Mr. Nose, was homeless, as no one else carried new information.

After that, Queriven convinced her to stop by the library and study since she was waiting for dusk. She did so. The elf joined her several hours later. Still not finding anything under books about the ancient races, they shifted to the history of

Dyara.

The books were few, but the information plenty. Blair quickly became an expert on the town, from the moment someone decided to build a town there, to when rokians destroyed it. Still, there was nothing mentioned about a horn.

Blair patrolled the streets for several nights. Kerna remained positive, though one could tell she was struggling. While she stayed with them, she would go by the shore, using the abilities she had even in human form to catch plenty of fish. She then sold them, helping the two with some money intake. Sometimes she would even patrol with them.

But they haven't seen the thief nor has anyone recently.

However, not all was hopeless. It was late afternoon and Blair and Queriven were at the library as they usually were. Blair had patrolled late the last night. She was struggling to stay awake. An open book was lying on the table in front of her and she held her head up with a bored hand, her eyes drifting.

But a disturbance off by the shelves set her sitting straight again. "I found the horn!" It was Queriven, and he came to her table with an old book in his hands. The binding was threatening to peel right off. Already, pieces of it were lying away from it as he set it on the table beside her. Blair could just make out the worn title on the cover before Queriven flipped it open. "It's so unlikely to find it here. I wasn't expecting it."

"What is it?" Blair asked, interested but her voice was drowsy.

"'Remarkable History of Fairdraisha'. It's a category of noteworthy occurrences. Look," a slender finger glided over the open page and pointed at a particular entry. Blair leaned closer and began to read. "It was entrusted to the town of Dyara, but the person who held onto it then was a man named Chester," Queriven explained.

Blair read it through carefully. The heading even had a sketch of the artifact. It looked the same, like a sibling to the other two horns she's seen, with the only difference the carving of the body itself. Just like Rocanu said, there was a meeting with the humans before they entrusted the horn to the people. It mentioned how this alliance brought the two people to fight alongside each other to defend Fairdraisha from disaster by the rokians' hands.

"It doesn't say anything about where it is now," Blair responded after reading it through.

That wasn't news to Queriven. "No, but it's a start. We found something and now we have a heading. I'm going to try and find this Chester."

Blair looked up as he rose to his feet. "He could be anybody. Despite having been there to retrieve the horn, he was more than likely just a small-town peasant like me. I doubt you'll find anything on him."

"Maybe not," Queriven agreed, "but what about his family? Where did he go after Dyara fell? All that I have to find is a Chester originally from Dyara."

Blair shook her head as he retreated back to the shelves. Out of all the people living in Fairdraisha, and after an event that happened a thousand years ago, it would be like searching for a needle in a haystack.

She closed the book she was on and brought over the still open one Queriven left behind. Then she returned to her last position and began reading more of the articles.

◊ ◊ ◊

"Blair!" a voice called her through the empty void. "Wake up. It's after sunset already." Then she remembered Queriven's voice.

Her head was resting on the open book she was reading, her dark golden hair draping over the edges of the table. Blair bolted upright, startling Queriven who had his hand on her shoulder. She stretched, pulling her arms up high over her head. "Did I fall asleep?" she asked no one in particular.

Queriven still leaned forward, his gaze remaining on her. "You were pretty tired when I left you. Are you all right?"

"I'm fine." She rubbed her tired eyes. "Sorry. I didn't mean to fall asleep."

"Why don't you go back to the inn and rest? I'll handle the

streets tonight."

"No," Blair answered immediately. "I can handle it for a while." She stood up from the table and giggled, "Especially now that I've already had some rest."

"Are you sure?" Queriven asked. "It's fine, really. I can look for the guy on my own."

"I got it," she groaned, giving another quick stretch. "Have you found anything else important?"

He shrugged and gestured to the book under his arm. "Not yet, though I'll like to go through this one really quick before I take to the patrol tonight."

Blair nodded, the light of the waking world returning to her eyes. "Good luck then."

Queriven gave her one last call as she was heading for the door. "Don't stay out too late! I'll meet you back at the inn."

A light flurry of snow was falling gently on the pavement outside. Blair shivered and pulled in the other sleeve of her jacket. It wasn't terribly cold tonight like it has been, but it was certainly a change from the warm library. Blair picked a direction at random and went for a walk.

She made sure, as the night grew older, to walk by the streets with the most taverns. The snow continued to float gently the whole time she was walking. It was already building up, starting from the cracks in the stone road. It was quiet, almost like the night and the snow soaked up the rest of the sound. She couldn't hear the ocean tides from here. No creatures chirped or cried. Blair was alone.

She used to be afraid of approaching the tavern doors alone at night, but it didn't bother her anymore. The light that spilled from the open doors of the bars was bright and lively, the only sound reaching her ears. It was full of boisterous voices and calls, music, clanging of mugs, and so on. Very few men who left these doors at this time of night were sober. Blair easily pushed away and ignored those who flocked to her. And those who tried to give chase didn't make it far for one reason or another.

The chilly air came with the scent of fresh dusted snow, and it ached her lungs to breathe in very far. There were clouds in front of her with every breath. There was still no sign of Mr. Nose. No progress was being made tonight, Blair concluded. The night was growing late, even a lot of the drunkards were setting themselves in their rooms. Perhaps, she should just head back to her own? She wondered if Queriven was there already, or maybe he found the man they were looking for.

Blair took a turn around the block, making a round back to the road that'd take her to the inn. She was done with the patrol for the night, so, of course, this is the night where she found Mr. Nose accidentally. She saw him first, taking a few steps every minute but mainly looking down at his palm. He was holding a few coins there, and he was staring down at them. It was almost like he was considering if he should purchase something or not. He was just like Blair had imagined him; long face with eyes so low he could hardly see from them. The few steps he took were going opposite from hers. If he kept going this way, he'll reach one of the busier bars.

Blair took action, waiting for him to come nearer to her. "Are you Mr. Nose?" she asked. His face left the coins and met hers. His lips trembled. She wasn't sure if he was cold with old age or if he was trying to respond to her. But then something else caught her attention. He had a sealskin tied to his belt. Blair pointed a finger at it. "Is that yours?"

Those old eyes widened and he turned, nearly throwing the coins from his grip. Then he sprinted back where he came from. Blair wasn't too far behind, and she raced for him with everything she had.

For an old beggar, he was quick. It was almost like he's done this several times before. Whatever the reason, he wasn't just running; he had a plan. Blair was certain of it. She chased him down several streets. The darkness was like an obscured cloud before her eyes, and she worried about losing him in it many times, but she followed him close enough to see him a moment later. Now the breeze she pushed through made her face hot with rushing blood.

Finally, the man's breath came in painful gasps and he took

her into a dirty alleyway. There, it seemed like his next plan was to hide in a pile of trash, and he was in the process of climbing over a box spotted with mold.

Blair didn't hesitate; she gripped the man's bony shoulder and ripped him from his perch where he sprawled on the snowy ground. He couldn't even control his trembling as this woman who stood over him. He whined and begged in such a high tone she couldn't understand. She nearly had to yell to talk over him. "You stole something from a friend of mine. Why did you take it?"

"Please Miss," he continued slowly but still whining. "I'm nothing but old homeless scum. Take pity! I didn't do anything, I swear!"

Blair growled. "The sealskin! You tore it from a little girl! Now answer me before I do something I'm going to regret."

He held up his hands in front of him. His gloves were worn and torn in many areas. "Fine, I took it. I did! But she didn't need it. She had plenty of furs and skins on her."

"But why would you commit a crime for it?"

His next sentence came with an explosion of spittle and tears. "I wanted it! It was calling to me. I don't know why I took it, but it was special. I had to have it. That's all." He calmed his breathing as Blair didn't move against him. "You're not going to take it back, are you? I'm just a poor man living on the streets."

Suddenly, a spear flashed in front of him, glittering before his bulbous nose. "You stole it first," Blair answered. "Why not think of the little girl you took it from? It's important to her. She was in tears without it."

"Fine!" he cried out annoyingly. His hands went to the sealskin on his belt where he loosened it and tossed it at Blair's feet. "Just don't hurt me. I won't do it again. I swear!"

Blair picked it up from the dirty ground and returned the spear to her back. The man was still cowering on the ground before her. She turned, leaving the alleyway without another word.

Now with the alleyway far behind her, she continued back to the inn, staring down at the skin in her grip. A bit of guilt was starting to build in her mind. Was she too mean to Mr. Nose? She brushed it off as she thought about it again. The man was clearly sick, wrapping himself up in everything he can get his hands on, and spending so many nights drinking away the money he could use for his own blankets and food. This was his choice, and he was fine with it.

Blair looked down at the hide in her hands. For once, she had some good news to tell the others.

CHAPTER FOURTEEN
LONELY STREETS

"You found it! I can't believe you found it!" Kerna cried as Blair came through the door. With much excitement, she ran and wrapped Blair in a hug. She took the skin in her arms as she did. "Thank you. This is wonderful!"

"You found Mr. Nose?" Queriven asked from his seat by the window. "Was it hard to convince him to release it?"

Blair smiled. "Not really, though he'll think twice before doing something like that again."

Queriven's first reaction was confusion, then he sank back in his seat with bewilderment.

"You two are the best," Kerna continued. "Now I can finally return home as a selkie. How can I ever repay you?"

"You already did," Blair replied. "You helped us off the island. Now we're even."

Queriven spoke next as Kerna wrapped the skin around her shoulders. "You should stay with us tonight and then you can head back home in the morning if you want to."

Kerna nodded. "I'll never forget this. You two are my best friends for life!" She giggled as she took the skin from her shoulders again, inspecting it closely and walking away from the door. Blair just shook her head, grinning widely as she settled in the room.

◊ ◊ ◊

Blair woke up the next morning feeling refreshed, which hasn't happened in a long time. She yawned, escaping from her sleeping corner and rising to her feet. Kerna was still asleep on the single bed in the room, hugging the returned skin tightly.

Then, the door to the room opened and Queriven strode through. Blair tilted her head and watched him. "Don't you ever sleep?" She never remembered seeing him rest, either before she sleeps or after she wakes up.

He returned her an even more curious look, like she should know the answer before asking. "Of course, I do. What do you think I am?" And he returned to the stash of pouches set on the table, organizing the contents. "Oh, good morning to you too, by the way."

The answer didn't change her question, but she shrugged it off. Her hair was in knots and she tried to straighten it with her fingers, but that only ended in frustration and pulled hair. It was considerably longer now. She made a mental note to cut it later.

In the bed, Kerna began to stir. She yawned and sat up. The skin was still in her arms. Blair knelt down, picking up her jacket and turning it over. That's when she noticed something odd about her curse. At first, she froze, hardly able to breathe until she found out what it was. The three strings going around and around her wrist were down to two. Why was it different? This wasn't an illusion. It was true. There was one string missing. She turned her head back to Queriven, her heart racing, but words failed her and she was quiet. Queriven was too wrapped up in a conversation with Kerna to notice.

After they were ready, the three went out and had breakfast, then they walked to the edge of town by the shore to see Kerna off. She was quiet and serious the whole way there. The ocean spread out far into the horizon. Gentle splashes and bird cries welcomed the group near. She looked ahead. The water was beckoning her home. Kerna was suddenly torn in two directions. She turned to Blair and Queriven who stood beside her. "What if I don't go home right away? What if I stay and help you break the curse?"

Blair and Queriven exchanged glances. Blair spoke next after a thought. "You owe us nothing, and your family is waiting for your return."

She looked back down at the skin again. "I just don't want to say goodbye."

"Then don't," Queriven answered. "You said it yourself; we're your friends for life. When will be the next time we need to reach Lyfíhana?"

The girl smiled and hugged both of them tight. "You're right. I expect to see you guys again; both of you."

The two agreed, and Kerna stepped closer to the water edge. She wrapped herself in the skin and morphed into the form of a seal and waved with a large gray flipper at her friends before she jumped in and disappeared in the waves. Blair and Queriven watched until she was surely gone over the horizon, heading back home.

When she refocused, Blair looked away and saw Queriven. His face was pure and joyous for the first time ever. She wanted to point it out to him — that she's never seen him so happy before — but she also didn't want to take it away. Instead, Blair decided to appreciate it quietly.

There was an unsettling growl from Queriven's side of the table. Clearly, that beautiful spark of joy was gone and he was back to his serious, expressionless self.

They were back at the library, soaking up page after page of useless script they would never need in their lives. Queriven had tasked himself with following the life of the mysterious Chester while Blair followed the progress of the sister city, Penacha, after the fall of Dyara.

Blair glanced over to the side from her open book, just in time to see him toss his current one off on the stack he's been through already. He sighed and caught her looking at him. "Maybe you're right. Despite owning a magical horn given to him as a sign of friendship between two races, Chester is nothing but a peasant." Tired, he picked at another book on the other side of the stack, but then just left it in front of him like he couldn't bear to open another one. "The family hasn't done a single noteworthy thing in their histories. Please tell me you're doing better."

Blair wished she could give him some hope, as he'd done for her, but she had nothing. Regrettably, she shrugged and gave him a look as if to say, "I'm sorry."

He growled again and flipped the book open to a random page. Then he froze. "I should be reading more about the destruction of Dyara," he realized out loud. "Chester had the horn, but it belonged to Dyara. Where did it go?" After closing the book again, he pushed it aside and dug in his assortment, looking for something about Dyara's fall.

Finally, Blair paused in her reading. "No need to push yourself too hard. It's been many hours now. Why don't we stop and find some supper?" The shifting of books stopped and Queriven looked back at her. Again, the shock was evident on his face. It was that look that said he must have heard her wrong though he knew it was correct. He didn't even have a response to that, either positive or negative. "You're tired, I can tell. We've been digging through books in this library for days now. It's taking a toll on both of us."

"Yeah, and we need to find an answer soon. I thought you were always the one to push us into finding the next piece to the puzzle," he scoffed and the shuffle of leather bindings continued. "That I'm tired doesn't change the point. I'm always tired. It has nothing to do with finding the horn."

Blair left him with his search and drifted back to her pages, though she couldn't help but think about what he said. Seeing him so deep in research and working so hard on his last nerve made her mad with guilt. Like this Chester, she was a useless peasant. Nothing was important about her. And Queriven, though she still didn't know too much about him, was an elven knight, and he was giving his all to protect her. "You wouldn't be so tired all the time if you actually rested every once in a while."

Queriven had a different book open, and he responded without lifting his eyes from the page. "Let's not make this about me right now."

But it was too late. Blair had grown too curious to drop the subject. "Is it because you struggle to sleep at night? Does it have something to do with your past back home?"

She had stepped in dangerous territory and the whole atmosphere of the library changed when Queriven fell into a temper. He tried again to warn her gently. "I'm not discussing this with you. It'll be better for both of us if you don't speak of it again."

"You always change the subject and there's a good reason behind it. Am I going to stay unaware of your life this whole time?"

"Yes, that would be preferred."

A moment of uncomfortable stillness passed and Blair's eyes tried to return to reading, though her mind wasn't following. Finally, it struck her. Of course! She knew why he was so shifty about his past. It was right before her. "You were in the elven military. You've been in terrible battles, haven't you?"

That was the final shove. Queriven tore away from the book. "Tell me, do you want to find the horn to break your curse or not? Stop digging around in something you don't belong in!"

Blair retreated back to her pages. Curious as she may be, making him angry was not on her agenda and she was sorry to bring it up. For a while, the two sat quietly at the table, but the silence didn't bring much comfort to Queriven's anger. Finally, he rose and disappeared in the aisles.

Blair sighed. Now she made it worse. It was true that Queriven was a difficult person to deal with a lot of times, but she pushed him into that one. She was no way knowledgeable when it came to war, but she knew violent battles can take hold of soldiers in more ways than one. Queriven was struggling with a rough past. Blair decided then she would try to stay out of it. It only brought both of them pain anyway.

◊ ◊ ◊

Queriven was quiet, but his terrible mood was gone when Blair retrieved him for supper about an hour later. Still unhappy with the lack of clues they found, they left the library and picked up some food at a nearby tavern.

The elf sat at the other end of the table with his hood up. It was casting a dark shadow over the top half of his face from there.

Blair tried to organize her thoughts, but couldn't. She knew she didn't want the argument to affect them anymore. She lifted her eyes and spoke her thoughts aloud. "Listen, I want to apologize for what happened earlier." As it turned out, Queriven also seemed lost as he stared down at his plate while chomping on a meager slice of mushroom. His eyes jumped up at her when she spoke. "You clearly told me to stay out of your past, and you're right. I was poking around in something I didn't need to. I tend to be too curious for my own good."

Queriven shrugged like it didn't matter anymore. "I understand. I'd be curious too if this was my first time meeting a human."

That answer kind of surprised her. She didn't really consider how different she would be in his eyes. That thought alone took her to imagine it further. Humans were everywhere here, and he probably didn't know too much about them when he first met them. He was in a world so different from home. The experience would be exciting, but home sickening at the same time. She never thought about it, but elves and humans were a lot alike in different ways. Meeting an elf was less magical than Blair thought it would be. That made her angry, as the imposter who cursed her made it feel more magical than it really was just to attract her to him.

"Of course, I tend to be quite selfish," Queriven said next. "I hardly ever thought about what others think about me, and not just humans. I let down many of my friends back at home. My pride was in the way. I never really appreciated them when I had the chance."

Blair went back to her soup. Her head was filling up with more questions, but she didn't speak them. It would be inappropriate after what she just apologized for.

Queriven still watched her though, and he picked up another mushroom. "I was in the military for many years and a knight too before you were even born. I've tried to block many of the battles from my memory, but yes, many of them were terrible." He sighed and looked away. There was a strong hurt in his eyes. "I was young and naive. I had no idea what I was getting myself into when I began training as a soldier. I just figured I could pick up and do it with no costs. I was never so wrong." He lowered the mushroom back to the plate. "The worst part is, that's who I am now. I was never a good enough leader, and with the title of a knight, so many people expected the best of me. It just wasn't something I could deliver."

"Well," Blair began, quiet and a little shy at first, "for someone who's nothing but selfish and lets down those around him, you were certainly different for me. To me, you were extremely selfless. You involved yourself in a cause that brings you no gain."

Queriven exhaled slowly and said nothing. He wished she spoke the full truth. He wished to help her since the curse was his fault. He didn't know much about the curse or the reason behind it, but he held back information from her. Why wasn't he telling her everything? He didn't rightly know, though he was afraid. He buried that story far behind him for a reason. It was why he left home in the first place.

Queriven shuddered, thinking about something to break the uncomfortable pause, but Blair was already back to her meal. She was smiling, the return of joy breaking through the wall of anger and sadness. It touched his heart. The mushroom lifted back up and he took a bite.

Silence closed in around them and the smile slowly melted from Blair's face as the two ate. "There's something I was meaning to tell you. There was something odd about my curse this morning..." And looking around them for anyone suspicious, she laid her arm on the table and pulled back the sleeve.

Queriven inspected it. "One of the strands is missing," he concluded. "Why?"

She shook her head, bringing her arm back. "I don't know. Do you think this is a good or bad thing?"

He pondered for a moment. "No idea."

Blair brought her wrist to her face, thinking. After a minute, Queriven spoke again. "But if that mark is like a chain holding you to the curse, maybe it's weakening."

"But what happened? That would make it good news, but what made it weaker? Maybe it's growing dim to show I'm running out of time."

"We still have until the changing of autumn," Queriven reminded her, leaning on the table surface. "I don't think we'll figure out the cause on our own. All that matters is that we know when the deadline is."

Blair sat back in her chair. The bit of truth rang in her head and gave her comfort against the unpredictable future. The rest of their supper was pleasant again after that.

The two tried their best to stay pleasant and were back in the library a day later. The never-ending search for answers was tiring.

Blair browsed the aisles, staring at every binding. Her current subject ran dry, but she didn't even have an idea of what to search next. She leaned on the shelf behind her, scanning the row of books. Her face dropped when she still came up with nothing a minute later. She glanced over to the end of the row where Queriven was quietly standing by the shelves on the wall. She couldn't see his face from here, but he looked just as clueless.

They've tried everything. There was not an entry about where the horn moved to. It was gone, just as lost and forgotten as Lyfíhana. The only place it could be now is in Penacha. That was the only thing that made sense, unless it was either left in Dyara when it fell, or it left Fairdraisha entirely. That was it, she decided. Their best chance was to try Penacha. If the horn wasn't there, then they gave it their all and there was nothing left.

Giving up on the choices in front of her, she moved away from the shelf and came to Queriven. He didn't move to greet her right away, though he knew she was there. So instead, Blair spoke her thoughts. "We're wasting our time here in this city. I think we should head to Penacha. It's our only logical path."

The elf had his hand up to his chin and didn't move even when she was talking. He responded, "I was so stupid not to have seen it before."

Blair gave him a moment to elaborate, then realized he was talking more to himself than to her. "What?"

Almost like he didn't believe it himself, he finally turned to meet her and said, "I know where the horn is."

CHAPTER FIFTEEN
REFLECTION

Darkadus has been watching the pirates carefully since he released them from the brig of the Enchantress. Their morale has suffered since the incident at Lost Sanctuary, but the captain, in particular, had changed the most. He carried a grudge for the girl who killed his best first mate before escaping, but even more so, he had vowed revenge on the people who took her away. The crew of the Enchantress was the first to suffer before the pirates tossed them to the open sea, but there remained one person who still lived, the elf who organized the plan of attack. Queriven.

Darkadus sneered at the fuming pirate. The captain was more personally involved with the rokian's goal than ever, but Darkadus couldn't trust him to leave Blair and Queriven alive. Yusen was a strong ally, and he hated the thought of sending someone else to do his work.

"Sir," Captain Nashögan called when he found Darkadus out of his tent. "Correct me if I'm wrong, but I feel as if you've been leaving us in the dark." His deep eyes were studying for a reaction. "What is our next plan? You said yesterday that the two were back on the mainland."

"Yes," Darkadus answered with little change of expression. "I was scrying on them. They left the city this morning."

The captain went silent for a second before taking a step back. Even Darkadus could see his rising anger. To avoid confrontation from curious eyes of those who remembered the captain of the Enchantress, the group made camp outside the city. The ship they had stolen wasn't even docked at Seadrake, but just south of the eastern river not far from the elven border. "They were in Seadrake? Why didn't we stop them?"

The answer came first with a pause, showing he wasn't in a hurry. "Because you want vengeance. I need someone else to take the job now," Darkadus answered. He knew manipulation was his best tactic now. He still needed someone to stop the girl, and he couldn't do it himself. He needed his magic to stretch as long as possible.

He moved to go around the captain, but he stepped in the way. "There's no need for that. They beat us, but we're standing free again." Yusen was pleading now. It would have looked bad if any of his crew were watching him in this state. "We had a deal. Let me keep that part. For a place of power and treasure, I'll set aside my own deeds to follow yours at the time being. This I know will take me and my crew to a better place than we were before."

For just a moment, Darkadus looked away. He didn't try again to go around the pirate. "All right. If you swear I can trust you, then I'll sweeten the deal. Not only will I protect my kind, but you'll be respected. We'll reward you with more in valuables and territory. But these rules I say next are more important than ever; you may hunt both the girl and Queriven and slow them down, but you may not kill them. I need them both alive," he smiled, "though, of course, after the change of autumn, I'll no longer have a need for the elf. You can kill him if you wish after that."

The captain clenched his fists, the notion of that last promise bringing a spark back to his spirit. Darkadus finally walked around the man. Yusen didn't even turn to look back as the rokian's boots clomped on the little bit of snow on the ground.

But then it stopped and the rokian called him. "If you find

yourself defeated again, I'm not releasing you at the expense of magic," Darkadus chimed. "Remember, the more magic I use, the weaker the curse becomes. I'm not sure if I can catch her a second time, so we have to give this everything we have."

"You have my word, sir."

◊ ◊ ◊

"How do you know the horn is in Dunverhart?" Blair asked.

"The name we found, Chester, was the name of a family who lived in Dyara. They were the holders of the horn for several years," Queriven replied. They were just north of Seadrake and traveling up a steep hill on the side of the road. "But one day, there was a break-in. I don't know many details, but the article said the entire family was found murdered in their home and the horn was gone. Do you have any idea what happens to stolen artifacts around here?"

She shook her head, growing frustrated. Blair raised her voice. "I don't know! Why don't you just tell me?"

Queriven stopped and lowered his tone almost to a whisper. He leaned close enough to her so that no one could overhear him. "Anything with a considerable enough value ends up in the hands of your king, King Brenmor. I believe the king in that time hired someone to take the horn when Dyara wasn't willing to give it up." Then he moved away again, allowing her to soak up the message.

"Why do you think that?"

He shrugged, regarding her like he didn't know why that didn't answer the question. "Because that's the kind of people who sit in your throne. The Brenmor line takes and controls. It's even more likely he took it because it was originally owned by a peasant family."

Blair finally saw the point he was trying to make, but she stayed firm. How much bias did Queriven have for the human rulers? The elves and humans have been rivals for many years after all. "We didn't always have bad kings, you know! Some of the Brenmors we had were pretty decent. That was a long time ago too. How do you know that was one of the bad ones?" She glared at him, now mad by his hateful assumption.

But Queriven has never been so sure. "He has it. I know he does. As for how we'll get to it, I don't know. We'll figure that one out when we're there."

Blair still wanted to argue, but instead, she remained silent. They didn't have any other clues and she wanted to trust Queriven knew what he was doing. Even if the family wasn't killed by Brenmor at that time, Raek Brenmor may have gotten his hands on it since then. With another sigh, Blair allowed the subject to drop. Queriven turned back to the road again, but he took only a few slow steps forward. To the left of them, there were a few trees lining the entrance to a thick wood. The place was familiar to him and he thought for a while. "Actually, before we leave... I was wondering if I could show you something first."

That held Blair's attention, but again, he didn't elaborate. "What is it?" she prodded.

He was almost lost in thought. It was like he was wondering if he should or not. "It's a little out of the way, but it won't take us too far from the bridge." Finally, he made his decision and veered off the road going into the woods.

Blair scoffed but followed him anyway. "Where are we going?"

"You'll see."

All the times he's been vague with her, she always wanted to argue. Then, she always had to remind herself how pointless that is. Instead, she just insisted they were quick.

As they entered the thick trees, Blair took a quiet moment to take in the light chill in the air. Spring usually arrives late almost every year, but it was already beginning. It was cold, but not terrible. Even the snow was thinner than normal. It came up to her toes instead of her calves. The winter would soak up every sound as well, though here, she was already listening to some chirps of early birds. It wouldn't be long for the wildflowers and herbs to sprout up again. She was sure Queriven would appreciate the return of spring as she heard him many times complaining about how much he hated snow.

She took in a deep breath, taking in the scents of wood and the earthy ground fixing to sprout new life. Then she noticed a slight gurgle and bubbling. They were near a river, and as she heard it, she saw it moments later. The water was low, but the ice was just on the edges.

Then, her step faltered and her heart jumped. This wasn't just any woods; this was the woods near her hometown! She could see the hills between the trees on the other side of the river. "Is this near Bailiese?" Blair asked suddenly. "This water is flowing from a lake nearby, right?"

Queriven showed a bit of surprise in his tone. "You're right. Bailiese is on the other side of those hills." There was a moment of silence as he understood a second later why she mentioned that. "Your hometown. I remember that now."

He didn't say anything else and Blair was staring back at the hills again. She hasn't been so near the place since she left all that time ago. But other than that thought, she didn't know what else to make of it. Her thoughts confused her more than ever. Maybe she should be sad, she thought, but that really didn't express it either... Then she thought of her parents. She's been gone for so many months. How much have they changed? Or did they even change at all?

Maybe she was the one who changed...?

Then she was a little sad. Her mom would be planting flowers soon, her dad taking the goats out in warmer weather. She wasn't a part of it anymore. Even with the reminder, she held on her emotions for home and took them in. She wasn't alone now, and she was glad for that. She was no longer a lost peasant girl. So instead of feeling sorry for herself, she took a silent oath to tell her parents the truth when all this is said and done. That is, if she was still here to tell it by then.

When she refocused, they had walked for nearly a mile and they were still going. "Are you sure it's only a little out of the way? I still don't know what the reason behind this is."

Queriven answered without looking back. "We're almost there."

And indeed they were. Queriven was slowing his pace even

as he finished speaking. The slower he walked, the more Blair was fixing to shoot an angry retort, but she kept her mouth shut as he came to a stop. At first, she looked at him in confusion. They were still in the middle of the woods and she didn't note anything interesting at first. His face dropped and grew shallow, and finally, she understood.

She didn't see it the first time because it was blending with the scenery around it, but on the second impression, she saw a man-made shelter. It looked like it was made from nothing but thick branches, twigs, and vines. They lined up almost in the shape of a tent. Despite being a little shoddy, she saw an incredible effort there. Brownish moss filled in any spots that may include openings. The back of the shelter was against a good sturdy tree, and from here, it looked like it was a part of the wall of the shelter. "What is this?" Blair whispered, but the answer came to her before she even finished the question. She looked again at Queriven who didn't respond. "Did you make this?"

He took in a breath, finally finding his voice again. "This was my sanctuary when I left the forest. I haven't been here since summer."

"When you left the forest...?" she echoed, staring at the little shelter. Blair wanted a better look at the design, and Queriven followed a little behind her. Even with all the padding and different methods the elf had tried to seal any cracks, sunlight was still seeping through. It must have leaked terribly in rain. Blair inspected it, going around it to take in the detailing. The door was small. They would have to crouch just to go through it.

The elf remained by the front of it as Blair went around. "Back home, the elves would enchant the trees to grow them tall and wide, then we carved them out into rooms. Since this kingdom doesn't grow any trees like this, I had to improvise." He chuckled bitterly. "And I'm not much into construction."

Having gone in a complete circle, Blair stopped by the entrance. "May I?" she asked, pointing at the door.

Queriven shrugged. "Go ahead."

Inside, Blair found a few basic furnishings. In the middle of the room was a wooden chair held together with thick plant fibers. It was next to a matching little rectangle table. Against the rightmost wall was a hanging hammock made from a sheet that looked like it was bought from a store. As a matter of fact, many of the objects here were bought from a store. Blair moved further in, looking down at a chest sitting by the other wall behind the chair.

Queriven came in behind her. The space was thin. It would have been too cramped if there was another person here, and the two were already taking up a lot of the room. He didn't say a thing even as Blair blew off the layer of dust that gathered on the surface of the chest. At first, she seemed like she was going to open it, but she was shy and decided against it. It was amazing to be here at all. She didn't want to poke in his belongings.

Finally, he did speak. "Most of that is just blankets I bought to fight off the cold. I don't make much money, but I would sometimes have enough to save me some trouble."

Since he was open to the idea, she flipped the lid up. It was true. The box was stuffed with many different kinds of blankets, most of them thick and heavy, but there was a little thing sitting on the top that caught her attention. It was a little book. Blair carefully picked it up and ran a careful finger against the front. She took a peek on a random page. It looked like a personal diary, but she couldn't make a word of what it was saying. It was in a language she's never seen before. There was no doubt it was the written speech of the elves. Some pages were filled to the brim with the characters, while others were not even filled halfway. It was like he gave up writing every once in a while.

Blair flipped through the book one last time before closing it. "How long have you been out of the forest?"

She fully expected him to argue and shut her down like he always did when she asked those questions, but he was fine with it this time. "Time escaped me so quickly after I left. I'm not sure exactly." Queriven was standing closer to the hammock now and he took a second to ponder. "It must have been a decade at least; not quite two."

Blair took in a breath. For an elf, that wouldn't be very much at all, but still considerable. She would have been a little baby back then. "Why would you be gone that long? Don't you have family and friends there?"

He turned away. Queriven had no strength to argue with her now, but he didn't answer that question. Instead, his speech stumbled a few times before falling silent for a moment. "Like I told you before, it's complicated. If you don't mind... I'd prefer not to talk about it."

Blair turned around, her stomach aching as she imagined being so far away from home for more than a decade. "Why not? I might be able to help."

Queriven returned her eye contact. There was a glimmer in his eye for only a second. "I know you will, but there's nothing to do about it."

She wished he would accept it. After all, he's been helping her. If it wasn't for him, she wouldn't have made it this far, and the rokian would win and she would never return home. Blair wished she knew more about the cause of Queriven's bitter past. She set the diary down on the blankets and closed the lid of the chest.

Blair then noticed that the tree made up part of the far wall, and he had a clever way of using it. At the top near the roof hung drying herbs, but it was the floor level that got her attention. The inside of the tree was carved out and there was a small open area inside. It looked like a closet, as it wouldn't be big enough for much else.

She placed a hand on the bark and leaned inside. It was being used as a closet too. She saw several different articles of clothing inside, some folded on the floor and others hanging on a notch made by a knife.

But one, in particular, stood out from the rest. Among all of his worn-out and faded traveling gear, there was one fancier than the others and more foreign. Over the shoulders was like a bright white metal that caught and shone in brighter colors from the smallest source of light. Then it occurred to her that she's seen that metal before, both on the tip of Queriven's spear and the arrows. The outfit looked well-made and sturdy, though it looked like it was made from many different kinds of plant substances. The belt around the hips was just twisted plant fibers. Overall, it was more than just traveling gear, though it seemed flexible and light enough to still be comfortable.

"That was one of the very few items I took with me."

Blair turned back and saw Queriven looking at her. "That armor, my spear, and my bow and arrows. That armor is the outfit of ranking knights."

"It's beautiful," she replied, giving it another look. "Why does it shine like that? I've never seen anything like it before. It's on the weapons too."

He chuckled out of disbelief and gave her a serious, wide-eyed look. "You don't know what that is? Has it really been that long since the trading stopped that humans no longer know it?" He shook his head and came closer where he took the drying herbs off the wall around the closet. "You've seen it before, but it's now in an unrecognizable state. It's pure starlight."

Blair frowned. "I don't understand. It's made from stars?"

Queriven immediately discarded her last question like it was ridiculous. "Starlight. We have talented wizards back home who can gather the light the stars give off on clear nights. It starts in a liquid form, but it can harden in any shape. It imitates metal, but better." One by one, he picked off certain herbs from the string. "It never dulls or rusts." Then he hung the empty strings back up. "It used to be a very popular item back in the day of trade. I never once thought the humans would forget about it. We use starlight for many things, both for important uses and decoration. We even held a starlight festival once a year to appreciate its uses." He paused, taking a moment to dismiss the returning memories. "The material was irreplaceable there. We never mined anything on our own; that is, beyond a few stones that were on the surface level. So, it replaced strong metals like iron and steel."

Blair found it all fascinating and began to wonder why that's no longer passed down in stories. More than likely, it was a victim of the falling friendship of humans and elves.

"That armor has never left that tree for many years. Before, I just couldn't stand to look at it, though I couldn't bear to think of it going unused all this time. I couldn't throw it away, though I'm not fit for it anymore." He approached the closet and Blair moved to the side as he leaned in and retrieved the knight's armor. Now that it was out from that dark corner inside the tree, it looked even nicer. Queriven went quiet as he stared down at it. Blair couldn't even imagine him in it. It was too proud and honorable for him.

He took a breath and looked up at her. "This is the reason why I brought you over here. I thought maybe you could give this armor renewed purpose. I'll like you to have it."

She was blank for the longest time, as if the statement didn't even register in her mind. Then she blinked, "What did you just say…"

"I want you to have it," he repeated. "It's still good armor and you need the protection more than I do. As it stands, you've been wearing that dress to shreds. I'm honestly surprised you've been doing all right with the remains of it. A dress is not a really good garb to travel or fight in."

What he said was true. Blair has been wearing the dress she left home in. It had so many stains and tears. It definitely wasn't the best thing to wear for this kind of journey, especially in the terrible winter they had. But this was not just an outfit; this was a knight's armor. It belonged in the elven military. She backed away. "You said you were no longer fit for it. What makes you think I'm anything more?"

He was still holding it before him. "Don't think of it as high-rank honor. It hasn't been that for a long time. I'm giving this to you in better hopes for the future," he shrugged. "I'm not sure what that means for me anymore, but since I came to help you break your curse, I felt as if I'm working toward something important again. I haven't done anything but exist and survive since I've been in this kingdom. This means something to me more than you can understand."

Still unsure, she took it from his hands. Encased in the fibers and thread, Blair smelled clean air and healthy trees. She could smell the many scents of a fruitful summer all in one breath. It was overpowering to her. This is what the Aven Forest smelled like.

Queriven gave her a final comment. "I can't force you to use it, but I think this is a good chance for you to change into something better. I'll be outside when you're ready. You can use the armor or any of the other garbs in the tree." Without waiting for a response, he moved away and left through the door.

Blair was by herself with his old knight armor. She brought it to her eyes, studying it and wondering if she could even fit in it. Then she took a final look inside the closet. After a few more seconds, she made her decision.

Queriven waited outside for a good long while, but he stayed patient. Blair had some choices, and he wanted to give her all the time she would need. After this, there was nothing left but to return to the road and head up to Dunverhart. He had no idea how they'll retrieve the horn. They couldn't ask for it. No, that man was beyond reasoning. He feared they'll have to risk legal matters to reach it.

But those thoughts could wait and Blair crawled out from the makeshift home. Queriven turned as she was standing up. She had gone with his old armor, and she looked fine in it. Better than fine. The shape and size fit her well, and the solid starlight on her shoulders glittered and shone like new. For her, not only did it fit comfortably, but it was nice to wear without having to worry about the ruffles of her old dress. "What do you think?" she smiled shyly and turned in a circle.

He took a second. The old life he left behind returned when she came before him, but the pain then ebbed away, leaving behind the pleasant memories of his knighthood. Queriven also noticed how it looked like it was made for her, as they were similar in size. He nodded, not exactly sure how he wanted to answer. "It looks wonderful."

She thanked him and replaced her jacket on top of the

uniform. The jacket, scarf, and gloves she kept were still in good condition. Then they left the shelter for the walk back to the road.

Dunverhart was far north of the continent, which would take them many days to travel. Blair was no longer afraid of the road, not with Queriven to lead them. Despite her new confidence for travel, Blair only became more nervous as they came closer to Bailiese. They were still far enough away. The road came only to the start of the hills. It was still many miles away from the town itself, but it was like the village was watching her, and it made her uneasy.

A part of her wanted to break free from the path and see how it was doing, but she was also scared of it. She was scared of what people may think or say, and she was scared to answer them. Blair reminded herself of how she broke free of home and how it would be best to leave it like that until she was free to return.

Luckily, the days were growing longer and slightly warmer. Spring was just around the corner. They still had plenty of time to summon Rocanu and break the curse with many months to spare. They had plenty of time and daylight to travel.

The two made good progress each day, and they camped after dusk, but roads were seldom quiet. They'll see a few others on the road every now and then. None of them was a problem until one unsuspecting night.

It was dark; well past midnight. Nothing but a handful of embers remained of their fire. Blair was asleep ages ago, and now she was nothing more than a heap of lightly snoring cloth. The sky was clear of obstructions and stretched wide above them. Queriven was lying just to the side of the campfire. His shoulders were against a rock, so he was leaning up and staring at the sky. The hills and trees were nothing but a black silhouette. So black the night sky looked colorful and blue. The stars and quarter moon shone an intense white.

Queriven was fully awake as usual, but he remained quiet and still. Beyond the burning embers, the grass smelled sweet. Thinking to himself, he predicted the hard winter was bringing them a lush summer this year. He breathed again and closed his eyes. There was nothing but the wind and chirping of various animals to remind him where he was. Though he was awake, he chose to take a welcoming peace from the twinkling sky, as before his mind made him suffer from the past. *I give this to you in hopes of a better future.* He remembered hearing his voice speak those words. It was so unlikely. He'd never thought he would have hope again until he was already saying it, but it wasn't a lie. Rather than deny the sentence, he decided he should use every bit of it.

After he made a silent vow to remain hopeful rather than fearful of the future, he let his mind drift away. He was already settling into sleep when something woke him to his senses again. The dried grass crunched and he realized he was being watched. Whatever it was, it was only a few yards away.

Queriven opened his eyes and saw a figure coming closer. The figure was hesitant, like he wasn't really sure about what he was doing, or even if he should be doing it. He came closer and looked around the campsite. A young man's voice whispered, "Blair...?"

Too close, the elf thought. He needs to draw him away, but Queriven didn't want him to run. "Hold it there," he said to the man. "What are you doing?"

The figure froze and began backing away. "I'm sorry. I didn't mean to intrude."

Queriven rose slowly and saw the figure ready to bolt away. A shiny spear jabbed forward in the man's line of retreat, blocking him. "I said hold it right there. What are you doing sniffing around our camp?"

Light from the embers and Queriven's elven eyesight saw a few of this intruder's features. He had a head of copper hair, a short but protruding nose, and handsome eyes spaced evenly apart over high cheekbones. The young man emitted a high-pitched squeak and tried hard to keep his tone calm and steady.

"Look, I said I was sorry. I'm not looking for any harm. I was just looking for a missing person."

Queriven studied him carefully, though he believed he was telling the truth. "What's your name?"

"Hector," he answered.

The spear retracted and Queriven paused, watching for any sudden reaction. "It's extremely dangerous to approach camps in the middle of the night, Hector. Whatever your reason for coming here is, there are better and safer means to do it."

The man grew annoyed. "Yeah, and I already apologized for it. What else do you want from me?"

Queriven didn't seem to regard his response. "Now, when you came up, I thought I heard you say something. Who is the person you're looking for?"

But it was a different voice that answered. "Hector?" Neither of the two noticed, but the unfolding event, despite being as hushed as it was, brought Blair back to awareness. The bed wrap was shaken off and Blair came to her feet. "What are you doing here?"

Hector saw her and his eyes opened wide. Suddenly, he forgot about Queriven and took a step closer to see Blair a bit better. Hector had to clamp his gaping jaw shut as he tried to recognize who she'd become. His eyes fell to the spear still lying nearby where she slept, over the noble and foreign attire, and finally to her face. He couldn't believe what was standing before him, but that was Blair's face for sure, even though she was so different. "Is that really you?" he asked, dumbfounded. "What happened to you?"

Blair responded with her own shock. She laid a hand over her chest. "To me? Why are you so far from Bailiese?"

Queriven interrupted, "You know him?"

Blair didn't look back at the elf for longer than a glance. "He's from my hometown. We used to herd the goats together."

Hector's only focus was on Blair. "Do you have any idea how upset people became after you disappeared? Your parents took the worst of it. I've been looking for you for a long time!"

The last part both concerned her and made her doubtful. "You've been looking? Did my parents send you out for me?"

Hector nearly shook himself crazy. His hands flew up in the air. "No! I took it on myself!" A silence broke through and Queriven stood to the side, unable to do anything but let the two sort out their problems. Blair's blank stare beckoned Hector to continue. "Your parents wanted to look too, but with the goats and the village... They could only do so much. I wanted to help, so I've been checking around the road and hills. I've been to Dunverhart, Penacha... I've even been to the cities of the northern mountains one time."

Blair turned her head. "You've been that far? But what about your work or your master?"

His eyes finally shied away. "I've tried to keep up with the work, but this was far more important. I knew how much you liked Bailiese. I thought it was odd for you to leave. I never doubted there was a strong reason for it. As for my master... He passed away early winter with that really strong blizzard. It was just too much for his poor health."

In turn, Blair lowered her gaze in respect. "Oh, I didn't know. I'm so sorry."

Queriven, still waiting quietly as the two talked, began tossing fresh wood on the campfire, thinking to relight it.

The movement reminded Blair of her surroundings and she sat down on the cold ground. "What now? What about your practice to become a blacksmith?"

Hector followed and sat down next to her. The fire was now burning again. "I've been thinking pretty hard about it, and all this time exploring Fairdraisha has helped me come to a decision. I'm moving into a house in Bailiese. I'm not returning to Dunverhart to find another blacksmith to train under." His next breath caught in his throat when he studied her beautiful expression. There was a calming crackle coming from the fire. "As you know, I moved into Bailiese to help give my master fresh air and space away from the city capital. I was going to return to the city after he recovered, but things changed. I fell in love with the green hills and the goats. I wanted to stay there forever already, but I didn't have the heart to quit my training either. My master would want me to keep his talents alive, but he would also want me to live my dream. I'll like to think he approves of my decision. I still don't know enough of his works to take control of it anyway."

Blair said nothing, and the silence made him want to keep talking. "I know it wasn't much, but I loved our time together. Herding the goats with you is a peaceful memory of mine." He laughed at his foolishness. "I kind of hoped you felt the same too. Even if you don't, I still want to stay in Bailiese, though I would love if you were with me." His ears were turning hot pink now. It was steadily becoming worse as he went on. "I never had the chance to tell you how I really feel for you. I... Well, I liked you from the beginning." Hector looked away awkwardly and began running his hands over his knees. "I thought, maybe one day, we might be together."

Blair had nothing to say. She had always suspected he might have a crush on her, but she never thought he would admit it, especially out here. Her lack of a reply made Hector anxious. He hurried to correct himself. "I mean, only if you wanted to as well. I would never push that on you! But... If you ever needed a place to stay, my house will always be open."

Another uncomfortable silence. Blair pushed it away with a laugh and looked away. She came back to him a second later, thinking to say something. Hector spoke first. "So what do you say? Should we go back to the village?" The question made him even shyer of Queriven, who gave him a half-smile, pretending he was unaware of their conversation.

Blair knew otherwise. He was listening to the entire thing. She winced. "I can't."

Hector held his arms out in confusion. "Why not? Why are you out here?"

She stumbled, unsure where to start. "It's complicated..." she began, but instantly thought of Queriven who always gave her the same excuse. Now a part of her understood why that word was easier to use. She sighed, silently scolding both her and Queriven for lack of information. "Fine, I'm trying to find a cure to a curse someone placed on me." She showed him the mark on her skin and his expression went from curious to wide-eyed. "I only have until autumn to remove it."

Hector was about to ask more, but Queriven was the one who spoke. "The cure is a horn. I'm pretty sure it's somewhere in Dunverhart."

Blair could see Hector's mind turning in circles. It was like he was fighting to speak only one of a thousand questions, but then gave up and hopelessly gestured to the elf. "Who is that guy?!"

The question went unanswered as Blair had one of her own. "How are my parents? I know they must be scared to death over me, but I must know."

Hector shrugged. "They're in good health if that's what you mean, but they are as distraught as you say they are. Isabelle is trying her hardest to keep positive, but she struggles every day. As for your father, he asks me about what I find on the rare occasion I'm in town. A part of me fears he's going to sell a lot of the goats so he can take my place in looking and do so with enough money."

The words struck Blair like a knife. "They're falling apart. Hector, can you do a favor for me and help them keep their heads up?" She studied him for a reaction, but there was none. There was only concern and disappointment. "I'm not running away from home forever. We're so close to finding the cure now. I'll come back on my own when I'm free."

He stuttered. "Of course, but what should I tell them?"

Blair was blank for a while. For a second, she looked back at Queriven, but he was unable to help her with that one. "Don't tell them I'm in danger. They have enough to worry about. Tell them..." Then, there was a spark of inspiration as she settled on Hector's face. He marveled at the swirl of hazel in her eyes even in the low light. "Tell them there's something I have to take care of. I know what I'm doing and I'm coming home soon. Tell them I have plenty of help," she finished, looking at the elf who gave her one of those content smiles. "Remind them I love them both and I'm not mad." She had to look up at Hector now as he was rising back up. "I wish I could see them for myself but I can't just yet."

With him up on his feet, the other two followed. "Are you leaving already?" Blair asked him. "It's so dark out."

"I'll be fine. Besides, I should return home as soon as possible to give them the good news," he answered, the look in his eyes showing more understanding.

Queriven had come around the fire where he shook Hector's hand firmly. "I suppose it was a good thing you invaded our camp." He even gave a short bow as he let go. Then, to Blair's horror, he flung back the hood from his head. "The name is Queriven by the way, and you mustn't worry. I give you my word. Blair is safe with me."

Hector nodded at first, then his eyes lingered on the elf's exotic face. Blair and Queriven watched as Hector changed from calm to panic, especially when he finally noticed the tips of Queriven's ears protruding a bit from his hair. He let out a gasp and fell backward. He cried out something incoherent and looked at Blair for support. He was expecting her to be just as frightened as he was. He panicked even more when she wasn't bothered. "You're an elf!" he whined and crawled back. Queriven looked pleased. "Did you…Did you know?!" He aimed at Blair as he stumbled back to his feet. "Is this the elf you saw the other day? What would your parents say, Blair? This isn't right!"

Blair approached him and had to raise her voice over his continuous cries. She patted the air and waited for him to calm down. "This is not the man I saw before. That man wasn't even an elf. He was only disguised as one. I made a really big mistake, but trust me when I say I know what I'm doing now. Queriven's here to help me, not hurt me. I know this is the truth."

Hector quieted down but still looked upset. He pointed a shaky finger at the elf. "I can't leave you out here now. Those people are not safe. Remember what your books say about them? They seem safe and charming at first, but they're really not!"

Queriven choked up a laugh. Blair ignored him and continued. "Most of what the books say is wrong anyway.

Queriven has already proven his intentions to me. He saved my life. Twice." She waited for him to relax, but he was still tense. "Just trust me on this one, all right?" Then, without a reply, she came and wrapped her arms around his shoulder.

Hector forgot how to breathe then, and he returned to a state of calm. Finally, Blair withdrew, but Hector held gently on her hand like it was the highest prized jewels. He sighed and looked back at Queriven for only a moment. "Fine, I'll trust you. You're certainly the smartest I've ever met." When he came back to his senses, he let her go and focused on her face. "But promise you'll come back home. Bailiese and I will be waiting."

Blair was hesitant, but he didn't need anything more from her. He took a step back and turned, walking for the darkened hills. The night sky was a little brighter than before, and the moon edging closer to the horizon. Hector's form walked slowly at times and he would turn back to look over at the campsite again. It was not quite half an hour later when he was swallowed up by the darkness of the night.

CHAPTER SIXTEEN
A BANDIT TO BE

"How long have you known that Hector?" Queriven asked.

They weren't walking very fast and they were only a few more miles from Dunverhart. The tall castle sitting up against the hills closer to the mountain behind the city was just in view. The days have been quiet and long. If Blair had more energy, she would have been so excited to see the city on the horizon.

She yawned. The walk was taking a tiring toll on her. Then she thought about his question for a moment. They had walked in silence for quite a while now and she didn't imagine that the next topic would still be about Hector, especially because it's been several days now and Queriven hasn't really spoken about the boy who intruded their camp. "Not long," she answered. "He was in Bailiese for a little over a year before I left."

"And... How do you feel about him?" came the response.

Blair snorted a laugh back at him. "What do you mean by that exactly?"

"Well, he was wishing you would move into a house with him. Is that the future you're hoping for after you go back home?"

There was a falter in Blair's step. She slowed down a little and Queriven caught up with her. She was suddenly somber when she looked at him. "I...haven't really thought about it. I never thought he would ask me, really," she shrugged and looked down at the dirt road under her boots. "I don't know. He's a nice guy, I suppose, but I don't think I feel for him quite the way he does for me."

Queriven pondered her response for a short while, but he said nothing. She brushed off the discomfort and lifted her eyes. There was a smirk on her lips. "I was rather surprised when you took off your hood in front of him. Why did you do that?"

The elf was trying to hide a smile, but those mischievous eyes gave him away. He didn't answer right away. "He wasn't a threat to me and you already knew he was. I figured it was safe."

Blair didn't miss the playfulness in his tone. "You just wanted to pick on him, didn't you?"

The elf chuckled. "Maybe a little. His reaction was pretty funny though." He took a second to appreciate Blair's laugh, then he tugged on the ends of his hood again. "I suppose I was a little excited to learn a little more about you."

That caught her off guard. She didn't expect to hear something so honest from him. He's been doing that a lot lately. It only made her wish she knew more about him in return. "I'm not that interesting really. I'm just a peasant from a small town."

"That doesn't make you ordinary" came the reply.

Blair took that as a compliment, but it only reminded her of her mistake with the rokian. "Don't misunderstand me. I love Bailiese and I love my family. I never thought anything this extraordinary would ever happen to someone like me." There was a bitter taste of irony in her mouth now. "I wasn't planning on leaving either. I only left because of the curse. All of my books had such amazing adventures. I always wanted to be a part of something like that. Now that I'm here, nothing's as magical as I thought it'll be." She shook her hair back, trying to chase away the bile from her throat. "They say to be careful what you wish for."

Queriven pressed on beside her, his gaze drawn into invisible surroundings. He shook his head. "You should have looked more closely. What's ordinary to you is a wondrous new find to me. Every culture and town is rich in its own stories and style. You just couldn't see it for yourself because you grew up in it."

Another surprising thought. Blair regarded him honestly. "I never thought of it like that before."

Queriven shrugged. "Me neither. The first time it occurred to me was well after a year of leaving home. It made me realize just how special and beautiful the forest really was."

Blair fell silent, unsure of what to say after that response. The city of Dunverhart was closer than before. Slowly but steadily, they'll make it with plenty of time to spare this day.

Unknowingly, the two were staring at the castle up the hills. They both imagined the horn sitting there somewhere in that castle. But if it was there, how will they reach it? Any idea they may have will not be anything but illegal. And an illegal act against the king would result in terrible consequences. Blair and Queriven knew they were facing their toughest trial yet.

"I don't know why I should ask this again, but how will we find the horn?" Blair broke the silence over them. After a second, she added, "If it's even here."

"Oh, it's here." Queriven remained looking at the castle. "I know enough of your king." The last bit he spat in disgust, then he thought for a moment. "As to how we'll retrieve it? I have no idea. We'll need to find out where it's being kept first, then..." He fell short of using the word "steal".

But Blair caught on to what he was saying. She took another dare and spoke the obvious. "If we fail, we'll be put to death."

After glancing at the ground, he met her eyes. "It's a risk we have to take." And he marched forward into the city. He was still just as hopeless, but he tried to show confidence in front of Blair.

They didn't call on the royal court nor did they leave for the castle without a plan. So, after wandering through busy streets aimlessly for a while, they stopped for an early lunch.

The restaurant had only a few patrons at this time of day, and Blair and Queriven took a seat near the quiet portion of the room. For the longest time, they ate in silence. Then Blair, casting a glance away from a chunk of roasted lamb, leaned forward. "You've been in the military for a while. Do you know of a good method of sneaking by patrols and guardsmen?"

Queriven dropped his wooden spoon in his green vegetable soup. "Unfortunately, our military and how we station it is really unique compared to yours. I have no idea what to expect."

Her gaze caught in the void ahead of her. She thought aloud to herself. "So I guess neither one of us has enough experience to go through with this."

Queriven didn't reply and went back to his meal. Blair also went to hers, but slowly as her mind was still distracted. "How do you know the horn's here? You seem to show a hateful bias toward King Brenmor."

The elf chuckled with genuine surprise at her accusation. "It's not biased. It's the truth. Are you going to tell me you think any different of him?" he asked, but Blair only dropped her eyes to the table. He brought up another spoonful. "I have my reasons. Your king's great grandfather was the one who ended the friendly trades between your people and the elves, and he did it over a ridiculous matter," he scoffed. "That man is no different than him. Believe me."

"Were you ever a part of the trade wagons back then?"

Another pause and he thought for a moment before answering. "No, I was just a child back then. I had more important matters to take care of. I had to look after the house and keep up with school."

Blair's face beamed and she laughed. "You have school too?!"

His expression showed slight insult, though he took it in good stride. "Of course, we do. What do you think we are? An uncivil band of forest dwellers?"

Blair's hand wove over the table and she steadied her singsong giggle. "I'm sorry, you're right. I just wasn't sure what to imagine." She dropped the topic and they went back to a silent meal. Blair still thought of him as biased, especially after hearing him admit he was never involved with the trading. Whatever he would have learned about Fairdraisha in that time was from the other elves. He wasn't able to build a viewpoint of it himself. Still, she said nothing more about the matter.

The pleasant air of laughter was gone and Blair sighed solemnly. "I still don't know how we'll go about pulling this off. It's not like we can go by the library and find where King Brenmor keeps his treasures. We'll be going about this task blind."

"We won't be doing it blindly," he assured her. "It'll be difficult, but we'll have a plan. Somehow, we have to sneak by the guards, reach the treasure room, take the horn, and escape. We have to do all this without them catching us. All that we have to figure out is where the horn is being kept and the best way to avoid attention."

"That still sounds like a lot of work..." Blair hushed her tone as she noticed a single man sitting at a table in the far corner looking at them.

Queriven, taking the hint, shifted in his seat and saw the suspicious person before settling again. Not only were they being watched, but the man was forthcoming about it. He stood up from the table and began walking the distance to their table.

Blair prayed their conversation wasn't overheard, but of course, that would have been too lucky. The man was dark and shady. He wore dark colors and a concealing cloak. Those eyes were wise and carried knowledge beyond his years. His hair was black and he was unshaven but handsome.

His boot scuffed to a stop and a mild odor of oily and sweaty skin ran over the table. The two sitting there tried not to meet his face, but he spoke anyway. "Breaking into the king's treasure room, I see. Mind if I cut in?" His voice was rough but harshly quiet. Without waiting for an answer, he slid a nearby chair to the table and took a seat.

Blair spoke next, "It's not what you think..."

Queriven also tried to cover their intentions but the newcomer interrupted, "Well, that's a shame." He folded his arms on the wood and looked at the two. "I was hoping to join you. Believe it or not, I have my own business to take care of."

"What do you mean? You want to join us?" Queriven asked. "You're saying you want to steal from King Brenmor?"

"How clear do I have to be?" he teased lightly, showing his palms in open conversation. "The king is a nasty trickster and nobody tricks me and gets away with it!" His tone was meaner now and he stuck a thumb to his chest. He settled again and continued, "Last spring, I stole some valuable jewels from a wagon by the northern mountains. I then sold them to King Brenmor. He paid me a lot less than I thought he would and sealed them up in his filthy treasure hoard. I demanded them back, but he threatened to hang me."

A spark of realization crossed Queriven's face. "You're one of the highwaymen he hired."

"His ex-highwayman," the man agreed as the shock showed on Blair as well. "Now I want those jewels back, but I can't do it by myself. From my understanding, we have the same goals. You help me and I'll help you."

"Hold on," Queriven cut in. "How can we know to trust you? You might abandon us as soon as you find the chance."

"Fine then," the newcomer chimed, unaffected. "I don't need to offer my help. I'll find someone else." As if to prove his point, he shifted, about to rise from the table.

Blair was the one who stopped him. "Wait!" she pleaded, and he froze for a second, then settled back in the chair. "We really do need some help. There is a special horn we believe the king has in his possession. It's made by the vayen aray. It has a russet tint in the ivory. Do you know anything like that? Or maybe where he would keep it?"

He thought for a minute. "I haven't seen it, but I've been in the castle before. I've seen the king with my own two eyes. I know where his treasure room is, and it's heavily guarded with soldiers and locks. But I have no doubt what we want is there in that safe together."

"Great! That's just what we need," she replied. "So if we help reach those jewels, you'll do the same with the horn?"

He placed a hand over his heart and smiled. "You have my word, Miss." He leaned over the table, meeting the eyes of both his new cohorts. "This is better than I could have hoped for actually. Since all that you want is an old horn, I won't have to split the jewels with you. I tell you what...we can get started on this right away. The best time to hit them is tomorrow noon. First, we'll need a good plan. Can either of you pick locks?"

"Why noon tomorrow?" Queriven asked.

"Because the king will be distracted with a council meeting. That'll keep him busy with many of his trusted advisors and men too."

Blair stuck out an arm on the table to interrupt. "But how do you know this?"

He looked at her with dark eyes. "Tsk, so many questions. But I suppose I deserve that for being a hired thief. I've been waiting for the perfect time to sneak in since spring, and so I've been watching the king's schedule carefully. As for what I asked earlier, I sure hope either one of you has done this before. That will surely be a great help."

The two exchanged empty glances. The man sighed. "Ah, that's a downer. Whatever. I'm sure we can make it work. Maybe we can learn a thing or two on the way, eh?"

"What's the plan?" Queriven asked, his finished soup bowl pushed out of the way.

"Simple," the man answered. "You follow my lead and we watch each other's back until we reach the safe. Then we break in, grab what we want, and get outta here." He was a master of making the impossible sound simple, but that was the best Blair had. Luckily, he sounded like he knew what he was doing. This might just work. "Of course, it'll help if we know who's who. I'm Barram, trained in trickery for over ten years. You're in safe hands if you're on my side." He shook their hands with a good grip.

Blair introduced them in turn. Barram nodded in a surprisingly kind manner. "Great to meet you both. We're going to try our hardest to do this without spilling any blood from either side, but do keep your weapons close just in case. Meet me by the gates at the end of town early in the morning, and wear dark colors. We need to sneak in while no one can see us. Then we'll wait for the council meeting to start before we hit the safe. Sound good?"

There was still doubt, but both agreed and Barram pushed away from the table and exited the restaurant. The pair of eyes met. Finally, Blair spoke first before Queriven could. "I know what you're going to say, but I think we should try it. He has experience and he knows the castle. We wouldn't have stood a chance on our own."

"Perhaps, you're right," he replied. "But we need to be cautious. He has every means now to trick us. After he has his jewels, he may leave us behind, or worse."

The severity of the task before them was sinking in with dread. "I know, but we already knew this would be risky. We might as well have someone who knows how to do this."

The rest of the day was uneventful and quiet, and the two of them retreated to bed early in order to remain focused on their mission. Even then, early morning came without a moment's notice, and they ate a quick meal on the way to the gates.

There was only a single streak of light blue in the cloudless sky overhead. Blair thought she smelled a light scent of nectar, though she wasn't sure if she was making it up or not.

True to his words, Barram was there waiting patiently at the gate. At first, she didn't see him reclining back on the wall in the dark shadow, but then he stood up and stepped out with his normal smug smile on his face. "There you are, finally! I didn't think you would make it for a second. Glad you came through." He glanced up at the top of the wall and met their faces again. "You ready to do this? Just know that after we climb over the gate, there's no turning back."

Suddenly, Blair's breathing became irregular and anxiety

battled her mind. She nodded. Barram held his hands in front of him and hushed his tone. "All right, stick close to me. Stay quiet and avoid being seen. I'm going to lead us past patrols as we head up the mountain." Then, he looked for prying eyes before judging it was safe. The gate was taller than the wall and made from firm materials mixed with clay. Across the double doors were wooden bars. They were thick and heavy. These he used as a foothold, and he climbed easily from one to the other, then flung himself up on top of the wall where he crouched. Barram glanced down on the other side but quickly sat up again. He placed a finger over his lips and pulled in his other arm, asking Blair and Queriven to follow him up.

Queriven went first, swinging up with even more grace than Barram showed. Blair admired the move, but grew frightened as she knew she wasn't nearly as good as them. Queriven didn't forget about her though. Once at the top, he reached for her hand and helped her keep her balance on the way up.

Barram led them a little way up on the wall, staying low and watching the ground below them. When he decided they were far enough away, he hopped down and rolled in the grass. There was a figure moving in the dark, but it was quite far away and Barram went unnoticed. He cast back to Queriven and Blair, who were already following him down.

Once they were together again, Barram told them they were veering off the path and were going to make a wide circle back to the side of the castle. Those sides were bound with rougher slopes and cliffs, but they would be safer there. Then, after reminding them to stick close, he skittered away, running on the grass like a weasel.

Queriven wasn't holding Blair's hand in this mission, but he also knew she lacked the experience in the job. He watched her carefully as she sprinted ahead next. As planned, Barram took them for a wide arc, moving further and further away from the path. There were still a few patrols here and not a lot of places to hide, but so far, they remained unseen.

Blair couldn't help but feel exposed given that the guards were everywhere around them. Just when she thought they were clear, she saw a silhouette moving by. Queriven, on the other hand, saw the forms even clearer than either of them. There was a time when he stopped Barram from moving because of a nearby guard that no one saw until he was already safely away. Barram offered a compliment before moving forward.

The green grass sloped into a grey rock. Barram checked their surroundings before reaching for a hold and pulling up. Then he dropped back down before the others came up. There were voices right above them, and Barram quickly rounded the rock. Blair and Queriven were right behind him. Blair's heart was racing so fast she worried those around them would hear it.

A moment of still silence. Blair thought Barram looked afraid as he peered over the top. It was clear but awfully close. He pulled up again with the two close behind.

The slope only grew steeper here, but he led them on. They were closer to the castle now. Blair could barely make out the front gate in the growing sun. Up here, there were a few more patches of cold snow than there was at the bottom. They had to make sure not to step on it. The sun would bring it to melt as it was wet already. The grass, flowers, and plants were already beaming with sparkling moisture from fresh dew. They were spreading a fragrant earthy smell in abundance. It was even warm enough for the insects to still be out. The hearty chorus helped to muffle their movement.

After climbing a long way and sneaking by some more close encounters, Barram brought them to the side of the castle. Once there, he parted a neat row of shrubs and revealed a brick more chipped than the others. "I noticed this when I was walking down the halls once," he whispered before anyone asked. "This is our best way in. Any of the doors would be too heavy with soldiers." He glanced up at the others standing over him. "I need you two to take a careful watch. I'm going to make us an entrance and we'll go in at noon."

They obeyed with no questions, each taking a post on either side of the wall. The sky was brighter blue and gold now. The sun was blazing in Blair's direction. She leaned her side on the wall and imagined the same sun rising over her home. Again, she thought of Hector, of the promise she made when she said she's coming home soon. *I never thought I would make it this far. I'm almost close enough to break the curse, then I can go home.*

For several hours, there was no activity around the wall. The sun was almost at the highest point in the sky and Blair, though she stood doing nothing for a long while, remained restless and fidgety. She still couldn't believe what they were about to do. It was unreal. Her light nerves had her jumping and spinning around when Barram called the two back to him.

The chipped brick was gone now, revealing a hole into a fancy hall of some sort. "Now," Barram was still crouched on the ground and was looking at the two carefully, "this will be our entrance, but I'm also hoping this would be our exit route as well. I think it'll be smart to leave someone here. We need to make sure this hole is still an option."

Blair immediately volunteered, thinking this would be the best she could do to help. After all, these two knew what they were doing, but Queriven countered her suggestion by stepping in himself. She met his eyes questioningly and he answered, "If something goes wrong, I'll make sure there's still an exit. Then I can help if I need to. Take Blair with you. She's cunning enough to fight her way through if she needs to."

At first, she was going to counter again, but his calm gaze assured her he will be fine. Maybe it was for the best, she decided. If they're discovered, they'll most likely be killed, but she worried Queriven's people would take a harsher treatment since he's not supposed to be here in the first place. Barram crawled through the wall first. She hesitated, thinking to say some words of encouragement or at least something to lighten the severity of her thoughts, but nothing came. Queriven nodded and placed a slender hand on her shoulder, supporting her silently.

"It's clear," came the call from the other side.

Blair tore away and followed Barram into the castle. Immediately, she choked on the perfumes of the carpet. It only became worse when she rose up to her feet. The colors in the paintings, floorings, and curtains were so rich they must have bathed in pools of rare dyes for days. The hallway was so impossibly clean. The unlit sconces on the wall didn't hold even a pinch of ash. There was no way King Brenmor needed his home like this unless he was allergic to everything from the outside world.

"There's not much to hide in here, but take your best chances if you need to. Other than that, follow my lead and try not to poke around."

Blair kept low, watching and trying to mimic exactly Barram's moves. The long hallways, in particular, were empty of guards. It was odd, but she reasoned it was because of the council meeting. She couldn't hear any voices at all, not even from the few soldiers they've seen to this point. How many rooms did this place have?

A part of her doubted Barram before, but he looked like he knew where to go. Even if he has been through these halls before, though, it was amazing he knew which door was which. Whatever the case, Barram never turned back and never took the wrong door.

Further in and past the long hallways, there was a rich aroma of lunch. In one breath, Blair smelled everything from baked bread, roasted beef, and steamed fruit cobbler. She winced as her belly rumbled quietly. She hasn't eaten since early this morning.

Barram, after judging it was safe, kept close to the walls through a seating room and to another door Blair swore was thick gold. Inside, the warm orange glow of a candle on a nearby desk flickered on the dark stone bricks. This was yet another seating area. "Barram?" Blair whispered after he stepped in. "Why are we in these rooms? Wouldn't the treasure room be in a hallway or something?"

"It's in a smaller, personal hallway. I don't know exactly where it is in comparison, but it's not far from the king's bedroom. It is most likely on the next floor." He pressed his palm against his face as he mumbled next, "Those stairs will have more traffic. Why didn't I think of that earlier?!"

Now the curiosity was digging on her. "But how do you know that? Do all of the king's hired highwaymen know the way through the treasure room or to his bedroom?"

Despite the situation they were in, he couldn't help but chuckle. "I have enough evidence to know where the rooms are. Sometimes it's pretty obvious. I came to report to his advisor, Gistal, once and was sent upstairs to the man's study. From there, I took in my surroundings. As I was leaving, I saw a maid going into a room. It was a large room with double doors and there was a bed so soft and spread out it would have made a duke's bedroom look like a lowly peasant's house." He paused and shot a guilty look her way. "No offense." Then he took another step forward and continued. "No doubt that was the king's bedroom. As for the treasure room, I saw them carry some of our goods up those very stairs."

Blair said nothing in response. Barram went back to his complaining. "I was taking us to that room, but I wonder if there's a different set of stairs going up." He scratched his nose and pondered, then he whispered to himself. "Maybe on the other side of the castle..."

With the talk about all the rooms in this place, they might become lost. Blair worried they'll never find their entrance again. "I thought everyone was busy with the council meeting."

"Not everybody," he corrected. "And that council meeting is taking place near those stairs. Between lunch and the calling of servants, there's too much attention there. We need to reroute our course."

Blair sighed in frustration as Barram turned and walked past the orange loveseats. He was taking them deeper into the heart of the castle. Blair couldn't tell what was more dangerous about this — heading for their original target that might have more activity or turning back around and risk spending too much time here. She silently wanted to remind him of his goal and that he should do everything they can to remain unseen, but she decided that was pointless to say out loud.

Barram opened the door just a crack and looked either way before ducking back in the room. There was a cart rolling on wheels. It had fluffy pastries and delicate cups of tea. The maid didn't even look back at the sitting room as she continued away.

It was safe now and Barram stepped into a small kitchen. If Blair thought the smells of lunch was heavenly before, now marvelous temptations overwhelmed her. The baking bread and fragrant pot roast almost blew her back into the previous room. Her mouth watered and she wondered what it would be like to eat like this every day. Did they ever become bored of this or was every meal just as enticing?

There were a few more plates carrying pastries left on the counter. One look at the fluffy breading and Blair could almost taste the pockets of cream and sweet fillings rolling over her tongue. It took her a moment to notice that Barram was also staring at the food. He regained focus. "We mustn't let our stomachs fail the mission. We'll eat after we leave. What a sweet reward that would be!"

Her belly was reluctant to agree, but she knew it was a wise choice. The single door to the side led into a cute tearoom. The little table in front of the lounge was dripping in delicate lace. This area was different from the last two seating rooms they've passed. Instead of dark brick, these walls were bright and cheerful. This brought a new distraction for Blair. On either side of the lounge were shelves filled to the brim with casual books for light reading. Just from the titles on the spines, she wished she had a few of these in her collection. At the end of the shelves and tea tables were two doors. Barram hesitated.

The fear of losing themselves in this place grew real. "I hope you know where you're going," Blair whispered.

Barram was as still as stone, but he chuckled. "Not anymore. I'm hoping to find a staircase somewhere back here."

"The longer we take with this, the more dangerous it becomes. And that's not only for us but for our planned exit," Blair reminded him, finally growing impatient. "It's only a matter of time before they find that hole in the wall. Queriven may be fighting to protect it even now."

His hand flew up in awareness. "I know, I know." Then a finger pointed at the closest door and he jogged to it.

At least there were fewer people over here in this part of the castle, but that brought Blair to ask aloud a new question. "How long do we have before the meeting ends anyway? The whole place is going to be swarmed again when it does."

Barram led them into another hallway. "Uh, royal matters take a long time. I'm hoping several hours, but I don't really know." The far end of the hallway was tight. This area had a rather large laundry room. "Aha! We found it," he exclaimed when the narrow hall turned to stairs leading up. *Finally*, Blair thought. They were making progress now.

He was still careful, but he took hold of more confidence and began walking faster again. The maids' quarters were upstairs. Unfortunately for them, a lot of the maids were working here. They carried fresh sheets and quickly came and go throughout the rooms. Barram and Blair hid behind carts, in closets, and behind doors. They could barely move a few feet at a time before having to hide. *We have to leave now or this is a bust!* Voices of panic yelled in her mind as Blair pushed Barram into another corner behind an armchair. They waited for the maid to finish sweeping the floor. Finally, she left, and Barram rushed to leave the room.

There was a maid standing wide-eyed right behind the door frame.

For a second, nobody moved. Then Barram came at her, dagger in hand. The woman opened her mouth to scream and Blair stepped forward. He was going to kill her! The dagger flashed, and before she could make any other noise than an alarming squeak, he rammed the hilt into her neck, then the top of her head. He successfully rendered her unconscious and Barram hoisted her up in his arms.

Quickly, he rushed through the hallway and opened a large double door room. There, he stuffed the girl in a closet on the other end of the wall. Not sparing a second, he tied the knobs together. Relief came to Blair even though they were still very much in danger. "You scared me for a moment. I thought you were going to kill her."

"That would be too messy, but we need to hurry before she wakes up or someone finds her." Giving the closet one final look, Blair turned as Barram ran by her. "We're not far now. Keep close."

She did so, and Barram took them down the rest of the hall. This led into a large foray with two sets of swerving stairs coming up to them. Blair heard a group of voices talking below the floor. This must be the first set of stairs Barram was trying to come to, and that was the meeting taking place. A bypassing man in a suit made them duck under the railing, and Barram headed to the left. There was another hall in the center of the wall. After a short distance; it jutted to the right and Barram stopped by a heavy-duty door with several locks in place. "This is it!" he declared as he ruffled in a pouch on his hip. "This is the safe. I'm going to try and pick these locks as quickly as I can. I need you to watch my back. Alert me if you see someone coming."

Blair obeyed without question, flicking back wavy strands of her hair as she retreated back to watch that end of the hall. Meanwhile, Barram pulled a set of lockpicks from the pouch and set up to work. The locks, as he quickly found out with no surprises, was a king's lock. It would be very tricky. He moved with fake confidence, as inside, he was wondering if he could pick every last impossible lock in time before they're discovered. He cursed his luck. Perhaps, he should have invested in help that could pick as well as he could. Still, he decided to make the best of his time. He slid the tool in the first keyhole.

So far, there wasn't much activity, but that didn't give Blair any comfort. She watched the space around them with the unflinching eyes of an owl. She even checked the hall opposite of them, treading a quiet pace. As watchful as she was, she didn't take notice of Barram's struggle.

The minutes passed into double digits. The two criminals were beginning to grow anxious. The meeting downstairs was still in progress, but Blair noted moving forms over the foray. "How's it coming?" she sidled up to him.

He groaned in response. "Not well." His hands were sore and tired from the work. "But we are making progress. I've managed one so far."

One lock was a great achievement indeed, but a small number to how many they had left. Blair looked over her shoulder, already feeling the stares of the guards on her back. Barram looked up at her from his place near the floor. "I might need some help if we're to do this in time," he admitted.

Blair snapped back to him, showing features marked with worry and confusion. "What?"

Holding the lockpick with one hand, he retrieved more of the tools from the pouch and handed them to her.

She could only uselessly look at them. "You want *me* to help you?" She held her hands out before her in astonishment, but she didn't take them. "I don't know what I'm doing. I'll only hold up some of the locks."

Barram nodded like he knew exactly what he was asking of her. He wove the hand again to her. "You have to try. I don't think I can make this by myself. Just try. You can't lock them tighter." When she hesitated, he added, "There's a first to everything, and if you can learn quickly, here and now, any other lock is going to be too easy for you."

She sighed, took the tools, and began working on the other side of the door. Barram didn't offer any advice until she slipped the pick in a higher lock. "Don't force it. There are springs inside the lock that the key matches to. You need to align those springs and turn it open." He watched her for just a moment as she fumbled with it. "Don't rely on your sight, but your touch. You can feel when they're in place."

He could see she's never attempted this before, and after many failures, she would pick up and check the hallways again, only to come back and fiddle with it some more. She was giving it her best despite her doubts. Barram was glad, even though her efforts didn't open one lock. He focused again on his own task. The time ticking by drove their minds deeper into tough focus, and a click between his fingers took him to another lock.

None of them were focused enough on their surroundings to hear the lack of voices downstairs...

Nearly an hour had passed and another lock clicked open. Throughout the next few minutes, Barram's work became easier. He was finding a niche in the task, but Blair was still on the same one as before. She groaned in frustration. Another click and Barram rose to the last one. Hers.

"I just don't think I'm any closer than I was when I started," she cried, sweat from the unease lining her face.

Barram inspected the lock and turned her hands slightly to the right. "I believe you're closer than you think," he said. The lock agreed and clicked free. Her eyes went wide and Barram pushed the door swinging in.

Inside were pedestals and shelves spilling over with various valuables. Jewelry, gems, richly colored satin and fabrics, ancient artifacts stored for over a hundred years, and other items lined the room as soon as they stepped in. The material was rich and abundant. An entire city could live in wealth and comfort for many generations! It seemed a waste to keep it hidden away.

Barram leaped into the room first, giving out a quick remark about how they need to grab and go. He started with the boxes on the shelves, looking for those jewels he was after. Blair entered next with an image of the horn in her mind. She hasn't seen this one before, but she figured she would recognize it if she saw it. The gold and treasures clinked and chipped behind her as Barram went through his own corner of the room. Blair ignored it and first scanned for the horn sitting out in the open. *Where else could it be hidden*, she wondered? Would a horn, specially crafted by the vayen aray for the humans, be hidden in an unmarked box, invisible to the world? Something as proud as that gift should be sitting out in the clear.

And indeed it was. She just didn't see it the first time. The curving, red-tinted ivory was sitting in a holder on the back shelf lined with trophies and carved figures. Blair reached up and took it safely in her grasp. The wide, brightened smile she wore was because of the blessed cure in her hands. Like a little girl, she wanted to hop up and down on her feet, squealing with delight. She was as good as free and she was never more joyous in her lifetime.

She turned, ready to leave. Barram stood just behind her, gripping a leather sack in his hands. "You have what you need?" he asked and turned to leave the room before she answered. Blair couldn't help but notice there was more than just a sack of jewels in his possession, but she shrugged it off. He helped her rob the king's treasures after all. It wasn't her place to judge what he took with him.

Barram stopped right outside the door, making sure it was clear to leave. Then he hissed a curse. "The meeting stopped! We have to get out here now!"

Along in the sudden quiet, Blair's heart dropped like it got caught in its own strings. Dread followed, and she pushed her legs under her.

They galloped like a greedy wildfire, anxious to eat up all it can before it's halted by a drowning splash of rain. Their footsteps pounded silently on the wooly carpet, their breaths coming in quick huffs. The council was downstairs, but they won't be for long. They might already be loose. Neither one of them knew exactly how long the silence went on.

If they didn't know before of the intruders, they would now, as the thieves left the treasury door open in flat-out panic. Quickly, they found the evidence of a break-in and the alarm sounded off to a hundred soldiers. They rushed in action to catch the thieves.

What seemed like a wonderful dream to Blair quickly became a deafening nightmare as she followed Barram. It was all hopeless. The castle was a maze, and the only way out was a tiny exit in a hallway almost identical to the other halls. At this point, she thought to cry out to him just to take the front door if they could, but she didn't. This was chaos, and in the midst of all of it, she needed to trust the man with the most experience.

That wasn't the worst of it. They cleared several of the maids' quarters and made it back to the first floor. That's where the guards had them cornered. Blair was running so fast, her vision so blurred, she almost didn't see the first few soldiers coming around the edge in the hallway. She skidded to a halt and Barram yelled. He tried to turn around, but there were even more men at the other end now. They were closed in from either side. Blair drew her spear, her desperate nerves wanting to fight for her freedom.

"I wouldn't do that if I were you," a voice responded. The criminals turned. The speaker was standing back by the guards. Queriven was in the man's grasp, his face one of defeat. There was a sharp knife over his throat.

Blair hesitated. She didn't move against them as the soldiers slowly took her spear and the horn. Barram surrendered as well. The man in the suit spoke again as the guards restrained their hands. "Your friend gave us quite a fright. We couldn't believe our find until he was finally captured," he stated, gesturing to Queriven. A hand reached up and pulled down the hood from his head, revealing sharp ears protruding from light brown hair. Queriven didn't fight him. "I have to say I was expecting it to be harder to capture one of these. Elves are not allowed in Fairdraisha. This is a serious crime, and if that wasn't enough, you had to try and steal from His Majesty." He shook his head. Those squinted eyes looked corrupted and evil, if one could make such judgments. The knife retracted from Queriven's neck and Gistal pushed him forward. "Clap this elf in tight irons!" he spat and a guard came forward. "We have to make sure this one doesn't escape."

His polished boots carried him with confidence as he came closer to the team. "As for you, Barram, the king expected you to do something like this. I did hope he was wrong. I wasn't convinced you were so terribly foolish."

"Gistal," Barram growled in return, "you'll pay for this one day. I swear it!"

The man revealed as Advisor Gistal chuckled. "The one thing His Majesty wouldn't be expecting this day would be this..." He cast a disgusted eye at Queriven. "...this forest scum.

Carry them off to the dungeons." Gistal turned his back, his hands neatly behind him. "I've got to visit the king."

They escorted the three criminals away and the other soldiers followed Gistal around the corner with the stolen goods in tow. Blair could see the horn that was her only salvation swinging in the hands of one. She dropped her head, her hair covering the despair on her face.

CHAPTER SEVENTEEN
STANDING BEFORE POWER

Unlike the royal likeness of the castle, the dungeon was the opposite of the rich comforts. The floors were sticky and the cells smelled of unclean bodies and disease-carrying pests. If Blair was thinking more about how it soaked her up like a sponge, she would have feared it'll never wash off. But for the moment, she was too dragged down in sorrow to care. The horn was gone. There was no way she could reach it now. All that was left was to wait for a pointless trial that wouldn't be fair anyway. She would have laughed at the irony of her curse being broken by death before it could take her. The only regret she carried now was the weight of the promise she made to return home.

For the first time here, she slowly pulled her hair back and took a look at the cell. Without a care, Blair was sitting in the middle of the nasty floor. There was an old, torn bed sitting in the corner, but that didn't mean it would have been a cleaner place to sit. Other than that, there was only a little empty bedside table. She turned her head the other way and looked over in the next cell.

Queriven was in there, and he was as defeated and still as she was, if not more so. In fear, he was bound tighter than the other two. His hands were stuck tight behind his back, and the chain around his feet wouldn't allow much movement. They even stuck him next to the wall so he couldn't approach the door.

He was as still as a corpse. His hood was at his shoulders, showing his elven ears openly. If Blair would have paid closer attention to him earlier, she would have noticed the bleeding slash near his shoulder. "You're hurt," she said, breaking his drowning silence.

He narrowed his eyes. For a second, he didn't know what she was talking about. Then, he inhaled a response. "It's nothing really. I was lucky they didn't gash me worse for fighting back." He shifted a little bit. The chains holding him jingled in protest. "I'm sorry I failed you. There were too many of them."

Blair shook her head. "You did the best you could. We all did."

"So..." a piped-up voice broke in from the other side. Blair turned behind her and saw Barram. He was up on his feet, observing every angle on the locked door to his cell. "You're an elf from Aven Forest. I gotta say, that sure does explain a lot, and I count myself a fool that I didn't think of it before. Word says you guys are pretty scary. Personally, I think it's pretty cool I met one." He laughed and continued to ramble. "The name gives it away, but I guess us humans don't think too hard on names, to begin with. It's almost like elves are nothing but unseen legends now." He turned, dropping a hand into the folds of his shirt like he was looking for something. "Now where did I put it...?"

Blair watched him like he was a madman for a moment. "You don't seem too upset about this. What are you up to?"

She didn't catch his nonverbal response, but he regarded the question seriously. "Nothing yet, but I'm hoping to change that. Let this be a lesson to everybody who hires a criminal to do his dirty work; you can't double-cross them without them working their magic against you. I plan to hit them where it hurts," he shrugged. "Then... Who knows what else? Maybe I'll leave the country and start over again. I always wanted to set foot in another kingdom. Maybe it will be better for me there."

Suddenly, there was a twinkle of hope. Blair rose to her feet.

"You're breaking out?" she said out loud. She trusted he could do it if he wanted to. "We're doing this together, right?"

"Uh-huh," he answered her, bringing out a handful of thin wires from the inside of his shirt. A few of them dropped from his grasp, chinking and bouncing on the floor. He swore, picked them up, and began working on the lock. By then, even Queriven was watching him carefully.

The lock was easier than the safe's, and within moments, he was out.

Blair excitedly clapped on the iron bars. "Great job!" she chimed. "Now help us break loose. Then we can take back the goods they took."

But her heart sank when he declined. Barram slung the cloak over his shoulders. "It's too risky even with one person. Wait here, I'll take care of it!" He winked back at them and dashed off as they called desperately for him to help. He didn't even look back over his shoulders. It was too late. He was already gone.

Blair sighed, the despair coming back with a lump in her throat and tears to her eyes. Her voice cracked. "He's not coming back, is he?"

Queriven's head dropped again. He cried a few words in his native tongue; his voice was straining with discomfort. "I didn't think it would come to this. We have to find a way to break out now or we'll be put to death."

The sound of his helpless tone made her want to break down and cry. Queriven was always so wise and strong. She never thought she would see him bound like an animal, unable to help himself. If there was *anything* they could do, Blair had to take it herself.

She twirled around the room, testing the bars and gathering the smallest details about her cell. She was scanning the floor when a bit in Barram's cell caught her attention. With a closer look, she realized it was one of the wires he dropped on the floor. Looks like he missed one. "Wait," she beckoned, her voice clear again. Blair knelt and slipped her hand past the bars.

It was just barely out of reach. She groaned and strained her arm as far as it could go. A fingertip poked at the wire and it turned just a little bit. Because of that, she could now pinch the end facing her. She brought it closer. With the wire in hand, she rose again and slid it in the lock.

Queriven watched her as she fumbled with it for many minutes. *Don't focus on sight,* Blair reminded herself. *Trust your feelings...* She closed her eyes so they wouldn't distract her. She could feel it fighting the lock, but it still refused to give in. She only managed to scratch her finger accidentally on the wire. She growled, retracting her hand and the pick from the door. "I don't think I can do it. It's too tough."

Queriven said nothing, but she could feel him encouraging her silently. Blair huffed angrily and stared from the weak wire to the taunting lock. As hopeless as she was, she gave it another try. Then there was a clank, but it wasn't from Blair.

"Someone's coming," Queriven exclaimed, and Blair hid the wire and stepped away from the door.

The guard unlocked Blair's door within a heartbeat and took her arm. The jingle of chains behind her suggested Queriven was alarmed, but another guard was already at his door. "Where are you taking me?!" Blair cried.

The man didn't even regard her question. He was staring at the cell where Barram was. "Where's the highwayman?" he asked the other at Queriven's door.

The second shrugged. He seemed hesitant about entering the room with the elf. The first guard then turned to Blair. "What happened?" When his question was met with nothing, he directed an order to secure and search the castle to the other. The man hastily agreed, happy to take any order to be away from the elven foreigner. After he sped off, the guard led Blair out of the dungeons. "The king wishes to speak with you personally. Don't worry," he added when she looked back. "The elf will be coming as well."

Blair was having a hard time keeping her breath steady. She was going to see Fairdraisha's king firsthand? That wasn't a good thing. Surely, he didn't meet with every criminal. She began to worry for Queriven, as they would give him a harsher treatment.

Her heart began to pound louder and harder with every step. There were guards everywhere now, and they all seemed to be busy and stressed. They were looking for Barram, but they couldn't find a trace of him.

The soldier escorting her didn't slow down, not even when they came to a large set of doors. Blair was suddenly very afraid and the soldier had to stop to push her along. The doors swung open. It was as she feared. This was the mighty throne room.

It was just as she expected it would be — large, fancy, and unnecessary. She was surprised and a little confused to see King Raek Brenmor sitting in the wide carpeted chair at the far end of the long hall. She never thought he would be so young! He was barely even an adult. His eyes were prideful and filled with youthful ignorance. This only made Blair even more nervous.

Finally, the guard beside her stopped. Blair kept her head lowered. She was too scared to look up at the king. She wasn't sure if he was waiting to hear her speak or if he wasn't interested. Either way, it was a good several minutes before he spoke. "So you were the one with that highwayman," King Brenmor reported in a voice louder than his own. It occurred to Blair that he was trying to intimidate her. It was working. "I believe the elf was also with you in this plan to rob me. Am I correct?"

Blair winced. That made her sound so bad. No wonder the king was upset. She tried to speak then, but her voice came out as a little whimper. She didn't really know how to start. Before she could find her voice, the king interrupted her. "I thought this was an average attempt to steal, but then I learned this involved the elf. Is this some kind of conspiracy from Aven Forest?"

Blair dared to raise her eyes. King Brenmor was piercing a dagger stare at her. His smooth hand was up at his chin as he considered her. Blair took a second to marvel at how big the crown looked over his head. If he had any more dark hair on his head, the headpiece would be pushing it over his heavy eyes. "No sir," she whispered barely loud enough for people to hear. He was already leaning forward. "I know this looks very bad, but we have a very important mission. Please understand us."

Her plea was cut short when the door opened up again. Blair turned her head and looked behind the guard still by her. There was a loud rattle of chains and Queriven slowly edged forward in the room. She wanted to yell at the guards as they strode behind him. They were totally paranoid of the elf and compensated by keeping him locked up with an incredible amount of chains. When the nervous guard behind him stopped, Queriven rolled his shoulders forward and back. He was very uncomfortable.

Now the king was more interested at the sight of the elf. He left his throne and came closer for a better look. "Wow, what a catch!" he cried out. Blair was suddenly forgotten. He came up and marveled at the elf, as if he was nothing but a trophy on the wall. Queriven's eyes were glaring angrily away from the king. "He doesn't look very scary, does he?" King Brenmor leaned down and met the elf's face. "You are here from Aven Forest, aren't you? Why did you come here?" He spoke each word slowly, like he didn't think Queriven could understand him.

Queriven only raised his eyes. There was a deep scowl there, but he said nothing. It was Blair who spoke next. "Your Majesty, we came because we needed something in your possession. He was helping me find an old horn from your treasure horde. I need it to break a curse."

King Brenmor shot to her. From the look on his face, Blair guessed he only listened to the first half of her explanation. "And why are you with him? You're no thief; only a girl." He spread his arms out wide and turned in a circle. "No one's giving me an answer here! I'm starting to grow angry," he yelled.

Finally, it was Queriven's turn. The dark tone in his usually beautiful voice made Blair flinch. "Didn't you hear her? My companion just told you we came for something in your possession."

King Brenmor spun back around. There was genuine surprise on his face. "So you can speak. Tell me then, elf, what is the meaning behind this? I can't seem to remember... All of your names sound the same to me. Was it the lord of Aven Forest who sent you? What is his name?"

Queriven growled with hate. "I didn't come here because of Aven Forest! You're not even listening."

Blair winced. She knew Queriven wasn't going to hold his tongue back. She wished he would. It might be safer for both of them if they controlled themselves. Amazingly, King Brenmor didn't even seem upset with his retort. "Foradue, was that it? Is Foradue *still* the lord of the forest? Anyway, I don't believe your excuse. Why would an elf attempt to steal from Fairdraisha if it has nothing to do with Aven Forest? Are you upset about the dropped trading rights? Is it finally catching up with your kind?" He laughed and came in close to Queriven again. "Do you think you can really make up for it by stealing from me? You may tell your Lord Foradue I'm not accepting his apology. It's too late."

Queriven lurched forward with rage. "We never needed your help, and we don't now! The elves have adjusted just fine after the trade. It's the humans who are missing out!"

King Brenmor didn't back away, but came closer. His face was now inches from the elf's "Then tell me again, what are you really here for, hmm?" For whatever reason, Queriven's silence satisfied him and he returned to his throne.

Blair wanted to speak up again, but every time she tried, she went unheard. The king was more interested in Queriven. She met his eyes and silently asked him to try again. He growled and looked up. He wasn't shy under King Brenmor's judging stare. "It's the truth. We came for the horn of red ivory. It was crafted by vayen aray hands, and the only way to break a curse that's set on her by a rokian."

That gave everyone pause. For just a second, the king was silent and looked afraid. His wide eyes moved from the two captives to the guards holding them. Blair took a breath and stood straight. They finally pushed the message through.

Just when the silence threatened to contain them, King Brenmor's mouth turned up into a grin and laughter broke through. The unease was gone and the guards followed along with him. The only ones who didn't move were Blair and Queriven.

If there was perfect quiet before, the whole room was shaking from all the laughter in the room. King Brenmor was practically crying. He wiped his eyes on his sleeve and hugged his belly. Once he recovered, he yelled down at them. "A rokian?! That's the first time I've ever heard that one! Do you even know what a rokian is?" The amusement left his face and he was scowling again. The rest of the laughter was calming to a few controlled chuckles. "You can't play that one on me, elf! I know you think me a fool, but I'm better than that!"

King Brenmor cleared his voice and sunk back in his chair. He pointed a proud finger at the captives. "Maybe Foradue will realize how much of a mistake he made when I kill his messenger. As for the girl..." He pondered that one for a minute, then continued. "Actually, execute both of them in the city. We have to show Fairdraisha what happens to those who try to mingle with the elves."

Blair froze at that statement, and her next breath came hard and ragged. There were already tears in her eyes. Queriven cried out as the guards turned the criminals away. "You're no king! You're a terrible tyrant just like your forefathers before you. You filthy human!"

Blair was also screaming out once more for the king to change his mind. King Brenmor ignored the two and the doors to the throne room closed.

The guards marched the two back quietly toward the dungeon. Blair didn't want to make a scene in front of the elven knight, and she tried to control herself. There were still sobs escaping between the sliding of metal chains. Queriven, however, didn't make a sound besides the metal holding him. If one could see the look on his face, they would see a maze of emotions. There was no escaping this one. He was going to die in human territory.

For Blair, there was more shock. This was even worse than the time of the curse. She was not only going to die in front of the entire city, but she condemned her own friend to death. There was no apology that would soothe herself for Queriven's fate. He gave everything to help her, and now they will die together. She cried out her internal pain. She wished she could see her parents again. If this was really happening, she hoped they would never find out about all this. It was just another terrible mistake. She refused to look at Queriven entirely. She was too upset and ashamed to face him, but he didn't even look at her. He didn't look at anything.

The stairway to the dungeons was in view now. The guards didn't slow down, not even with the sound of footsteps behind them. Finally, a voice spoke up and they stopped. "Mind if I take over?" asked the man in full armor.

The two guards met each other's gaze until one answered. "We're returning them to their cells right now. We have it."

The man laughed. "Of course," he retorted like he thought himself a fool for asking. "Carry on," he said. The guards shrugged and turned. That's when the man spoke again. "Changed my mind. Sorry 'bout that." And before they could respond, there was a loud impact and Blair's guard fell over. The last guard yelled and went for his sword, but it was too late. The imposter slammed a hilt to his forehead. He joined his friend on the floor.

Queriven turned and watched as the newcomer dropped and picked at the fallen men. "Barram? What are you still doing here?"

Blair had to blink away her tears to see his rough face behind the shadows of his helmet. Barram laughed and came back up with a set of keys. He went to unlock Queriven's chains. "What do you think I'm doing? I have to release my partners in crime, of course!" he answered. The two went to object, but he interrupted. "I'll explain later. Right now, we have to escape."

There was no disagreement there, and Barram dashed back down the hall after he set Queriven free. The elf groaned aloud after those constricting bonds fell free. Blair stuck by him as they followed the highwayman through the castle.

They only went down a few halls before the chaos was stirring up around them again. Someone either heard or found the guards by the dungeon entrance. Barram stopped before a room suddenly, leaving Blair and Queriven to stumble behind him. Barram then grabbed the two by the sleeves, pulled them toward the room, and flung a dusty old blanket over them. "I've got to lead them away or we won't make it! Be still, I'll be back!" Then he rushed back out the hall.

Blair tried to steady her breathing, but it was hard to do between the running and the stress. There were so many footsteps around them, and now some were coming in the room where they hid. She held her breath. The dust was settling in the back of her nostrils, burning them. The corners of her freckled nose flared in disgust. What was a blanket like this doing in the room anyway? She didn't get a good enough look to know where they were.

Blair couldn't see anything from under the cover, but she knew the guards were coming closer. Whatever they were doing, they were noisy. Things were falling over and clattering. She wasn't sure if they were flipping things over or if they were really clumsy. She shut her eyes tight. Queriven was tensing up beside her. She could hear his racing heart from here.

Just then, there was a clamor back in the hall, and the feet in the room ran after it. "This way, men!" called a guard just inches from the blanket. Within seconds, Blair and Queriven were the only ones in the room again. Blair released her held breath and fell against the wall behind her. Even so, she didn't dare to say a word.

Seconds passed and she looked back to the elf. It was dark. She could only make out the outlines of his face. Still, he looked much better now that he was free. His gaze matched hers quietly. There was so much curiosity there. He seemed to be asking her what was next. Blair turned away to the other end of the blanket. Everything was still and quiet and has been for too long. She poked at the grungy end of the fabric and lifted it up a little.

The edge of the door was within arm's length. It was a little dark in this room as well, but she could see now that it was yet another laundry room. The blanket they hid under was like the ones in the stack a few feet over. This must be some unneeded or forgotten fabric of some sort since it was unwashed and dusty. She held back a cough and leaned forward, thinking to peek out the hall.

She barely caught a look when Queriven pulled her back up. She then noticed the approaching footsteps. It entered the room and stopped just before them. "It's only me," Barram's voice whispered.

He lifted the fabric and helped them to their feet. "I've led most of them to the other end of the castle, but we must hurry. We can't leave out the main gates or the way we came in, but I think we can escape through the courtyard." With that, he handed them their weapons and crept out the room again. This time, he didn't run, but he hurried as quietly as he could. It was the best he could manage with a full suit of armor anyway.

They followed silently behind him, doing everything he asked them to. As stressed as she was, Blair couldn't be happier with Barram's reappearance. He came back for them. He didn't leave them to die. They were still very much in danger, though at least Blair was more confident with the thought of escape.

He led them down many identical halls and corridors and tried to stay far away from any guards. He would stop and swear every time they caught a glimpse of anyone. Then, he would lead the team away.

The walls were pressing tighter. Blair's lungs were burning for the fresh air of freedom. There were guards at almost every turn now. Every minute marked the possibility that they were never coming out. It was amazing they weren't seen yet.

The yells of the soldiers were growing louder. Blair didn't know if they were upset at losing the thieves or if they were found out. She didn't see any of them here so far. "This is it!" Barram breathed aloud. But yet again, he stopped short of the corner and swore. There were guards watching the door to the courtyard. Barram turned and met Queriven's eyes and pointed back down where they came. There was a split in the path there. Queriven nodded, understanding at once. Then he vanished.

Waiting for just a short minute, Barram jumped around the corner. Blair gasped and followed him. Barram and Queriven quickly cornered the two guards together, taking the weapons and knocking them out. It wasn't quick enough. However, the screams alerted the already nearby soldiers. "Quickly!" Barram yelled and unlocked the door. He checked to make sure the two were behind him before he dashed outside.

They were spotted. Blair only ran faster at the yelling and cries for them to stop. Luckily, none of them carried ranged weapons. The royal courtyard, filled with various statues, fountains, and gardens alike, was nothing but a blur to Blair as she hurried to stay with the two guys in front of her. Later, she would remember very little details about her experience at the castle.

Barram was the first one to the wall and he scaled it with ease. Queriven was next, and he leaped up higher. He didn't drop down though; he turned again, holding out his hand. Blair was close. She refused to look back at the guards she knew were catching up. "Just behind you!" the elf cried out to her.

She jumped and took his hand. Within a heartbeat, he pulled her up and she kicked her legs behind her. Something metal crashed against one shoe, and something grabbed the other, yanking her from Queriven's grip. Stone paving smashed into her belly, and before she knew it, a shadow fell over her, but it wasn't from what she was expecting. Queriven was soaring down from the wall where he landed right on top of the guard who pulled Blair down. The elf used the shining spear to choke the man until he was unconscious. Then, he helped Blair up the wall again. The first guard who grabbed her was lying dazed on the ground. Blair successfully hit him while she was on the wall.

The two dropped out of the courtyard where Barram was waiting. His face brightened and he gestured them to follow. Like before when they entered the grounds, Barram led them out in a wide arch. There were already several guards out here as well, but none of them were this far out yet. The three criminals didn't run into any more confrontations after that.

Now that the city wall was in view again, Blair could breathe a little easier. She was still a little paranoid about running into more castle men for a while, but her adrenaline was slowly fading. Her senses were returning to her again. It was late afternoon and her legs were aching.

"We'll drop in a quiet alley," Barram decided. When they made sure it was clear, Queriven scaled up on the wall and waited for the others to join him. They were high up now. Anyone could see them in this daylight. They made a point not to stay long and dropped down as quickly as they could with a safe landing. By some miracle, they weren't seen. They descended the city until they came to a deserted alleyway where they finally stopped.

Neither one of them said a thing for many minutes. Blair and Queriven were busy catching their breaths. Barram was as well, but he played off the terror of the siege with a grin on his face. He began stripping the armor off and retrieved the red ivory horn from a pouch at his side. Queriven immediately took it from him, his eyes were wide with disbelief. Barram patted the pouch proudly, and there was a high chinking in response. He only laughed and grinned wider when Queriven didn't reply after seeing the horn. "Something tells me you weren't expecting me back."

Queriven was forthcoming and honest with his answer. "Why should we? You escaped. It was very dangerous to come back for us. Why didn't you leave?"

Barram stuck a hand to his heart in his old, wild attitude. "That stings, my elven friend. I do appreciate the honesty though. Truth be told, I was struggling to find a way out as it was. In the end, I decided to disguise myself in plain sight. So I took the time to reclaim the goods we stole. It wasn't easy. After that, I saw you two were on death row and I took the chance to rescue you. I've never met an elf before, and so I figure I should stay on your good side. Remember me, will you?" he asked, extending a hand in good friendship.

Queriven was content with his answer and returned the gratitude. "Of course, we're in your debt."

Barram wove the notion away. "Eh, don't worry about it. I'm not sure if we'll ever see each other again after this. I plan to be far away before the next dawn. That's for sure."

Blair was leaning over with her hands on her legs, trying to recover from both the stress and rush. When she looked back up, Barram was looking down at her. "Hey, keep working on those lockpicking skills. You'll get it eventually."

She smiled and said nothing. Barram turned back to Queriven. "I suppose I should get going if I want to make it to the docks. You two should be moving as well. This place is going to be swamped."

Queriven and Blair wished him a farewell once more and he flew down the streets. There was already an uproar starting on the streets, but Queriven was confident he could find a safe way out of the city now that they were away from the castle. "I dare say, for a thief, Barram kept his promises," he stated to Blair. She nodded her agreement and they hugged the quieter sides of the city on their way out.

CHAPTER EIGHTEEN
QUERIVEN'S PHANTOM

"Is something the matter? You've been awfully quiet." The soft sweet voice of the elf cut through Blair's dazed thoughts. She looked at him and caught a glimpse of the horn at his hip.

She was quiet for a moment more. "I'm just still a little shocked about what happened at the castle." She hung her head. There was a sorry dullness in her eyes. Her lips were too relaxed and restrained from joy. Suddenly, her voice broke and filled with sorrow. "I never thought I would be a terrible criminal. This affects my home and my future. I can't allow punishment to come to my parents."

Queriven didn't seem half as bothered as she was. "As long as you're not found out, I'm not too worried anything bad will come to them. King Brenmor doesn't know who you are or where you're from." He tried to encourage her with his confidence, but she only sighed. He could see the memory writhing below her skin. Her innocence was dying right in front of his eyes. As much as he hated it, he knew there was little he could do to help her. "We had to do this. We had no other choice," he answered hopelessly.

The look on her face suggested she was beginning to think otherwise. "I don't know. I guess I'm feeling a little guilty." In truth, she was more than a little guilty, and if she didn't look away from the elf, she would have seen sympathy. He related to her pain. He knew what it was like. Queriven remembered losing innocence at a young age when he first became a soldier. It was never coming back. The old Queriven was dead. His history was now stained with terrible mistakes and regrets. He didn't wish that on anyone, especially someone as young and sweet as Blair. He moved closer to her without a word. His shoulder was now inches from hers. He walked in silence.

Blair looked back at him and noted his voiceless support. Then she inhaled a deep breath of spring nature and tried her best to relax. The warm sun cast itself into the wide blue sky, taking down the last patches of snow. Flowers of many colors bloomed and new life was abounding. In her hands, Blair carried her scarf, jacket, and gloves. It was too warm for them now. Too nice. Nothing covered Queriven's old elven armor now and she seemed to fit in it more every day. Blair took in the joyous chirps of birds and the soothing whisper of wind through the trees and grass. The beautiful scenery was certainly helping, but she kept recalling a vision of King Brenmor of Fairdraisha, deeming execution on both her and Queriven. Before, it was like she was falling into a deep abyss of no recovery. She was wailing and pleading to the young king. It was like a terrible nightmare she couldn't shake. She wished it was just that. At least it would be fading away quickly. That, and she wouldn't feel like such a fool. The memory resurfaced and she relived the time they snuck in to the time they miraculously escaped. She looked back at Queriven. Many bruises and cuts marred his skin; but if any of it bothered him a fraction it did her, he was excellent at hiding it.

She was uncomfortable now and wanted to break the silence. "I remember you yelling back in the castle. You said the king was a tyrant like his forefathers before him. Is that why you seem to hate him so much?"

Queriven regarded her with a surprised glance. His pace faltered until he stopped. Now Blair was curious. She turned to him with her hands together shyly, her warm clothes still wrapped around her arms. Queriven thought back to the time before the king. He blurted that comment in a furious rage. He didn't remember exactly what he yelled. He blinked and rubbed a shoulder as he watched Blair patiently waiting for him to speak. He didn't want to release further rage on Blair's kin, but he wanted to be honest with this one. "I...don't know much about Raek Brenmor in particular, but I do remember the lines before him. As I said, I was a young child when the trading stopped. Foradue was still lord of the forest at the time and argued with the king over our relationship. The king was arrogant and wanted to argue over little things. It was stupid, really."

Blair focused on everything; the way the light caught his eyes and how he adjusted his hood between pauses and the like. The answer made sense to her. Queriven was of Aven Forest, so it was only normal for him to side with Foradue in a political matter. He continued, "I learned a lot after I came to Fairdraisha. My views on the Brenmor line was only supported when I learned of the various highwaymen and his choice in guards. That was only a partial reason why I disliked him though." He was a little more nervous now. He pressed his lips together and sighed, his hand going to the back of his neck. Blair didn't move or interrupt. "I learned a lot about humans too, the same way you have with the elves. It made me respect them better. There were a lot of terrible things I thought was true about them. I was wrong. Well, about most of it anyway. They're people, and they feel emotions, happiness, and fear just like we do. But twenty years ago, before I left..." He looked away, his voice was quiet now. "I actually had a strong hate for humans. I hated all of them. I thought they were all terrible, selfish beings. I've since learned that you can't take someone's action and use it as a representative for everyone else."

He must have feared that would bother Blair, but she only respected him for it. She smiled. "Well, I'm glad you don't feel that way anymore. It would make traveling with me a lot harder. Besides, I really enjoy your company."

The elf relaxed the tension in his shoulders and began to walk again. He was glad that didn't upset her. Blair picked up the pace beside him. The stress over what happened at the castle lessened. Now they were able to walk in confidence again.

Little did they know, but Blair and Queriven were being watched from afar. Captain Yusen Nashögan and his men were waiting for them to leave the safety of Dunverhart and were now plotting an ambush. He found it unfortunate he couldn't kill the elf at least, but he still took pleasure in the idea of inflicting severe pain.

The captain knew what he had to do. His master was furious when the elf and the peasant left the city with the horn in hand. "They're summoning Rocanu to break the curse!" he had cried. "You must take the horn from them or the spell is broken!"

Captain Nashögan marked that as his first priority. Vengeance was his second. The pirates spread out on either side of the road, clutching bows and swords, waiting patiently for the perfect time.

The sky was beginning to glow a clean golden hue. The grass and hills were brighter than day in the fading sun. Blair and Queriven were coming at a steady pace, their destination being a lodge further down the road.

"I wonder what I will do after this," Blair pondered aloud. She didn't meet Queriven's eyes as she continued. "How do I return to my old life after something like this? How do I continue getting out of bed in the morning, eating breakfast, and going to work with the goats?"

She didn't mean to ask anyone in particular, but Queriven answered anyway. "I don't know. I actually hope to find that answer myself. I've lived away from home for so long; I still don't know how I'm doing it." A breath escaped his thin lips. "I suppose we have little choice. No matter how hard we hang on to the past, it's always running further and further away from us. You either move on or you don't. It's a decision one has to make for themselves," the elf said after the long pause.

Blair opened her mouth to reply but then changed her

mind. Even if she does return home after this, will it ever be the same again? Would she even see the elf or will he disappear again into the wilds? Blair loved her life in the village, but she feared she was no longer simple enough for it anymore. She's seen too much and cared enough for her new friend she didn't want to see him leave. But he can't really hang around though, can he? Queriven is an elf, and the royal officials of Fairdraisha already found out about his heritage. It will be harder for him to go unnoticed in these lands than ever before.

They didn't know it, but it was already too late. The pirates had them surrounded now. Blair looked to the side, noting Queriven's hesitance. He knew something was wrong. Before he could say anything, the band of pirates jumped out and charged.

Queriven responded immediately and brought his spear in front of him. Blair tried to do the same, but she hesitated. After all this time, she's only trained with Queriven. Never once did she have to do battle. The elf took his fight to the nearest pirate. But by the time Blair recovered from the surprise, she has spent all her valuable time. The fight came to her. She dropped her winter accessories and ducked low. Now ready, she came back up and flailed her spear over her head. She knocked the blade away and a kick sent the pirate back on an unbalanced leg. Despite him leaning far back, his weapon arm came forward. Blair matched it. The sword struck the rod and held. Blair wanted to topple him further, but they were locked with matching strength. Adrenaline took her. It was purely on instinct that she released and dived under his reach. The sword continued in a movement driven by momentum, and it dug into the back of a nearby pirate.

A band of ruthless pirates couldn't hope to possess the speed and grace of an elf, let alone one of the military. The tip of solid starlight was as bright as the sun when it twinkled right before a jab. Queriven's war dance was not without trained skill and balance. His face was calm and focused on each challenge set in front of him, but that didn't mean he wasn't struggling. Captain Nashōgan still had a lot of men left on his crew, and they came out like a field of scattered ants.

Queriven leveled the spear before him, blocking an attack from one pirate and pushing aside another. Then, the tip swung down and he spun it in a circle. He released the momentum toward the first man. The tip plunged forward into the man's heart. Blood gushed and washed over the spear as Queriven pulled it free, but the starlight seemed to reject it and it dripped down like it was dew on a bird's feather. The spear, clean like nothing's touched it, whipped around and clanged with the next offender.

That offender was none other than the captain himself. He snarled at the elf with pure hatred but didn't see recollection in return. The sword retracted and stabbed low, but Queriven was already out of the way. Not slowing, the weapon struck high, and again the spear blocked it. Captain Nashōgan spat. "I'll be! Don't you recognize me, elf? After you came and slaughtered my crew the last time, I didn't see anything then either. They say you're losing your mind. I suppose they're right."

But Queriven's expression remained unchanged. "I remember you." The spear spun and knocked the sword free, then the butt of the weapon came up and smacked the captain's jaw, staggering him back. "I just don't care about you or your crew anymore."

The spear came in for the last strike, but the sword came up quickly, just in time to lead it away. The pirate wiped his lip and spat blood from his mouth. Then he did the unexpected; he laughed.

Queriven raised a confused eyebrow and pierced the shiny tip forward. The captain, though a little unbalanced, sidestepped from one side to the other as the flat side of the spear came after. "Surely, you know who you're up against!" he yelled, still laughing. "You already know it's a rokian's curse? Sure you do! You already know who it is!" Then, the laughing stopped and the captain brought his sword forward, forcing Queriven to block. They were neck and neck, and Yusen dared to bring his face inches closer. A deep growl came from his throat. "Why do you remain with this girl when you have to know who's behind this? I was under the impression you were running from your past, so why are you here?"

It was Queriven's turn to respond angrily. He shoved the captain back. The spear came forward and brushed by his shoulder, more cutting through fabric than skin. "You know nothing about me! Not like you think you do!"

Now that fueled the captain for the battle and the sword sliced through the air on either side, but it was hard to reach Queriven in close combat with that spear. "Come on!" Yusen yelled, casting spittle as he did. "Queriven, you know of the rokian already. You met one all those years ago! How are you so oblivious? Don't tell me you've blocked it out!"

But Queriven hasn't. All along, he dreaded the answer. He knew what he was wrapping himself into. He only prayed he could help break the curse without having to see the cruel man behind this. Blair was his last hope to regain a piece of himself, and he took the mission knowing the risk behind it. In the end, he wasn't sure why he did it, but he had to for his own sake as well as Blair's. A name came to his mind; a name he tried so hard to forget. "Darkadus."

It was too late for denial and Queriven pushed on, swinging the spear madly aside. The captain was nearly swept off the ground with it. Another part in his jacket ripped, this time casting blood from his upper back. The captain cried out and charged forward, dropping under the range of the spear, but a boot came up and kicked him in the face. Down again came the captain, and Queriven followed, pointing the tip to his chest.

"Captain!" a pirate cried and drew the bow. He quickly shot an arrow into the elf's thigh. Queriven cried out and fell to his knees. Yusen rolled out of the way and came up, smacking the back of his head with the hilt of the sword.

Meanwhile, Blair was too occupied with three pirates to see her friend fall limp in the captain's hands. The girl was quick, too quick and underestimated by the pirates. They teased her and called her pretty. She responded by snapping their jaws on their nasty tongues. One lunged at her as she poked the spear at another, but she waited. Then, she turned gracefully out of the way and stomped on his foot.

He was down for now but not out for the count. She focused on the other two. They glanced at each other for a second, then charged as one. But Blair prepared herself. She ducked under the first blade and while still down, poked at the other's legs. The spear sliced from his knee to his groin. Her spear slid free. There was crimson on the metal. She hesitated, now watching the man press down on the wound. Blair gave him a nasty gash, and the sight of it horrified her. Never once did she cause such a wound. She only used her spear to train. This was the first time she used it to hurt someone, and it took too much of her attention.

She came up, now aware again of the first man she dodged. He was already swinging again and it snagged her hand. Using the injury to her rage, she screamed and dug the spear in the pirate's chest. Those wide and dying eyes stared at her in disbelief as he slipped and fell to the grass. Blair could hardly keep her breath, but she wasn't done. The wounded man was pulling a dagger from his boot, which he aimed to throw. "I'm sorry!" Blair cried genuine tears as she flipped to the side, slicing a line over his throat.

That left one more; the one she stomped on. She went to face him. That was when she saw Captain Nashögan behind him, helping the men haul the unconscious figure from the ground. Her eyes opened wide. "Queriven!?" She took a step forward and yelled at them to stop. She won their attention, but it only spurred them quicker into flight.

Blair wanted to give chase, but the thug in front of her stood in the way, grinning and bearing a scimitar. The pirates were running further away. Blair started to panic, but she needed a focused head. Fighting with panic wouldn't do well in her battle with the threatening man in front of her. She had no other options. She sighed and leveled her eyes. "Come on then. I don't have all day."

Still grinning, the man chuckled and lashed forward. Blair pointed the spear at him, keeping him further away. That didn't stop him for long though as he batted the weapon aside and came around it. Blair took a step back again and swung the spear into him. The wooden pole smacked the pirate and nearly sent him to the ground. He kept his footing and turned again to bat at the spear, flipping it over. But Blair used the move to drop it down on him and it sliced open his collarbone. Blair took his hesitation and ran him through. The sight of the bloody body clouded her vision again, but she let him drop down and she ran past him. "Queriven!" she cried as she came over the hill.

But no one was there, not even a dark movement further in the distance.

She ran a little more, stricken and lost. Blair flicked her head to and fro, looking for any sign where they might have gone. There was nothing. Queriven was gone, along with the horn he carried. Blair couldn't move on even if she wanted to, nor did she have any means of finding where they took him.

Blair wandered back to the road. The bodies were strewn about it in elaborate positions, bloody and filled with holes and cuts. She played a good part in this massacre. They may have been pirates, but they were people, nonetheless. She killed them, ran them through like a piece of meat. Defeated and not sure what to do, Blair lowered herself on the ground. She spotted her winter jacket and scarf then. They were all soaked in the blood that spilled on the ground. Deep down, she couldn't help but imagine the dropped clothes as her innocence. Just like her, they were scuffed, dirtied, and stained with blood from humans who died at her hand. It'll be impossible to wash out completely.

She sat in the grass for only a little while before she wiped her eyes and stood back up. Crying about her situation wasn't helping. Now she needed to try something else. There was a lodge further down the road, and after that was a small town. That was Blair's best chance. She had to be strong for Queriven's sake.

Blair gave the bodies another solemn look before she left them behind, her winter clothes and innocence among them. None of those things were ever coming back. The horrible death she brought was like a knife in her own gut. Even with them out of her sight, she could feel their final breath over the hairs on her arms. A few minutes ago, they were alive, and now they passed on. A part of her died with them when she left there.

She tried to let it rest. She needed Queriven back, even more so than the horn. She won't be able to find him on her own; she needed to find help. For now, she could only pray he'll be fine on his own.

Queriven fought to clear his vision. His head pounded profusely, though after a second of trying to come through, he realized the pain in his leg was worse. He groaned aloud, surprised past his blurriness as he forgot how to speak properly. Finally, his vision slowly cleared enough for him to see a little bit.

His legs were resting on a hard stone floor. The one in pain had a bandage wrapped around the thigh and he could tell it was soaking up quite a lot of blood. Was that where the arrow hit? He wanted to evaluate it further, but he couldn't pull his hands free. For the first time, he noticed his hands were chained to the wall.

That brought him to his full awareness and he rattled the chains. How long has he been here? He had no idea, but his chafing wrists told him he's been there for a while at least.

He was in some sort of building, though it wasn't exactly airtight as part of the wall was missing entirely. Perhaps, that was for the better since the room was dark enough as it was without the light of the moon shining through. There was a light reek of blood, but beyond it was freshly watered soil and a pit-pattering outside. It must be raining. Queriven's speculation confirmed it as there was a dripping puddle in the middle of the floor. The sprinkle of rain was finding its way inside. This must be one of the old ruins.

The elf strained his neck, trying his hardest to gather as much of the room as he could. That was when he noticed footsteps coming closer from outside. A gray-skinned man followed through as he stopped once he entered the hole in the wall. That gaze burning amber was wide as he regarded the elf chained to the wall. "Oh, so you are awake," he exclaimed.

Queriven, still groggy and throat parched dry, met the speaker's face for a long time before recognition kicked in. His heart skipped a beat and his breathing came more ragged. The nightmare that haunted his sleep for years was finally standing before him in the waking world.

Unable to voice a response past a long tortured mind, Darkadus spoke first. "So you do remember. Funny, the pirates weren't sure if you really did or not. It has been a long time. Considerable at least for you, right?" There was a pause, and the elf was still too stunned to speak. His jaw was tight, but he couldn't tear his gaze away. Darkadus sighed. "You really shouldn't be too surprised, Queriven. Did you think you were trying to break another rokian's curse? What made you decide to help this girl and stop running away?"

Still nothing. Darkadus raised a dark eyebrow and turned away. Queriven took another ragged breath and spoke. He was afraid, but he tried not to show it. "It's been a long time, Aswren," he said the name slowly, referring to the first time they met when Darkadus was under the disguise of another elf. He called himself a friend of Queriven's for a time before he learned of his real form. Queriven remembered how sickened he was when he learned the rokian killed the elf after he was done using him.

Darkadus turned around and looked down at the helpless victim. "That's a little better," he said quietly. "For a moment, I worried you'd stay silent." A hand came up and rubbed on the side of his face in unrelated thought. "I am sorry for leaving you like this. I do hope you'll understand my reasons for bringing you here, my old friend. I wouldn't have to do this if you weren't carrying that horn."

"The horn!?" Queriven bolted upright at that, or at least he tried to. The chains twisted his arms painfully with the forced action and he slipped back down again. Then he spotted his equipment leaning against the far wall, the horn among them. Without it, Blair had no hope to break the curse. Queriven cursed his bad luck and wished he gave it to her earlier.

"You two were clever, I'd give you that," Darkadus continued, looking back at the horn sitting by the shining spear. "A blessing from one of the vayen aray may be the only thing that can break my spell. When I came to this world, I thought I was invincible, as I was free from the vayen aray. And yet, you found a way to summon none other than Rocanu himself." He laughed. "I didn't think it was possible! You really are magnificent! It's only a shame such power and wisdom has to be wasted on an elf."

His flattering nonsense only made Queriven sick. He barked at the man through teeth gritted under pain. "Release your spell. Blair has nothing to do with this. It's me you want. Take me and leave her alone."

Suddenly, Darkadus fell into all seriousness as he processed the request. His eyebrows lifted and his lips parted slightly. Flabbergasted, he found an answer. "You still don't get it. To think, I thought you changed after that day in the forest, but you didn't. You still think this is about you, don't you?!" The amber flashed dangerously as Darkadus raised a thundering voice. "There's more to it than that. The girl is everything now! I didn't do this because of you; I did it because of my people!"

He now looked angry enough to harm him. Queriven flinched, but nothing came. To vent his anger, the rokian turned and began to pace. "Many years have passed... Many generations..." he mumbled and then elaborated as he came closer. "And the people of Fairdraisha thrived after their terrible mistake. They thrived!" His chest heaved as he took in a full breath to bring about emphasis. Queriven listened quietly, but he was slowly shrinking back in fear. "They cast the vayen aray and rokians into a low plain of existence and went on with their happy lives while we lived in misery. Those were my ancestors." The further he went, the more he continued to break down into insanity. He continued past rage. "There was always little food among the tribe. The land was almost too barren to produce anything. There were no seasons, no wind, no change of weather and little water. The barren plains of the dead ground stretched for eternity with little change. The humans pulled us there. They even pulled in their so-called heroes, the vayen aray!"

The rokian's face shot back and Queriven thought he caught tears building in his eyes. "There was no regret." He froze, catching a breath. Then a hand rose up and a gray-skinned thumb poked his chest. "Surely, you can see how wrong that was — to leave us there. The vayen aray remember that day. They live forever, but my kind is different. We're not the same ones, and we did nothing to deserve poverty. My ancestors paid for their mistakes, but it's time for the sentence to be done. I took control of the tribe and gathered my wisest mages. Together, we were able to bring enough magic for me to grip this world, but it wasn't enough for all of us." His arm dropped along with his face as he remembered the ordeal. "As I clawed up to this beautiful and fruitful land, I knew I had to lead my people back to their former glory. I alone have the power to save them from that dying world. It took me years to find out what I needed to do. Even once I knew, it was no simple task." He was so still and without eye contact. Queriven feared he would fall over. The face lifted and he was calm again. "The magic the vayen aray used was so complex but incomplete. They needed more time and focus to use it, but their hands were forced. It was the fault of humans. They interrupted the spell and because of that, the magic went rogue. I found I needed to find a human to break the spell, but it wasn't good enough to work on just any human."

The pause seemed to stop time, and Queriven thought he wasn't going to continue. But finally, his eyes, burning with rage and passion, met the elf. "I needed a particular blood to take my people's place. I needed a descendant of one of the human families who were there. Thousand years have passed since that day. The families have scattered or moved on. I followed many leads and they all led me to a dead end."

Finally understanding, Queriven looked away, already knowing where this was headed. Darkadus' tired voice went on, "That was when I heard about the horns the vayen aray crafted in the day. They enchanted the horns to call for their help over miles away. I was lucky enough to find one." The sickness returned to the elf and he squinted against the painful memory that surfaced. That was when Darkadus took the horn from his hand. "All that I had to do was turn the magic to a different target. That is the gift of my kind — to manipulate and enhance with magic. So I turned it to call the bloodline I was looking for. Nearly twenty more years have passed, and I was growing desperate. Then, I finally found what I was looking for."

"Blair..." Queriven breathed. "She's a descendant from one of those families?"

"The Tripps, yes," Darkadus agreed, obviously hearing the remark. "They are the last ones in this land who stayed. It was a good thing I found her too. In my own world, I have no trouble casting spells. But here, I've only a limited amount of magic before it fades. It's like I'm only partially anchored in this world."

Silence tore the room. Seconds ticked like minutes, minutes like years. With a new tone of voice, Darkadus spoke again. "I was trying to convince the girl to follow me willingly. It would have taken much more magic to force the curse on her, but in the end, I had to do that anyway. After the colors of autumn, the curse will suck her into that terrible world and my people will be free."

Queriven dared to raise his temper. "She doesn't deserve to suffer in a dead world just as much as your people. The humans were not completely in the wrong to banish your kind. Your kind was wicked and the humans couldn't sit around and allow their families to die."

Darkadus took a step closer. His foot landed with a thick thud before the elf. Then he knelt, meeting Queriven's face closely. The elf shut his eyes, though he could feel amber piercing his mind. "You dare say that about my people when you hate the humans as much as I do?" He nodded, studying the elf's face even though his eyes remained shut. "This is only a little human peasant. Why do you want differently? Wouldn't you do the same after everything humans have done to your family?"

The answer was already given when the elf didn't reply even after Darkadus stood back up. "We should want the same outcome. When you think of it, we're pretty alike. We've both suffered at the hands of humans."

No response.

Darkadus responded with anger once again. "What makes you so inclined to help this girl?" Dead silence ripped for just a second. "You're falling for her just as she did for you. Or should I say, as she did for me?"

Finally, Queriven's eyes opened and he looked up in stark curiosity.

Darkadus matched the look and chuckled. "She didn't tell you the full story? When we met, she was head over heels for me. Her eyes sparkled with the idea of the forest, the elves, and the magic. True, the horn I used to call her made her more interested in finding me. That's the way it works. But the intrigue and fascination for me, she carried on herself. After a while, I decided it would be best for me to play along. After she thought we were in love, I tried to convince her to run away with me, but the peasant chose to stay in her little village!" He growled and flung his arm to the side in anger. "The nerve! I promised I would take her to the forest. It was something she always dreamed to see in the first place, and yet she chose to stay in the ordinary!"

That burning gaze landed on Queriven as he spoke to the elf directly. "Queriven, she's a human; of all things, a human! I don't need to tell you about the relationship between humans and elves. It's not good. It'll be best if you don't bother with that one, trust me."

Queriven huffed and drifted his gaze away. Darkadus turned and walked to the far wall where the elf's equipment sat. Queriven couldn't react to the idea of Darkadus trying to flounder for Blair. It settled like a rock in his stomach, though he wasn't sure if it was the idea or his general discomfort. "So what's your plan now? Are you going to kill me?"

"Sadly, no. If I kill you now, I'll lose my disguise" came the answer. Darkadus bent down and selected the horn they picked from the castle. "But I can't have her finding you either. You bring her too much hope. Besides this," he paused and rolled the artifact in his hands, "there's no way to summon Rocanu, none that I know of at least. I need to be sure. The vayen aray were full of tricks and I don't want to miss anything."

"If it weren't for us, you wouldn't have known about the bond in that horn," Queriven reasoned. "You've been spying on us the whole time."

Darkadus laughed and took a step forward. "I'm flattered, but no. It takes too much magic to watch you all the time." His attention again on the artifact in his hands, he spoke again, "I need the girl hopeless, and this gives me another chance to make it certain." He dropped the horn and took a breath, a magical wave spreading from his head down to his feet.

Queriven realized what he was doing but it was too late. "No!" he cried. The enchanted boot was already in the air, and it came swinging down like an iron hammer. There was a loud crack. When the foot lifted, the horn was in several pieces. The chipped edges rattled to and fro uselessly. The lovely engravings were smashed and torn apart. Queriven sat with mouth agape, the sight of the broken artifact sinking in a dull vagueness like a disturbing vision.

The shattered thousand-year-old artifact did nothing to change Darkadus. He looked at the scraps like it was nothing but littered trash under his foot. He looked again at Queriven, who was too horrified to match his gaze. "The pirate captain, though loyal, is quite useless. Looks like I have to handle this myself." From his belt, he took up a pouch and drew out the other horn, originally hidden from sight.

When Queriven finally lifted his eyes, the sight was like a stab to the gut. That artifact was once his. He remembered everything about it. The sketching whispered of a lifelong dead.

The elf was brimming with sorrow. He could remember the trees, thick in the summer heat. The wind rustling through the deep green gently, a hundred scents mixing sweetly of nature. Everything once counted as precious, he tried desperately to forget.

Darkadus inhaled and closed his eyes. The vision of the rokian changed briskly. Now standing in his place was the exact look-alike of Queriven. The false elf opened his eyes and strolled back to the wall, gathering Queriven's equipment and spear. The tip sparkled none the brilliance in his hands as he held it tight. Lying eyes flashed back with a smirk that made Queriven sick. With a deepened tone still belonging to Darkadus, he breathed in. "It's wonderful to be back in the land of my ancestors."

Disgust made Queriven want to yell once more that this was not the land of his ancestors. It was a useless retort though, and he remained silent. Like a phantom lurking in the mirror, Darkadus rounded back and left through the missing wall without another word.

Queriven remained chained to the wall, his terrible emotions swirling around his head like an ugly beast. Blair's only hope was still in pieces on the floor. A part of him wanted to take pride in how he gave it all so far to help her, but a pang of bigger guilt remained. The elf wanted to help break the curse he was in the fault for allowing. He should have killed Darkadus those years ago when he could. His motive was different now. No longer was he concerned for his own choices, but what would happen to his new friend. Blair was no longer the unfortunate victim of a curse, but someone far more precious.

When he first entered the borders of Fairdraisha, there was a dread for the humans who lived here. But unlike Darkadus, Queriven had moved beyond that. Never should one judge an entire race as good or evil when it's easily a mix of both. Queriven has met both sides of the coin at this point, and he was wiser for keeping an open mind. Never will he see the young peasant girl in the same way as the terrible human thieves who came in to hurt the elves. Blair had a heart of gold and Queriven loved that about her.

And now Darkadus was trying again to trap her from freedom. There was nothing he could do about it but pray she can handle it and break free by herself. Will it be too late by then? She was much stronger than she used to be, both mentally and physically, but Darkadus was so convincing...

As the conflict began to ebb, it released into a pounding headache. Nothing could comfort him than the hard stone floor. He shifted his weight to the other side, a wave of pain striking his leg when he did. The elf grimaced but continued anyway. Now settled into a position less comfortable than the last one he was in, he stared up the towering ceiling. He imagined he was swimming in the open sky beyond it, offering prayers. It was the only thing he had left.

CHAPTER NINETEEN
ALONE IN SPIRIT

Blair made the wise decision to rest rather than work through the night, though that didn't mean it came easy. Even if Blair had the horn with her, her main concern was Queriven's safety. Wherever he was right now, she was sure he wasn't well, or at least, he won't be for long. The pirates were trying to halt her progress, but they won't be letting him go anytime soon.

She had to find him before it's too late; if it wasn't too late already.

The next morning, Blair ate a quick breakfast in silence and gathered supplies for a trip in the wilderness. The little town she stayed in was hardly a town at all. Most of the homes were farmsteads. There was little else to do or check here. Blair still spoke with many of the farmers there, desperate to find some help. Pirates were holding Queriven. It would be hard for one person to retrieve him without the pirates' attention.

In the end, she found no help. All the people she spoke to, while most were farmers, didn't want to spend the time or effort to offer assistance. The few who could not come but were sympathetic enough offered their prayers and bread. This brought a frustrated sigh to her lips, but she gratefully took the supplies anyway. Leaving Queriven was still not an option. She left the community. *Looks like I'll have to set out and find him myself.*

Several hours later, she was back on the road where yesterday's battle took place. No one must have crossed it recently because the blood and bodies were all in the same position. Blair gave the scene one glance before averting her eyes. The torment was still there and she had to shake loose the turmoil that grasped her. Instead, she looked at the hills just off the road. The last she saw her elven friend was when they carried him off toward Taleena Hills. But where did they take him exactly? Was he in the midst of a camp or maybe a base? Surely, they ran through the hills, but where were they now?

Blair was no good at tracking. She stood helpless in the field of bodies, not even sure where to start. She took a slow breath in, not just to clear the start of nausea but also to try and remember the fight. Where was Queriven when she last saw him before he was taken? *Right over here.* She walked closer to the growing grass over the edge of the road. He was lying down here.

Blair knelt down for a better look. Even with her lack of skill, she studied the crushed grass and spotted some blood by the end of it. She gasped. There was an arrow shaft in her fuzzy memory. Was he hit by an arrow? Was this his blood or a pirate's? She wouldn't have been able to tell, but she stood, thinking to check for a trail. Sure enough, she found some more further up the first hill. Why didn't she notice this before?!

The droplets weren't always an easy thing to see. Blair had to stop every now and then. Now determined not to lose her path, she kept on and rounded the first few hills. The trail stopped again and she stood still, scanning the ground carefully. There was a good wind building up and it carried the sweet scents of new leaves and flowers. The grass under her feet caught the breeze and ruffled with it like a green ocean.

Her brow furrowed in focus, and with a steady hand, she pulled back, wavering gold locks to the other side of her head.

It was then when she realized she wasn't alone. There was a figure coming down the hill more to Blair's right. She squinted past the sting of the wind. He was coming closer. Then she recognized it to be no other than Queriven himself! He was leaning heavily on his spear, walking every careful step with a pronounced limp.

"Queriven?!" Blair shouted, jogging to him.

Those pitiful eyes lifted and softened at the sight of her. "Blair," he answered and hugged her tight. "Oh, Blair. I'm so sorry."

The sound of his voice brought her sorrow. She looked down. His leg was bloody underneath the wrapping. It took her a moment to respond past her shock. "Are you all right? What happened? How are you here?"

He lowered himself down in the grass, a terrible wince on his face. "I escaped when the pirates weren't looking," he declared sadly after a moment. "They kept questioning me if there was anything I knew about breaking your curse, but I insisted I didn't." He shook his head. "They already knew about the horn though. There was nothing I could do. I'm terribly sorry."

"What?" Blair asked, kneeling beside him. "Did they take it?"

The elf swallowed. "They shattered it. There was nothing I could do."

With her breath caught in her throat, Blair plopped down in the grass and stared down at her lap. The reality didn't settle right, almost like she couldn't comprehend the meaning of his message. The wind whistled by them as they sat in silence. "It's gone?" she mouthed, the only thing she managed to let out.

"It's all my fault..." Queriven replied.

An empty gaze veered to look at him. "How can we break the curse now? That was our only hope."

"I don't know," he insisted, just as lost as she was. "We did everything we could."

But his words did little to comfort Blair. She looked at him for help. "What do we do now?" But he had nothing to offer her. The mark on her wrist never seemed tighter. For the first time in a very long time, like before she headed for the Limadia Estate, she felt her doomed fate creeping up on her more than ever. The mission was already lost.

Despite the fresh green hills around her being a temporary and short haven, she looked back at her friend. Even after she's gone, he'll still be here, moving on in this world. She gave him a broken and sad smile. She was still thankful he was safe. "This is not your fault. You helped me more than you can ever imagine. I'm glad I had the chance to meet you."

She dreaded to think the expedition in the castle was worthless, but she allowed it to come anyway. She leaned back and rested her head in the soft green grass, trying not to show the tears building in her eyes. Queriven also leaned back and relaxed. Both stared up at the string-like clouds crossing in and out of the sun.

Nearly two hours passed by and neither of them said a thing. Blair didn't know if she was becoming mad or if the reality still hasn't settled right, but she dared to think about the first time they met Rocanu on the mountain of Lyfíhana. He was not something she could simply conjure. He was still out there somewhere in that dimension, waiting for her to summon him. If he was still out there, then maybe she shouldn't be so hopeless. Maybe there's another way to bring him forth. Why not try? The rokian did it, and she still has until autumn.

As if he sensed she was about to speak, Queriven spoke first. "Perhaps, we can retrieve the shattered horn? I don't know if we can still fix it or not."

Blair already made her decision. "I want to go to Dyara." There was a breath of silence. Queriven didn't reply; he only stared at her curiously as she sat up. "From my understanding, Dyara is the strongest link between humans and the vayen aray. If we still have a chance, we'll find something there."

Queriven wasn't convinced. "Blair, there's nothing over there. It's just a mound of forgotten buildings. Why should we search the broken ruins when we can try something better? The pirates haven't moved yet. We can retrieve the scraps of the horn and figure out how to fix it."

But Blair shook her head, her dark hair brushing radiantly over the starlight by her shoulders. "They want to stop me from breaking the curse. I'm sure they disposed of the pieces by now, or at least, they know I wouldn't be able to use it anymore. The horn carried magic. Fixing it wouldn't restore that. No, it's too late to turn back. We can only go forward, and as long as I have time on this realm, I'll keep looking for answers." She smiled at the little glimmer of hope she found, proud she will continue doing everything she can. Blair looked back at Queriven, who was still leaning back and watching her. "Will you be by my side even if I fail?"

"To the end," he assured her. That wide gaze showed surprise in her steadfast decision.

Blair pushed to her feet and brushed the loose dirt and grass from her clothes. The sight of the bandage over the elf's leg made her wince. "How is your leg? Do you want me to look at it?"

Before she even finished, her hands hovered over the wound. Queriven pulled away. "I've already treated it. The arrow didn't land deep."

Blair gave him a look that said she didn't believe him, but she didn't question it further. She swept her hair in a smooth arc and breathed in the sky. "The sun will be setting in a few hours. Can you walk with me to the lodge? It's not too far from here."

"I'll try my best," came the answer. He brought the spear closer, rooting it firmly into the ground. Blair also lent a helping hand and pulled him to his feet. Queriven strained with effort but made it back up. He leaned on the spear and waited. Blair hesitated; the hand still in her grasp was slender and warm, his breath breathing life over her skin. Finally, he retracted his hand from hers and Blair refocused. She turned and walked slowly back over the hill to the road, checking back behind her every few minutes.

They didn't exchange many words after that, save for Blair's good night after they reached the lodge. The impostor stayed in his room for a good long while until the night was growing late. Then, casting away the appearance of the limp or injury in his leg, he quietly left the room.

No one even drew him a suspicious look as he crossed the counter and disappeared outside. He left the span of lantern light and traversed into the dark. Though disguised as an elf, Darkadus possessed no abilities of one. If he chose, he could enhance his eyesight himself, but he didn't. He didn't need to see in the dark to know the shadow moving from ahead was one of Yusen's pirates.

"Darkadus, sir" came the greeting. The voice sounded tired and a little irritated, like he had to respond to the summons, though he would rather be asleep right now. The pirate carried no light source so as to not draw attention.

Darkadus didn't bother with formalities. He went right to the point. "The girl didn't fall for the plan. We need to prepare something else. She's insistent about reaching Dyara even without the horn. Meet us there and we'll make sure she wouldn't be able to escape again."

The shadow bowed his head and the figure turned, but the false elf grabbed his arm and spun him back around. "Don't take the roads. Go around far enough so she wouldn't suspect anything, and don't stop in Penacha. This will take you longer, but I'll slow her down."

The man sighed in response, but agreed to the plan without question and vanished in the darkness. Then, Darkadus returned to his room and rested.

He stayed in his room even after daybreak and waited. Finally, there was a knock at his door. It was Blair, and she was curious why he hasn't come out yet. "May I come in?" the voice asked and the door swung open.

After she stepped in, Queriven hobbled back to the chair he was sitting in and fell in it. "I'm sorry," he answered piteously. "I guess moving around has been a struggle for me this morning."

Blair stood in the center of the room for a few minutes. She looked down at the wrapped leg. "The injury?" she asked.

"Grown worse, I'm afraid. I pushed it pretty hard yesterday." Enveloped in silence again, the two were already thinking the same thing. Queriven gave her a look of sympathy and sadness. "I know we should head out today though. I'd hate to slow us down."

"No" came the immediate reply. "That won't do. I can't let you push yourself any further."

Queriven looked up at her face. "Blair, we still have a deadline. I don't care if this kills me; we're going."

That seemed to bother her further as she didn't even give it a moment's thought. "We'll leave as soon as you're able. Until then, we're doing all we can, like we always have. Take today to rest and we'll see how you're feeling tomorrow." She looked away and glanced outside, her eyes looking at something she couldn't see. She folded her arms. "It could be that we can borrow a pair of horses when you're well enough. That seems to be the wisest."

Queriven said nothing at first, as her change in tone stunned him. He didn't remember her being more like a fighter. He nodded. "That would be wise indeed."

She smiled, her pink lips brightening with the colored shimmer in her eye. Blair's arm dropped as she swung them back at the door. "Do you want some breakfast? I'll bring some when I come back."

The elf nodded. "I'll like that. Thank you." When she left, he chuckled and shook his head. She was very sweet to the elf. This shouldn't be too hard.

A few days later had them on the road. Blair successfully acquired a pair of horses by herself, and they started at a slow pace as to not bother Queriven's wound.

Blair didn't speak aloud or show her fears. She didn't want to bother Queriven further, but the delay was setting her on edge.

Summer was not very far away, and that just left her a few more months before the danger of the curse. She didn't blame the elf though. She believed he was doing his best to push things forward.

There was nothing to do now but continue forward. If there was nothing in Dyara, Blair wouldn't know what to do next. She swallowed the unpleasant taste in her mouth and glanced over at her companion. He was riding on a solid brown mare, his wrapped leg draping down her flank. Queriven neither met her gaze nor said anything. Blair found that odd as he usually breaks quiet gaps and would usually ask her if she was all right. Maybe his leg was still bothering him more than it should? His face didn't show even a slight grimace, but he probably knew she would catch it if he did show it. He was good at hiding things.

Blair let the thought go and stared ahead. The days were already growing longer and warmer. Spring didn't last long this year... She resisted the urge to race her old paint into a gallop. Penacha was still a few days away. She tried to hold on to the hope that they could find something there, but she was thinking it unlikely.

Blair was almost free from her curse. She was almost home, but everything was gone now. She longed for some encouragement that she was on the right path, but she dared not to be the one to break this silence.

Night settled in quicker than Blair wanted it to, and they set up camp on the side of the road. The quiet was slowly killing Blair. It was warm enough that evening that they didn't even need to build a fire, so Queriven leaned back and relaxed.

Blair had enough. "Have you ever been to Penacha before?"

"I have" came the response.

Blair sat down on the ground and folded her ankle over the other. She waited for him to say something else, but apparently, he was finished. "Is it a big city? Do you think there's a chance we'll find anything there?"

Without much of a thought, he answered again. "I'm thinking not. If a bond between races is the only thing to summon Rocanu, then what else can we use?"

The sour tone caught her off guard. The stern but accepted hopelessness was unlike him. Queriven wasn't always the most joyful person, but he would always hold out a goal for Blair to strive for, no matter how small it may be.

Content with letting Blair stew in bewilderment, Queriven lowered the hood over his eyes and turned to the side. But confusion burned brighter and brighter as stunned seconds passed. Blair couldn't let this sit. "What's wrong with you? We have just the same chances for success as when we first started all this before we knew we were going for the horn."

"Well, those chances weren't high to begin with, were they?"

Blair marked her surprise with a well-placed scoff as she sat straight and stared at the figure across from her. He didn't bother to turn. "What happened? I'm being serious. Did the pirates do something to you? Or maybe you'd rather be on your own. That's fine too. I wasn't the one to bring you in on this."

Finally, the hood stirred and a darkened face lifted. "Go to sleep, Blair. I have my doubts, but I promised I would stick through with this till the end."

Blair was too uncomfortable to let the topic go, but she didn't feel right staying where she was either, so she stood up angrily and pretended to scout for a better spot in the grass. "Out of the two of us, you were always the one who had the most hope for success. Who told me to keep fighting when I was on the verge of giving up?" She found the best patch of grass in the field, and now she watched him, standing awkwardly in the middle of the open. "This I promise you; *I will* find a way forward and I will show you what you were like for me when I was at my lowest."

The head turned again, burrowing down in the cloth without another remark. Blair scowled and lied down in the grass again. There wasn't as much as a smile from him. This was not the Queriven she knew, and the longer she pondered it, the more it bothered her. There was something more to this and she wanted to figure it out. Blair gave him one final look before finding a comfortable position to sleep. As she closed her eyes, she vowed to watch him more closely.

Alone in Spirit

Queriven was still awake. She was nagging him with frustration. The more he wanted to dumb her down and insist there was no hope, the stronger she believed there were answers. Blair was no longer something he could crush between his fingers. Just wait and see — once they leave Penacha, the pirates will take her and she will find him right when he said there's nothing she could do.

◊ ◊ ◊

Before, the silence between them bothered Blair, but now she was glad it stayed that way. The morning did nothing to soothe Queriven's stewing temper, but at least he kept it to himself.

Blair gave a loving stroke to the strong paint. His thinning coat of red and white was soft and fuzzy on her skin. She climbed up in the saddle. Queriven did the same and they were back on the road.

After nearly an hour later, Blair found a wave of sadness. She missed the old Queriven she once knew. She missed their conversations and his rare but beautiful smile. It was almost like she was on the road all by herself. Still, she didn't want to draw his attention and make him mad. If she did or not, she was sure it wouldn't help her case, so she rode on in utter quiet.

The next collection of days passed by uneventfully. He was becoming more suspicious of her, but she couldn't find out exactly why. She watched him very carefully. On the occasion when she was brave enough, she asked him questions. Queriven was still reluctant to talk much and he still wouldn't give her a hint about what was going on.

They rode into Penacha in the dimming evening. Unlike Dunverhart, a city Blair has been to before when she was little, Penacha was quite unique. It was smaller than the big city, but it was bigger than Bailiese. At first glance, it was a comfortable size. Front doorsteps had space to breathe, and a large stone plaza in the center of town gave plenty of room to walk. The buildings, a lot of them tall, were mostly shades of brown and other dark colors. Something about it was very beautiful in a way Blair's never seen before. The golden hue of twilight seemed to match it so perfectly. It was like a little haven away from the chaos of the world. She couldn't imagine any other time it would look more perfect. With Dyara once being a sister city only several miles away, she wondered if it looked similar.

Queriven seemed unchanged as they trotted into the plaza. The hooves of the horses clinked on the stone with every step. Blair brought hers to a slower walk. "We should stay here tonight. If this city was once alike to Dyara, then I think it's also worth to check for answers here too."

Without either agreement or denial, Queriven also slowed his horse and dismounted. They bought more supplies and food, found a comfortable inn to stay for the night, and searched for information about the vayen aray. Neither the residents nor the library knew a thing they didn't already know. Queriven was still not surprised and also not too helpful. Though the lack of a new goal wasn't bringing Blair down, she still wanted to search the old ruins of Dyara.

Queriven didn't show a change in response again, Blair noted. In fact, he resorted to not saying anything other than he was turning in for the night. Blair thought to grab his attention and demand what changed, but she stayed silent and allowed him to leave.

That next morning, Blair was ready to hit the road again, and she came to Queriven's room to gather him for breakfast.

He was already gathering up his belongings, but something odd then caught her attention. Queriven was at the other end of the room where his spear was, while a few of his bags remained near the door. With them was a pouch Blair was unfamiliar with. What's more? She could see that the seam of the flap was slightly askew. There was something hiding inside. It was merely a shadow. She couldn't see the colors or material, but it was like a long tool of some sort.

Before she could take a better look though, Queriven came back with a spear in hand and picked up the last pouches before her eyes. He shattered her attention further by asking her if she was ready. She nodded and turned around.

They ate a quick breakfast and took to the road. The mysterious pouch hung over her thoughts. When did he pick it up? She didn't remember seeing it before. Either she just didn't remember right or he found it recently. Maybe he picked it up from the pirates? Then why didn't he tell her about it? Maybe she was only being nosy. But there was something different here, and she was going to figure it out on her own if she needs to. There was something unsettling about that pouch.

CHAPTER TWENTY
RESCUE MISSION

Blair noted that Queriven still had the mysterious pouch with him as they rode along a few hours down the road. She decided she wasn't being nosy but was centering on her suspicion. In light of Queriven's odd behavior, she vowed she would watch him closely, and now she found something of interest. The thought was setting her on edge and now the whole thing wasn't right.

"Wait," she said, pulling her horse to a stop. Queriven, who was ahead of her, did the same and turned the horse to the side so he could look at her in impatient confusion. "I have a bad feeling about this."

Queriven sighed. "You've been pushing us to go to Dyara so hard and now you're not sure? What's wrong this time?"

"I don't know," she admitted, releasing her nervous tick in the reins she held, which she twirled in her hands. She wanted to say something more, but there really wasn't a reason for the pause.

The pause extended as Queriven didn't have a response. His firm expression softened a little and finally, he spoke. His tone was light and not judging for once. "Do you want to turn around?"

Blair hung her head for a moment longer. The paint snorted and shifted his weight to a different side. "No," she decided, though her tone was still short. Blair then urged the paint forward. Queriven turned his horse around and continued on.

But it was only a few minutes after that when Blair snapped, her heart stopping in sudden amazement. The sun parted from the clouds and shone down a warm golden ray on the rolling green hills. There was a hint of red ivory showing in Queriven's bag. The shape Blair made out earlier suddenly made sense now. The object was a horn. Either Queriven was lying when he said the horn shattered or he wasn't Queriven at all. Besides the horn they captured from Dunverhart, there was one more, one Blair saw herself many months ago in Bailiese. Like a punch in the gut, Blair became sick as she realized who she was with.

Her falter slowed the horse.

It took Queriven a moment to notice this, and again he turned around. "Why are you slowing down?"

Her lips parted and her hands began to shake. She stared at him in quiet bewilderment. "Queriven?" she whispered almost like she was asking for help. When he didn't respond, she withdrew the spear on her back and pointed it at him. Her expression suddenly changed in a heartbeat from shock to determined and angry. "Where is Queriven?" she demanded.

Like last time, that sweet tongue filled with a voice of soothing music broke apart. In its place was a dull tone, enriched in a deep accent. "Clever girl." The person before her mused honestly as he viewed her as an object in a market. "You've grown quite considerably since we met last. If I didn't already know you were traveling with that elf, I would be wondering if I had the right person or not."

Blair wasn't fazed. "Where is he?!" she demanded louder. "Tell me now or I'll run your black heart through!"

The intruder wasn't the least bit bothered by her threat. "You won't find him in time. Why bother? Your salvation to the curse is already destroyed." He rolled false eyes when she didn't move from her position. "Is he really that important to you? Take my advice; don't trust that man. He's a terrible, selfish coward."

Blair scoffed. "Like I should trust you when you've done nothing but lie to me."

He poked a finger in the air like he blocked the accusation from passing through. "No, I've told some truth before. Just because you wouldn't listen doesn't mean otherwise. Tell me, how much do you know about that elf? About his history? Can you even tell me why he left home?"

There was a second of hesitation before she threatened him again. "Why do you think you know him any better?"

There was a prideful gleam in the intruder's eye. "Because I was there that night."

Another bit of hesitation, this time with a drawback of stunned disbelief. Then Blair refocused the fire. "I don't believe you."

"Maybe not now, but you will sooner or later. Queriven drew his soldiers into a losing battle knowingly. He let them die, and now he's running away from the monster that he is." He jabbed an accusing finger at Blair's chest. "That armor you're wearing was worn by a knight who betrayed his friends and then gave up the horn he carried to spare his own useless life. He never should have been a knight in the first place! He's nothing but a selfish coward!"

"Get off the horse!" Blair yelled. "I'm finding the real Queriven, even on the occasion you might be speaking the truth. This is your last warning."

The intruder choked up a laugh, making the image of Queriven a distorted lie. "You don't scare me, girl. You have no idea what I'm capable of. If I wanted to, I could take you away right now. Alas, that would take effort. It'll be too much effort than it's worth, and considering I have no help and you're already doomed to your fate, I suppose I should be on my way."

Before Blair could repeat herself, the brown mare took a few steps back and leaped up and over Blair's own horse. The height could have easily scaled a barn! As the horse landed, it sped faster than a wild stallion, touching the horizon edge in merely a moment. Blair looked back in astonishment, unable to respond on that time. Suddenly, she found herself all alone and unable to even think about following up on her threat. That imposter is uncatchable! How did he manage such a spell like that?!

Something happened to Queriven, and it wasn't good. How will she find him now? She didn't have a single lead. Warped in confusion and uncertainty, she sat in the middle of the open road. What were her options? Should she turn back and try to relocate the area where she ran into the imposter, or should she continue on to Dyara in search of answers? The last one made her shiver uncomfortably. If that fiend has been with her this whole time trying to hinder her plans, then she wasn't sure about going ahead; not on the road anyway. He wouldn't allow her to get away with it.

This whole time, he's been trying to convince her that this trip was worthless, so maybe that means there is something there? Blair sighed in the breezy spring wind. There was nothing else to go on. She was unable to help her friend right now, so she might as well continue with what she had.

The red and white paint responded to the click of her tongue and trotted off the dirt road and into the grass. She was going to enter from the back of Dyara.

Dyara was literally at the end of the road. It was the last town on the southwestern part of the continent. It rested near the edge of a cliff that dropped a long way down into the sea. The waves were particularly rough today. Blair was nearly deafened by them far below. It must have something to do with the thick clouds gathering. She could almost smell the rain still in the sky, and she thought she heard a roll of thunder hiding behind another crash of waves, but she could be mistaken.

She was really close to Dyara now. She could see the nature overgrown buildings, but that wasn't the only thing.

Along with the mix of dirt and cobble road, there were

figures moving to and fro. Looks like they were using some of the still-standing buildings as shelter. Who were these people and why were they here? Whatever the case, she needed a better look.

Blair led her horse to a safe grazing patch and dismounted, stroking the beast's face calmly. "Wait here for me," she whispered softly before running off to the town.

There wasn't a lot of coverage on this cliffside, but she managed until she reached an old house where she hid and watched. Upon closer inspection, there weren't a lot of them; maybe six or seven at best. They carried weapons and she thought she recognized some of the faces belonging to Captain Nashōgan's crew. Of course! The rokian set them here as a trap for her. It made so much sense now.

But how will she search the ruins for answers with them here? There weren't many of them, sure, but still too many for her to go unnoticed. That's especially considering they were already here to capture her.

Slowly, a tall, bulky man was approaching two shorter men playing a game with dice. He stopped before the game and stared, looking between the two like he didn't know who to address. "You go on watch," he finally chose, looking at the man sitting on the right.

The shorter man didn't respond right away, almost looking like he dared to argue he was in the middle of something, but then he merely growled and released the dice from his hand and stood up. Laughter erupted from his opponent once the dice landed and the man growled again before tossing a handful of coins at him before leaving.

There was too much to risk here. If they find her here, her chances of exploring and rescuing Queriven would be nearly impossible. The latter was more important. All she needed was to find out where he was being kept.

If she wouldn't be able to find anything here, then she'll need to help Queriven's cause somehow, and she was in the best place to do so. If these men worked with that rokian, then perhaps they know where he's keeping him.

All she had to do was wait for a moment of weakness...

It came nearly an hour later. The men were in the midst of an argument about having to wait at the site for so long. One man, barely old enough to be called so, was fed up and left with the excuse to relieve himself.

He was marching this way and he was by himself.

Blair made a final scope to make sure none were close enough to see him disappear, then she hid behind the corner and waited.

The kid kept walking, unaware of the trap waiting for him just behind that last building. Blair was carefully watching for a hint of movement. She could hear the grass under his footsteps as he came closer and closer.

And finally, he came in front of her without suspicion. Blair leaped at him, one hand wrapping around his chest and pulling him back while the other muffled his scream. The last thing he remembered was knocking his head against the wall and seeing the sharp spear tip before he looked at the girl holding him down. Dark golden hair swung in front of her face and a face full of freckles did little to soften her intimidating glare. Blair held her ground firmly, even though his dark eyes were welling up with fearful tears. "I'm not going to hurt you," she whispered to him. "I promise." With a palm still over his mouth, Blair sheathed the spear on her back and studied him a little longer. The boy's rapid breathing was brushing across her hand. "Don't make a sound or we'll both be in a lot of trouble. Do you understand?"

His expression didn't change, but he gave her a quick nod. "Great," she responded, releasing his mouth. "I only need some help." With her last grip, she pulled him to his feet and he pressed his back against the wall. Any tighter and he would have melted right through it. "A few days ago, the pirates took an elf hostage. Do you know anything about this?"

Again, he nodded. "You mean the elf they called Queriven? They took him to an old watchtower in the north." His voice was wavering with fright. He was light and young. Blair was a little regretful for scaring such a young kid.

She gave him a smile. "That's the one. I'm going to need you to come with me."

His eyes widened further and his lips parted, but he didn't refuse or yell. Blair removed her grip and looked back around the corner. No one back at camp seemed to notice anything amiss. They should leave quickly before they began to wonder where the kid ran off to. Blair turned back to see the boy still standing behind her. She pointed to the open clearing ahead and followed behind him.

Once they were far enough from the pirates, she led him to her horse, who was grazing peacefully right where she left him. "Leave any weapons you have here. You won't be needing them."

Without a word, the boy took a small dull sword and dagger from his waist and dropped them and then removed a few knives from his boots. He then waited for Blair to double-check, but he wasn't hiding anything else. Then, she climbed up in the saddle and beckoned for the boy to ride behind her.

Once settled, she brought the horse to a trot, heading back to the dirt road she left nearly a day ago. "I'm Blair by the way. What's your name?"

The boy hesitated for a moment, as if he was afraid of talking too much. "Medahai, though you can call me whatever you want. I know the pirates do," he answered.

Though his response was negative, Blair responded with a light tone. "Medahai is a fine name. I think I'll call you by that." Like the rest of the crew, Medahai was from a foreign country. He had dark eyes and hair, an exotic face and skin the color of dark desert sand. She turned back to look at him and saw he was too shy to lift his head. That left her a view of fluffy overgrown hair on top of his head. She turned ahead again.

The sky finally dropped the rain it was holding just before they reached Penacha. The two were soaking wet, but most of all, Blair was starving. With all the stress of finding the truth about the imposter, Blair hasn't eaten much. So with the excitement for supper, she left the horse at the stable and returned to the same inn she and the imposter stayed just the other day.

The rain continued throughout most of the night, though it continuously stopped and started. Blair woke up early the next morning. To deter Medahai from escaping, she latched the door good and tight and slept near it. She could barely see beyond the knotted mound of blankets on top of her, but could hear the rain hitting the window. She pushed the blankets past her and sat up.

Medahai was still asleep in the bed against the far wall, his light snoring matching the pace of his breathing. The boy has been quiet all night long, barely saying anything to her unless he really needed to. If anything, Blair hoped he could eat with a better appetite than he did last night. She sighed and stretched. It was quite natural for him to be scared. After all, what she did was no less than kidnapping, but she still hoped he would warm up to her a bit.

She rubbed her hazy eyes and stood up, her hair still in a mess. It was time to hit the road. She wasn't going to wait the rain out, not while Queriven was still in danger.

Luckily, the rain slowed down yet again to a pleasant sprinkle by the time they retrieved the horse. Medahai was still quiet on the back of the horse, only staring absentmindedly. Blair caught onto it quickly. "Medahai, you mustn't worry. If you have something to say to me, then say it."

Finally, shapely eyes looked up at her. "I know who you are," he paused, thinking long and hard. Just when Blair thought he wasn't going to say anything else, he spoke again. "You're the cursed one, the one who killed Nekene."

Blair hesitated, unable to even respond.

Medahai continued. "I was an apprentice to the first mate. Now that he's gone, no one's really had the patience to show me how things work. Not like he's really had much in the beginning anyway, but at least he was nicer than the others."

Blair wanted to forget the subject, but she knew, for his sake, it was best to say something. "I...I'm sorry about your loss." She swallowed the harsh memory from her gut and looked away. "But I didn't kill him. Nekene...killed himself. After seeing the destruction on the Sapphire Reef, he was quickly losing his mind. He blamed the attack on me and threatened to kill me. But when help from the Enchantress arrived, he didn't let go."

"Oh," Medahai whispered, "well, that's not what the pirates say. But then, I don't know if they've even heard the whole story of it either. That, or they didn't listen to it when we were aboard the Enchantress."

"I really was sorry for him," Blair stated again. "I believe, despite his piracy and wrong acts, he was a good man deep inside. He was nice to me when I was on the Sapphire Reef too." She turned back again. "Have you known him for long?"

"No," Medahai answered. "I've been a part of the crew for only a few years. Before, I was trying to make it on the street without a home. It was Nekene who brought me aboard. He said if I worked hard and followed orders, I can have food and shelter."

Blair pondered for a second. "How old are you?"

"Almost fifteen, Miss."

This young boy wasn't involved in pirating for long, Blair realized. He was still marked with crime-free innocence. She had no place to judge him. Life on a ship was a better option than living on the streets, but the record over his head will stain forever, and he will live a difficult life because of his choices now. It was a good thing he wasn't involved in it long. It wasn't too late to turn back.

Blair said nothing about her thoughts. She shivered in the still dripping rain as the horse continued to trot. In just a day and a half, they were past the farmsteads and were in the location where Queriven disappeared. Someone must have found the battlefield because the blood, weapons, and bodies were all gone. Blair was glad Medahai didn't see such a terrible thing.

"The old watchtower is straight north of here, but we might

continue on the road toward Dunverhart first. There is a river we have to go around," the voice behind her said.

Blair knew the river he spoke about. The Limadia Estate was just in the middle of the Taleena Hills, and the river was at the edge of the territory. She nearly fell into that river when she tried to run from a bandit then, but a tree caught her fall instead. That was when she met Queriven. The memory sparked a pang of regret. She was so mean to him back then. She never even apologized.

Queriven was true and selfless. She didn't care what that imposter said. He's done everything for her and she never had a chance to return it. She prayed he was still all right... If it was the last thing she could do, she wished he could see how important he was to her.

The rain was starting to fall a bit quicker with more of a roar. She sped the paint along, fearful they may have to stop and find shelter. Blair blinked away the drops that fell in her eyes. At least it was warm still, but it's possible one of them might catch a cold before too long. "Medahai," Blair asked, looking to distract herself from her thoughts. "How much do you know about the rokian? The one who ordered Queriven's disappearance?"

"Not much really," he admitted. "And I've never met him myself. He mainly gives orders through the captain. What I do know is that his name is Darkadus and he promised us a future where we won't be killed for our crimes or choices. He'll give us treasures, land, and freedom. That's something a lot of the crew always wanted — freedom. Most of us were chosen to be part of the crew without much to say about it. It's just who we are now."

"Oh," Blair remarked, quite disappointed with the lack of information. At least she now knows what his name is. A shudder ran down her back and arms and it wasn't from the rain. She imagined the man she met, who wanted her to run away with him, as one with such a name as Darkadus instead of Queriven. She dreaded to think of him as something other than a nefarious spirit, but as something like her, something real and out there still. She looked behind her and saw clear eyes.

For a second, she considered not trusting his word, but she disregarded it quickly. Medahai was young, and though shy and scared of talking to her, he wasn't fretful. His gaze never wandered and he didn't pause or stumble when he talked. If he was a liar, he was the best one yet, maybe better than Darkadus himself.

"I understand if you had no choice to join a crew like that to survive. I will not blame your past, but I do not believe those circumstances make who you are. After recovery, there is a time when you can make a choice. You can shed off a crime-filled past and move on to something better. If you don't, then that's the choice you made. You can choose to stay in the same place." She waited for him to lift his head. "You're young, but not too young to take care of yourself. If you wanted, you can leave the pirate life behind and find honest work elsewhere. It's a big world. I'm sure someone needs a worker like you."

He didn't say anything and Blair wondered if he took it in or not. She shrugged. It wasn't her decision if he moved on or not nor was he her responsibility.

Medahai was growing a little more comfortable with Blair being around. At least, he wasn't scared of her hurting him anymore. The rainy late spring days leading up to Dunverhart was long and torturous for Blair. Every day, hour, and second, Queriven was in serious danger. Blair really hoped Darkadus wasn't trying to move him somewhere else. He was smart, and Blair wanted to reach Queriven before anything could happen to him. Unfortunately, it was just taking so long.

They barely spent any time in Dunverhart when they finally reached it. Blair was thankful they made it quickly through. She didn't want to face the king again.

As for now, the rain had ceased, leaving only rushing water

of the nearby river. "They say Darkadus uses the watchtower when he wants to lay low or have a meeting away from prying eyes." Medahai pointed a thin finger to the west. "After we cross over the bridge, we should leave the road. The watchtower is only a few hours away, next to a small wood against the cliffside."

Without saying anything, Blair spurred the horse to a gallop and nearly knocked Medahai from the saddle. Rolling green and colorful wildflowers moved past them like a daze. The speed of the overflowing river raced them straight for the sea. Blair focused ahead, her legs already growing tired from being in the saddle. *Please be all right. I don't know how I can do this without you.*

CHAPTER TWENTY-ONE
AGAINST THE TICK OF TIME

Not soon after they crossed the bridge and left the road, Blair could see the mountains in the distance. They were tall and capped with snow, even in the hot summer. There was a hardy city just at the base. As a city that lived off the harvest of the mountains, she always imagined it to be totally different than she's ever seen before. But that trip was not today. There was something more important waiting for her. As she rode, she prayed over and over that Queriven will still be here. If he was already moved, it would be so hard to find him again.

Her heart skipped a beat as she made out a tower in the distance. Like most of the ruins, it was made from stone and was still up despite being over a thousand years old, though it looked like one side of it did collapse. There was a large open hole in the wall and a few at the top. Even though it otherwise looked safe and sturdy, she wouldn't want to try climbing up to the top.

"You must be careful," Medahai said when she slowed the horse down. "If your friend is still here, someone else will be as well."

As eager as she was to find out, Blair dismounted the horse and stayed nearby. "Do you know of any other locations they might take him to if he isn't here?" she asked, not bothering to look at him. Out of the corner of her eye, he briefly shook his head, and as she looked at the watchtower again, she had her confirmation. A figure was standing right outside the broken wall. Even from here, she recognized the odd-looking hat atop his head. It was none other than Captain Yusen Nashögan himself.

Queriven was still here.

Blair took a step back and faced the boy. "You've done your part, Medahai. You're free to go wherever you wish." Like the first time she took him away from the camp, his eyes grew wide with disbelief. "Can you make it from here on your own?"

He cleared his voice and began checking his pockets. "I believe so. I've got money and food that will last me some days."

"Good. Be on your way then," Blair responded with a smile, glancing back at the watchtower every now and then. "And Medahai, this is the time for you to make a choice. I will not pick one for you. You may go back to the pirates, though you may be questioned and perhaps land in trouble for helping me, or you may use that money and food looking for a better job." She paused and glanced at the paint as he snorted. "You may take the horse if you like."

Blair wasn't expecting him to decline the last offer. "Oh no. You're going to need him when you're breaking out of there with your friend." He sighed, crossed his arms, and turned to the road that was out of view. "I've always appreciated how the pirates took me in when no one else will, but I know they never liked me. They were mean too." Medahai finished his thought and addressed Blair again. "Well, good luck, and thank you for not scalping me or anything."

She would have laughed at him if she wasn't so drawn in the situation. Instead, she agreed she was glad she didn't either, then she broke away for the ruins. She kept a fast pace forward. Luckily, there was more to hide here than by Dyara. There were more hills, trees, and bushes.

The captain was entering the broken wall. Blair sped up, stopping only when she was against it. She took the spear and clenched it tight in both her hands, then pressed her back into the wall. She might have to fight the captain, she realized silently. It only scared her a little. Her skills were improving, but were they well enough to compare against his? She listened closely for anything on the other side.

"...Against me," the captain's deep voice came in. "Now I have something against you. You destroyed my ship and hurt my family."

Blair forgot how to breathe when another voice responded. She recognized it easily even though it was strained and tired. "I suppose that makes us even then."

The captain snapped back loudly. "Not even the slightest! You're only alive because Darkadus needs you to be. After the curse takes the girl, you're dead. And I'm going to kill you nice and slowly."

"Why do you care what Darkadus wants? He's the one who's pulled you into all this. If it weren't for his orders, you wouldn't have been involved and your 'family' wouldn't have gotten hurt. If you ask me, I'd say you're blaming the wrong person. Maybe you shouldn't trust him like you do."

"Shut your mouth!" Yusen yelled, his voice alone scattering a flock of birds from a tree not far from Blair. There was a metal scraping that sent Blair to her toes. "Don't tempt me to break my promise."

"Go ahead," Queriven whispered quietly. Blair almost didn't catch it. "I'm not afraid of dying anymore."

A growl came from the pirate. Blair peered around the edge and caught a peek of the captain's side. He was leaning over the floor, but she couldn't see anything else. "When I'm through with you, you will be." Yusen was turning back around and Blair retreated back to safety just in time.

The captain was coming through the open wall to place some much-needed space between him and the elf. Blair rounded the corner quickly, once again disappearing from view. She was growing paranoid with discomfort. Beyond the wall against her back, she was standing in an open field. She feared someone might be sneaking up on her from either side.

Blair crept away from where the captain was, watching carefully in case he came back. Then, she looked away and tiptoed to the opposite side of the ruins. If that broken wall was being treated like an entryway, then surely there's a proper door somewhere else.

She rounded the next corner and nearly bumped right into the captain. Her heart was racing so fast she didn't even flinch at the terrible body odor on him. "Why, if it ain't the girl," Yusen remarked, a wide smile over his face. Blair hesitated as his hand went to retrieve the sword sheathed on his belt. "I thought something was creeping around the tower."

With a flash, he thrust the sword forward, but Blair was ready. She brought her spear up and caught it. With a twist, she pushed him aside but he came rushing back in. The shaft blocked, but her hand slipped and the sword came through. Yusen's aim was off and he missed her face by inches. The captain was close now and Blair sliced the spear aside, gashing his chest. Yusen fell back and pressed his free hand on the wound.

That took only a second before he rushed forward again. His sword snapped in, front, up, and right. Blair followed each, her feet and spear flowing with the grace not belonging to a human. Surprisingly, she was one step in front of him, and she curved the weapon to catch his sword. Then she slung it to the side. The blade whistled and thudded in the grass.

Disarmed, Yusen backed away and fell to his knees. Blood spilled from his chest, but it wasn't fatal. Even with the spear in front of his face, he didn't flinch. His expression was tight and unregretful, almost daring her to finish the job. Blair retrieved the sparkling sword from the grass and moved for the door of the watchtower, watching Yusen as she disappeared inside.

When she looked away and the door closed, she glanced ahead and froze. Her breath was once again caught in her chest. Opposite her was the broken wall, and a figure slumped on the floor, his hands bound to the wall. It was Queriven. Blair cried aloud, unable to use words to express herself. She jogged to Queriven's side and dropped down, her spear landing just beside her. The elf raised his head, though his hair was still lying in front of his face. "Blair?" he whispered. His tired eyes didn't change until moments later when she fretted over the lock on his wrists. "Is that you? How did you find me?"

Blair lamented the lack of a key, but it was too late to turn back now. What she did find was the wire she'd taken from Barram. Every attempt of picking a lock has failed her so far, but she needed to free Queriven as soon as possible. She brought the wire up and to his wrist. "I found someone among the pirates who knew where you were." Blair was in an awkward position as she leaned over him, trying to pick the lock from his wrists. "Are you all right?"

Queriven looked up at the chains. They clinked and rattled as Blair struggled. His chest heaved with a long breath. "I don't know. My leg was hit with an arrow. I haven't had the chance to walk on it." As he finished, Blair looked down at the wrapped leg. She didn't see any blood on the bandage and it looked like it was freshly wrapped. Darkadus was a smart man to fake the same wound. He surely was a good liar. If there was any chance of escape, she needed Queriven to be able to walk well. "How long have I been here?"

She thought for a moment, clenching her teeth in frustration as the lock still refused to give in. "It's been almost two weeks."

He sighed and shook his head. "Then perhaps it is healed up enough."

Blair prayed so, but her frustration was starting to turn into panic. If she couldn't free him soon, they would capture her as well. If they were escaping, the time needed to be now. "Come on!" she urged it under her breath, giving the wire a violent shove.

The lock clicked and fell open.

The slackened hand fell by Queriven's side and Blair went to the next one. Now that she had a better feel with it, the second lock was easier than the first and she wrenched it open within a few heartbeats. Blair examined the red chafe marks on either wrist and searched for the horn Darkadus had. Finally, Queriven turned his head in confusion. "What are you doing?"

When she couldn't find it, Blair smiled and embraced him tightly. "Just making sure."

Queriven choked with surprise but returned the hug. When she released him, she took his hands, stood up, and helped him up as well. Gently, Queriven allowed his weight on the injured leg. It didn't seem to bother him much at first, but as she took his arm and led him toward the outside, there was a stark pain in the wound and he yelped.

"We have to get out of here!" Blair remarked, still tugging on his arm. "Before others arrive." When he still limped, she came beside him and allowed him to lean over her. To her surprise, he allowed the help without a word and they escaped from the watchtower.

They made it past the clearing with no pursuers. Blair was glad she still had the horse not far from here as she struggled to continue carrying Queriven forward.

But to their dismay, they were already caught. As they rounded the last tree where Blair hid her horse, Darkadus was already waiting for them. Immediately, Queriven stepped back on his own and Blair withdrew her weapon.

Darkadus didn't respond in kind. He remained calm and relaxed. Blair didn't recognize him, for the rokian was without any kind of disguise. "I'm impressed. Even though I left nothing behind, you still managed to find the elf." He took a breath. "But now you have me curious. What's your next plan?"

That deep voice sent a shiver through Blair, but the face didn't belong with it. Then, it came crashing down and she tensed up. This was the voice of the intruder, belonging to either time she's seen him. Like she was afraid to be right, she asked anyway, "Who are you?"

There was a spark in his eyes and he tried to hide a smile. "That's right. This is our first meeting with the truth. Allow me to introduce myself properly. I'm Darkadus." He bowed down with his prideful arms swooping to the side. "You may not remember me now, but I was the one you met at the lake near Bailiese before you met him." He directed the last part toward Queriven. The elf didn't move at the notion. He remained still with his head down.

"I'm not afraid of you. Step aside or I'll strike!" Blair returned, taking a single step forward with her spear ready.

Darkadus moved out of the way. "By all means, I will. If I can avoid fighting today, that'll be ever helpful." He gestured to the horse. "Run along if you wish. You're nothing but a waste of time and magic for me, though you would be wise to be afraid. I've never lost a fight."

Blair scowled as she moved beside him with Queriven leaning on her once again. She helped him in the saddle then climbed up in front of him. Darkadus watched them without interrupting. "I just thought I should remind you how pointless this is. I smashed the horn to bits. You may ask Queriven about that if you wish. You're already falling into the curse. Even if you can find another way around it, it's too late to act. You have no time left before the change in autumn."

Blair sped the horse into a quick trot without a response back. That left Darkadus quickly fading behind in the distance, watching them. Then he turned and headed back to the watchtower.

Blair rode back to the road, a silent dread in her soul. She tried to take comfort as her dear friend was safely behind her, but she feared Darkadus was right. She was already doomed to the curse and the only thing she achieved today was making sure Queriven would survive after the deadline. With him safe, she was ready for the future, whatever that would mean.

The dark clouds were finally parting, revealing a golden twilight sky. The two were quiet for the longest time. The watchtower was nothing but a memory. It's only been a few hours since Blair broke her friend from the place, but it already seemed like a long time.

She knew after a strained groan from Queriven that is was time to stop. Blair slowed the horse to a walk and looked for a comfortable place to stay off the road. She settled with a location quickly and took the horse far enough to be invisible from the road. Then, she helped Queriven to dismount and he laid down in the grass.

A shock rolled through her when she noticed the condition of the bandaged leg. The escape must have reopened the wound as dark crimson seeped through the wrap. "Oh no!" Blair cried as the elf winced again. "I pushed you too hard. I'm so sorry!" She took a deep breath to steady herself. "What can we do? Should we continue to Dunverhart? It's not much further."

"No," Queriven answered through clenched teeth. "We can't risk being arrested again."

Already, Blair was going down a mental list of the things they would need. Luckily, she had spare bandages with her. "We can't treat it with medicine after Darkadus ran off with all your equipment."

Queriven pushed himself up and began searching through his pockets. "He didn't take all of it." Finally finding what he was looking for, Queriven tossed a wrapped object on the grass. "I'm going to need your help, Blair. Clean the wound, treat it with a mixture of those herbs, and wrap it back up."

Blair's eyes widened. She never imagined he would seek her help in this, but she didn't complain. She sank to the grass and took out a clean rag. *All right*, she whispered to herself. She gathered her courage and unknotted the bandage before carefully removing it. Blood was already pouring from the wound. It spilled into the edges of the ripped fabric and gathered in a pool on the grass. It was worse than she thought. Blair pressed her hand to her mouth and tried not to be sick. The arrow caused a lot of damage to the muscles. She hesitated for only a short moment and finally pressed the rag against the wound.

"I've got it," Queriven said, taking the cloth from her shaking hand. "Mix the herbs I gave you."

Blair obeyed without question and took the wrapped bundle and bowl from him. She added the plants and broke them apart. Once she blended them to a gooey pulp, she applied them to the wound and took out a fresh bandage, wrapping his leg back tightly. She shook her head as he groaned again. The stress of tending his leg was over for now, but she was still a little lightheaded. "Will it heal back completely?"

"The herbs will help speed it along, but it's still going to take time, though that's something we don't have."

Blair sat back with the bloody rag still in hand. Not like that mattered anyway. There was nothing for them to do now.

Queriven sighed and laid a hand on the injured leg. He tried to clear the pained look on his face, though it remained. "We'll find something. We always do. If there was one way to summon Rocanu, there'll be another one."

Blair gave him a broken smile and looked down at his bruised and swollen wrists. She knew he was only trying to cheer her up, but it wasn't working. Instead, she changed the subject. "Is there something I can do for your wrists?"

He looked down and examined them. "They're not as bad. You've done everything you could, and I thank you." He gave it another look before dropping it again. "The herb that would help them the most is *lininea*, or mulicer to the humans, which I don't have anymore."

"Mulicer?" Blair pondered aloud. "My mother grew those in her garden once. It's a tall white flower. They're in season if I remember right." Her eyes lit up. "I bet I can find some here. I'll like to go look."

Queriven turned his head. The wince in his eyes was finally replaced by fatigue. "I forgot you knew a lot about flowers," he marveled. But before he could tell her not to worry, Blair excitedly stood up.

Before leaving him, she laid out a wrap in the grass and handed him some bread and water, telling him to rest and wait for her to return. Queriven relented, crawling into a comfortable position after she ran off.

Blair fell into her thoughts as they slowly constricted her. She didn't even know how tired she was herself, but a lot of stress hit her at once and she began to crumble. The world was quickly changing around her. In her heart was a mess of emotions. They clashed like cymbals and made her want to sing and cry all at once.

They've come so far. She couldn't even believe she rescued Queriven on her own like that. She was certainly more capable of defending herself. Yet, she was already defeated. The reality of her surroundings was too strong for her to grasp. The true face of Darkadus sat in her thoughts like an ugly blister. She didn't want to think of that man behind the disguise she met him in. Blair could hear him ask her to run away with him and she nearly gasped in disgust. He was the man who cursed her.

Blair shook the hair from her shoulders and looked down at the mulicer she carried in her hands. Best not to think much about it, she thought. Darkadus was a monster. Why should she bother herself with him? All that she had to worry about was the curse. Despite the growing fears, she tried to hold her head up high.

Summer was already beginning. Was it really too late to try a new lead? There wasn't even a lead for her to take now anyway.

A tired sigh escaped her lips and she returned to the clearing. "Queriven," she announced with a little less enthusiasm than she had before. "I find some mulicer. What should I do now?"

But no answer came to her. Blair turned around to the wrap and saw Queriven lying down, asleep. The gentle rising and falling of his chest comforted her, and she chose not to wake him. Instead, she set the flower next to the bowl and sat down in the grass. The light green plants were soft and young and the evening air was warm and pleasant.

For a long moment, she watched her lush surroundings. A few early crickets began chiming a night song, and nearby bushes rustled with activities of new, fluffy animals. Blair watched a glimmering sap ooze from the stem of the mulicer, then her heavy eyes fell back to Queriven. He seemed so peaceful. This was the first time she's ever seen him sleep. Either being locked up twice in chains totally exhausted him or he trusted her more than he used to. Blair decided both were likely. After all, he wasn't nearly as defensive with her as he was once before. He even allowed her to change the bandage on the wound.

She sighed again, but this time, she breathed out her problems and tried to relax as he did. She wanted to crawl closer to him, just to be near. She wanted the comfort of his presence. She wanted to take in the aroma of plants he carried on him and listen to each deep breath he added to the noise of dusk.

Instead, she looked down at the grass and caught a glimpse of the cursed mark on her wrist. There, she found something new tugging at her interest. A second strand was lighter than the other. It was slowly fading away. That's odd. Maybe she didn't see it right? She lifted her hand in the better light shining through the fresh leaves to see it better. There was no denying it. It was disappearing. That will leave only a single strand left.

She wanted to be happy about this, but it only left her mind more chained up than ever. She breathed deep past the tension and laid her head down, wishing for the escape in sleep.

Blair awoke in the exact place she fell asleep in, though a ray of light beamed right in her face. She blinked and sat up. Her sleep was mostly of a restful deep nothingness, though as she refocused back into the real world, she remembered seeing a memory of chasing a stranger into the woods near the lake. It played out exactly the way she remembered it last fall, but this time, the stranger was Darkadus, not the fake Queriven.

Disturbed that she once thought she loved that intruder, she tried to think about something else. Then she found the real Queriven. He was right where she left him. He was still asleep, though he moved from his original position.

Blair stood up and yawned, taking time to stretch before deciding to fetch some fresh water. When she came back, Queriven was already on the verge of waking up. Blair was a little surprised as she thought he would be sleeping for the rest of the day. His elvish eyes opened and he looked up at the trees before looking at her. He was still lying down inside the wrap. The edges went up to his shoulders. "Good morning," he greeted before he regarded the sky once more, "if it really is morning already."

"Did you have enough rest?" Blair returned. "How do you feel?"

Queriven looked like he wasn't sure at first, then he sat up and looked around before rubbing his face. "Still tired, like I'll never wake up properly again." He carefully moved the blanket back to reveal a bandage stained in blood. There wasn't much like there was last night, but it was still more than Blair wanted. "Hurts quite a bit too," he concluded. Then his face dropped to the grass. "I see you found the mulicer. I'm impressed."

Blair approached and kneeled over, undoing the bandage and bringing back the rag and the bowl to treat it. Queriven noted her solemn expression as she tended his leg. From the look in her eye, he knew she was losing strength again. Lightheartedly, Queriven joked past a spark of pain. "Something about all this seems familiar, but I remember you being in my place right now," he continued, but she didn't regard him. "The funny thing is how cold you were back then. I'm glad we've both learned a lesson since."

She breathed out and finally met his eyes, her hand still dabbing softly on his leg. "I wanted to apologize for that time. You were just trying to help and I was nothing but mean and hurtful then."

"No harm was done," he swiftly answered. "You learned the truth quickly."

Blair dropped the rag aside. "Not fast enough. I had all the evidence to know he wasn't the real you, but I was just so mad I didn't want to see it." Neither of them said anything else until Blair finished treating the wound. Next, she brought the mulicer to his reach.

Finally, she spoke, the memory of Darkadus pressing too hard on her mind to ignore. "He said he knew you, the rokian.

He said he was there when you left the forest."

There was a horrifying spark in Queriven's mind and he looked away. Focusing on the mulicer again, he pressed the sap from the stem and shredded the petals between his light fingers.

Blair noted the hesitation and fought back, growing concerned. "Do you know him? I don't want to believe what he told me before I hear your side of it."

Again, the answer took too long. Finally, his eyes lifted and met hers. Blair watched him carefully, but couldn't read the mystery in his eyes. In his heart, Queriven was trying to decide what the best answer would be. "I... I don't have a clue."

Blair leaned closer, as if she didn't catch his reply.

Queriven repeated his response and went back to the broken mulicer. The elf's voice was slow and unsure. "I suppose he thinks there's a connection because he's worn that disguise for so long."

Blair sat back and pondered. "But he described you as a monster. He said you left your friends in a losing battle."

The notion struck the heart, making it skip a beat long enough to kill him from inside. Queriven shook his head and nearly dropped the flower from his hands. "He lies. He's only trying to turn you away from me." Queriven tossed the plant aside and took the sappy moisture to his wrists. "I don't know who he is and I most definitely didn't know him before I left the forest."

Blair was unsure herself, but she wanted to trust him. Perhaps, there was a shred of truth somewhere. Maybe Darkadus was telling more lies, trying to paint a bad image of the elf. "I believe you," she answered out loud. Queriven was a dear friend to her now. She trusted him. After everything they've been through, she figured he deserved as much.

He nodded absentmindedly, though her trusting spirit hurt him. He couldn't do it. He couldn't tell her the truth. He was just too ashamed of the experience himself.

Several hours passed and the two have barely said a thing. Queriven stood from his place in the grass a few times, though he limped every time he did so. Blair provided more bread for him later and she sat beside him again.

Queriven studied her before taking the first bite. He was still trying his best to move on from the previous conversation they had. "Something is different, but I don't know what. Besides the curse, what's bothering you?"

There it was, that connection between them. Somehow, Queriven knew when to break the brooding silence. It was her first cue to the intruder's false identity. "There's so much all at once," Blair lamented, allowing her heart to spill before him. "The curse, the loss of the horn, the kidnapping. Yet, on top of it all, I fear I can never return back to what I once was, even if my family was before me."

Queriven's eyes regarded her for a moment and swallowed. "Well, we already knew that. You spoke about it before."

"But it's different!" she snapped back. "I killed people in that last battle."

"Ah!" Queriven exclaimed. "You did what you had to. I've killed many people in my days in the military. Some of those faces still haunt me. It broke me down the first time I had to do it. You have to remember your reason for fighting."

"I was afraid you'll say that..." Blair slumped, her shoulders rolling forward and dipping a head full of thick hair over her face. Her response was deep and full of regret. "None of this is worth it. I'm only fighting for myself. Why would it matter if I just disappeared?"

"Don't say that!" Queriven answered, jumping forward in his seat on the wrap. He thought back to the uncomfortable watchtower. He knew now why she was important in all this. He had to tell her something even if it wasn't going to be about his past. "This is bigger than you! I don't claim to know everything about this, but Darkadus has his reasons for cursing you."

He failed to retrieve her attention. Desperate, like he was about to lose her forever, he came close and gently grabbed her arm. "We must stop the curse," Queriven stated strongly. "If it takes you, you replace Darkadus and his kin. They'll come back to Fairdraisha. All the work of the vayen aray would be lost. Not only that, but they won't be here to help lock them away a second time."

She was fighting back tears when she looked at him again. "He wants to release the rokians?"

Satisfied she understood, the elf nodded. "He claims his new generation is a better people, but if they were fine with a bounding curse on an innocent, then I'm not too convinced. If Darkadus can do this with no regrets, what will he do to the people here? Blair, we're fighting for more than your future; we're fighting for the world at this point."

She wiped her face with her fingers and refocused, matching him eye to eye. "So I'm not the only one in danger? My family is involved in this too?"

"As is the rest of Fairdraisha, if not bigger."

Blair blinked and Queriven retracted, returning to his previous seat. As the message sank, Blair remained quiet. Then, like she wasn't exactly aiming anything toward anyone, a spark of confusion hit. "Why me then? There are bigger cities and thousands of people here. Why would he pick me?" She looked away and tried to stem her discomfort by picking at a blade of green grass. "It doesn't make sense. Why was I tuned to that horn he had?"

Queriven answered immediately. "Because he was looking for a particular bloodline. The only one who could free him from that dead world is if he takes a human descendant from the line of witnesses who betrayed the vayen aray's trust. He said your family was the last."

"My family?" Blair echoed. She couldn't even process the shock properly. Her thoughts jumbled up in a string of chaos. "That would explain why my father reacted to it too." She sat up straight again. "I knew my bloodline's been here for a long time, but I didn't know we had that kind of history. What do we do about this?"

With a strong certainty, he answered, "We make sure he doesn't succeed."

Blair only shrugged. "How can we do that? We don't even know what to do."

"First, we need to be able to return to the road. That means my wound has to heal even if it heals just well enough to ride. We need to extend our distance from that tower before someone goes looking for us. Second, we find another way to summon Rocanu and act quickly."

Blair rose to her feet and dusted off her clothes. "Sounds like it'll take too long."

Queriven didn't budge. "It'll be faster than you think."

That brought a more genuine smile to her face this time. "I hope so. Thank you for your support. I wouldn't have made it this far without you."

The elf returned the smile but wished he could do more past his lies.

CHAPTER TWENTY-TWO
A DANGEROUS GOAL

Queriven was right; the next step came quicker than Blair thought it would, and it came in the most unexpected way imaginable.

Two quiet days passed since their conversation. Queriven walked as much as he could, though he was wise not to push his limits. His leg was already looking better. It was hardly bleeding when Blair cleaned it. Finally, he decided to try riding. Blair allowed it, though she had the paint walking slowly at first. When Queriven didn't show any pain, she took it to a trot.

The dirt road was only a few minutes away. Once there, they talked about what they should do. They both spoke of Lyfíhana, but it just wasn't an option anymore because of the approaching deadline. The only option remained with research or a return to the scholar, Aen Vidwal, who knew more about rokian curses than anyone.

"I'm worried about being caught in Dunverhart," Queriven stated behind her. "Let's go right through it and not enter the main part of the city."

Blair agreed and they rode on.

In this time of year, with the bountiful season of summer just beginning, the roads were busy with many caravans and wagons as people carried goods from one place to another.

This road was no exemption, and Blair and Queriven remained cautious of each traveler.

The red and white paint snorted shyly when Blair tugged on the reigns again, making him sidestep off the path. An open-faced caravan was coming closer. Blair immediately recognized it. "I can't believe it. That's Anita and her gang."

Queriven started, confused as Blair kicked the horse forward again. Even though he said nothing, she reassured him as they came out from hiding. "Don't worry. I know these people."

Fergus hesitated and slowed the caravan upon seeing them. "Hey!" Blair called, catching everyone's attention. "Fergus! It's Blair. Remember me?"

There was a spark in Kain's eye and he stood up in the stopped platform. "Of course, we do. You stayed with us for a while last fall. How are you?"

Blair stopped the horse against the side of the caravan and met the riders directly. "I'm... Surviving so far. Everything all right?"

Kain looked back with content lining his face. "We're doing great. Thanks for asking." He took a step before sitting on the seat opposite him as to be closer to the two riders. "Did you visit with Vidwal? My wife told me you were suffering from some kind of curse?"

She could feel Queriven's eyes piercing the back of her head, but she couldn't imagine what he might be thinking right now. "Uh, yeah, I did. He was quite helpful."

Anita's voice popped up before them. "He is a little confusing at times, but I'm glad you found him all right. So are you free now?"

Blair shrank back, not knowing how to answer. As much as she trusted the group, she found herself wondering if they still really believed a rokian cursed her or not. Still, she decided to continue being honest. "No, well... I'm working on it. He told me only the vayen aray could break it. I had to act out a bond between them and the humans with an old artifact, but I guess..."

"I know of the bond," Anita chimed. "They gave us a horn to

call them with. It was a symbol of friendship. A powerful bond indeed. They did similar events for all their allies, including the elves of the Aven Forest."

That caught the attention of both riders on the horse. "What?!" Blair breathed, nearly falling from her perch on the horse's back.

The passengers on the open caravan regarded her reaction like they've deeply offended her. "The elves are allies of the vayen aray," Anita repeated. "They were also given an artifact with the same purpose."

A hot mix of renewed hope and anger burned in her. Of course, why didn't she see it before? The horn Darkadus stole from Queriven was that exact artifact. She already knew it was made by vayen aray, but she didn't consider it was also a gift. If that event was like the one in Dyara, then perhaps there's a site in the forest as well. She could summon Rocanu from there.

Blair blinked. The group of musicians was still regarding her quietly. She spoke simply to break the tension. "I didn't know that about them."

Kain nodded and Blair suddenly felt like an idiot. "Thank you for stopping for a while," she said, not knowing what else to say. "It was great to see you again. We'll be on our way."

Anita smiled more genuine than awkward. "We wish you the best," she replied and Fergus took that as a farewell. He urged the horses to pick up the pace again.

"Oh, I almost forgot!" Blair cried, looking back at the curious eyes on her. The caravan stopped again. "Vidwal wanted another show from you. He told me that was the only thing he wanted for his help."

Lynny broke into laughter and Kain shook his head. "Ah, what a character. All right, we'll make sure to stop by at some point."

She thanked them and continued on the road. The sound of turning wheels behind grew quieter until it wasn't there after a while.

For such a breakthrough in her quest, the two on the horse

shared no discussion. At first, Blair was still trying to grasp the reality of what she heard, but then, she realized something wasn't right. As usual, she expected Queriven to speak first, perhaps even speaking one of her unspoken thoughts, but there was nothing.

She couldn't see him well enough by turning her head, so she stopped the horse and adjusted her position to see him better. The elf had his head lowered, but his gaze snapped to her after a second. Blair didn't remember ever seeing him so pale, as if the blood in his face drained out. "The Aven Forest. That's our next step," Blair said evenly. She finally gave in and spoke first since he didn't. Queriven opened his mouth, seemingly to protest, but he shut it before a single word came out. A discomfort seeped into Blair's mind. The elf has been away from that place for twenty years. With a subtle fear, she wondered if he would go through with it. "Are you all right?"

The elf merely blinked and looked away.

"I know it's been a long time since you've been there, but I think this is our last hope. I want to take this chance."

"It's better if we didn't," he mumbled quietly, still refusing to look at her. "They should think me dead. It's better if I stay that way."

The notion slapped Blair in the face. She stared with her mouth agape. Of all the things he's never shared about his life among his own kind, Blair never expected she would hear those words from him. "What do you mean by that?"

Queriven snapped his head around angrily. "Forget it. It doesn't matter."

But Blair wasn't ready to change the subject this time. "But it does!" she yelled back, startling him enough to draw his eyes on her. "You told me this concerns the entirety of the continent, if not the whole world! If we don't go, I may never return." In a heartbeat, there was internal turmoil in his face and she flinched. "We struggle together. This time is no different."

Nothing changed in his expression and he looked away again. "We're wasting time. Let's be going."

Blair refused. She was angry with him now. "So that's it? You're just giving up and letting me go alone?"

He tried to respond several times, but when he couldn't, he inhaled a large breath and shook his head. "I can't go back there" was his only response.

Blair huffed. This was important. She couldn't let this one go. When she spoke, her voice was deep and rough. "And why not? What happened that was so terrible you can't return home for two decades?"

Queriven flinched and looked away yet again. He was terrified. Blair's never seen anything like this before. "Well? Aren't you going to say anything?"

He didn't fight with her. "I can't."

Without thinking over her argument, Blair barked at him. "So why did you come this far?!" she yelled. Queriven blinked and shrank back. Blair was usually quiet and sweet. Seeing her yell such accusations was new to him. "You fought the pirates over the winter ocean to save me, came along to help me find a cure for my curse, and even stole an artifact from the King of Fairdraisha. You did all of this without a lot of motive and we were strangers when you first saved me. Now all of a sudden, you're calling quits?!"

Understandably, Queriven didn't answer. Like usual, he wanted nothing more than to run away, or at least dismount and get away from her. If it wasn't for the pain in his thigh, he would have, but he knew it would only make this worse. He wanted to give himself a better excuse, but that would have angered Blair further. He stayed quiet. The last thing Queriven wanted was to give up on the mission, especially now. They've been working on lifting her curse for so long. He didn't want her to fall victim to Darkadus. He never wanted that in the first place, but certainly not now.

At the same time, it was hard for him to come back and help knowing that Darkadus is the one who cursed her. That alone was personal to him, and now it was worse. At least, he was already expecting to face the rokian one way or another. He never thought he would be asked to go back to the Aven Forest. "It's asking too much of me to go back. It became too personal."

Blair gasped. His delayed words were like a sharp weapon he jabbed in her heart. After everything that happened, he didn't care about her outcome anymore. She turned her head away, tears on the brink of dripping from her eyes. She spurred the horse on and tried to move beyond the hurt of his statement.

For Queriven, dusk didn't arrive soon enough. They safely stopped many miles from Dunverhart. Blair helped prepare supper and set up camp. Queriven, though he didn't refuse her company like she thought he would, still didn't eat or talk much. He didn't seem nearly as upset about this than she thought he would be. He still refused to talk about it, but his calm behavior stood out like a flag. Would he make the mistake of running again? She dismissed the idea. He was better than that now.

After cleaning up, Blair laid out the bedrolls, though the pleasant evening made her think she may not need a lot of covers tonight. She looked up and caught Queriven staring at the sky. The first twinkling stars were just starting to appear in a canvas of dark blue and pink.

Blair was still uncomfortable from their discussion earlier. She regarded him with turned lips and sorrowful eyes. She broke away without a word and climbed in the wrap.

Queriven was almost too scared to look at her. In the end, he didn't need to because he could feel the unpleasant emotions in the air. He didn't know what to do about all this, but her pain was beginning to affect him. He slowly stood up and limped closer. He didn't want to turn in for the night just yet, but he didn't want to remain standing either. So he slowly sat down on a mound of dirt and faced her. Blair was trying to ignore the fact that he was looking at her. The damage was done. Nothing he said now will help her.

He spoke anyway. "You're still planning on going, aren't you?"

Blair didn't look at him. Her lips were taut and her eyes looked the furthest away she could. She tried to control the sound of her voice to make sure she wouldn't cry before him.

"Of course, I have no choice." The question was stupid for sure, but she knew he was just trying to strike up another chance to talk.

Her answer was legitimate. Queriven knew she really would go out there on her own if she had to. He hesitated and tried to use a minute to think of something helpful. Despite their failing friendship, he thought maybe he could give her hope. "You and I both know we'll need the horn Darkadus has to break your curse. Should we set off and find that first?"

Blair silently wished he would leave her alone, but she didn't want to push him away just yet. She answered the question. "No. Darkadus always has it with him. With his powers, I don't think we can take it from him without a plan. We'll have to set up a trap, and even if it works, he'll know it was us. We'll have to break the curse right away after taking it." For the first time after Queriven's hurtful words, Blair finally looked at him. There was a spark in her eye he wished he could connect with again. "It'll be better to find where the vayen aray made that bond first. Once we have everything we need, we can then focus on grabbing the horn."

Queriven rolled back with awe. She already had a strong plan made up. This was not the same girl who found herself in trouble all the time without his help. He only wished he could be as powerful as her. Blair noted the way he slumped over, and for some reason, she wanted to apologize to him. There was no reason to because she was right. Still, her mind was on him now and she pushed herself up. Her long hair flowed with each motion. "The Aven Forest is a dangerous place for humans. None of them ever made it through the wilderness without an elvish guide." She didn't have to tell him this, of course. He already knew. "Queriven, I need you."

Once again, he shied away from her, wishing he could just disappear. Blair's heart broke again. "It's not going to be easy, but I'm sure we can push through this together no matter what happens. Don't you remember what you told me before the pirates attacked? You said you either move on with your life or you don't. No matter what happened in your past, I promise I will not judge you for it."

A hurt beyond comprehension showed on his face and he scoffed with frustration. Blair was expecting him to back out then, but he didn't. "To state it simply, my family gave me everything and I took them for granted. My fellow soldiers held me up with respect and support, and I let them down. I was nothing but selfish and prideful, thinking only of myself even with all the love around me. I couldn't see the errors of my ways until it was too late. I don't deserve such compassion from them; I never did."

Blair furrowed her eyebrows. "So... What Darkadus said was right?"

"No!" the elf yelled. He regretted it instantly seeing as how Blair was already bothered. He took a steady breath and spoke again. "But I deserve no less than exile. That may have been my sentence anyway. I won't ask for forgiveness. My actions were too much for that."

Conflict arose in Blair's head. She respected Queriven and saw him as one of the strongest people she knew. Was she wrong about him? "You're a fool to think that."

She stunned him breathless for a second. His face went blank and he opened his mouth, but Blair interrupted him. "You should never assume those things, especially when it comes to family. Forgiveness is never out of the question for anybody, no matter what they did. I've done things I wasn't too proud of as well, but I never ran from it because I knew they would love me anyway." There was a tight scowl on her face now, and she balled her fist. "This whole time you've been running away because you were afraid of being sent into exile? What if that wasn't the sentence?"

The elf suddenly wished he never spoke to her. His heart pounded and his face grew red. Queriven frowned and pounded a fist in the dirt before looking away. "I don't care if that was the sentence. I couldn't face them anyway! Like I said, I was selfish and proud."

Blair was back on the brink of tears. Watching him was only making it worse. She waited for something else to come up, but when nothing did, she softly asked him a question. "So what are you going to do now? Are you leaving?"

Queriven was honest. He stood up again with a quiet groan. He didn't like the disappointment written on Blair's face. "I don't know. I need to think." His unfinished tone suggested he wanted to say something else, but he couldn't. So that marked the end of this discussion and his face dropped as he marched away, like he usually did when he was mad or upset.

Now that she was finally alone, Blair could let her tears free. She laid down her head again and cried. Even if he did leave, she would go to Aven Forest by herself. There was no decision for her to make. She shut her eyes and wished sleep would take her quickly so she could forget her approaching deadline and her emotions over the argument. A part of her still wished she could chase him down and change his mind, but she decided against it. This was his choice to make. She couldn't force this on him.

Eventually, her mind was restful enough for her to fall asleep, but it was hardly the forgetful abyss she wanted it to be. She hasn't slept like this since her first few days away from home, where she heard every second ticking away. It only secured her to her doom. It made for a long night, to the point where she was glad to wake up to the sunrise.

But that hardly brought her any relief when she rose to her feet. Queriven was still gone along with his bed wrap. He wasn't planning on coming back. Looks like he finally came to his answer.

In the midst of a breath, Blair realized there was something in place of his wrap; a single white flower placed carefully on the grass. Blair bent her stiff knees to pick it up. It smelled of sweet syrup. She couldn't see it from away, but closer up she saw thin stripes of lavender on the petals.

Holding the mulicer close, she breathed and looked to the still dark western horizon, wondering if she would ever see Queriven again. Wherever he may be, she wished him a better future, one filled with less hurt and more joy...

CHAPTER TWENTY-THREE
LOST IN THE EASTERN FOREST

Going to the Aven Forest alone was suicide. Blair would become entangled in the overgrowth until death or the curse took her, but she had no other choice without just giving up like her elven companion did. She still thought this was a better alternative anyway.

The red and white paint was strong and loyal, and she stroked the thick neck to keep herself from seeing Queriven's eyes. The pain of betrayal stayed long after she left the morning she found the mulicer. She didn't cry again after he left nor did she think about turning around. She was a fighter now. She liked to think she might have a chance at reaching an elven city in the forest.

"Come on. Let's be on our way," she whispered, giving the horse's neck a pat. The already thin fur was shedding. It was going to be a hot summer.

The forest was far, and she spent many restless nights growing lonely without her once trusted friend. When he left, he took with him a piece of her soul, leaving Blair with a hole in her heart. The air felt empty and meaningless.

She rode toward the border of the elven kingdom as much as she could. Though when it finally came in view many days later, she was hardly any different. The horse snorted, drawing out her focus. He's been working hard and the thickening air foretold yet another rain shower. The ground was still moist from the last one and the horse was sweating from humidity.

Blair wiped off her own damp head and continued along.

From afar, it looked nothing more but a thick span of trees covering the eastern edge like a vast green sea, but with it carried suspicion. From here, she could smell the foreign soil.

Not a lot of people of Fairdraisha came this close to the border, though she wasn't sure why. Maybe they didn't know either. It was clear their relationship wasn't close. Elves weren't supposed to be on human soil and neither were humans supposed to be on theirs. As for the border, it was like either race was nervous to approach it. Therefore, nature grew wild and uncultured here. In some places, the grass was so tall it itched at Blair's ankles. She resisted the urge to scratch her legs as the horse trotted.

The trees were becoming more common along this trail, along with buzzing beetles and other bothersome insects. She could smell rushing water not far south. It was then when she noticed something rather unique about the trees ahead. She couldn't tell before, but compared to these trees, the ones in the forest seemed mystic. Many were taller than possible. They were thicker and stronger and rich in colors of hearty browns and fruitful greens. What would the Aven Forest look like in winter or even autumn?

It wasn't soon after when another sight stole her concentration. For an overgrown trail taken almost completely by nature and animals, there was what may have been a formation made by human or elven hands.

Blair frowned and slowed the horse to a stop. The trail took them right through it, and it looked like it had influences in both human and elvish design. The dirt path went right through an old broken gate attached to a tall stone wall that wrapped around the entire site. There were two trees on either side of her, right outside the wall. At first, she noticed they were impossibly wide and tall; no tree could naturally grow to this size. Then, she saw something in it further up. Was that a window carved right into the tree? It was, and she could see a circling staircase inside. Looking at the leaves, Blair thought there were several perches where someone could stand to see a clear view. Obviously, this was an elf's make. Blair lowered her gaze back to the ground, finding herself quite dizzy from looking so high. Those trees reminded her of Queriven's little sanctuary. Not only was a tree part of the wall, but he also carved enough inside to make it a closet. Blair supposed that type of sculpting was typical of his race.

The horse was walking again, but slow enough for Blair to inspect and look around. Here looked to be an old fire pit, and there a stable made from sanded wood, though it was almost buried in plants and tall grass. There was also a fenced-in field where the horses could run. The fence reminded her of the belt around her armor. It was the same tightly sown, green fibers.

Then came the houses...

There weren't very many of them nor were there a lot of shops, but someone lived here. It was like a tiny village. The homes were falling apart, however. Roofs were caved in and moss and animals were taking over. There were also a few ripped tents, a dried well, and some more tree towers.

Blair turned her head to the left and a sudden tug on the reins stopped the horse yet again. Before her laid a huge stone garrison. Despite traveling vines making their way up the walls between the cracks, it wasn't nearly as destroyed as most other things here.

Struck with awe and curiosity, Blair dismounted the horse. Something important was being protected here, but what? With all the tents and wagons, this didn't look like much of a town at all, but someone was staying here long enough to build houses.

What was the purpose of this place and why was it abandoned? This was obviously a place for both elves and humans. Perhaps, that's why nature was taking over. Elves and humans no longer interact with each other. That answered one question, but she still had many others.

A part of her wanted to investigate, but she was so

determined in her mission she decided not to. The Aven Forest will be thick and deadly. She wanted to go through it as quickly and safely as possible.

Blair tore her gaze away from the moss-lined stone walls and focused again on the forest. It reeked of mystery, the kind that made Blair shrink in fear. She still couldn't believe her elvish friend would leave her alone to deal with this when he knew how to go through the right way. As upset as she was about it, she still couldn't help but feel a little sympathetic toward him. She couldn't hate him after everything she's been through with him.

She didn't realize it, but she was stroking the thick shoulder muscles of the horse. She swallowed the bitter taste in her mouth. The forest would be no place for him, but she wished she could keep his company. Alas, she knew she wouldn't have a need for him there. He'll only be killed or trapped likely the same way she would.

Blair sighed and began unstrapping the saddle and bridle from him. She quietly whispered love and wishes to him. He only picked at the grass and snorted. The skin over his back shuddered when he realized the confining equipment was gone. Blair buried her face into his fur one last time before encouraging him to go on freely. The animal didn't go very far back, but she was satisfied and went on without him. She was aware of him watching her until she disappeared in the trees.

Blair stepped each step as carefully and quietly as she could. She tried to keep her hands and legs from trembling. She wanted to think back on what she read in her books about this part of the kingdom, but she knew by now she couldn't really rely on it. After all, she thought she knew everything about elves without really seeing one. Queriven was often very different from what she's learned from books. She'd figured by now the forest would be the same way.

Suppose it was really the only thing she had to go on. Not a lot of the books would state exactly what was in the forest, as the people who entered never came back, but she knew it was dangerous. Even Queriven agreed with that. The only thing she knew was that there were a lot of monsters as well as magic in this area. Everything was a potential hazard here — the trees, the plants, vines, water, and branches. Just about anything could be aggressive or enchanted.

She couldn't exactly place it, but this forest was unlike any she's ever visited. The trees seemed to be talking about her behind her back. Everything was so tight together. The sunlight couldn't reach much of the ground. Time didn't make sense, but it always seemed to be late afternoon before the colors of sunset here. Blair knew it must be no later than late morning, though the time she's spent here was also blurred.

Blair couldn't help but feel as if the entire forest was alive. She was constantly under the impression she was being watched. There was a rhythm lining the air, though she heard no music. There was a rustle or a dash of movement with every turn of her head. Blair flexed her fingers and stood on her toes. She very well could have eyes on her this very second. So far, she's encountered nothing strange or mystical, but she was already wanting to draw her spear.

She tried to ignore the fact that she was already lost and had no idea which way she was going now. She'd figured that if she just went straight, everything will be all right, but her worry about her environment made her lose her sense of direction.

The Aven Forest was a different world entirely. But even at that, she never once imagined it to be anything like this. Just like how Darkadus warped her mind into thinking elves were more magical than they were, her impression of the forest was just the same.

She brought up her hand to rub her stressed eyes. The aroma of the forest blended with the thick and moist air. This place was so overgrown and unnatural. It was almost too much to be called a forest. Did she still have a chance at finding civilization? She tried to not think too hard on the answer.

It was too late now. She'll either make it to the city or she will die out here.

Blair must have been going crazy, but she thought the forest was showing a little more color the more she walked. She couldn't really understand it, but it was like a muted flowing light of reds, greens, blues, and others. There were even a few sparks around them that caught her attention. None of it was really affecting; her that she could tell, so she continued on. But was she even moving? She couldn't help but feel like one step in front of the other was not doing anything. It was like the ground and trees were moving around her instead. The forest was in control. There was nothing she could do to fight against it. It already swallowed her too far in.

Finally, something different happened. At first, Blair thought this was just another alien occurrence within the forest, but then she recognized a face looking at her from a thick trunk. The head of the little man was about the size of a fingernail. His ears were taller and more pointed than Queriven's, and his hair was spiked and dirty, though he didn't seem to care. His face was also painted with different patterns and colors. For such a small being, he had good muscles. Blair froze and stared back at him. His expression was also one of interest and confusion. A clear wingtip appeared around the tree. Then she realized this was some sort of fairy.

Blair couldn't help but be a little disappointed despite seeing one for the first time. She wished it was one of those crystal animals. That would be much more helpful. Isn't this the type of place they would come to help her through anyway?

Blair kept her distance and watched the curious fairy carefully. There were many different types of fairies in the world, including many dangerous ones. She had no idea what his intentions were, or even if he had any at all.

The two must have stared at each other for several minutes, then the fairy came out of his place behind the tree. Blair withdrew her spear, but she didn't need to use it. A light bubbling voice spurred from the fairy's mouth, but it was in a language she couldn't understand. He seemed to be asking a question. Blair bit her lip and let her hair fall to one side. He didn't seem very dangerous, or at least, he wasn't trying to hurt her.

Blair soon picked up her feet again and walked around him. He let her go on with another questioning chirp and flew a few inches behind her. Then, she turned her head and told him she had no idea what he was saying. She already knew the feeling was mutual.

The little fairy continued to follow a little distance behind her. With every silent thought, Blair wondered what he wanted and why he kept following her. She became more and more nervous as time went on and wondered if she should chase him away. It didn't matter in the end, because the few times she tried she knew he still followed her just a little further away. After a while, she gave up and ignored him.

The sparkling clear wings quickly became a normal sound she expected to hear behind her. She prayed this was the only interest he had with her. But if she was still worried about him, she would soon find something else a little more intriguing.

There was something moving again up ahead, but it was bigger than an animal or fairy. It was a young man just standing in the middle of the forest. Then, as she came closer, she realized he was holding out his hand for her. Another bout of hesitation caused her to exclaim her emotions. "Queriven!? What are you doing here?"

The elf smiled and came closer. Blair's eyes burned from the air and she rejoiced at the idea to leave the terrible wilderness. "Blair," he answered, still holding out his slender arm. "This way."

Blair held out her own hand. Her heart was leaping up to the sky. He came back for her. Her safety was important to him after all. But yet again, she hesitated. Why did he come back and how did he find her? Still, the image of him standing before her made her relaxed and happy. When he asked her to go with him again, she couldn't resist.

He took a gentle hold on her wrist and redirected her a little to the right. She had no idea what direction they were going now. Queriven was also going pretty slow, and it seemed like he was pulling her a little closer to him. When he turned to her, his expression was serious and calm. She couldn't take her gaze away. She allowed him to pull her in closer.

Finally, the forest began to move again. It was like they were leaving the ring she's been running in. The light was pooling down with sunshine. It was fresh and breathable. Blair sighed. The songs of birds were playing out above them, and Blair took note of several normal-looking animals skittering to and fro. It was like she was under a delusion after all. Maybe the forest wasn't as alien as she first thought. It was very beautiful. Soon after, she could hear the voice of a bubbling stream.

Blair looked to the side at the determined elf. He had a goal in mind judging from his unwavering stare ahead. Only once did he look back and smile warmly at her. She wanted to voice a question to him, but she didn't know where to start. In the end, she wanted to enjoy their resurrected friendship quietly. She will ask about the city once they reach it.

She was unaware now of the fluttering fairy still following her. His almond-shaped eyes were complete circles and he rested a finger over his lips as he flew. He zigzagged ahead and watched as much as he could.

If Queriven noticed the fairy far behind Blair, he didn't show it. The stream was rounding the last few mystical trees. Clean water ran and spilled over many rocks. The stream wasn't very gentle, but it wasn't too rough either. Blair took in the smell of the wet soil and stone, but she stopped when Queriven continued his slow walk ahead. He was only about ankle deep now, and he turned and regarded her curiously. The stream was fairly wide and looked like it would go deeper. Why was he wanting to wade in it?

Blair had her hands on either side of her as she watched him. "Why should we go through the stream? Isn't there another way around it?"

The elf only smiled bigger and held his arms before him like he was coaxing a young child to trust him. He only pushed it further when he began giving her light words of encouragement. Blair didn't know what to think about this at first, but her joyous heart began to fall as he continued. Her face displayed unease, but her foot scuffed a step forward. She wasn't sure if she was in control of that or not. It was like she was falling in a dream. She couldn't stop and she couldn't draw her weapon. Blair whimpered quietly as she was falling slowly toward his outstretched arms. She lifted her hands and braced for him to take her.

Just then, there was a light sparkle of glowing wings and the two flinched. It was the fairy, and he was very angry. He targeted Queriven and began to strike and throw some kind of powder at him. The elf blinked and staggered backward. When he rose again, the fairy continued his assault. The bubbly voice of the fairy was angry and rough, like a cry of battle. He swooped in and out.

Blair has fallen down back on solid ground. She was too dazed to understand what was happening. She only saw Queriven swiping at the fairy while trying to regain his footing. The fairy struck him in the forehead. Queriven cried out and was in the midst of falling backward again when his form changed. In his place was a gigantic black horse. Blair could only make out a bony narrow face with sharp teeth as it whinnied in a dark dissonance, kicked up its feet, and galloped downstream. It was out of view in a heartbeat.

The air fled from Blair's lungs and she sat, gasping for steady breaths. She nearly fell victim to a water horse. She was so close to death. Blair rolled over, whimpered, and tried to compose her senses. She knew something was wrong since the beginning, but she had no control of herself, either emotionally or physically. She hugged her arms tight and looked up at the fairy floating down to her.

He didn't flinch and he didn't speak until her breath evened out and she sat up. Her freckled but drained face fell with relief. "Thank you," she praised him. "You saved my life."

The fairy still had no idea what she said, but he recognized her relaxed tone and posture. He crossed his arms over his chest and stated something back to her. Blair sighed and pushed back up on her feet. She was very lucky he continued to follow her. She was no longer afraid of his intentions.

The dirt-covered man hovered closer to her with caution. He seemed like he was willing to test her level of comfort. Blair held her hand up, trusting him. In response, a little dark arm reached up and he placed his hand on the tip of her finger. He cried out happily and started doing flips in the air. Blair chuckled as he squealed with joy. Then, he directed a hand over her eyes and pointed back the way they came. Blair looked behind her. The forest was thick and jungle-like again. The mysterious pound of the air and her sense of loss returned to her. She looked back at him. He continued to poke forward and zipped a few feet over.

Was he trying to lead her somewhere? He came back to her then and began pulling on her finger. Blair obeyed. She stood up and allowed him to lead. Her spirit was rising with hope. He knew the way out, and he was taking her away from these terrible dangers.

Unbeknownst to Blair at the time, Queriven was making his way toward Aven Forest on a racing steed. He knew he could only blame himself for letting her go. He gritted his teeth and cursed against the wind. Why did he allow this to happen?! He was nothing but a fool. In the few days he spent without her, he quickly came to the realization that he had to follow her to the end, no matter what that meant. Unfortunately, she was already long gone when he tried to catch up. She may already be in the forest by now.

The horse under him was panting, but he encouraged it to keep moving. Like the coward he was, he ran from her yet again. This time might be the death of her. He pushed that last thought away. If she died in there, it would be his fault. It would be the worst mistake and one he couldn't live with. He could only pray he will find her somehow before it's too late. One thing was for sure; he was never running away again. This he promised on his own life.

He was hoping, for whatever reason, Blair stopped in the

remains of the Forest Border Trading Post. But he knew that would be asking too much. That still didn't keep his heart from dropping when he didn't see her there. He growled. Even for an elf, a human girl would be nearly impossible to find in the forest.

He swung himself from the bare back of the horse and encouraged it to run away before dashing into the forest himself despite his still weak leg. Every second was a chance on her life. He had to find her in the quickest way possible if it wasn't too late already.

CHAPTER TWENTY-FOUR
SEELIE VERSUS UNSEELIE

The thick trees swallowed Queriven up in a heartbeat. It was then that he came to a sudden stop. His thudding heart was leaping in his throat and his head was cloudy with adrenaline. He needed to focus. He wasn't going to find Blair in time if he kept this up. The elf exhaled a long breath and looked around. What could he do? Tracking her was useless and she wouldn't have reached the city on her own. It was also impossible to learn what she's encountered so far.

He tried to keep calm, but it really wasn't helping right now. Then he tried to think back to his life here and remember what he could do. Finally, it occurred to him. There was someone who would know of any intruder who dared to step into the wilderness. There was more than dangerous monsters here. Blair would be a target. The fairies would have taken notice of her as soon as she took her first step in. Queriven knew exactly what to do about that. He picked up his feet and took off once again.

Even though he was away for about two decades, Queriven remembered exactly how to reach the city. The fairies didn't live too far south from it. He tried to hurry, but he also had to stay safe and wise.

◊ ◊ ◊

The forest was timeless. It wasn't any different from the last time he was here. He thought the memories would come flooding back to him as soon as he reached the old trading post, but he hasn't been thinking about it much. Maybe that was because of his important mission.

After what seemed like a lifetime, he reached the mushroom glade. Queriven stopped and tried to catch his breath. His leg allowed him to travel pretty far, though the pain reminded him it was still there. He wasted so much time already. If Blair was still alive in these woods, the fairies would know for sure. They could lead him directly to her.

Queriven was still stressed and his breathing was still a little hurried, but he needed answers fast. He took care as he stepped into the perimeter as to not disturb any property belonging to the fairies. A lot of the mushrooms were big and colorful, but there were also some plain ones. The grass was lush and soft. This didn't look like it, but this was the city of the seelie fairies. If he was their size, he would be able to see more evidence of civilization. But right now, it was nothing but a mystery. He knelt by a tree stump in the center and waited.

It wasn't long until they alerted the others of his presence and the queen was sent. She appeared before him within a minute. Her face was young and majestic despite being many centuries old. Her lovely wings sparkled a warm white light as she landed before the elf's eyes. Atop her bright blonde head was a crown made from twigs and flowers. Queriven politely bowed his head. She spoke to him in a high voice, one not belonging to her wise nature. "Why elf here?" she asked in his native tongue. It was simple and broken, but he respected her by answering in the same language.

"I need your help. I'm looking for a human intruder somewhere around the forest. Do you know anything about this?"

She calmly nodded. "Yes. Fairy looking now. Why elf looking?"

The queen did know. Queriven found a little hope in Blair's safety. "The intruder is a friend of mine. I need to find her before anything bad happens."

He figured that would give her pause, but her facial expression was suspicious of him. It occurred to Queriven that it would be difficult to convince her to help him. "Human intruder. Elf visitor," she pointed out to him.

He nodded. "I was supposed to come with her, but I let her get away. It was my fault she became lost in here."

Again, her confusion gave her pause. "Human came by self. Human not with elf." She was visibly growing upset now, as if he was trying to pull some kind of trick on her. "Elf not thinking. Human is fairy bait, like every other."

He feared she would say that. The unseelie and seelie fairies have been battling for many years. Since this was also elvish territory, they usually didn't involve Queriven's kind, but they liked to involve any other outsider. Both kinds of fairies would be looking to side Blair to their cause before turning her into one of them to use against the other. The queen was wanting to add her to their kingdom. She wouldn't be wanting to help Queriven find her. He was starting to grow desperate again. He held his palms open on the stump. "Please help me. You know where she is. I know you do. Is she already in the custody of your people? If not, anything can happen to her. What will change if I was also looking around?"

The Queen stroked her long gorgeous hair and hummed. Her wings were twitching in thought. She was truthful with her answer. "Fairy lost human. Fairy trying to find before ugly cousin do. Don't know where human is, but somewhere upstream. Far north of elf city."

Queriven staggered to his feet. He had his answer now. He was fixing to toss her a thank you before she stopped him and flew up at eye level. She pointed a light-skinned finger at his face. "Elf find human before cousin. Better that way. Fairy be mad if cousin find human first!"

"Of course. Thank you," he responded, bowing his head yet again and carefully exited the mushroom city. His senses told him it was already afternoon. He needed to find her before dark.

Blair remained positive with her new companion. At least she had a little bit of direction now. The fairy was also pretty comfortable with her now. He continued to point and talk to her, but he was now resting on her shoulder. They still couldn't understand what they were saying, but Blair didn't need to. He made his expressions and inflections recognizable. He guided her away from danger with warning chirps and screams.

It's already been several hours since she nearly fell into the hands of the water horse. So far, nothing has changed since then. They were still in the thick of the forest for what Blair could tell. She hoped to reach something different soon. She was growing tired from the walking and lapse of stress. She only wanted to reach the city...

The fairy on her shoulder watched her rub her eyes and yawned. He caught her attention with a string of words and hopped up and down. Blair then looked ahead again. "I really hope you're excited because we're almost there. I don't know how much more of this I can take."

Little did she know, but he was trying to encourage her because they were nearly at their destination, but it wasn't the elven city. He was directing her to his campsite, where she would remain with him in the forest forever.

In the meantime, Queriven finally found the creek that was flowing from the north. He followed it close enough he could hear it at all times. He was confident he was in the right place. She was here somewhere, but the location of her whereabouts was too vague. He'll have to look for more clues.

Finally, he found what he was looking for. He didn't see it at first, but there were fairies everywhere. Most of them were seelie, but he did spot one unseelie arguing with one of the other kind. He only noted for a second though, because they went silent when they realized they were being watched. They were slowly beginning to float away. Queriven called to them once again in his native tongue. "Wait! I need to know what this is about. Was there a human here?"

They exchanged glances and the little rogue fairy pouted. It was the seelie that answered, and he stood tall. "Kelpie almost eat human. Ugly cousin save it. He take human to camp."

Both fairies darted upwards when Queriven pounded a boot next to them. "Where?!" he cried.

The man shrugged and turned to the rogue fairy. The dirt-covered, darker fairy shook his head. "Too late!" he yelled in a scratchy voice and folded his arms. "Mitmaj has human! Human belong to unseelie now!"

The fairy next to him tried to grab the front of the shoddily made tunic, but the unseelie slapped his hands away. The attacker was yelling at him in the seelie dialect now. "You do not know that for sure. We will find her before your people can take control! You can count on that!"

Queriven yelled at the two to stop them from fighting. "But do you know where they went?"

It worked, but just barely. The seelie shoved his palm into the rogue's face and answered. His wingtips were beating with rage and he didn't even bother slipping back into the elvish language to respond. "They were last seen heading that way, but we do not know where the camp is." He took a second to point out to the northwest before the unseelie rubbed his face and lunged at his opponent. Queriven was quick to leave the fighting fairies and ran to the northwest. Fairies were fast flyers, but Queriven knew his eyes would cover more ground and catch more clues. If he hurried, he could reach Blair. He was already so close.

He pushed forward and raced by the trees. His quick movement had anything in his path staring or hiding from him. Some appeared to be normal animals, but he didn't know if they were the predictable or the crazed kind. He also noticed there were others among them like the curious dryads. None of them bothered him, so he ignored them and continued on.

Finally, he slowed down again. There was movement up ahead, and he heard a woman's voice speaking soon after. There was a sparkle of light that caught his eye, but it wasn't from a fairy's wing. It was pure starlight radiating off of Blair's shoulders. The excitement was quickly replaced with anxiety as he realized she was talking to the unseelie fairy hovering next to her.

Queriven stepped out of the trees and called to her. "Blair, don't listen to him. I'm back!"

Her gaze immediately snapped back to him and her eyes widened, but it wasn't from the joy of seeing him. As a matter of fact, she seemed more than a little scared. The elf didn't know how to act when the fairy pointed an alarmed finger his way and Blair continued walking her own, almost like she was pretending he wasn't there. Queriven held his hands on either side of him. "Wh...where are you going? I came back for you."

He was still being ignored. The elf raised his voice and walked after her. "That fairy's not helping you. Chase him away!"

But the further he walked, the tenser she became. She looked back over her shoulder and quickened her pace. "No, not again," she cried out and was only encouraged to run faster by the fairy.

What did she mean by that? Queriven wondered. Whatever was going on right now wasn't going to convince him to give up. "Stop!" he yelled and jogged ahead.

Blair did what he asked then, but then she spun around with her spear in hand. Queriven nearly fell back from the dangerous look in her eye. He fell silent. Blair's hand was barely shaking, and by her intimidation, he knew she would strike him if she needed to. "Please..." he asked her, but she didn't respond. The forest has taken all her reasoning. The fairy beside her stuck a pink tongue out and blew at him. Queriven was worried now. He came out all this way to help her, somehow found her inside a dangerous forest, and still couldn't protect her from her fate. He couldn't give up on her; he made a vow. However, she wasn't going to allow him anywhere near her. He began fearing for the worst. "It's me. It's Queriven. I just wanted to tell you I'm sorry. I meant to reach you earlier, but I..."

"Queriven's not coming back," Blair spat. "You can't be him. He left me to fend for myself. You're only another monster trying to trick me."

Her words hurt more than the spear ever could. "If you truly believed that, you would have run me through already. I know you're still in there."

For just a second, her expression softened on him, but it didn't last long. She lifted the spear and backed slowly away. He couldn't do anything else. He took a single step after her again. Like before, she turned around, but this time she jabbed at him. The elf jumped back and had his weapon before him in an instant, but then he hesitated. Blair took a swing at his legs and almost caught him. "Go away!" she cried.

"No!" he answered and came back up, aiming to dislodge her weapon. "You need to hear me out. How can I convince you of the truth?!"

She allowed him to hit the spear, but she used the momentum to turn it around and she used it to attack him again. This was something he showed her, unfortunately. Everything he taught her was being used against him right now.

If that wasn't bad enough, the fairy decided to involve himself then. Queriven was in the middle of trying to block an attack when he flew up and showered him in a powder that went right in his eyes. The elf stumbled back with a hand to his face. Surprisingly, Blair has not thrown herself at him but was instead backing away.

When he regained his focus, the fairy was attacking again, this time shooting some sort of shiny missile at him. It exploded like a small bomb when it hit his shoulder. Queriven shot his spear in an arch above him but missed. He tried again with his free left arm in the same movement and swatted the fairy from the sky. The rogue fairy screamed and disappeared in some weeds somewhere off the side. Blair gasped and came at Queriven even harder.

Both fighters matched the other. It was like watching a synchronized dance between them. They swung, parried, and sidestepped all the same ways. The elf underestimated her ability to match him like so. He thought he could disarm her easily, but he was really struggling just to protect himself. With each swing, Blair was becoming angrier. After he attacked the fairy, which Blair saw as a friend, it gave her even a better reason to see him as a monster. If she wasn't looking to hurt him before, she was now.

A hit from the shaft alone would be enough to unbalance him. Queriven kept moving. He just needed to hit harder and faster than he has. If he was a little more aggressive, he could probably outmatch her, but that was what he was afraid of. Too much hesitation might cost him his life, but if he tried any harder to fight, he might hurt her instead. That was something he couldn't allow.

His soft reactions on Blair gave her the upper hand. She parried a high strike, then came down low. Queriven hit it back, sending it up, but Blair used the angle to cut just under his arm. He didn't let that keep him down for long though, and he used his rage against her. He jumped ahead suddenly and batted Blair's spear to the side. Finally, between the sudden movement and the horrified look on her face when she noticed she hurt him, the weapon almost fell from her grip. Queriven ducked low and grabbed the wooden shaft, yanking it from her hands. Then he tossed the weapon behind him.

Blair shrieked and did the only thing she could to protect herself; she ran. Queriven darted after her. He wasn't sure if he was actually faster than her or not, but he was quickly catching up. Maybe it was because of the rough terrain slowing her down. Either way, he tackled her to the ground and tried to restrain her. He called her name many times over her screaming and struggling. Blair chose not to listen, though she heard each word and could feel his every breath on her ear. She continued to struggle. Queriven had her hands penned, but she squirmed and smacked her elbow into his face.

Somehow, Queriven held on, but she was putting up a fight he couldn't win for long. She was a lot stronger than she looked. His lip was already going numb. "I don't want to hurt you! Please just listen for one second!"

Finally, she freed her hands and pushed him off. Before he could even realize what was happening, she came to him again, but she somehow had his spear in her hands. He didn't even know she took it from him. She was already back on her feet while he was sprawled on the ground. Beyond each rugged breath he took, he dared not to move. Blair was too unpredictable now. Queriven had no idea what she will do next, but he was afraid she might be so far gone as to strike him.

Blair's eyes narrowed to the tip made of pure starlight. Her expression was unreadable. Finally, she pointed it down on him. Still, he didn't move, and he wouldn't. If she was the death of him, he would have kept his vow. He came back for her, no matter the costs.

Surprisingly, she didn't attack him and spoke instead. She paused often as she was also trying to catch her breath. "If you are the real Queriven, then tell me how we met."

There she was. He wasn't sure why she decided to give him a chance, but he didn't take it for granted. He adjusted his seating on the ground but didn't stand. "You came to me in Dunverhart, in a lodge I was staying in at the time. We didn't actually speak until I rescued you from some bandits in Taleena Hills."

Blair wasn't quite satisfied. "And our mission? Why did I come into this forest?"

He didn't hold back. "We were trying to break your curse by stealing one of the horns crafted by the vayen aray from your king. When it was smashed, you came here to find where they passed another horn to the elves." Finally, his honesty came through and her expression softened on him. Though he still had something he wanted to say. "And I'm such a terrible person for letting you come in here on your own. I should have been by your side from the start of this. I've said some pretty terrible things and abandoned you when you needed me the most. I'm so sorry."

The pain there was raw and genuine enough for Blair to see. The spear lowered and she went slowly from sympathy to regret. She came closer and offered her hand. Queriven took it and retrieved the spear once he was on his feet. Blair half turned from him and placed her hands over her face. "I...I don't know what came over me. I just didn't think. I didn't know you were..."

She didn't have to finish for Queriven to know she didn't think he was ever coming back. He came around to stand in front of her, where he reached for her attention. He gently took either arm. "This wasn't your fault. The dangers of the forest crawled in your mind. I'm the one to blame. This wouldn't have happened if I came in with you."

Blair's eyes lifted open and she stared down at the oozing cut she gave him earlier. Queriven brushed it off. "It's mainly ripped cloth than anything. I'll be fine. I'm just thankful this was the worse of our fight. I was really afraid of hurting you." When her expression didn't change, he chuckled. "Though I underestimated you for sure! You're quite powerful, you know?"

She still didn't smile, but she lifted her head. Wordlessly, she gazed into his shining face. Those green eyes were brighter than she's ever seen them and that smile was free from the shadows of the hood he usually wore. He no longer needed to hide his heritage here. This was his home and he seemed to fit in perfectly with the mystery and beauty of the forest. Blair had daydreamed before of seeing the forest with him, but those were always rich with light emotions and safety. Despite what nearly overcame them, this reality was somehow more beautiful. Maybe she was just happy to see him come back for her.

Queriven finally let her go and rubbed the back of his neck. "I suppose we should head back for your spear before we go on to the city."

Blair nodded and fell beside him. She couldn't wait to be out of the wilderness. For now, she could only imagine what her eyes may see when they finally reach the elven city. She was even more excited to see it now that she had her old friend beside her.

CHAPTER TWENTY-FIVE
A GHOST FROM THE PAST

Queriven knew exactly where he was going, and it was a good thing too. The woods were growing darker and darker by the minute. The nightfall in Aven Forest was unlike any other in Fairdraisha. The grass, bushes, and flowers didn't sleep once the sun fell, but released a collection of glowing lights. There were blues, greens, pinks, oranges, and plenty others just floating harmlessly in the air. They didn't seem to be anything living, or at least, Queriven wasn't concerned with it. When she asked, he said it happened in the forest every night and was merely a release of mysterious magic from the plants. On their way to the city, which he called Sylinna, Queriven explained his dash into the forest to try and find her.

Blair understood then why trusting the fairy was such a big deal. He wasn't trying to help her after all. That display against the kelpie was to take her for himself. Her speckled face paled when she considered what might have happened if Queriven didn't come back in time. She would have been stuck with the unseelie forces until the curse took hold.

Again, Queriven apologized, but Blair already forgave him. He was done living on the fence and done with his selfishness. This mission was important to him and he'll see the end of it. Blair couldn't have been happier to hear his newfound determination. To him, she was worth the fight. She was worth everything.

"I was wondering," Blair started after he finished with his story. Queriven listened. "Before the Aven Forest, there was an abandoned campsite of some sort. It looked like it was made by a collaboration of human and elven hands. Could that have been a mixed village maybe?"

Queriven's smile turned upside down and he sighed. "That was no other than the meeting point between the elven and human merchants. They simply called it the Forest Border Trading Post. It's heartbreaking to see it really. It's so forgotten even after all this time."

That certainly explained a lot. Blair silently wished she was more aware of it before now. The trading post was right on the border of both Aven and Fairdraisha. Her people should at least acknowledge that history. She looked at her companion and found sadness. "Of course, since it was the exchange of goods, it became a target for the evil-hearted. It was fortified enough to hold against most attacks. A lot of the thieves never came in, except for the night that caused the break between our relations," he continued with memories hanging over his head. He didn't even notice his pace was slowing down. Blair didn't interrupt, though she noticed his joyful mood disappearing. "The Trading Post was bustling with activity one summer evening, but they were unaware an organized attack group lied just outside the walls. With a signal, the thieves stormed. It was unlike any attempt before. These guys were smart and brutal. They were willing to murder outright. After the whole camp became a field of dead elves and humans and the goods taken, the thieves fled." His voice darkened with dread when he added, "They were never found."

Blair didn't know what to say, though the space around her suddenly became gloomy. Queriven wasn't finished, though he didn't match her face. "It was after that terrible slaughter that Lord Foradue and King Brenmor argued. Foradue screamed outrage and blamed Fairdraisha for the attack since all the thieves were human. King Brenmor declared the merchants would have been protected better if the Trading Post was inside Aven Forest than on the border. The fight only grew worse when Foradue said he wouldn't allow such a thing, as humans couldn't be trusted. Finally, penchants and treaties were broken and the kingdoms, though on the edge of each other, tried to ignore the other's existence." Queriven shook his head. "It's all nonsense... I was only a young child when this happened."

For some reason, Blair took it on her shoulders like she was responsible. "I'm sorry. I never knew this was the cause of our separation."

"I know," he answered. Finally, he looked at her again and moved a strand of brown hair from his face. His calm gaze told her it wasn't her fault she didn't know what happened. "Neither Foradue nor Brenmor wants to talk about that event. It's easier for Brenmor to forget about it since it's been several generations of your people. There are still many of us who remember it. Unlike your king, our Foradue is the same man from that day."

Blair was glad this was something they could talk about now, rather than him trying to hush her whenever she had questions. "Do you personally remember it? Were you nearby when it happened?"

The look on his face suggested he hasn't thought about it in a long time. His eyes darted either way on the ground, like he's forgotten the answer. "I wasn't nearby on that day. I was only an adolescent and my class had a long field trip we had to take. But I do remember hearing the news of the attack."

"That must have been awful."

Queriven nodded and didn't say anything else. His sharp and handsome face was staring ahead into something Blair couldn't see. He was gone for only a short while, but he was already different. She didn't know what it was. Maybe it was his decision to come back for her or maybe it was the familiar forest itself waking up his senses of a home he left long ago. Whatever the case, she's never seen him like this before.

The hesitance in him only increased the more they walked. Blair knew they must be close.

As it turns out, she was right. The thick trees suddenly

parted without warning and Blair gasped. The trees in the city were different than the ones in the wilderness. They were even larger and wider than the towers at the trading post, and taller than Fairdraisha's castle. Of course, not even these compared to the one further in the center of the city. Summer leaves flourished on top of every tree, even the large ones. There were no houses or dwellings; just the towering trees with carved-out windows. The ground was mostly free of roads, though there were dirt paths and even the major ones were lined with rich ebony and the radiant starlight shining like beacons. It was like an exotic paradise hidden away inside the terrible dangers of the forest. The sky was deep blue. The stars and moon were like pure silver, even in the remaining light.

Blair breathed in and tasted the fragrant breeze. She only grew more excited to see what was ahead! Her pounding heart was the only proof this wasn't a dream. She edged a step forward before looking behind. Unfortunately, Queriven didn't share her enthusiasm. It was like he couldn't budge his legs a step forward.

Blair stepped back and waited for him to recover on his own time. His breathing was anxious and uneven. Finally, he remembered he wasn't alone. "I haven't been this close to it in twenty years... What will they do once they find out the truth?" he asked no one in particular. He didn't even move or look away.

Blair wished she could offer him more comfort, but this was out of her hands now. She shrugged. "We'll just have to take it one step at a time." She wasn't sure if that helped him or not. He exhaled a long breath but still refused to move. She needed to coax him a little further.

She gently took his arm and tried to lead him, but he stopped her. "Wait," he replied. She obeyed, though he was still for a moment longer. Finally, he unbuttoned his cloak and removed it. The fabric flowed sweetly in the breeze as he then wrapped it around her shoulders and pulled the dark hood up. "Here. You need this more than I do. You're the foreign one now."

Blair accepted it with thanks. She didn't feel any more exotic than her usual self, but she supposed he was right. The cloak will also hide the knight armor from sight. It would have drawn in some unwanted attention otherwise.

Finally, Blair began to walk ahead when Queriven finally started moving along, though she quickly realized he was already lagging behind. Blair came up beside him and gently took his hand in hers, keeping him by her side.

The city opened up to them immediately, though Blair knew it was because they didn't enter from the main entrance. Compared to what she's seen in the forest so far, this city was much more welcoming and clean. Even the birds seemed safer and happier here. The thick clouds from earlier never dropped rain, but the air was moist and a rough wind kicked up in its place.

Their surroundings were still growing darker, but there were a few elves seen at this time. Blair marveled at the fields spanning between roads and land. There were amazingly lush farms of growing herbs and vegetables between the gigantic roots of the trees being used as homes. The homes were spread apart from each other, allowing room for the farms and roads. The elves were like Queriven with their thin builds, pointed ears from long flowing hair, and beautiful features. Blair was never so out of place in her life, though she was still ecstatic to be here in the main capital of the forest.

Even without pointed ears, her features lacked that soft elegance, and her body was bigger-boned and more padded than their slender forms. Their skin was fair and free of blemishes. Queriven didn't look quite as unique anymore. Even safely under the hood, she was beginning to grow a little self-conscious. "This is Sylinna," Queriven hushed his voice beside her. "I spent many years of my childhood here before trying to become a knight."

He already explained to her what this city was to him, but now that it was before her, she feared her heart would stop. She never would have imagined she'll be able to see where he came from. She looked up again. This is what she always wanted to see with her own eyes. The city of the elves. Her dream came true, but unfortunately, it was a living nightmare for her friend. Queriven pointed up at the biggest tree in the center of town. "That is what we call the Center Tree. It's like Sylinna's castle, but a little different. Foradue lives there and watches over the city. It's where I trained to be a soldier and later the first knight."

Blair found everything he said fascinating, and she wished he continued talking. He was merely trying to hide his growing fear from her, though she noticed every bit of it. They were in the heart of the city now. What he called the Center Tree was climbing over their heads like a mighty tower taking up the sky. The rustling leaves suggested there was much more wind all the way up there. *What was their plan now,* Blair wondered? The hardest part was reaching the city, but she didn't know what to do next. Suppose they needed to find a place to stay the night? She was sure she was the one leading Queriven around the city. His mind was so swarmed with emotions and memories. She would have to ask him, since he knew the place best, what they should do next.

But when she turned to look at him, he stopped yet again, this time with his jaw hanging open. Blair followed his gaze ahead and saw another elf on the road, this one a woman, giving him the same look. Slowly, she stepped forward, her hands on either side of her. "Queriven...?" she whispered like she forgot how to talk.

Queriven didn't respond or move when she came closer. Blair looked at him again, silently asking him what this was about. He was too stunned by the elf to even notice her. The woman's feet quickened. "Queriven, is that really you?" Her voice was beginning to break and Blair was forced out of the way as she jumped into his arms. Her dark hair showed a rich red sheen as it spilled over her face and onto his shoulders. Blair watched the scene, confused as to who this woman was.

"Kielle," Queriven spoke back, holding her tight. Blair waited, forgotten and awkwardly standing on the side. The longer seconds of no explanation was starting to bother her and she found herself growing angry with this Kielle. Who was she?

How does he know her? Of course, this was his hometown, but Blair was growing annoyed with neglect.

After a lifetime, the woman let go, but she couldn't look away from Queriven's face. "Where were you all this time?!" she cried aloud, her jeweled eyes too stunned to drop tears. "We all...I thought you were dead! What happened to you?"

Blair folded her arms, a lingering distaste in her mouth at how Kielle cared so much over Queriven.

Queriven opened his mouth to speak, but no tangible words came out. Kielle finally dropped her gaze on Blair. Her beautiful hands released the folds on Queriven's sleeves. "And who is this?" she asked, stepping forward slightly. She measured Blair from the feet up, then her eyes stopped on her face for a long while. Even with Blair's hood up, the woman seemed alarmed. "Is this girl human?" No one gave her an answer. Now she was just as confused as Blair was. She spun back to Queriven. "Is this a dream? Queriven, what's going on?"

"There's a lot to explain, Kielle. I'm not sure how much of it you'll understand," Queriven finally answered, his voice already dipped in regret and sorrow.

"Of course," she answered. "But whatever it is, I'll listen. Why don't we head back to my home and talk about it?"

Queriven looked like he'd rather not, but he nodded anyway. Then, he fell in place beside her. Blair followed behind the two. She was out of place again, and it only made her angry. "I suppose the human can come too," Kielle said, offering her a quick glance. "But there needs to be a good explanation of why she's here."

Blair scowled but said nothing.

"We need to tell Sirnah and Finhaus about this," Kielle continued. "They'll be amazed. We were all so worried about you."

"We don't have a lot of time for visits," Queriven answered. "We're on a tight schedule right now."

Kielle looked at him, baffled. "Queriven!" she replied with confusion. It didn't seem like she knew how to respond to his statement. "They're your brothers."

That caused a spark in Blair and her step faltered. Queriven has two brothers?

The remark didn't change his mind. "I didn't come back for them. This is an important business."

His tone hurt her now. "What do you mean you didn't come back for them? Is your family not important anymore?" She watched him like she wanted a reply, but Queriven didn't say a thing.

None of them knew this, but they were being watched by an elf from afar. His face twisted with angry pain as he glared at the knight who once served the kingdom long ago. Burning tears lined his eyes, but he refused to let them drop. The elf didn't cry out to the three but decided to bide his time. Then he sank away, tearing his dark eyes away, though he still struggled to breathe properly. He had to do something about this. Justice must be served one way or another.

Kielle's home wasn't too far away from the center of the city. The front door on the towering tree had no doorknob, but she pushed it and it swung open. She allowed Queriven in first, then Blair, who was staring up so high up the tree. It was like she was as small as an ant, staring at the stretching top. The branches and leaves were so high. It was almost too far for her to make out. She hesitated. No human ever had the honor of entering the home of an elf. Perhaps, she should be more grateful?

Still, Kielle burned her with a look of displeasure as Blair moved past her and into the room. Neither Kielle nor Queriven was nearly as awestruck as she was. While Kielle offered them a seat, Queriven remained standing, his eyes fixed on her. Blair tried not to examine the room too hard as to not offend their host. The floors and walls were the smoothly carved innards of the tree. On the far wall, a sofa made of soft cotton and wood trim faced them. Its body curved with the shape of the tree, making it look quite elegant. In front of it was a low circular table, dyed to be a pearly white. Further to the side was a long counter. It looked like it was carved out of the room itself, making it a part of the wall. There was even a wide rug in front of it. It was a deep bluish purple with a swirling design made with thin lines of sparkly starlight. For a tree, it wasn't bare or empty. Even the walls had decorative designs on it, including a few windows she noticed earlier. It dawned on her that Kielle had all the proper living accessories she needed. Many were serving the same purpose Blair's own house would have, even though they did look a little different.

Kielle folded her light arms, not pressing her offer for them to sit. "Are you going to tell me what this is all about?" she barked, her strong features masking hurt.

Queriven held his hands out, blocking her temper from boiling over the top. "I will in due time, but I need you to listen. Blair needs help. There's a curse over her and she doesn't have much time to break it."

Kielle's eyes flashed. "You came back to help the human? What about us, your family? Were you ever going to come back?" She blinked away weakness, her arms dropping as she accused him again. "Where have you been all this time? I need to know!"

Queriven shrank back, words caught in his throat.

She nodded, anger only rising when he didn't answer. The elf snapped, her finger pointing to his chest. "It's been twenty years. Everybody accepted you weren't going to be found and one day you just show up with no regards to those who loved you?! What if that was me, Queriven? How would you feel if I just showed up in town after two decades, then treated it like it was nothing?"

"Kielle..."

She turned away, her red hair waving in its place before she walked away. "I suppose I should prepare a late meal." Then she stomped up the stairs and disappeared.

The two remaining were speechless — Blair especially, as she felt like she was intruding in personal matters. She was standing well off on the sides, watching Queriven as he stood there hopelessly in shame, his head dipping downwards.

Every second was like an hour and Blair clawed for comfort. She finally took a seat on the sofa. "Who was that?" she whispered after a while.

Queriven's eyes lifted and he glanced her way, almost like he forgot she was there. Blair already asked him the question, though now she was a little scared to hear the answer. He studied her expression before he gathered his courage. "That was Kielle, my sister."

For the hundredth time that day, Blair flinched. "Your sister?!" she exclaimed. That was certainly a surprise, as she thought they shared a different kind of relationship.

Queriven only nodded slowly, not otherwise bothered by her response. "Are you surprised?"

Blair shrugged and leaned back in her seat to hide her shock. "A little," she muttered. "I mean, you don't look like you're related."

He sighed and sat down next to her. His hands were together over his knees. "As you can see, she's quite stubborn. She wouldn't even want me telling you she's younger. The two of us always bickered as rivals. She always wanted to prove herself as the stronger. Because of this, she tried to do everything I did. She even followed me into the military, wielding a spear no less!" He laughed weakly. "I admire her courage."

As stunned as she was, Blair had so many other questions she wanted to ask. "What about your brothers?"

Queriven leaned further into the seat. "Sirnah and Finhaus? They're good kids. Sirnah's the youngest. He's fascinated by plants and makes a living as a royal herbalist. Unless something's changed, he lives there in the Center Tree. He's gentle and quiet, sometimes coming across as awkward at times. As for Finhaus, he's content in following Father's footsteps in being a farmer. He's headstrong and has a real thing for animals. Finhaus is the only one of us not working for the military. Sometimes I wonder if that bothers him a little."

Blair was still shocked to hear him talk about such a big family. She didn't think about it too much. She just figured he was always a loner. "You have a lot of siblings," Blair said out loud. "Are there others?"

There was a smile on the corner of his lips, but he shook his head. "Just the four of us."

Blair almost scrambled to her feet when she heard footsteps coming down the stairs. Then Kielle poked her face in the room. "Supper is ready," she said. "Are you two coming to eat?"

Queriven was the first to stand up and he waited for Blair to do the same. Kielle disappeared upstairs again. Then, the two followed her up into the kitchen.

It matched the theme of the first room well. Everything was clean and tidy. In the center was a large white dining table, already set with wooden plates filled with leafy greens and mushrooms.

Kielle leaned her slender body over the table and set down a cup by each plate. Blair couldn't believe it; the cups were made from nothing but large leaves. She pulled out a chair and sat down.

As the two elves did the same, Blair had calmed down a little and was thankful for Kielle sharing her meal. She wasn't even as angry with Kielle as she was a while ago. Instead, she saw her for what she was; a concerned sister. Blair not only understood Kielle now but respected her.

Unfortunately, Kielle was still cold toward her. "I don't have any human suitable foods, so I hope this works for you. What do you guys eat anyway? It sounds like you devour meat with sharp teeth like some kind of monster."

Blair shot her eyes off her plate, staring up at Queriven who seemed to have the same response. The way Kielle said that was unsettling and rude, but Blair didn't want to return the notion. After she recovered from disgust, she forced a smile. "No, not really. I mean, we do eat meat, but not like that. We eat all kinds of things." Blair chose a nice rounded mushroom, then smiled again and looked at Kielle. "This is wonderful. Thank you for letting me stay."

Kielle's red eyebrows furrowed in confusion. She wasn't expecting that as a response. Queriven cleared his throat, wishing to change the discomfort of the table. "So Kielle, are you still a spear wielder of the Center Tree?"

She nodded, moving from Blair to her brother. "I go in for the night patrol actually."

That certainly explained why she was out so late. She was heading for work, which means she'll be running late. Queriven offered a glad approval and silence caved in again. Kielle dropped her gaze, then lifted it again a moment later. "But I'm no longer a soldier," she said with a bit of shakiness in her tone. "I'm the first knight."

Again, the two looked up, the food on their plate forgotten. "You're... a knight?" Queriven clarified and Kielle shied away. Her brother smiled. "That's wonderful. I always knew you would make a great leader."

Come to think of it, that made sense too. Kielle had patches of starlight on her clothes not unlike what Blair was wearing now. "Thank you... I never thought I would ever have the chance to tell you."

Queriven sighed and fell back in his chair. "I guess it's easy to say I'll never be a knight again, nor anything else. They're more likely to exile me as it is." His tired eyes lifted back up to Kielle, who regarded him sadly. "That's why I can't have everyone knowing I'm back. We need to find answers to break Blair's curse before it's too late. Can you help us?"

Kielle sighed, her fair features showing fatigue and stress. She turned from Queriven to Blair, both watching her. She lowered her head, looking down at the table. "Of course. For you, I'll always do everything I can to help." She allowed the silence to come back in. Neither Blair nor Queriven said anything else.

After the three picked up and cleaned the kitchen, Kielle took them further up the tree. "I only have one guest room, one I also use as a study. I'm thinking Queriven can stay up there and I guess the human can stay in my room." She turned her head back as she continued up the stairs. "If you're fine with that."

Blair had to refocus her attention as she was once again drawn to the design of the home. She was more than a little upset Kielle was still cold because of her being a human. "Sure, but you can call me Blair if you'd like."

Without a reply, Kielle stopped on the next floor. This one had a lovely entryway made of dangling vines like a curtain. "This is my room. You may wait here as I set Queriven up. I'll be sure to bring down a spare hammock."

Blair made sure to thank her as she and Queriven continued up the stairs. Blair slowly moved into the entryway and carefully past the curtain of vines. As she did so, there was a breeze of sweetly scented flowers in the air. Kielle's room was fresh and beautiful. Her windows up here were wide and brought in the forest. Just outside, leaves were sailing on the nighttime wind. Blair stepped closer for a better look. The first few stars were already twinkling behind the roof of trees, but they weren't the only sparkling lights. Instead of the dark silhouettes that normally swallowed the earth, the city had lights of its own. Blair leaned forward. She didn't notice anything down there before when the entered the city, but they looked to be floating puffs of easy blue light. They were all around the roads of the city. They were a little more organized than the floating lights in the wilderness, but they reminded her of them.

She stepped away and returned to the room. Some colorful flowers of blue and purple were sitting nearby. Like the cups at the dinner table, Blair marveled at the vase they were growing in. It was as hard as glass, but she swore it was nothing but a few giant green leaves.

There were some more over by the bed. The bed itself wasn't too unique, although it was different from what Blair remembered. There was no frame except for a thick body of wood as the bed itself and a soft material wrapped in a dyed fabric that lined the top.

There were footsteps coming from the stairs and into the room. Then Kielle appeared past the vines and came inside. She was already holding a wrapped hammock in her arms. The elf moved past Blair without even making contact and began setting it up.

She didn't even look back when Blair moved closer to her. There was still a passive-aggressiveness lingering in the air. Blair hoped to soothe it even if it's just a little. "Thank you for this. I know we came so suddenly. This is a big change for you too."

Kielle didn't reply. Her fingers were picking at a tangled knot in the strings. She finally dug in and released it. Blair wondered if she might be cruel enough to tie the hammock so it might fall, but she shook the thought away, not wanting to think of such things of Queriven's sister. Instead, Blair took the other end of the hammock and tried her best to help.

Tying the roped ends to the notches in the wall was easy, and Kielle turned away. It then occurred to Blair just how upset she was still over this ordeal. Blair followed behind her to the window looking out on the forest. Silence ticked on like a disease. Blair wanted to break it, even if that meant tempting Kielle to lash out again. "So what's up with all these lights? I've never seen anything like this before."

Surprisingly, Kielle's response was neither snarky nor hurtful, though it was still sorrowful. "The Center Tree is under control by a lot of magic users, so they use a lot of their magic to improve the city. The lights from the wilderness are another story. They've always been there. There's a lot of magic in that forest and a lot of magical creatures. Some carry light; others create it, and sometimes it just shows up for other reasons. The forest is beautiful but dangerous."

Blair took a second look at all the colored lights and the city. "It is beautiful," she agreed.

Kielle's next words stewed with even more hurt. "Has he ever talked about me?" She looked at Blair for a second and stroked the ends of her hair with her fingers. "I still can't believe he's been alive out there this entire time. Why didn't he come back?"

Blair wished she could answer those questions, but she didn't know them herself. "Queriven tried his hardest not to talk about his personal life at all. It's amazing to me that he has such a big family. I guess he was too ashamed of himself."

Kielle didn't seem surprised and returned to the room again. Blair saw her ruffling through a dresser, where she drew some light folded blankets from it and tossed them on the hammock. "I have to take my night patrol. If you'll excuse me, I'm already late."

She was already moving for the curtain of vines before finishing. "Kielle!" Blair cried, stopping her in her tracks. The elf turned and Blair gave her a nice smile. "Thank you again for letting me stay here."

Kielle pondered the message for a moment and then turned to leave again without saying anything back. Blair wasn't bothered though and climbed up in the hammock. Despite the stress from today and the unfamiliar environment, the gentle swinging of the hammock and fresh night air coming through the windows gave Blair comfort. It took her only a short while to fall asleep. As for now, she was unaware of the challenges they will face that next morning...

CHAPTER TWENTY-SIX
SYLINNA'S ONCE TRUSTED KNIGHT

The room was still empty when Blair awoke. Birds were chirping in the already warm morning, some even perching on the open window sill. Blair sat up, stretching with her freckled arms against her tangled head. The hammock began to swing when her feet searched for the floor beneath. When she finally found it, she stopped. There were voices downstairs. It sounded like Queriven and Kielle, but she couldn't make out what they were saying. Something told her it wasn't a pleasant talk though.

She stood up and reached for her shoes, deciding to investigate.

The voices became clearer as she moved by the curtains and came downstairs to the kitchen. "I thought I told you not to bother them!" Queriven exclaimed with bewilderment. "Who else did you tell about us? This will do nothing but hinder our deadline!"

Kielle snapped back. "They deserve to know just as much as I do. We're your family and I didn't talk to anyone else. I promise." They stopped as Blair came down into the room, regarding her for just a moment before Kielle addressed her brother again. "Are you going to see them or not?"

Queriven sighed angrily. "I guess I have no choice now." Then he stomped away from them and headed downstairs.

Kielle grabbed a piece of fruit from a basket sitting on the table and looked at Blair again. "I'll be awake for a little while, but I'm going upstairs to rest. Help yourself to some breakfast or scout around the kitchen for something else if you wish." Then she also disappeared. She was behaving herself, but she still stared at Blair with anger and distrust.

Blair stepped closer to the table, going through the options of fruit. She wanted to go downstairs with Queriven. She imagined they were talking about his brothers earlier, but maybe she should stay out of this for now. Queriven had enough stress as it was.

Queriven's pace slowed as the living room came into view. Two elves were sitting quietly on the couch, but they stopped when they saw Queriven. Eyes were wide like they were looking into the face of a ghost. Finhaus, the one closest to him, stood up and approached. The young elf wanted to say something and was thinking about what he might say in this entire time, but all words were gone. Instead, Finhaus cried aloud and hugged his brother tight. Finally, he choked his first words out. "It's been so long," he said barely above a whisper. The elf's voice was cracking.

Then came Sirnah, and he also greeted Queriven with a hug after waiting for Finhaus to back away. Queriven noted his brother's shaking shoulders. They were all on the brink of tears. It was then when he realized they weren't the only ones. He really missed his dear brothers and silently forgave Kielle for telling them about him being back.

Sirnah retracted but placed a hand on Queriven's shoulder. "Kielle told us you came into town yesterday," he said quietly. "I didn't believe her."

They hardly looked any different from the last time Queriven saw them. It drove him back to what he remembered as the good days when they were kids before he took his family for granted.

Queriven smiled at them. "It is good to see you two."

"So if you weren't killed," Finhaus started, sitting back down, "then where have you been all this time?"

Queriven drew up a seat on the other side of the table, but he didn't answer the question right away. It slowly sank in like a pointed knife in his consciousness. He swallowed and looked away. "I wanted to come back, but..." he shrugged, twisting with shame. "I couldn't. Not after what happened that day."

The two brothers regarded each other for just a second before Finhaus replied, "You know that doesn't matter to us. You're family. We would have forgiven you."

"It's not that," Queriven answered. "It was all my fault. I couldn't forgive myself."

Finhaus was about to respond again, but the three turned when someone was coming slowly down the stairs. A second later, and Blair's curious face peeked around the corner. She was growing too interested to ignore them any further. She wanted to see what was going on.

The elves, especially Finhaus and Sirnah regarded her with just as much curiosity. "I'm sorry," Blair said shyly. "I'm interrupting something, aren't I?"

"No," Queriven answered, rising to his feet. "You're fine. You wanted to meet Finhaus and Sirnah, didn't you?"

She nodded and came off the last few steps, twiddling her fingers.

Queriven aimed a question to both brothers. "Did Kielle tell you about Blair? The human girl?"

Again, both pairs of eyes went wide. "Uh, I do remember she said something about that," Finhaus stuttered, looking at Blair like she was some kind of strange animal. Blair didn't reply as she looked to either brother. Like Kielle, they had rounded youthful faces and large eyes. "You know you could be in deep trouble for bringing a human in, don't you?" Finhaus said again. Light reflected a dash of sea blue in his eyes and his long hair, dark with a slight reveal of purple, which he tied back loosely.

As for Sirnah, his round face was stuck in a curious, innocent expression. His hair was shorter than his brother's, just enough to touch the top of his shoulders. It was so dark it was almost black. His long dark blue robes reminded Blair of what Queriven said; how Sirnah was a herbalist of the Center Tree. She could also tell these two, especially Sirnah, were way younger than Queriven. Of course, she didn't really know what that meant for the long life elves have, but they looked like they were barely entering adulthood.

Finhaus politely, though nervously, rose to his feet and approached. He quickly looked her over and bowed down. "Forgive me," he said. "I've never seen one of your kind before."

She pardoned him and he made way for Sirnah's greeting. Sirnah was even more nervous than his brother was, almost like she scared him. He too bowed down before her.

"She's here because she needs our help," Queriven said. "Young Blair has been cursed and we may be the last hope she has."

Both elves shot back at her with worry. Finhaus reacted next. "Curses are nasty things! Why do you think we are the only ones to help? Are there not wizards who can break it in her world?"

"No wizard of humans nor elves can break this one," Queriven assured. "It was a rokian who did it. We need to speak with the vayen aray."

Both elves flinched. "A rokian?!" Sirnah asked in bewilderment. "You mean one of the two races, ancient in time even to our long lives? The ones who were banished to a different realm? Those rokians?"

"The same," Queriven confirmed. "But we know what we have to do. It'll be difficult. All we need is a plan."

Just then, footsteps were rushing down the stairs and Kielle dashed past the table for the door. She was mumbling something about an inconvenient time for a visitor, and she opened the door. No one in the room was aware of a knock. They were all caught off guard by her panic.

A guard of the Center Tree stopped in his tracks, surprised

Kielle appeared before he even reached the door. The elf cleared his throat and acknowledged her. "Kielle, it is the Center Tree's understanding that a past knight of the combat unit by the name of Queriven returned to Aven Forest yesterday evening. Is this correct?"

Kielle's expression said it all, and she nearly fell backward into the room. Instantly, she darted back to look at her brothers in the living room. Her astonished face swore she didn't share the news.

The guard took the confirmation. He nodded and continued. "Since Queriven is tied to honor the Center Tree, he must report before noon with an explanation of what happened on the night his commanded combat squad was found slaughtered south of the city. The trial will listen openly and the Center Tree will give a fair response to his word of truth." He paused for a minute and looked at the people gathered in the room. "It was also said he brought a human girl into our city. She needs to stand before judgment as well."

Then, without waiting for a reply, he bowed and marched back the other way.

Everyone back in the room remained with a horrified silence long after he left and Queriven's was the most terrified. His light tan face was so pale that Blair worried he was suddenly sick. His voice was quiet and gone with inflection. "I thought you said you didn't tell anyone else."

Kielle spun at the accusation, her mouth still agape. She shook her head and held her arms open on either side of her. "I promise I didn't!" she cried, but Queriven didn't seem convinced. Her hand gestured to the other two elves. "Sirnah and Finhaus were the only two I told." Finally, her wide eyes furrowed with steam and anger. "You just walked into the city entrance openly without a disguise and with the human girl no less. You could have easily been recognized."

Sirnah calmly replied, "Or someone could have overheard when you were telling us about his return."

Queriven spilled a frustrated sigh and stood up. "Well, it's too late to fix it now. I have no choice. I have to stand at the trial." He looked at everyone around him before he stopped on Blair. "I don't know what this means for our mission. We still need to break that curse, no matter the consequences."

Before Blair could speak, Kielle jumped in first. "I'm sure Foradue will understand. Perhaps, he can help us?"

Queriven nearly turned away as he disagreed before she finished. "No, he won't, not after he hears my explanation."

"Why?!" Kielle demanded. "What happened that night?"

He pressed his eyes closed, trying to snuff out the pain before he addressed Blair. "I'm sorry. I don't know why I hide the truth when I know it has to come out in the end."

Blair tried to reason out his response in her mind. Then finally, it hit her. "So Darkadus was right. You knew him; he was there when..."

Queriven nodded and apologized again. "Yes, but I didn't know who he was at the time. He was under the disguise of an elf named Aswren when I met him."

Blair wanted to understand. She wanted desperately to empathize with his pain. But her anger was boiling. Queriven knew important information concerning her quest and has been keeping it secret from the start. He's been lying to her for quite some time now.

"He was telling the truth about me."

A second later, and Blair barked a reply that turned everyone's attention. "You didn't think it was important enough to tell me about this sooner? You didn't think I needed to know as much as I could about my attacker?" Her face was glowing red now and her freckles compressed tighter in furrowed wrinkles. "I know he might have said some truth, but the fact that you lied about what you knew from the start is unacceptable! We're supposed to be in this together. That's what you told me once!"

Queriven was reaching now to calm her, but Blair backed away. "Why do you hide? What's the point of trying to help my curse when you hide so much from me?"

The elf's features softened and his eyes filled with

unbearable sorrow. "Blair, it wasn't you. I was just..."

"You know what?" she interrupted, trying not to spill the tears lining her eyes. "Maybe what he said was right. You are selfish and a liar," her voice broke at the end and a single tear dropped. She avoided the heartbroken look on her friend's face and disappeared upstairs.

Queriven didn't run after her but slumped in his sorrow. He backed away and sat on the sofa. His siblings regarded him sadly, wishing they could comfort him, but they either had no idea how to or they didn't understand the conversation enough to have a proper response.

Instead, they gave him space. One by one, the three meandered away, leaving Queriven in the living room, his head dipped toward his knees.

Several hours later, the four elves and Blair were on the road toward the Center Tree as they were told. No one said a word. They were no words of comfort or hope; just uncomfortable silence. Almost like the word has gotten out to the entire city, elves around them stopped to watch with judging eyes, but the four moved on.

Blair's soft face was no longer stained with the burn of tears, but her mind was still ravished with anger and disappointment. As the Center Tree, taller than any mountain on Fairdraisha, towered closer and closer, fear and dread started to build higher. Blair had no idea of what to expect of the elvish government. What actions would arise against these crimes? Should she expect them to be gentle or harsh? What could she do or say that might not be offensive? Silently, she decided to listen and watch carefully without doing much else unless asked.

The road ended with stairs going up to the tree, where it was hollowed out to provide more room, but the court was outside on top of the stairs. The middle chair behind the desk was no throne. It was not unlike any of the others, and yet, a wise elder with stark, light gray hair and wrinkles sat there. His clothes and shining circlet of rich sapphire suggested he was of high rank. Was this Foradue? For a leader, he didn't hold himself any more important than a normal elf. Around the table, there were more elves of the Center Tree to hear the trial, but it was the elder paying the closest attention at the moment.

Those old eyes followed the younger Queriven as he stepped before the table first. Without a change of expression, Queriven bowed his head and fell to his knees. Foradue's lips parted, and a firm and confident voice came forth. "Queriven, former knight of the Center Tree's combat unit?"

"Yes," Queriven answered, not moving from his place on the ground.

"Stand," Foradue beckoned, "so that the forest may rightfully judge your actions."

Queriven did so without complaint and waited. The ruler of the Center Tree didn't continue right away, but rather scanned the observers silently. Blair wondered what he was looking for...

Then, the elder sighed and propped his head up on his hand. "We wish to hear your story." He didn't speak from a formal script but talked like he spoke with a long lost friend. "Queriven, I respected you as both a knight and a friend. When I heard you led your teammates out where they were not given permission to be, I was both concerned and confused. I didn't think you would have forsaken them, or left them there and ran away yourself." Then, he sat up, his face genuinely sad. "I always thought, even after all this time, there was a reason behind this...behind you disappearing."

It was time for Queriven to answer and Blair looked away, suddenly not wanting to hear the story about his battle, not after learning that Darkadus was right. He approached the desk and held his arms on either side of him. "I wish I had a better story, Your Honor, but I'm afraid I have to disappoint you on this one." Queriven watched for a response, but there was none. "Before I begin though, please understand I carry utmost regret over what happened back then. I never should have taken them there in the first place." He nodded solemnly and couldn't meet Foradue's face. "If I could change the outcome, I would in a heartbeat," he whispered.

An unsettling shiver coursed through his body and the only way for him to start was with his eyes closed...

"Twenty years ago, I met a strange elf. He said his name was Aswren and he told me he was a new soldier under my rank and we would be working together. It didn't mean much to me at the time, so I accepted his friendship. He worked and obeyed without question and would visit after duty with the rest of us."

Blair furrowed her brows, the anger mixing in with a stirring pot of sympathy and sadness. She remembered telling her story when she first met with the real Queriven, and she remembered how he denied knowing anything about it other than the horn. Queriven already lied to her on the day they met.

"Aswren became interested in my past and started to ask me about it. He was also very intrigued over the ancient horn I carried with me at all times as a sign of my knighthood. After a while, I became annoyed with his constant pestering and released my anger on him." Tense shoulders slumped and thoughtful eyes sparked open. "I know now he was trying to find the right time to steal the horn from me, but none of his attempts worked. Instead of giving up, he decided to try something different. First, he apologized so he could gain my forgiveness, then he found my weakness; my reason for becoming a member of the Center Tree in the first place." He paused, as if he suffered an interrupting itch he couldn't reach.

Sirnah, Finhaus, and Kielle all solemnly bowed their heads like they knew what he was about to explain.

"To find revenge on the people who attacked the Forest Border Trading Post. Of course, they were human, so their times have already passed, but that didn't matter to me. My soul needed closure after my parents were killed there."

Blair's eyes popped open. His parents?! His parents were killed at the trading post?! No wonder he seemed so upset when she asked him about the day the trade ended. Still shocked, Blair turned her head toward his siblings. They were all quiet and sorrowful. They were all just children at that time and

Queriven was the eldest. The other three must have been pretty little. It must have been hard for them to recover on their own. Blair couldn't imagine what it would be like if her parents weren't around...

"Aswren used that information against me," Queriven continued, hesitating more between sentences. "It was almost a year later, and he told me he found that group of thieves right outside the forest. I didn't know what to think at first, but I followed him and saw the group for myself. After I learned about the attack, I investigated this group and learned everything about them. Aswren knew this too and created them well. They were from the far southern continent. Their faces were exotic, not like the humans of Fairdraisha. They even carried the right uniforms and flag. Immediately, I brought the news to you, Foradue, and your response was wiser than mine. You told me they needed to be watched in case they were planning something, but they were otherwise not an issue since they weren't on our land. We were safe since they wouldn't be able to enter the forest without an escort.

"This is where my mistake set in. I believed I could take them. Some of my friends within the unit already knew that was my plan and tried to stop me, but I fought back saying if they weren't coming, I would go alone." He took a breath and rubbed the back of his neck. "They had my back and came with me, but it was a planned ambush." His voice raised a pitch higher now, almost like he wanted to split in sobs, but he didn't let a tear fall. Blair turned away again, too bothered to watch him continue. Even when he choked or sniffed, her heart hurt. "Aswren was there, and that's when I learned his true identity as Darkadus before he... had us surrounded by his men. Every elf in my unit died trying to protect me, and after I was the only survivor, his henchman, a pirate by the name of Yusen Nashōgan, was about to kill me as well, but Darkadus stopped him. He took the horn from my possession and said that I may be more useful left alive." His hands were shaking and he couldn't stop the tears from dropping any longer. "I thought he was taking me hostage, but then they all walked away and left me alone on the battlefield. An hour passed as I mourned my fallen friends in the quiet field around me. Then I made another stupid mistake; I ran away. I was too much of a coward to return home and face the consequences. I let down my friends, my unit, and my family. I owed the world to all of them. They gave me everything. I couldn't face anyone after becoming such a terrible disappointment."

Finally, Queriven's voice broke and he slowly fell to his knees again. "It's my fault they're dead!" he cried, though his voice fell so far he was barely understood. "I'm sorry, my friends. So sorry...!" His weeping echoed in the open around them and Blair wanted to go to him, but she stayed where she was.

No one saw Foradue's face drop in sorrow as Queriven's cries continued. Painful minutes went by, and Blair noticed Foradue turn toward the other elves beside him and started speaking in their native tongue. As they discussed quietly, Queriven's weeping also quieted down, though he still remained on the floor.

The discomfort was making Blair more and more anxious. What was Foradue saying? If only she could understand the elven language, she might have a better idea of what was going on. She turned to Queriven's siblings, but none of them offered her any clarification.

After what seemed like ages, Foradue turned again to the broken figure in the center of the floor. It was time for an answer. For only a second, Foradue hesitated, then he sucked in a breath before speaking. "After discussing with the heads of the Center Tree, I've come to a decision. Though it does pain me more than a little. Queriven," he addressed the elf before him, but he continued on when the subject didn't raise his eyes. "Because of your endangerment to your fellow comrades, and then how you abandoned your responsibilities and trust before the Center Tree, we've deemed it best to exile you from Aven Forest."

Blair's mouth dropped open and she shot a look to Queriven who still didn't respond. Foradue wasn't done. "And the human you brought onto our grounds has to leave as well. I am sorry, but it has to be done."

That was it then. That was the end of their mission. Queriven was forever lost from home and Blair's curse never felt tighter on her skin.

Foradue pushed his chair back, but someone had stepped in front of Blair and called him to wait. It was Kielle. "Your honor, if I may!" She waited for his response and Foradue turned to her. "The reason Queriven came back into the forest is important and needs to be addressed."

Foradue sighed but returned to his chair with an open face. "I'm listening," he replied calmly.

"He came back home to save the human girl from a threat. She carries a rokian's curse and only has a few short months to break it," she finished. Blair didn't expect Kielle to fight for her case. She supposed the distrust she had for her wasn't strong enough to stand in the way of important matters.

There was an uproar of gasps at the table, but Kielle didn't flinch. Foradue's eyes widened and he leaned forward over the table. "A rokian? How?! Those people have been banished for centuries! No elf alive has ever seen them or their magic."

"It's true, and she has the mark to prove it." Kielle turned and beckoned Blair to come up.

Still anxious, Blair obeyed and approached the table. She pulled back her sleeve and lifted her arm up on the surface. Foradue took it with a gentle hand, his light skin wrinkled with age. Wordlessly, he examined the mark, then closed his eyes and let his hand hover over it. A slow and soft light drifted from his palm and covered the area on her wrist, where only a single strand of the curse wasn't faded.

Finally, he let her go and opened his eyes again. Up close, they held much more wisdom than Blair thought and she shrank from his gaze. "It's real for sure. What more do you know about this?"

She hesitated, only to realize he asked her that question. She stumbled to give him an answer. "It's Darkadus. He's a rokian. He cursed me to take his people's place in that dimension. He's breaking them out."

He nodded. "And how long do you have? Do you know how to break it?"

"Until the change in autumn, and we need the horn he took from Queriven. With that, we can call Rocanu to our realm, a vayen aray, and he can break the curse."

"I see," he replied, and Blair could see he was giving this extreme thought. "This concerns the safety of everyone, both Fairdraisha and Aven Forest. There will be severe consequences if it's not broken."

Foradue changed his mind and Blair lightened up. "Fine, you and Queriven may stay to break the curse. Do everything you have to." He leaned back comfortably in his seat and addressed the unmoved Queriven next. "But this is temporary. No matter the outcome, both of you need to be out of the forest before winter, and of course, you understand your title in the Center Tree will still be revoked?"

Queriven was in the middle of agreeing when another figure stepped up to the table. This was an onlooker. Blair didn't see him before and she wondered if he's been watching this whole time. His face was glowing red in anger and he brushed back a strand of thick black hair, as if he was trying to occupy his rising rage. "You don't mean that, do you? This man is dangerous! We all saw the evidence. Why allow him to stay?" he yelled, trying to keep his voice straight.

Queriven finally lifted his face at the sound of the newcomer's voice. "Dakru..." he whispered.

No one but Blair reacted to his response. Foradue didn't flinch by the newcomer's disagreement. "As I said, this is only temporary. Didn't you hear me? They must leave before winter."

The protestor wasn't satisfied. "He killed our people! Our friends and family! He shouldn't be staying here at all. Get rid of him!"

Foradue finally snapped. "And ignore the threat of returning rokians? Don't you know how important this is, or do you want them to return and destroy us all?"

The elf flung his arm back. "Then let the human stay. I didn't hear she needed any help from this monster!" he yelled, pointing a finger at Queriven, who was rising to his feet.

Dakru was not the only angry one now, and Foradue yelled back. "I've made my decision! You've taken this too personally, Dakru."

"Our people need justice!"

"The only thing you're wanting is revenge!"

Like a child, Dakru could do nothing but stomp a disapproving foot in the ground. Queriven approached and was about to speak, but the other turned and dashed by him, disappearing in the street.

Foradue had nothing to say of the occurrence and stood up from his chair. "If you need any help from the Center Tree during this time, let us know," he calmly said, his other members of court following him away from the table.

The elven family and Blair gathered together and turned away quietly.

CHAPTER TWENTY-SEVEN
TEARS AND VENGEANCE

If one saw the family sitting in the living room that night, they would have thought they were in mourning. For the longest time, no one said a word. All eyes stared at the floor. The stress of the court was almost too much and no one knew how to act.

Sirnah was the first to speak. The silence bothered him more and more. "So how do we break this curse? What do we need to do?" he asked, almost like he was afraid to.

Queriven took a long time to process his brother's question. Finally, without lifting his face, he answered, "Somehow we need that horn Darkadus took back. Without it, we can't summon Rocanu, the vayen aray who said he would help us. Then, we need to find where those people originally passed on that horn and go there ourselves." He exhaled and shook his head, his hair floating down in front of his face. His hands sparked with frustration as his fists broke open in sudden expression. "Who knows how long that'll take us? Taking the horn Darkadus wears on his person constantly is impossible enough, let alone finding where that ritual of peace took place."

The other three elves exchanged glances and Sirnah spoke up again. "Brother, we already know where the vayen aray gave us that artifact. Don't you remember? We learned it in school."

Queriven glanced his way with keen interest. Kielle answered, "It was on top of the waterfall in Lettir." When there was no response, she shrugged. "You probably don't remember because you were focusing so hard on your training at the time."

He sighed and returned to his previous position. "I suppose that just leaves us with one job then, but that doesn't make this any easier."

Blair was sitting on the last stair step, and though she remained quiet all this time, she finally chirped in. "Darkadus is a trickster. Nothing surprises him. How can we sneak the horn away without him knowing?"

Queriven thought back to when he learned the rokian was spending his magic to watch their movements. He probably knew of their next plan already. It was hard to tell. The more time that went by, the less magic Darkadus was trying to use. "I don't know."

The silence returned, but too many questions were going through Blair's mind for her to endure it. "So who was that man who interrupted? He seemed pretty upset."

No one answered as they hoped someone else would. It was Kielle who gathered the courage to. "That was Dakru. Queriven and he used to be good friends."

Blair tilted her head. "'Used to'?"

Queriven interrupted Kielle, who was about to speak again. "How do the humans say it? He was engaged with a girl who was in my unit."

Ashamed she asked only to hear such a heartbreaking answer, Blair didn't reply.

Finhaus adjusted his position. "It's not your fault. You didn't want that to happen. You shouldn't carry their deaths."

Queriven stood up, taking everybody by surprise. "I disobeyed orders. I took my unit straight into an ambush! Of course, it's my fault!"

Sirnah stood, seeking to comfort him. "Queriven..."

But Queriven backed away from him, declaring he needed

some air before he bolted out of the door.

Blair stood, thinking to follow him. Tears were spilling from her eyes. Kielle grasped her arm. "Don't bother. When Queriven wants to be alone, no one can find him."

That did little to help Blair, but she slowly sat down again, fiddling with her fingers uncomfortably. Kielle gave her arm a supportive rub before moving past her, saying she was going to ready herself for her shift for the night.

Blair remained on that last stair even when everyone else left...

◊ ◊ ◊

Queriven wandered the city edge long after the last shine of sun left the sky. Now the only light in the landscape was the collection of bouncing colors in the wilderness and the organized orbs floating by the city streets.

He cried until he no longer had the strength to, and now walked with an aching heart. For the first time in twenty years, he allowed his mind to repeat his past actions, something he always dismissed. He remembered his friends he tried to forget, his training, and his station at the Central Tree. He remembered it all like it was fresh and recent. He soaked in the hurt like a sponge, taking it in even though it threatened him. The burden was heavy and bitter, like a hand that squeezed his heart, making it hard for him to breathe beyond what he desperately needed.

His mind was so internally focused that he didn't know of the figure hiding in the darkness.

An invisible wall flashed in front of Queriven's face, and before he even had a chance to understand what happened, the hiding figure pulled him from the streets and into the dark space between the tall trees of the city.

Queriven stumbled, too stunned to react with his weapon. He scrambled on his knees to face his attacker.

It was Dakru and he looked angry enough to kill.

"Dakru!" Queriven cried. "What are you...?"

But Dakru moved again, this time ramming his fist into Queriven's cheek. "You shouldn't have come back," he cried. "That was your last mistake!" Then, without warning, he withdrew a short staff, finely carved and beautiful. The wooden staff held a dazzling cyan orb cradled on the top. Dakru flashed it in Queriven's face. Sparks shattered over the smooth surface and popped forward, burning the elf's skin.

Queriven scrambled backward, drawing the spear from his back as he also worked on standing up. The weapon he held in his hands was nothing like the spear he used to hold. This one was human-made and wasn't as nice or sharp as his old one. It would have to serve for now. He tried to speak again, and again, his mad attacker interrupted. "If the Center Tree won't serve this justice, I'd do it myself!"

For just a second, Queriven launched the spear to attack, but then quickly drew it in. His hesitance made him realize he didn't want to hurt his old friend.

But Dakru was still intent on hurting him.

The staff was sparking again and Queriven rushed forward and grabbed it. Dakru wasn't expecting that, and he pushed and pulled, trying to free it. When that didn't work, he pushed it again, slamming it right into Queriven's mouth. The elf recoiled, falling back with a hand over his face.

Dakru stomped. "What's wrong with you!? Strike me! Fight me with the skills that made you a knight!"

Blood spilled from Queriven's mouth when he answered, "Please, Dakru, I don't want to..."

Sparks flashed again, but instead of attacking, the magic took hold and slid him toward the wielder. Dakru stepped back, allowing Queriven to crash into the tree home behind him. "You're a coward!" Dakru spat, waiting for his opponent to stand. "And just like a coward, you'd do anything to defend your own life. Take the opening. Fight me now!" He only continued to tease after Queriven stood face to face with him, still not defending himself though the spear was still in his hands.

Queriven's heart was racing again, this time because he

feared for his safety. Desperately, he tried to plead to his attacker. "This will not bring Fia back..."

Wrong answer. Dakru's thin face contorted with so much more hurt and anger than possible. In one swoop, the butt of the staff pummeled the elf in the stomach, knocking him once again to the ground. As he gasped for air, Dakru ran a boot into him, once, twice, and a third time. "She was my love, my future. Do you understand that?! We had a life before us!" Sobs spilled into his voice, making his words hard to understand. "You took her away. How could you?"

He continued to yell, but Queriven could no longer hear it beyond the beatings now aimed at his face. The spear was kicked away somewhere in the chaos.

At some point, Dakru must have noticed it too because he stopped and used the staff again, forcing Queriven back up to his feet. Then, when he was secured against the wall for support, the popping sparks drew the dropped spear up and before him. When he didn't move to grab it, Dakru pushed into his arms. "Use it!" he spat again. "Or I'll just kill you!"

Queriven neither moved nor breathed, only locking his swollen eye on him.

Dakru flinched, but an outburst drew a short shiny dagger from his pocket, which he pushed against Queriven's throat. "It's not right," Dakru whined, but Queriven held his gaze, knowing this could be the last sight he sees. "You shouldn't have lived when everyone else perished in that field. I have to kill you."

That night, Queriven believed he actually tried to. The hand before his throat trembled harder and he bared his teeth. Even in that awful state, Dakru knew a sharp spear was still in Queriven's hands. If he wanted to, Queriven would have already killed him.

And yet, he did nothing. He accepted the fate staring before him, even if he had something he could use to avoid death already lying in his arms.

Finally, Dakru broke into the unspoken question they both

had. "Why won't you do it? Why do you choose not to defend yourself?"

There was only one answer to that and Queriven said it with certainty. "Because if I were in your place, I'd be doing the exact same thing."

Deep inside that tormented gaze, Queriven saw a familiar spark of recognition, of old friendship. Weakness made the dagger drop from his hand and Dakru sank defeated to the ground.

The weeping grew louder, but Queriven didn't leave. Instead, he shrank to the ground and mourned quietly.

He didn't notice when his head first started pounding, and his chest ached with each breath, but still, he listened to every wordless cry.

On his hands and knees, Dakru glanced up at the victim he tried to kill a second earlier. Red eyes blinked burning tears as he glimpsed in perspective Queriven's bruises. "I loved her," he whined again. "We were starting a family. I just can't be the same again." He lowered his head, allowing dark hair to brush downwards. He pounded a balled fist into the ground. "I've never been able to love anyone else, not after her..." Dakru's chest heaved with sorrow. "I'm so sorry, my old friend. Please forgive me..!"

How could Queriven hate him if he related with Dakru's response? When he crouched closer, he grasped his friend in a tight hug. Both were weeping for the regretful past.

Time flew. It must have been an hour later when Dakru gave a final sniff before pushing up from the ground. Queriven rose as well, trying to be supportive in any way he could.

But Dakru said nothing. The smaller elf evaluated every wound he inflicted on Queriven, and he tried to respond with words. He had nothing and only backed away slowly. He gave Queriven one last look over the shoulder, who was still standing there watching him before he walked into the darkness.

Only when he finally disappeared from sight did Queriven turn. He picked up the stainless weapon and also walked. The first shimmer of light blue was showing in the sky. It was nearly morning. The elf wiped a drop of blood from his lips. If only he didn't have to show his injuries in front of Blair...

◊ ◊ ◊

Queriven only had a short time to sleep before morning. Not like that mattered anyway. He wouldn't have been able to. Surprisingly, Sirnah was already in the living room reading a book. He paused at the sound of the door and lifted his eyes above the fiber-bound book in his hands. He said nothing at first, but his horrified eyes told Queriven the truth of how he looked. "What happened to you?"

The elf shrugged it off like it was nothing and closed the door, really wishing his brother wasn't here to see this.

Sirnah wasn't convinced. He dropped the book on the table in front of him and stood up, coming to his brother's side. As much as this annoyed Queriven, he didn't have the strength to push him away. Sirnah examined each wound he could see before rushing out of the room, promising he would be right back.

Queriven chuckled, though it was more out of annoyance than joy. He slowly strolled over to the couch and took the seat opposite where his brother was a moment ago. Curious, he peered at the book on the table, only to see it was an old elven fable. Queriven leaned back, trying to rest as comfortably as he could.

Soon after, Sirnah came down the stairs again holding a neat woven basket of various items; everything from medicine and herbs, to fabrics and tools. This was Sirnah's medical basket, one he carried on him in case of emergency. As he dropped the last step, Queriven admired how Sirnah didn't change. Sirnah was always a genius with his remedies. He was shy and awkward with a lot of things, but he was confident and passionate about those skills at least.

Without asking permission, he sat down next to Queriven and set the basket on the table. In his other hand, he held a bowl of water, which he also set down. Queriven watched as he made a grasping motion toward the bowl and the water slowly crackled to ice. Then, he retrieved a thin piece of fabric and wrapped a handful of the ice inside it before finally bringing it to his brother's swollen face.

Sirnah always seemed so calm, but Queriven could pick out the stress underneath the surface. His brother's state of health worried him. Sirnah was the first to comment about it. "So...are we going to talk about this?"

Queriven wasn't dumb enough to pretend he didn't know what he was talking about. "There's no reason to."

He wasn't sure what the response would be, but like always, Sirnah wasn't mad. "I'm tired of tending your wounds all the time. Can't you look after yourself better?" He wasn't joking when he said it. But after he finished, he flashed a beautiful white smile, making his round face look wider.

Queriven chuckled and silence returned. Sirnah passed the ice to Queriven and allowed him to hold it where he needed it.

Sirnah was somber again, and he began to check for more wounds. Queriven's shoulders were tense and his heart was quick. "Can you relax a bit and steady your pulse?" Sirnah asked, placing a thin hand on Queriven's chest as he did so. He was breathing deeper, though each rise and fall of his chest was difficult. Sirnah focused in again. "Does it hurt to breathe?"

There was one more exhale and Queriven answered. "I'm just a little winded."

Sirnah sat back, folding his arms in his lap. He was smart enough to look past his stubborn brother. "You need rest and care. You have broken a rib."

Again, Queriven did not respond. Sirnah began rifling through his medicine basket, though it was more to distract his thoughts than anything. Like the approach of dusk, Sirnah's mood slowly fell to sadness. He swallowed, but a tear still dropped from his eye.

Queriven furrowed his expression curiously and sat up.

A long sleeve came up and Sirnah damped his eyes. He sniffed and continued picking out herbs. "I'm sorry, I'm just...

So glad you're home."

To Queriven, that seemed a little silly, but he didn't put it off. Sirnah picked the bundle he had made and dropped it in another bowl. "I guess it's just catching up with me, but you've been gone for so long. This family wasn't the same after you left. We mourned you for years."

Guilt played on Queriven's heart and he moved the ice from his face. "I'm sorry I didn't come back. Every one of you deserved the truth from the beginning."

"Yeah," Sirnah agreed. "But you're here now and I just want to tell you that we all forgive your actions. None of us wants you to leave again."

Queriven wanted to smile, wanted to feel accepted into his homeland again, but it didn't offer the comfort he was looking for; perhaps because, if he wanted to or not, he was still leaving. He must leave before winter.

Then, before either of the two could begin to speak of the unspoken threat, there were footsteps coming down the stairs. Both brothers turned their heads to see Blair enter the room. Her neutral expression shattered when she caught Queriven watching her. His usual smoothly toned skin was cracked, bruised, and swollen. One eye was almost shut entirely. Blair couldn't help but freeze and stare. Her lips parted and her brows lifted in shock. A ray of sunlight was beaming into the room from the window, catching her hair alight and brought the colors in her eyes alive. The tones of her hair and eyes seemed to match perfectly at that moment.

She couldn't say a thing and Queriven fell further on the sofa when she quickly escaped through the front door. He turned to Sirnah as the door slammed, who was watching the scene intently. Queriven brought the ice back to his face. "She hasn't said a word to me since that time she yelled at me," he admitted his frustration.

Sirnah wasn't concerned. "Give her space. She'll talk again eventually." With a bowl of herbs in hand, Sirnah rose from his seat. "I'll make you some tea. Just relax here for a while."

Queriven sighed, a rack of pain hitting his chest when he did so. He groaned aloud but sank back into the cushion. His mind was a loud mix, and the only thing it did to him was keep up his headache and made him otherwise miserable. He wished he'd died in that battle as well. None of this was worth it; not if it meant he had to argue to the death with his old friends. Who else in this forest wanted him dead? Surely, all the loved ones from his unit would want to kill him too, maybe with less hesitancy.

Before he knew it, as he was waiting patiently for his brother to come back, Queriven fell asleep.

He awoke sometime later with a steaming cup of tea in his face and a concerned Sirnah holding it.

Queriven jerked and sat up, but the cloth of ice in his lap had melted. Cold water spilled over his legs when he moved. Resisting to cry about the cold bite soaking his skin, he took the cup from Sirnah, who apologized to him. "I thought about letting you sleep, but I wanted your tea to be ready when you woke up. I didn't think you would still be out."

Muffled and tired, Queriven assured him that it was fine, though the pain in his chest, head, along with the cold water, made him uncomfortable. Sirnah leaned in and nodded to the stairs. "Just to let you know, Kielle's back home. She's mighty upset after she saw you on the couch."

Queriven pressed a hand over his injured face. "What time is it?"

"Almost noon. You haven't slept for more than a few hours," Sirnah answered, passing Queriven a dry cloth. Queriven took it, thanked him, and began drying the water on his lap. "Do you want to go upstairs to your room?"

"Not yet," Queriven groaned again, trying to process his thoughts. "Did Blair come back?"

To Queriven's dismay, Sirnah shook his head. "I don't know what she's doing, but I haven't seen her."

Queriven took a sip from the cup. The hot tea poured down into his empty stomach. "She's probably just trying to think of a way to move forward." With a second sip, he set the cup down on the table. "We're running out of time and we're not making any progress."

Sirnah wanted to offer some encouragement, but he had nothing to say. Queriven shifted. "How could we? There's no way we can steal that horn without the rokian knowing. He'll kill us all before we can reach Lettir."

Unable to share advice, Sirnah did the best he could to say something positive. "I'm sure there's a way. Rokians aren't perfect. They're powerful, but they still make mistakes. We just have to find out how to expose his weakness."

Queriven was about to ask how they might even accomplish that much, but Kielle entered the room. Sirnah was right; she didn't look happy at all. "Lunch is ready. Come up into the kitchen if you want it."

The brothers exchanged glances. Queriven was the first to stand from the couch, but he followed Sirnah to the stairs first. Kielle's eyes peered into Queriven as she warned him she wanted answers to what happened the last night. That was the dangerous stare she gave her brothers when they were in serious trouble. Her intelligent eyes were flecked with gold, only making her look more intimidating. He said nothing and marched up the stairs.

A sweet and hearty aroma greeted him when he came up to the kitchen table. There were steamed vegetables, elven-prepared bread and jams, and even a sweet syrup hardened into sticky treats. Queriven sat down with the others. "Where's Finhaus?" he asked.

Kielle reached across the table and began to portion food into her plate. "He's working at home right now. He might stop by later today." When she finished, she took a bite of carrot and waited for Queriven to load his plate. She watched him like a hungry shark. Finally, she had her chance, and she was straightforward about it. "Sirnah said you wouldn't tell him what happened last night. Who did that to you?"

Queriven lifted his bruised face and froze for a second. How much should he say? He grabbed a piece of bread and began spreading some thick jam over it. "I don't know. Someone jumped on me as I was coming back home. It was dark. I don't know who it was. He kicked me around a bit and then he left when I was able to retrieve my weapon."

Kielle hesitated like she knew he was already lying to her. She went back to her plate for another bite of carrot before she looked up again. "You should have known better than to stay out after dark. A lot of people are wanting to hurt you. Don't you see how lucky you are to be alive right now?"

Queriven thought that was funny because the last thing he felt was lucky. He shrugged off her remark, but she continued to watch him. "From now on, maybe it's best if you don't go out there alone. I don't want anything to happen to you again."

He planned on not saying anything, but that last part made him upset. "I'm not a child anymore!" he yelled, banging the table harder than he wanted to. Now Sirnah had his eyes on him as well. Guilt crept in again and the looks made Queriven uncomfortable. He chose not to give in. He held his firm stare for a while before the others began eating again. Queriven also tried to return to his food, but all of a sudden, he didn't have the appetite for it anymore.

The table was too quiet, and he knew everyone was still thinking about Queriven's temper. He took a bite of bread, though it seemed less flavorful than it did a moment ago. It now seemed like nothing but crumbles of dust with dull thick texture on top of it instead of earthy jam.

By the time someone spoke again though, Queriven would have preferred the silence. "Was that Dakru last night?" It was Kielle who asked quietly. It was always Kielle.

Queriven melted into the table, running a stressed hand through his ungroomed hair.

She was serious now. She leaned over the table at him, her eyes unconditional with love. "Why would you lie about that?"

Still slouching, Queriven answered, "Because he's innocent. He's only done what anybody would have. Dakru loved Fia with all his heart. I can't blame him for that." He brushed his hair back and sat up, now facing her. "Besides, he left me alive.

Don't take this to the Center Tree. He's had a rough enough time already. He doesn't need to face exile as well as me." By the look she gave him, Queriven couldn't tell if she approved of his decision or not. He continued to match her until she finally looked away. "Kielle," he said, taking hold of her again, "don't condemn him."

She held a hand out, either blocking him or trying to calm him down. "All right, I won't, but stay away from him. He might still change his mind. Let the Center Tree handle these things if they need to."

Finally, Queriven could agree with that. He went back to eating, though something was still picking at his mind. The flavor was slowly returning to his food as he relaxed, though he was focusing on a different thought now. He wished Blair was here so that he might discuss it with her. "We need to find a way to take that horn, or there's not going to be enough time left."

"Well," Kielle said with a full mouth. She paused so she might finish. "You said this Darkadus has it. Do you have any idea where he is right now?"

"No," Queriven replied. "He has a hideout on the western hill behind Dunverhart, but that's a long way away. He may not even be there." He sighed, pondering out loud now. "And as it turns out, he uses his magic to spy on us every now and then. He may even know we're trying to steal from him now."

"That's difficult," Sirnah remarked. Both Queriven and Kielle looked at him. "I suppose chasing him around in Fairdraisha isn't an option considering his nature and the time we have left. So what are our options?"

"That's the question. Let's not forget about his henchmen," Queriven added. "Even if we manage to trick him, he'll send his pirates after us."

Sirnah held up a finger. "What if we storm his hideout? We may find a clue to his location if he's not there, and if we gather in a large group."

"Then King Brenmor will blame us for invasion. That's the last thing Aven Forest needs."

Kielle gazed off into her thoughts. "Then what? We have to do something. We can't let the rokians take over again."

"I know," Queriven answered, picking up the syrup treat and resting his back against the chair. "But I'm not sure what we can do about it."

"We may have to prepare for the worst of it," Sirnah said. "Maybe this time we can push them back ourselves, even without the vayen aray."

Queriven was not too happy about that last idea. "You can't be serious! Thousands of people, both humans and elves, will be killed! Not to mention, Blair will be sucked into their dimension. I will make sure that doesn't happen to her. I will ensure her safe future if I die giving it to her."

Both of his siblings seemed shocked to hear him say that, and they watched him finish the last of the treat. Kielle was the first to give in to the stunning silence. "I never thought I would hear you say that about a human. I only remember you hating them because of what happened at the trading post."

"I've changed that," Queriven declared, drinking the last of his tea. "Don't forget, I've lived in Fairdraisha for twenty years. Once I hated humans, but now I see they're not that terrible. It's true that Fairdraisha is under the rule of a king who's less than good, but that doesn't represent their entire race. Back in the old days when our people traded with them, our cultures were inspired by the other. We celebrated and lived together. You wouldn't understand that because that was before your time, but it's true." He paused, and Kielle and Sirnah exchanged glances. This was not the same Queriven who left twenty years ago. Not changing his mind, Queriven leaned over the table and caught their attention. "I encourage you two to see Blair as one of our own. She didn't choose to be born human, nor did we as elves, but that doesn't mean we can't understand each other."

After another nervous glance between Kielle and Sirnah, Queriven stood up and started gathering plates. Quickly, Sirnah stood and took them from him. "Kielle and I will clean the kitchen. You just rest for today."

Queriven allowed him to take them, and he turned thinking he might search for Blair, but something stopped him. Maybe she didn't want to see him. Maybe she was still mad. How long will this last? Did he destroy their friendship forever?

"Are you all right?" a voice asked. It was Sirnah. He was staring at him curiously, holding a stack of plates and cups in his arms.

Queriven then realized he was standing in the middle of the kitchen doing nothing. He nodded, hoping they couldn't read the sorrow on his face. Then he slowly retreated up the stairs without another word.

No answers remained. Darkadus was right; time was already out and he knew it.

Blair needed time to comprehend her own thoughts and emotions. She moved freely around the elvish streets, awed once more about the rich culture in her new surroundings. It was so different and so beautiful in comparison to her own dreams about the forest. She wished she could see it in different circumstances. Now her mind blocked her awareness like she wasn't standing in front of it, and she tried to clear her eyes for once. As unique and beautiful as it was, Aven Forest had a scent of familiarity about it, something like home, yet not quite. She stood engulfed in a new world like she was on a new continent from Fairdraisha.

Slowly and half aware, Blair browsed around the sights of the city through streets of tall homes and fields filled with herbs and crops. The city certainly seemed livelier the further in she went, but she was still pretty clueless about the ways of the elves. There were several banners placed on homes as she went, though if it was trying to help with her sense of navigation, it fell short on her. Everything was written in elvish. As of the moment though, she wasn't afraid of getting lost and stopped only when she found a comfortable spot in the grass.

Her memory haunted her like a leech, reminding her every five minutes of a promise she made to return home soon. Now she might never make that promise at all. She nearly cried aloud. They were so close to breaking the curse! If only the horn from the castle wasn't broken, then they would have seen the end of all this.

She didn't blame Queriven for any of it, not even for a moment. She wasn't trying to avoid him; she just wanted to give him space as he handled these personal matters. There wasn't much room for her to butt in anyway. Never before did she feel like such a stranger. Everywhere she went, there were judging eyes on her. The only one who didn't look at her this way was Queriven himself, the one she yelled at.

He was trying so hard. How could she not see that when he came all the way out here again? He did it just for her and she only became upset with his shame over the past. He didn't deserve that, and Blair never wanted to yell at him again.

She sat there for several hours, drifting back and forth from her mind to the forest. She was sorry there wasn't another chance at a first impression on the forest. She wanted to feel a rush as her dream finally came true before her eyes. That wasn't important enough right now.

She wanted to talk to Queriven at some point and tell him she forgives him. There will be enough time for that much at least.

CHAPTER TWENTY-EIGHT
LORD OF THE FOREST

Several days later, and little has changed. Despite the amount of brainstorming, Queriven had no new ideas. He was growing more and more anxious. Summer was still young, but it won't be for long. He had to act soon if he planned on doing anything at all. Sadly, he was still in a lot of pain from his meeting with Dakru, and it would only slow him down. There was no way he could escape with the horn with his injuries. Though time was pressing, he had to wait.

Meanwhile, the others talked about searching for Darkadus themselves, but Queriven couldn't help but think that wouldn't work either. Surely, Darkadus knew of their plan by now. He wouldn't be waiting in the open for them. If a team set out, they would need someone who was familiar with his tricks and his horde of pirates, but foremost, they needed an airtight, quick plan of action. They needed to know exactly where he was and they needed to return home right after their attack.

They might need outside help, Queriven decided, and he set off one morning to the court of the Center Tree. Once there, he requested to speak with Foradue, who complied and met him within the tree itself.

The interior was spacious and clean. The room was wider than even Kielle's home. It was certainly fitting for the leader of the elves, but it was also modest as well. The Center Tree had no need for expensive rugs or sparkling candelabras. It wasn't drowning in heavy perfumes either but smelled like a fresh spring breeze.

Foradue gave Queriven a simple greeting, then settled in a soft armchair with green-dyed cushions and twisted branches as the frame. With an elegant wave, he gestured Queriven to sit on the matching one opposite him. "What may I help you with?" Foradue asked. "I'm assuming you came today to ask for my assistance."

"That's right," Queriven answered, trying not to be self-conscious about the bruises still covering his face. "Darkadus is still out there somewhere in Fairdraisha. I fear we don't have a lot of time to seek him out and make it back safely with the horn. We need help if we're to make it in time."

Foradue nodded, listening intently. "Very well then. What do you need me to do?"

After a second of hesitation, he answered, "For starters, we need to know exactly where Darkadus is, and second, we need to somehow reach there quickly and back. I don't know the best way to do that; maybe teleportation or a speed enchantment?"

Foradue stayed silent for a moment, taking in the message. "I suppose... The first part shouldn't be too hard. That is unless this rokian would be harder to find than others. However, the second request may be more difficult. How many are you planning on taking?"

Queriven shrugged. "I don't know for sure yet. Just a small group."

"Keep in mind that we would have to use our magic on each one of them. Also, it may be easy enough to cast it the first time, but how will we use it again to bring you back?"

Queriven had nothing to say about that and dropped his gaze.

Foradue wasn't finished though, and he thought to himself for a moment before coming to an idea of his own. "I wonder if it'll be best to send a few wizards with you. That way, they can be the ones in charge of your return."

Finally, some good news. Queriven raised his head again.

Foradue slowly pushed himself up from the chair. "Why don't we see where this Darkadus is?"

Queriven stood up as well and followed closely behind Foradue. He took them up a set of stairs. The first floor had a tall ceiling, and so they had to climb over a hundred steps just to reach the next floor. Foradue was not young. His hair was like a light gray waterfall cascading down his back and his skin wrinkled from many centuries of life. Yet, the walk barely seemed to bother him. He floated over them like it was flat ground. He didn't need an extra breath. Queriven took silent note of his amazing strength.

The next floor didn't look too different from the first, but this was where Foradue disembarked from the stairs. Queriven didn't say anything and only continued behind him. Against the opposite wall was an open door leading out onto a balcony. There was a small table outside, but what caught Queriven's attention was the shelves lining the wall. The shelves were carved right in the wood and ran from one side of the door to the other. Within the shelves though was an assortment of different sparkling gems. Everything from emeralds and sapphires to pearls and crystals lined carefully all over.

Foradue stopped here and pressed a pondering finger to his lips, browsing them carefully. "Each one of these has a magical purpose," he explained. "They were normal gems when the humans gave them to us in the days of trade, but we knew they could be important and helpful if enchanted right." He browsed a minute more before selecting a large pink sapphire and carrying it outside to the table.

Foradue set the gem gently on the table and sat down, and Queriven did as well. Foradue leaned over the table with his hands on either side of the gem. Then, he peered inside of it. The morning sun cast a bright ray directly on the balcony, making the pink gem glow all the brighter. Again, it didn't seem to bother Foradue. He didn't squint or look away.

"That's odd. Why can't I see him?" he asked with genuine interest. Queriven didn't answer; he only allowed him to peer deeper. Without looking away, Foradue asked, "You mean for me to seek Darkadus, the only rokian on the plains?"

Queriven quietly answered that it was, only for Foradue to grow more confused. Finally, he blinked away and sat back in his chair. "I don't know why I can't see him. I figured it would be easy to find him as he's the only one of his kind here, but I couldn't see him well, only his form. He had a lot of magic surrounding him."

Of course, that was the case. Queriven frowned. "He's setting up his defenses."

"Could be," Foradue said, raising a thin eyebrow. "But maybe not. The reason I could barely see him is that I was being redirected. It's like he's two places at once. Something is anchoring his soul in another world."

That made even more sense. Queriven cursed himself for missing the obvious. He already knew Darkadus was weakened here. He mentioned how he was only partially in this land. That explained why he had limited power. "Then we're back to square one."

"Maybe so," Foradue lamented, standing up. "But there may be other means of finding him. I'll look into it myself. In the meantime," he added as Queriven rose, "continue your search for action and come back if you have anything new to add."

Queriven wanted to complain there was nothing more to add. Nothing more would help him then, but he was polite and thanked the elven leader. Foradue bowed and led Queriven out the way he came in. "Oh, and I want to apologize for the harshness of the trial the other day," Foradue called to him, making the elf turn back around. "I don't like telling people they're exiled from the forest, particularly an old friend of mine... But I have a responsibility to the forest I have to hold. I hope you don't think badly of me for what happened."

Queriven looked off to the side. He was a little more uncomfortable than before, but he tried to brush it off. Personally, he didn't have any anger or blame on his old leader. He was only upset over his own actions. "I know why you made that decision," Queriven answered. His voice was quiet with shame and he couldn't meet his eyes. "And if I was the one judging, I would have come up with the same sentence."

There was sympathy in Foradue's face, but he nodded. Queriven wished him farewell and turned, not wanting to linger on the subject much longer. He wasn't really sure where he could go next. He didn't want to go home and do nothing, but he didn't have any ideas either. After close to an hour of wandering around aimlessly, he decided to visit Finhaus.

Finhaus' farm was further than Kielle's home, and nearly on the edge of the wilderness. Queriven hasn't seen his father's farm since he left the forest. He wondered how it was doing under Finhaus' hands. As it turns out, it was just the same.

Finhaus was already sitting right outside his door. As predicted, he wasn't alone, as he was sharing food with some small birds and a deer. It didn't take long for him to lift his head. "Queriven!" he remarked, his exclamation bringing attention to the animals. The birds on his shoulder ruffled their wings and the deer glanced over at the newcomer. None of them left though and settled down again. "I wasn't expecting you here. Did you need me for anything?"

"Nothing in particular," Queriven answered, stopping and taking in the surroundings of the farm. The grass was a healthy green and the tree stood on a small hill. The farmland next to it was lush and full. It was properly cared for. "Are you already done with your work?"

Finhaus matched his look over to the growing field of herbs and crops. He laughed. "Not quite. I was just taking a break. It's a lot of work, you know!" The food in his hands was gone, and he brushed them off, rising to his feet. The birds continued riding on his shoulder as he came closer to his brother. "I'm excited to have you here. It's been so long since...since you were here last."

Queriven didn't know how to reply, which led to a moment of silence. Not wanting to be too serious, Finhaus cleared the subject. "So what can I do for you? You want anything to eat? Drink?" he asked as he backed away toward the front door.

"Thanks, but I don't need anything," Queriven repeated.

Finhaus gestured to the bench he was sitting on a second

ago. "At least have a seat," he said, sitting down on one side and patting the other.

Queriven relented and sat down next to him. The young deer hesitated and stepped back, now picking at the grass. The breeze carried the hearty scent of trees off in the wilderness. Insects of many kinds buzzed by and called from somewhere in the grass. The sun was hot, but refreshing at the same time.

"So what are you up to today?" Finhaus asked. "Or did you come all the way out here from Kielle's?"

Queriven sighed, the stress of passing time returning to him. "I was at the Center Tree proposing an idea on how to catch Darkadus." A pause and Finhaus urged him on. Queriven continued, "It didn't go well. Foradue couldn't find the rokian because of the magic pulling him to his old dimension. I was so stupid to not consider that. Now I don't know what to do."

Finhaus thought for a moment, wishing he could help. "I know this is important, but don't push yourself. Something will come up. We're all working on it."

"There's only a few months left. The end of summer marks the end of any chance we have."

Finhaus didn't back away. "We're in the prime of summer. There's still a chance."

Queriven chose not to argue with that. He looked over at his brother, catching a glimpse of an ebony knife on the arm of the bench. "What's that old thing doing here?"

Finhaus followed his gaze to the knife and picked it up. "It's summer, Queriven. Have you forgotten about the Starlight Festival?"

Queriven remembered what it was for even before he finished. "Of course. You still milk the stars at the pond?" It was an old tradition to gather starlight at the festival, which is where they celebrated the use of the material. Elves who studied the magic needed to gather it would meet at the open field around the pond in the center of Aven Forest to cut open the rays on a clear summer night when the stars are brightest. Then, they take the light in liquid form home where it's hardened and molded into weapons, tools, and other things.

Finhaus nodded and examined the knife. "I was just tuning it, making sure the magic was sharp and fresh enough for me to use it." He chuckled nervously and set it down. "I know this sounds like an odd question to ask at this time considering there are a lot of important events going on, but are you planning on coming?"

Queriven raised an eyebrow. That was an odd question indeed. He shrugged, not knowing what his answer should be. "I don't know. I guess it just depends on if we can find Darkadus in time."

That only seemed to worry his brother. "The three of us only want to spend more time with you. You've been gone so long, and now the Center Tree has declared to exile you before winter."

The reminder smacked Queriven in the face like a wet towel. "I know, but this is an important task we're on. If we don't succeed, not only is Blair doomed to live in a barren world alone for the rest of her life but the rokians will be released. If I could choose between working on our mission and going to the Starlight Festival, I would choose the former."

Finhaus, looking solemn, shook his head. "You're right. I'm sorry."

Queriven placed a hand on his brother's shoulder. "We'll just have to see what the future brings. If there's a chance for me to be at the festival, I'll take it."

Finhaus' eyes brightened. "Really? That's means a lot to me. Thank you."

Queriven smiled and stood up. "I suppose I should be heading back. They'll be wondering where I left off to. Thank you for letting me stop by."

Finhaus looked up from the bench. "Anytime, dear brother. Good luck with the mission."

Queriven gave a final bow before turning around and walking back toward the city.

Shortly after that, Finhaus rose up and returned to his work.

CHAPTER TWENTY-NINE
THE STARLIGHT FESTIVAL

The Starlight Festival came sooner than anyone thought it would. Kielle and many other knights helped with the preparations. She was gone almost every single day. The streets were starting to look so lively with the set tables and colorful banners. The famed material drizzled like a night sky on the fabric.

And since this was a festival to celebrate starlight, the material became a focal point in many areas, displaying their many uses, both practical and beautiful. Like every year, the festival brought the elves of Sylinna much joy. This was a giant celebration, bringing in elves from other cities to witness the wonder of starlight.

Yet for Queriven, it didn't bring any joy at all. Foradue was still unable to find Darkadus, and no other plan has fallen through. The world was resting its weight on his shoulders until it took his comfort and sleep.

But for Blair, this has only enhanced her own dreams. She could hardly contain the excitement despite the stress of the curse. This festival has finally brought back the spark to her eyes. The city was so rich in culture and beauty. Desperately, she wanted to be a part of it, especially if this might be her last chance to see such an event. Still, she thought, she wasn't going unless Queriven and his family were. It was only fair.

Then she learned of Kielle's and Finhaus' place in it, and that only brought more excitement.

Finally, this was the day of the festivities. Blair has not talked to Queriven or his family about it. Up to this point, she only took in the lively streets quietly, but this morning, she woke in her hammock to some scuffling in the room. She turned her head and saw that Kielle was also there. It was only a little surprising as she usually wasn't present when Blair woke. The elf was too preoccupied to notice Blair stirring as she was going through a large chest next to her bed.

Blair watched her as she tossed aside clothes after more clothes. They were all fine and majestic, and she realized most of them were dresses. Blair asked her what she was doing, though she knew the answer. She was more curious about Kielle at the moment than anything.

Kielle wasn't startled despite not looking back at her. "I'm seeking proper attire for tonight," she responded. Each dress looked like it would be worth a fortune in Fairdraisha, though Blair had no idea what that meant here.

Blair didn't respond. She only watched from her place on the hammock as it slowly swung back and forth.

Surprisingly, it was Kielle who spoke next. "Do you have everything you need for the Starlight Festival?"

Blair pondered for a moment. The question was genuine, not snarky like usual. It was like something was tugging at Kielle's heartstrings. She was trying to be nicer.

Blair took too long, and Kielle finally turned to face her. "You are planning on going, right?"

Once again, Blair hesitated. "Um, I don't know. Maybe."

Kielle stopped and stood up, waiting for a better answer. Blair didn't have one. Her voice stumbled when she spoke again. "It just doesn't seem right, you know? My deadline is approaching, and... I would like to, but I don't..."

Kielle shook her head and smiled, returning now to the clothes she had spread out on the bed. "Now you sound like Queriven."

That response made her flinch a third time and Blair sat with a gaping jaw like an idiot.

"So what are you going to do instead then?" Kielle asked without looking, though the smile remained on her fair face. "You say you're worried because your deadline is approaching, so do you have any plans to help? Or are you going to continue to mope around my home?"

Now Blair was offended and she looked away.

Kielle wasn't finished, though her tone didn't grow worse. "Eventually, something would have to give, but that's not for now. Why don't you come to the party? Maybe you can convince Queriven to unwind a little. He needs it. I'm thinking he might explode if he doesn't find any answers soon."

Interested enough to lean in again, Blair finally spoke. "What makes you think I can convince him to do anything?"

"Because you two are close. I can see it," Kielle answered. She caught a flutter in Blair's eyes. "Believe it or not, he used to love coming to these events with family and friends. He seems like a totally different person now. He used to brighten with joy and he was quite outgoing. He was always making new friends."

That sounded different indeed. Was that really Queriven they were talking about? "He... Wasn't always like this then?" Blair whispered.

Kielle shook her head, taking a seat on her bed next to the clothes. "No. That battle has been killing him slowly over time; the one he ran from twenty years ago. It's pretty awful. I understand it, but I miss the old Queriven. Of course, I mean the one before he started his training to be a soldier. That's when he became serious about his revenge. He could barely focus on anything after that. He was prideful and pushy."

Blair shrugged, the thought making her a little uncomfortable. "One couldn't blame him, not after what happened to your parents. I don't know what would have happened to me if something happened to mine, let alone if they were murdered. I'm truly sorry your family had to go through with that."

Kielle sank, a sad chuckle coming from her lips. She started a new sentence several times before Blair could make sense of her, even muttering something in her native language. "It seems it still bothers him too much to talk about it." Both she and Blair studied the other before Kielle spoke again. "Our parents weren't killed that way. His were."

The message didn't hit her, and Blair frowned, trying her hardest to make sense of it.

Kielle tried again. "Queriven's not our real brother."

Blair was not sure if she wanted to attempt breathing again or if she should use the last of it to scream disbelief. None of it made sense. None of it connected, and yet all of it did. "What!?" she finally cried, her lungs finally calling back needed air. Her eyes went wide and a sudden gesture nearly flipped her off the hammock. "How? Does he know?"

Kielle waited ever patiently for her to quiet again. "He was an adolescent when we met him. We found out after his parents died in that battle that he ran away from home. It was only a small town in the northern peak of the forest. He came to Sylinna because he had nowhere else to go. Finhaus, Sirnah, and I found him and brought him into our home. Ever since then, we've treated him just like family. It took us a long time to understand him and his reasons for being alone. It nearly destroyed him. He was so upset he could barely talk about it."

Silence came in like a creeping hurricane. Kielle showed a bit of a wince as Blair continued to sit, staring at her blankets. In her twisting mind, Queriven was the strongest person Blair's ever met, facing complete and utter disaster again and again. He lost his parents to thieves, became adopted in a new family, only to lose that when his unit of soldiers all died in a battle he led. No wonder he struggled all the time. Now his responses to her seemed more powerful rather than weak.

One by one, the news became clearer and clearer as Blair thought on it. That's why he was so different from the others, not only in his actions but in his looks. Blair never thought he looked like any of his siblings. "It's best if you don't bring it up to him," Kielle said. "It'll only make him worse than he already is right now."

Blair silently agreed and looked up, her eyes still wide and driven as she was staring a second ago. She tried to recover and picked up her pillow, holding it in her lap. "He told me he's really the eldest. For some reason, he said you wouldn't want him admitting that."

Suddenly, a hearty laugh by Kielle made the room happier. "He said that? I swear he tells that to everyone just to annoy me." She brushed her deep red hair back and nodded. "But it's true. He was much older than us when we took him in. Before he was part of the family, I was the eldest, but I'm not anymore. How many people can say that? I never thought about it, but the family used to joke about that when he became my brother. Something about that sparked a childish rivalry. Even though it was gone, I competed for the title of the eldest child. I tried to do everything he did just to keep up with the big kids," she sighed, once again laughing at the irony. "And now I'm the first knight! I guess that game still continues."

In all seriousness, Blair added, "He had to adjust to so many things. Stress alone warped his personality until it's buried so deep inside. Will he ever be able to find peace?"

Kielle wasn't bothered. "He's still in there somewhere. I don't think he's lost for good. He only needs a little help." With that, she jumped to her feet. "Like going to an old festival he used to love. You'll help with that, yes?"

Blair thought about it for a second longer. This was her chance not only to go to the festival but to help Queriven at the same time. She nodded.

"Great!" Kielle yelled, standing up again. She studied Blair for a moment. "That means you need to prepare as well, and I'm guessing you don't have any other clothes with you. We'll need to find you something nice."

As Kielle returned to the clothes on her bed again, Blair climbed out of the hammock and stretched her arms over her head. Kielle spoke again, mostly to herself this time. "I wonder if I have something here that might fit you... If not, we can see about something else."

A spark ignited in Blair's chest. Kielle was trying to find an elvish dress for her! The idea made Blair joyful beyond belief. It was such a kind gesture, but she also doubted any of these would fit her anyway. Kielle was much smaller than she was. She wasn't even sure if she should grant that honor to a human anyway.

Again, Kielle muttered to herself. "I might have something." She stepped back for a second and pressed her thumb against her lips in thought. "What color do you like, Blair?"

For the hundredth time that morning, Blair staggered for a reply. She gave the pillow a squeeze. That was the first time Kielle used her name instead of calling her a human. For the first time, Kielle was talking to her like a person. "Uh, well... I like blue..."

Kielle nodded and pulled something from the chest. When she held it up, Blair could see it was a long, beautiful dress. It was a gorgeous blue near the top, though it became darker until it was almost black near the bottom. Showing like the night sky, the falling skirt shone with nothing other than starlight, and it sparkled when it caught the light. The loose thin sleeves were pure white and the dress even had a thin veil attached to the back, which fell down with the length of the skirt. She's never seen anything like it before.

What came next scared her more than anything. Kielle gave it to her. "Try it on."

Blair carefully took it like she worried it was going to crumble as soon as she touched it. Then, Kielle pulled out a few others that might fit her. "Go on. You're not going to hurt it. I'm going downstairs for some breakfast. Come show me when you're ready."

Even after she was gone, Blair didn't move for the longest time. She looked down at the draping dress in her arms before setting it slowly to the side, turning back to her hammock for a moment.

Kielle was in the kitchen for a good long while, eating fruit with Sirnah. Finally, Blair was ready, and she came down the stairs one step at a time. Her face glowed bright pink and she seemed to float through the kitchen. Kielle and Sirnah were awed to see her, which only made her more embarrassed.

The dress wasn't too small at all, and it flowed with her figure perfectly. She was radiant. The colors and shine complemented her well. Kielle's lips parted and she blinked. "You're beautiful. I wasn't sure how it would look." She brushed back her hair behind a pointed ear. "You still look human, but it works for you."

Blair smiled.

Later that evening, elves gathered on the streets of Sylinna. The summer sky beyond the canopy of leaves was softly colored with light blues, pinks, and yellows. The sun was just starting to set and no stars were out yet. It was still going to be a while before the starlight harvest. Blair left Kielle's tree with her and Sirnah, and they met with Finhaus soon after. Kielle's chosen dress was just as beautiful as the one she gave Blair. It was a deep forest green and it brought out the dark red in her hair that fell over her shoulders like a waterfall. Her brothers dressed nicely as well, with Finhaus wearing a rich gray tunic studded with starlight and Sirnah wore what looked like a more formal version of his usual robes.

There were many things to see in the city that night: music, dancing, magic displays, delicious food, and enticing wines. Queriven, however, was nowhere to be seen.

Blair lingered with the three elves for only a short while. She wanted to join in the fun, but finding Queriven was more important to her. She decided to look for him, and knowing him, he'll be away from the busy streets at this time.

Blair carefully moved through the thick crowds. Voices of nearby conversations filled her ears, most of which were in their native language. Most of the elves barely noticed her go by, as they were too wrapped in their own business. But the few

THE STARLIGHT FESTIVAL

who saw her judged her for her odd looks.

Blair ignored them and continued through. There was a sweet smell tempting to distract her from her mission. A large wooden table nearby contained many kinds of good treats, but the flutes and harps were even sweeter.

Slowly, the music fell away as she walked. It was a large city, but she spent little time worrying about it and only focused on walking down one path at a time. She still couldn't keep from looking at all the new sights around her. The whole city changed with the festival. It was like a whole different world! Many stalls and tables brushed the road, and elves lined them with goods up for trade. There were also a lot of free treats to enjoy.

When the main part of the crowd disappeared behind her, she looked down at her feet. Maybe it was all in her mind, but she thought the starlight on the edge of the ebony pathways was glowing brighter than it has before. Then again, maybe it did glow brighter on clear nights, but she didn't know for sure. The glowing starlight was everywhere now, making the city look so magical! There were sparkling banners on the sides of the large trees, but that wasn't the only thing. Magic orbs and enchantments were set everywhere, and if that wasn't enough, there were many entertainers displaying their ability with magic. Not too far, Blair spotted a dancer off in the open, twirling gracefully with her fingers lighting colors in the air. And ahead, a male conjured fluttering fairies and gorgeous dryads to the audience in front of him as he described the adventures of a brave elf who wandered in the wilderness. Temptation and awe soared through Blair again, but she carried along, making a silent promise to return to the storyteller later.

It didn't take her much longer to find Queriven. Passing elves heading toward the center of town didn't see her eyes brighten when she spotted her elvish friend sitting on a large stump ahead. His back faced her and he slumped forward, perhaps holding his head up.

If there weren't already people around, and if he was

focusing a bit more on his surroundings, he would have seen her coming.

As she came around and saw Queriven's relaxed features, she wanted to smile but tried to show it only a little. Finally, he lifted his head. She caught his lips parting and eyes growing wide when he realized that not only was Blair standing before him, but she was in a most beautiful elvish dress that sparkled when she moved. She braided her dark blonde hair loosely and decorated it with little white flowers. She couldn't help it. She beamed at him, her cheeks once again brightening hot pink.

Queriven sat straighter, though he didn't have any words. He wasn't even dressed any differently. She spoke first. "What are you doing all the way over here?"

Again, he searched for a response. Finally, he clapped his hands together and looked away. "I was thinking," he muttered. "I visited with Foradue again this morning to propose a new idea. It didn't fall through, so I was trying to come up with something else."

Blair gave him another smile and sat down next to him. "I know you're trying everything you can, but why don't you join me? Kielle, Sirnah, and Finhaus are enjoying the festival. I'll like you to join in as well."

He looked at her, thinking to tell her he was busy, but he didn't want to be rude. Blair took over his chance to speak. "Just for tonight, won't you? Tomorrow you can return to planning."

Still not sure what to say, he shrugged and studied her expression for a moment. He wished he knew more of what she was thinking. Finally, he chuckled softly. "I kind of thought you'll be mad at me — you know — after I lied to you and all."

She nodded. "I was for a while, but I can never hate you, not after you came all this way for me."

"I wanted to apologize for that night. I'm so tired of hiding things from you. From now on, I'll be honest about everything I share with you."

No longer dwelling on the past fight, Blair spoke again. "I need to apologize as well. It's not right to treat you that way, no matter what you hid from me. You're totally selfless, especially after you came back here when you vowed not to."

He shied away, blinking harsh emotions by. "I need to tell you something."

There was a pause, and he shuddered. Blair smiled. "Let me guess, 'it's complicated'."

He chuckled for a moment but was serious. "A little." He looked down at his fingers, as if he wasn't sure if he wanted to speak or not. "Kielle, Sirnah, and Finhaus are not actually my siblings. They adopted me into the family when I was a child after my parents died."

To Queriven, Blair seemed surprised. Truthfully though, she was only surprised to hear him admit this when she did nothing to bring it up. He told it to her himself. "I was such a fool," he continued. "They gave me everything when they didn't have to, but I let them down when I became a soldier of the Center Tree. I didn't realize that I already had everything I could have hoped for — a loving family. I shouldn't have sought revenge. In the end, it only destroyed me, and not the people I was looking for."

He was falling into depression. Hoping to catch him, Blair placed a freckled hand on his slender wrist. Startled by her touch, he looked at her. She didn't judge him for a second and he returned to his composure when he focused on the mix of hazel showing in her eyes at that moment. "I told you your family would forgive you, have they not? The past is gone. There's no changing it, and we can only grow for the future. You can still be a part of this city if you choose to and become a better person."

"Blair," he responded, baffled, "you heard them. I'm exiled. I can never return to the forest ever again."

"No," she corrected, "you're only exiled after the change of autumn, and who knows what can happen before then? No one can take account for the unknown, the good or the bad. We just have to do the best we can." She wanted to tell him if he's forced to leave that she would always be with him no matter where he'll go, but she knew in her heart that would be a lie if their mission failed.

Queriven didn't smile, but he still relaxed a bit. Now Blair had to shake off her discomfort. She couldn't imagine not being around him anymore. She wanted to be with him forever. "So," she fixed her inner frustration and asked, "do you want to hang out with us?"

He sighed and leaned back, taking a look at the clear sky between the dancing cover of leaves above. The tower-like trees set the canopies of leaves higher than mountains, and even now, beyond the voices, music, and entertainment of the festival, a brush of wind rustled the enchanted leaves. The trees in the wilderness seemed magical and alive, but they paled in comparison to the majesty of Sylinna's. The bodies of the trees were thick and mighty, and the patterns in the bark swirled up to the sky. Though the elves made their homes in them, they were all a little different. They were different shapes, sizes, and types.

Queriven took the wonder of Sylinna in his lungs. Peace overcame him and his worries lifted. "Sure," he said after a short pause. He stood up from the stump and Blair walked beside him. "And Blair," he added as he continued walking, "whatever happens at the close of summer, I want you to know it was all worth it. You taught me so much and I would do it all again for you. Our time meant everything to me when nothing else did."

Stomach full of butterflies, Blair took his hand again and followed shoulder to shoulder. Bliss filled Queriven for the first time since being back home. He was now glad he wasn't alone.

Together, they entered the main part of the city where the music was the loudest and the laughter was brightest. The time Blair spent with Queriven and his family there seemed too short to be fair. They were content and together. That was all that mattered that night.

The sun fell, but the streets only became lighter with the floating colored orbs of magic, now more plentiful than ever. The party continued, and the first few stars were beginning to show.

"Sorry, I should be heading toward the pond. I need to prepare," said Finhaus. The squirrel by his side scurried up to his shoulder as he snatched another nutty treat from the table. Quickly, he left.

"When more stars show, we should head there too," Queriven remarked to Blair. "We can watch the harvest of starlight."

Blair was giddy just to imagine what that might look like. She took some candied berries from the table. Sirnah came closer. "I know our culture is quite different from your own. As the first human to visit in over many elf generations, what do you think of it?"

With her eyes beaming, she answered, "I think it's amazing. It's even more than I dreamed it would be. I still can't believe it's real."

He seemed a little more nervous now. "Even though we don't eat any meat? How does the food compare to your own?"

Blair marveled at the sweet, juicy flavor of the berries. They almost melted right into her mouth. It wasn't like anything she ever had at home despite her mother's lovely home cooking. "It's really different even compared to our own crops. The forest has a lot of the same vegetables and fruits that we do, though they have new flavors in it. I don't know why, but it's just as beautiful as the forest."

She approved of his homeland. Sirnah held his chin up and beamed.

A new song was starting. A deep beat was setting off into the horizon by a single drum. Blair turned. The musicians were standing on a hill not too much taller than the road just in front of it. Seeing the elves with their instruments made her so joyful until she couldn't contain it anymore. She grabbed Queriven's arm and took him closer.

After the other instruments started, it was like a leap right off the ground and into the wide open sky. Blair twirled around with her arms outstretched, the veil on her dress brushing up on her arms like the green leaves of the forest canopy passing her by on her way up.

Queriven watched, a smile growing on his face. Seeing her so carefree lifted his heavy worries. He hasn't been this way since they arrived here.

The tempo was rising right before the melody. Higher than ever, Blair grabbed Queriven again, beckoning him to join her. He complied, falling into step. She matched his step, each one she made a short hop. Her waving dress bounced smoothly up and down with each one.

Finally, after her trip through the air, her eyes settled on him. He looked so...different. At this point, she didn't know what it was. Was it their growing friendship, her knowledge of his history, or simply the shine she's never seen before in those dark green eyes? Whatever it was, it was beautiful. Even more beautiful than the soft blue of falling dusk or the lights keeping the festival warm and inviting. It was more refreshing than the rich banners waving in the cool summer night breeze or the sweet ripe scent of flowers and that enticing wine.

The night was so young and fresh, and she wished time would stop.

For Queriven, it was the same. He didn't even care about the looks that came their way as he danced with the human girl. She pursued his heart, and he wasn't going to run from it any longer. She was more important than the forest. If he was to be exiled, he knew he would be fine if he was with her, even if he followed her into that barren wasteland.

Both hearts synced with the echoing drums that soared in the distance. Blair dropped down as the drums slowed, and the flute played like a soft river. With her breath caught in her chest, she placed her soft hands on Queriven's shoulders. Together, they floated over the pathway.

Too soon, and the music came to a close. Blair and Queriven stopped, though neither pulled away. Blair studied his soft expression. She wanted to say something to show the feelings that were sitting in her stomach, but she had nothing.

Queriven didn't look away, but he stayed silent as well. They didn't need words to express themselves. The look in the other's eyes gave away everything.

Blair suddenly wanted to draw even closer to him, but she didn't want to scare him off. To her surprise, he allowed it and pulled her in as well. Slow and shy, Blair was close enough to brush her lips lightly on his. It was only a short gesture though, as the baffled looks around them made her lower her head.

Queriven was about to speak to her, but a voice behind him made him turn. If he wasn't able to breathe before, he might as well suffocate now. It was Dakru, and he looked messy and ashamed just to be standing before him. The elf's dark hair was unkempt and his red eyes hinted he hasn't been sleeping. He tried to meet his old friend's face but was unable to keep it. "Queriven," he started, barely above a whisper, "I've been looking for you all day. I was wondering if I could have a word with you."

Blair moved beside Queriven. She didn't even notice that a new song had already started. Queriven looked over at her, unsure what he should be doing right now.

"You have a right not to trust me," Dakru replied to their hesitance. "The girl can come, as this concerns her too."

After another look, Blair was the first to move and Queriven followed. Dakru didn't take them far; just enough away from the party where they could talk. "All right," he stated, turning to face them. "I heard you've been consulting with Lord Foradue on how to find that rokian," he finished toward Queriven. "I decided I want to help." He paused, judging the stare on either face. When he couldn't read them, he picked up again. "I was so stupid. Even more so that I felt like I had to kill you. I've been thinking about things since then and I realized that Fia would have wanted me to help you. Leading that army into the ambush was a mistake, a terrible mistake, but that's the thing about Fia. She was good at forgiving mistakes. She was good at supporting our friendship too. I just know this is what she wants."

After another turn of the head, Queriven accepted his apology. He gave the elf a friendly clap on the shoulder. "Thanks, Dakru. It's good to have you back."

Dakru wanted to smile, but it was broken. He did relax a little though. "See, I've been thinking. This whole time you've been trying to find this rokian, but what if we drove him to find us instead?"

Queriven raised an eyebrow and folded his arms. "I suppose I haven't considered it before, but how do we do that?"

Dakru continued like he already had the answer. "I don't know much about Darkadus, but I know a little about Aswren. He claimed he had amazing skills in magic, though I didn't see him use any. You know more about him than I do. What kind of magic does he have?"

Carefully, both Blair and Queriven gave him an account of what he had used before. Rokian magic was different from any other, but Dakru stroked his face and began to think. Finally, a spark of inspiration struck when Queriven told him that sometimes he watches them. "We can use this..." Dakru said, rubbing a hand over his tired eyes. "If we upset him enough, he will come to us, but what can we do?" He suppressed a yawn. When he opened his eyes again, he was looking at Blair. He added her puzzled look to his thought process. Slowly, Blair could see him piecing things together. "You're the cursed one," he said, more of a spoken statement to himself than anything. "This Darkadus is trying to escape with his race through you. Maybe we can manipulate him, but how?"

Neither Blair nor Queriven knew what to say. Dakru waited but grew impatient. He sighed angrily. "Come on. What will ruin the curse? There has to be something that'll void it."

"Uh, something that'll void the curse...?" Queriven wondered, trying to remember everything he could. "Well, I suppose if we make progress toward breaking it."

For a second, Dakru seemed excited, but then he shook his head. His arms dropped back down to his sides. "No, that won't work. We're not going anywhere with that as it is."

Blair thought of something else. She was a little uncertain about speaking it out loud but shared it anyway. "There is another way. When his pirates caught me early last winter, he tried to maroon me on an island with another pirate. The captain ordered him to keep me alive. If I die, I won't be tied to the curse anymore."

Queriven winced, not sure if he wanted her to share that information. Too late Dakru exclaimed out loud. "That's it! That'll upset him for sure!"

Nearly jumping in front of her, Queriven objected. "What do you mean? We can't hurt her! The whole reason for this quest is to save her!"

Again, it took Dakru a moment to register what he meant by that. Quickly, he waved off any accusations. "No, and we won't. Hang on for a second. I can manipulate Darkadus through his own magic!"

Queriven listened, though he was quickly falling out of trust with his friend again. "How can we do that?" he asked, his voice deep and suspicious.

"If Blair's in danger, Darkadus might come over here to help her. Since he spies on you two, we can send him an image of her close to losing her life."

Queriven frowned again, this time out of anger. "We can't do that. We don't know when he watches us."

"We don't need to know when he does," Dakru added. "You don't even have to be involved. I can send him a message."

Queriven still didn't understand. He growled, thinking Dakru only needed more sleep. Somehow, Dakru caught on to his impatience. He continued. "I'll come up with a scenario myself. Perhaps, the elves don't trust Blair and when they decide not to help her, she runs into the forest to save herself. Out there in the wild, however, she finds herself in danger of the various monsters in there. As you know, a human doesn't stand a chance out there. Since Darkadus lived with us for some time, he knows about it just as we do. I'll create the image and send it through the rokian's field of magic. The next time he tries to spy on you, he'll automatically pick it up."

Queriven finally settled down. That idea made more sense. Still, he was no expert in magic and so he asked, "How do you make this image? Do we need to act it out or something?"

Dakru waved his arms in front of him. "No need to. Creating a magical image like that is simple as long as I have a good understanding of the situation, which, in this case, I do. Sending it to someone else though, is quite difficult, especially considering that this is a rokian and he's different from anyone else. Still, I think I can do it."

Blair smiled and looked up to Queriven with approval. Dakru spoke again, drawing their gazes back at him. "The only setback is that it'll take me a little bit of time to create and send that image, and then we have to wait for Darkadus to pick it up. We have to be ready at every corner. When he finally picks it up, which is up to his own timing, we need to catch him as soon as he arrives."

Blair then hesitated. She held her hands before her. "Darkadus doesn't travel alone. He has an army of pirates and who knows what else? It'll be too easy to simply catch him."

Queriven nodded. "She's right. We'll have to prepare for a battle. Tell me when you send the image out and we'll send out a watch throughout several points in the forest. If we snatch the horn from his grip, he'll try to stop us from breaking the curse."

Dakru agreed. "Will do. I'm going home right away to begin our plan." He bowed low to the two. Queriven returned it and Dakru began walking away.

"Dakru!" Queriven called again. Dakru looked back. "Take care of yourself. We'll need you to defend the forest."

He smiled and disappeared in the ongoing crowd.

Queriven turned back to Blair. "So what do you think?"

She nodded, watching him just the same. "I think it can work. It's not going to be easy though."

"No," he agreed, "we're still trying to fool a rokian of all people. No one's been able to do that before, or at least, it was never recorded. They're too clever."

"It's still a better idea than trying to go to him," she answered and went quiet. She was a little shy now thinking about the dance they had before Dakru approached them. Neither one of them said a thing about it, but it was on both of their minds. She looked away to their surroundings. Elves all around were leaving. Then she looked up at the sky and saw an ocean of clear bright stars.

"The starlight harvest," Queriven remembered. "We should go to the pond quickly if we're to make it in time." Queriven offered his hand and smiled the same way he did as he danced. "Are you coming?"

"Of course," she answered, taking it and following him down the path.

CHAPTER THIRTY
BITTERSWEET EMOTIONS

The pond was about a few miles south of the city. There were several wagons waiting for those who were going to see the collection of starlight. Horses stood at the lead of the wagon, waiting for the gentle order of their masters. Blair marveled at the animals. The elves treated them with the utmost respect and love like they weren't animals at all, but family. The wagons reminded her a little of human wagons, but like everything out here, it was different enough to throw her off.

Blair rode with the peace of freedom in her soul. It was like she was free from the curse for just one night. She captured every detail and locked them deep down, wishing the memory would last a lifetime. If this was the strongest freedom she would hold, then she will remember it for years to come. She enjoyed the ride every second of the way. Queriven and her exchanged few words, but she could have ridden on longer if the trip needed it. They weren't the only ones who were quiet as the crowds and wagons were as well. Sweet, calming accents and rolling wheels filled her ears and she barely noticed when Queriven shuffled a little closer to her.

The ride wasn't too long, and the wagon rolled to a slow

stop. As she and Queriven stepped off to walk outside the trees ahead, she looked again at the horses. Elves rewarded them with praise and treats.

Queriven moved along and Blair kept close. She was still excited when the pond came into view. It was the only open field in all the forest, and it was open to allow the stars to beam down freely with no obstructions.

Elves gathered all around with some still arriving, though there was hardly a word spoken between them. They seemed to rejoice in the starlight though, and many bathed in it with their arms outstretched.

The intense light of the night sky spilled down in purple, casting over the entire field. The reflection of bright stars and the wide, full moon floated perfectly still in the water of the pond ahead. It seemed to be casting even more color around it. Like earlier, not one cloud dimmed the sky, and even the nighttime bugs whispered in awe and respect. The calm twinkling lights of fireflies all around melted into the summer field like it was part of the tradition.

Blair wasn't sure what calmed her more — the lovely shining sky or the fact that Queriven was also at peace. She looked up at him. The stars were dancing in his eyes like she's never seen. His expression was quiet but lit into a soft smile. The captivating sight sent her spiraling down a flashback. When she first met Darkadus, it was a lot like this with the light filling Queriven's eyes as he stared into the lake. Even then, she wanted to be close to him, but yet this time was different. This was real and much more gorgeous than that time. She knew his heart and he kept nothing locked away. It was like opening a tight safe for the first time in decades and watching dust blow free from the contents.

When she came to her senses, Queriven was leading her through the crowd closer to the pond. Around the pond in the rich purple light were banners of fine cloth spread out over wooden frames. It lifted toward the sky and angled down where a large bowl-shaped bucket was sitting at the end of it.

She spotted Finhaus with one of these set banners. The

squirrel was still perched happily on his shoulder. Queriven leaned in and whispered to her. "He's preparing the magic needed to collect the light of the stars. The surroundings have to be at peace for him to focus."

Curious, she looked at Finhaus again. He didn't bother looking at any of them; he only drew a knife slowly from his belt. The light caught it, only to reveal the darkest black blade made from ebony. It wasn't even big enough for a dagger. He whispered to it, though Blair didn't notice a change and then he turned to the banner. As he looked at it, the fabric caught a sparkle, as if it suddenly repelled the purple light...as if the light was sitting just on top of it.

Queriven grinned as Blair watched with wide eyes.

With the knife in hand, Finhaus took it over the banner and sliced the air. What happened next was nothing short of impossible. Like cutting open a water skein, liquid spilled out from where the knife was, though it was not water. The liquid pooled thick and shiny, like colorful platinum, the same shine and color as the metal on Queriven's armor. It slid down the banner, the light above it running dark and shady like it drained the intangible light. Then, it dripped down into the bowl.

The other banners were dripping as well with the same draining light, and when the liquid form of starlight filled the bowl, Finhaus lifted the folds of the sheet up so that the last drop fell in as well. Finhaus placed a lid over the bowl of swirling white liquid.

"Let me help you with that," Queriven offered, leaving Blair's side and taking the banner from the frame.

Blair watched as the two brothers cleaned up the equipment and Sirnah came to take the folded sheet. Then both Queriven and Finhaus lifted the bowl together and headed back toward town.

A few elves still lingered, and it took Blair a second to realize that Kielle was chuckling right next to her. "The look on your face is like that of a young child's! Do you have any interesting traditions back where you come from?"

Blair didn't know what her response should be. "We have interesting traditions for sure, but nothing like this. Even when I dreamed about this forest at night, it didn't have anything like this at all."

Kielle folded her arms and nodded. "Yeah, it doesn't fail to awe me every time still. This is a lovely land we live in. I want to make sure nothing happens to it." The elf smiled at the reflective pond that was just as bright as the sky. A mysterious purple hue was still covering the field. She threw her head back to the northern trees. "Shall we head back home?"

Blair nodded and they meandered back to the path. It wasn't long after that when the rest of the elves started to head back as well, and the chatter around them grew. "Kielle?" Blair asked as accented voices speaking in the elvish language, as well as the humans', echoed around her. Kielle turned her head and listened. "Do you know why I can speak with so many of the elves here? I don't know elvish. Why do they know the language of the humans so well?"

Kielle thought about it for a second, her fingers twisted in the folds of her deep green gown. Finally, she answered, "The light of elves is more mysterious to the humans than the other way around. Think about it. We've already lived several of your generations. We remember a lot more about humans than they do about us. I wasn't born when the attack happened on the trading post, but at one time, we taught our language to humans and they taught us theirs. Most elves today still know their language as we remember humans. The same can't be said for Fairdraisha."

Blair looked down at the floating bits of dirt she kicked up. "Makes sense, I suppose... It's a shame King Brenmor keeps us away. The elves are amazing people and it was only a misunderstanding that drove our people away. If we wanted to, we could build our relationships back. It'll be better for both our people."

Kielle nodded again, respecting Blair's choice of words. She held a pleasant smile on her face and her step had a little bounce in it. Blair was thankful she was growing more comfortable with the elf. It seemed like her harshness to Blair settled a bit.

Blair picked up the dark ends of her blue dress to avoid it scraping some twigs on the road. When she lifted her head, she caught a slight glimpse of Finhaus and Queriven far ahead in the crowd, bringing the starlight to a wagon. There was a falter in her step and only partially because of the snagging plants at her feet. Memories of only an hour before flooded her mind when she came so close in his arms. She held her breath when she realized for the first time how close she was to pressing her lips on his.

"I hope Queriven doesn't overwhelm himself with work," Kielle broke Blair's fogged mind, bringing her back to the real world. "He still hurts from that attack the other night. It's going to take a long time for his wounds to heal, and we may need his help soon. I only hope he heals enough."

Blair watched as more elves crowded around them, blocking her view of the two brothers. She picked up her gown again and looked down. Queriven had a nasty habit of keeping things to himself, but she knew he could handle pain if he had to. He was powerful, especially when it came to physical injuries. "I'm not too worried about it. I'm sure he'll be fine."

A quiet giggle came from the elf and she added, "You know, it's been a long time since I've seen him so carefree like that. You did well at bringing him to the festival. I wasn't sure if he could still dance so well. I suppose his spear training keeps him moving that smoothly."

Blair blushed, her world getting sucked into a deep quicksand abyss. Her stomach turned when she considered Kielle was watching the two dancing together. At the time, she didn't take any account of the crowds around them. It was like it was just her and Queriven.

"It seems there's still hope for him," she continued without change. "I bet he was glad to be there with you as well. It made him upset when you didn't speak with him in some time."

Blair burned hotter, her blood now pulsing through her face.

She didn't know how to respond, so Kielle spoke again. "Even before he wrapped himself up in the military and forgetting what he had around him, it took him a long time to make such close friends like this. You wouldn't understand what he was like unless you were there to see it."

"Yes, well..." Blair added, decided to say something to make herself appear less awkward. "We've been through a lot up to this point." Once the words left her mouth though, she only felt even more embarrassed. "Where did you and Sirnah disappear to anyways? Were you watching me dance the whole time?"

Kielle laughed again. "We left shortly after. It was stunning to see Queriven dance again after so many long years, but I figured you two didn't want us staring, so we walked the streets some."

She wouldn't have seen Dakru coming to speak with them then. That also means she didn't see how she was wrapped tight in Queriven's arms, but it still sounded like Kielle knew of Blair's feelings.

She didn't bring it up again after that though, and they returned back to Kielle's home. Blair relaxed in her swinging hammock, warm and fuzzy from such a lovely summer evening.

The next morning, Queriven was with his family on the first floor. He shared with them the new plan on catching Darkadus. As predicted, Kielle didn't like it one bit when she heard it involved Dakru. "He's dangerous. I thought you told me you were going to stay away from that freak."

Queriven acknowledged her concern with the same tone he was already speaking in. "He's no longer seeking revenge, Kielle. Didn't you hear me? If he has the courage to forgive me after what I did, shouldn't he be given another chance as well?"

She scoffed and looked away, but didn't object.

"Should we tell Foradue then?" Sirnah asked.

Queriven met his gaze. "I already did last night before I came back here. He approves of it and told me to get back to him when Dakru tells us to be on the watch. The Center Tree has our back, which means we'll have the help we'll need."

Finhaus lifted his head. The owl perched on his shoulder fluttered its wings. "So when do we act? When will we be ready?"

Queriven shrugged. "Hopefully soon. We have to wait for Dakru to finish his spell, then we'll watch for Darkadus. There's no telling what might happen after that. If he attacks, we'll need everyone on the defense. That means you'll be there with your unit." He addressed Kielle. Then he turned to Sirnah. "And you will be in the back of the formations ready to treat any injuries."

Finhaus looked solemn, his eyebrows knitting in thought. "I wish I could help with this. I'm not sure how I'll handle seeing all of you on the lines while I'm here just praying for your safety."

"You will have a place in this as well, Finhaus," Queriven promised. "Even if you're not a part of the Center Tree, there will be work for you."

"Like what?" he asked, growing more upset. "I can't fight or treat wounds. I can't do anything."

Queriven was confident in his brother's abilities and wasn't afraid to show it. "You are talented in many ways. If anything, I may have the most important job for you. Just wait."

He sat straight and lifted his head. "If you say so then."

Finally, Queriven's gaze dropped to Blair. She sparkled back at him and responded at his glance. "We've already been through this several times. I'm sure we can do this," she assured him.

"We're aiming for the horn. If he doesn't have it, we'll make him help us. Darkadus is really going to show his wraith at this, and we don't know what group of ruffians he'll bring at our door," he countered, but Blair's gaze didn't change. "Summer's almost over. This is truly our last act."

"I'm ready," she responded. "And if for some reason we fail, we can accept that we did our best. That's what matters most to me now."

Queriven seemed quite proud by that answer, and shortly later, he sat down at the table with the others. Together, they brainstormed ideas and plans for many hours.

◊ ◊ ◊

Each day passed like a ticking time bomb. Everyone knew it was only the calm before the storm. Yet, it didn't seem to affect Blair and Queriven as much as the others. To a third party, they still seemed just as happy and peaceful as they were in the Starlight Festival. Perhaps, they already accepted the outcome of the battle that has yet to happen.

While they waited for Dakru to come back, Blair and Queriven spent almost every day together. They walked the edge of the forest wilderness and through the city as Queriven told her more about their ways and his past life. Blair learned so much about the elves and the city. He explained and read the banners on the trees as they went through the streets. It was then that Blair learned they were the homes of proficient elves. The banners helped to market their abilities, though there were no "shops" in the city. Rather, the banners marked who specialized in what, allowing opportunity for trade. Blair thought the lack of currency in the forest was not only fitting but freeing as well. Aven Forest has always worked off of fair trades. Something about that was pure and innocent.

Already, the sun was falling quicker and a light chill crept in after dark. It wasn't far until the tall trees of the elven forest would change to the colors of fire, and yet if Blair noticed, she no longer showed it.

In just a week, Dakru came back to their door. "I've sent it away," he chimed excitably. He looked a little better than he did at the festival, but his unkempt hair still brought a frown from Kielle. "Darkadus can find it anytime now."

They took the news to Foradue straight after that. He responded immediately. A watch was set around the entire western edge as far as the old trading post. The soldiers hid tight in the trees and watchtowers. Even a rokian couldn't hope to find them.

All they had to do was wait for Darkadus to reach the forest...

CHAPTER THIRTY-ONE
THE CALM BEFORE THE STORM

"What if he doesn't show up? Do you think he knows it's a trap?" Blair asked Queriven one night. They were sitting outside watching the sun set beyond the trees.

"He'll show up," the elf answered with all certainty. "I don't know if he thinks it a trap or not. He's smart, so he probably does. Even if he does know that, he'll come anyway." He paused for only a moment, and Blair's confused expression had him talking again. "We both know he's running out of magic. This is his last chance as well. If you die, he fails, and he doesn't have enough magic to withstand cursing another. You, Blair, are his last chance at releasing his kind. He can't take the risk that you may be in real trouble."

She supposed he was right and she pondered quietly. "So all that we have to do is fight him and his thieves? Then we can take the horn and retreat to the waterfall in Lettir, right?"

Queriven sighed. It wasn't going to be that easy. He shifted in his seat, already knowing this next plan wasn't going to make her happy. Carefully, he picked out his next words. "I developed a plan that Foradue accepted. It goes beyond attack because I knew Darkadus and his army would bring a hard battle. If we're still to break the curse in time, then we must do this. If you follow through on your part, maybe the battle can end sooner, though I'm not certain."

Curious, Blair nodded and prepared herself. Anything he wanted her to do, she would do. Her ability with a spear was just as impressive as his now, so if he wanted her to fight Darkadus himself, she wouldn't hesitate.

She didn't know he was fixing to ask her to do something even more difficult. "If he has the horn with him, we'll try to ambush him and take it in the heat of battle. Once we have it, we can't wait. You must take it to Lettir right away."

Blair was heartbroken. "What?" she asked. "You want me to leave you behind while you fight a rokian's army?! I can't even summon Rocanu on my own. An elf has to do it. I thought you were coming with me."

Queriven nodded. She responded just as he thought she would. "I've considered this already and that's why you're going with Finhaus."

Her shattered and upset stare didn't lighten. "Finhaus? Why can't you come with me?"

"Finhaus is not a warrior. He can't stand in the line of defense, but I can. We need all the arms we can get. Finhaus needs a role to help in, and I know he'll lead you safely through the forest too."

The look on Blair's face told him she was growing only more desperate. "I can fight too," she cried, her voice wavering a little. "I'm good with a spear. Put me on the line. We'll head for Lettir when it's over."

Queriven winced. He didn't want to make it sound like it would be too late by then, but he also knew how important it was for her to leave. "Blair, you don't... What if we can't take back the horn from him by then? What if he wins? Wouldn't it be better to take it away when we have the chance?"

She knew he was right, though that didn't make her feel any better. She lowered her head. Gently, he called her name. When that didn't work, he brushed her arm lightly. Finally, she lifted her eyes to study his. He was understanding, but he wasn't going to change his mind. "I'll like nothing more than to have you on the line with me. I'm not sending you away because you can't handle yourself. I'm doing this so you have a chance to be free. If you join me on the line, then we may lose. The curse may not be broken and Darkadus will win anyway," he paused, allowing a second of silence to fill in. "Who's to say he might not retreat early once he finds that the curse is already broken? You could be the one to call off the battle. You could save lives."

Blair continued to look at him and finally, he asked. "Or... If you have any other ideas, please share it with me. I've always relied on my own answers in the past."

She wished she did, but she shook her head. "Just be careful. I don't want you to get hurt."

Darkadus' hand began to tremble as he took in the scene before him. He hadn't dared to use any magic in over a month, but the waning summer was beginning to take over his mind. Blair was almost his, but he knew she wasn't going down without a fight. He made a terrible mistake in the past by underestimating her. She was powerful and very smart. She wasn't letting time tick by. She would come up with something.

And so, Darkadus used his precious magic to conjure his eyes on them. What was there enraged him. She dared to enter Sylinna to find out how to break the curse. As predicted, the elves weren't too happy to find a human in their midst and sent her away. Even Queriven was unable to help her. He let her down and now she had no choice but to fight for herself. Upset and blind with tears, the human girl wandered off into the wilderness to save herself from the curse. *Stupid girl,* Darkadus thought. *Didn't Queriven tell you how dangerous the forest can be?* Why would he let her run off anyway? He thought they had something special between them. Looks like Queriven was back to his old ways. He was letting mistakes unfold right before his eyes and chose to do nothing.

Would the girl be so dumb as to run off into the wilderness of Aven Forest by herself anyway? Surely, she knew better than to do that. Darkadus growled with frustration. She knew there wasn't much time left. Desperation can drive anyone to a bad decision. There's no telling what she'll do now.

This proved to be quite terrible though. Darkadus was hoping to stay away from them if they chose to approach him, but this was a problem. The girl could die out there, perhaps even before he can reach her. Her best chance now would be if the fairies find her first. Even if she fell into their hands, she'll be safe enough for the spell to take her. Can he really count on that? She could also fall to some other kind of monster and be killed. If that happened, his mission was through. He didn't have enough magic to do this all over again. Soon, he might not even have enough to go back home. He must hold some magic at all costs, or he'll find himself surrounded by both the people of Fairdraisha and Aven Forest. If that happens, he'll be unable to defend himself.

The scowl he held deepened the wrinkles on his nose and forehead. The image of Blair disappearing in the thick summer scenery faded away with a lingering sparkle. He tightened his silver fist until his knuckles whitened. If he used more magic at the start, he would have won already, but he was fickle and easy on her.

He only had himself to blame if she slips free from him now.

Darkadus stormed out of his tent. The flaps whipped wildly behind him and the light of the setting sun blinded him. The pirates within his view scrambled to the side, startled by his sudden appearance. The rokian didn't say a thing to any of them and continued to stomp through the camp. They settled their camp past the hills and closer to the mountains north of the elven forest, far east from Dunverhart. He had to move away from the old watchtower after Blair discovered it. Turns out, this was a fantastic place to stay. It was quiet and didn't bring in a lot of attention. The warm summer weather was also convenient considering their living habits.

The clean mountain air and vivid green grass the rokian coveted so much in this world didn't register with him right now though, and he didn't hide his rage from his growing band of thieves, though that rage was hiding a level of fear resting under the surface. Even Darkadus denied that fear to himself. Even if the girl was in danger, there was no way he could lose to them now. He was, after all, the most powerful man in the world. He was a rokian. He was the one to cause fear, not hold onto it himself.

He didn't stop until he barged into Yusen Nashōgan's tent unannounced. "Captain!" the rokian cried. "We must head to Aven Forest. The human girl has placed herself in great peril."

The captain had his back turned to him. His posture remained relaxed and solemn, and he didn't even turn to look at his employer. Thinking he somehow misheard him, Darkadus repeated his order. Yusen was sitting at a table, staring down at the surface. At first, Darkadus thought he might be looking at a map or some other kind of tool, but realized there was nothing on the table but a few unlit candles. Finally, the captain half-glanced his way, but there was no sense of urgency on his face. He sighed and leaned back toward the table. "So many have died already. What's the point in continuing the fight?"

Darkadus crept a step forward and raised a black eyebrow. He wasn't even sure if that was aimed at him or not. "What? Did you not hear me? I'm telling you to ready your men."

That barely stirred the captain from his seat. He muttered once again. "I've sacrificed everything I had to serve you — my ship, my resources, and my crew, and for what? We're fighting a losing battle. Even the reward is dull in comparison to what I once had."

The rokian was now more confused than ever. He snapped from the rising anger. "What's wrong with you?! I haven't lost yet, but if we don't get moving, we'll be done for sure."

There was a sudden scuffle when the captain pushed himself up from his chair and faced the silver-toned man. "I'm done following your commands. This is too expensive for me now. You'll have to find someone else to lead your rogues."

Darkadus grew red in the face and wanted to choke the pirate out of his arrogance. He held his hands tight in front of him. "You can't back out on this now! We had an agreement," Darkadus reminded him but didn't yell at him yet. "The rokians are almost freed, and when they are, we will take back what was once ours. With your help, you will remain among my kind, rich, protected, and powerful. Now that doesn't sound remarkable enough for you?"

"Sir," the captain responded calmly, not moving an inch from his master's rage, "it's been twenty years and all that I've been promised is falling short."

Darkadus scoffed and pointed an accusing finger his way. "You don't see any of the progress being made here? Summer is almost over and the girl will take my place in a little over a month."

Yusen tossed the notion with a turn of his head. He crossed his arms and remained tall. "I've lost too much for it to matter. I've lost a lot of my men. Most of them were loyal to me for years, including my first mate. We've wasted a lot of time and effort following your commands and often traded away our valuables and comforts..."

Darkadus wasn't finished though and tried to manipulate the man instead. "If your head was on straight, you'll remember it was Queriven who killed your first mate and sunk your ship. I thought you wanted revenge, but then you let him go."

That brought the reaction he was looking for. The captain scowled and barked back, tossing his hands to the side. "I did not let that filth loose! The girl came and took him from me!"

"Exactly!" the rokian spat back. "The girl beat you in a fight, didn't she? Maybe you are worthless. I can assure you neither of them will win against me. I don't need your help. As you'll soon see, I'll destroy all of them on my own." Without waiting for a response, Darkadus turned away from the steaming captain and calmly returned to the door of his tent. But before he left, he gave the captain one final thought. "Just so you know though, I'm taking back my offer to you and your crew. When my people come back, we'll treat you just like any of the others. You better sleep with one eye open at night, Captain, or better yet, move far away from Fairdraisha." There was a rippling disturbance in the air, and the rokian grinned at his cleverness as he exited the tent.

This wasn't the end. Yusen Nashögan was going to come back pleading for his position shortly. Darkadus already knew. In the meantime, the rokian had to prepare himself for the journey to the forest. He ignored the nervous stares of those he passed as he returned to his own tent. Once he reached it, he stopped before entering the flaps and folded his burly arms, taking in the golden sky. No matter what happens in the forest, he knew it would probably come at the cost of some magic. He had to carefully consider what spells he could cast, but that nearly seemed impossible since he had no clue what he would be up against. He sighed and dipped his head, his sight now on the horn of red ivory he kept with him at all times.

The sight of the artifact only made him fall into further thought. The horn was powerful, and he feared Blair may come back seeking this one next. If the last one could summon Rocanu, then this one might be able to as well. He held it in front of his eyes and tightened his grip around it. Despite being over a thousand years old, it held firm and sturdy like it was brand new. It would be foolish to appear before Blair with it on him. He couldn't underestimate her any longer. She may try to take it and run. Maybe that was her plan.

Darkadus then dared to think she placed herself in danger on purpose, knowing that would force him to come in and save her. He needed a plan... Even if she did it on purpose, he still has to go. He couldn't really take the horn, but he couldn't leave it behind either. Someone may sneak in behind him and take it if he didn't bring it with him. Letting one of the pirates hold onto it was also not an option. Darkadus was the strongest one here. If someone had to hold it, it would be best protected in his grasp.

That left him only one answer. He had to take the horn with him; but maybe he could still come up with a way to keep Blair from sneaking it off of him. There were a few ideas already coming to his mind.

Darkadus dropped the subject from his mind and went inside his tent. Once inside, he immediately began rummaging through supplies and bringing the important necessities together.

As he predicted, Yusen Nashögan came back before nightfall and asked Darkadus what to do next. The rokian couldn't even hide his grin at the pirate's return.

They'll leave at dawn.

CHAPTER THIRTY-TWO
TRICKING THE TRICKSTER

This was the day, and it came like any other. The call of the soldier at Kielle's door was urgent and filled with terror. "The rokian has been spotted! He's approaching the Forest Border Trading Post!"

"Were there any others?!" Queriven asked as he joined his sister's side.

"Many others" came the reply. "He's got enough men to alarm King Brenmor of Fairdraisha."

Queriven stepped out the door. "Round the others and have them hide in the trading post. We want Darkadus to come as close as he can without spotting us."

The elf nodded and rushed off. Queriven turned back to Kielle and Blair, who were looking at him for direction. "I've got to warn Finhaus. You two meet us on the road before the post."

Kielle nodded and looked back at Blair as Queriven ran off. "Stay close by," she said, referencing the walk through the dangerous part of the woods.

The only thing Blair wanted at that moment was to follow Queriven. Seeing him turn and run off hurt her, though she didn't know why exactly. She had nothing to say, and nothing new to add to the plan; she only wished she could stay by him and ensure he would do anything and everything to stay with her again.

"Are you ready?" a voice asked. Blair turned to see Kielle slinging a bright shining spear on her back. She was already in her full armor. Blair marveled by her warrior spirit. She was again wearing that armor that looked a lot like Queriven's. Blair wondered if he looked a lot like this when he was the knight of the spear-wielding unit. She looked brave and truly a proud knight under the service of the elves. Blair nodded and followed her into the streets, heading for the deep woods.

Many elves were already here and, despite the huge number, hardly did anyone make even a slight sound as they rushed through the brushes. Blair scanned the wildlife. She knew there had to be over a hundred elves here already, though she could see a slight movement here and there, and never directly. The trading post was just ahead.

Kielle stopped and turned to her. "I need to stand post with my unit. Wait here for Finhaus. He should be here soon enough."

Blair let her go without a word. But as soon as she left, Blair felt vulnerable and lost. All the others were preparing for battle and yet here she was standing in the middle of the road doing nothing. She clutched onto her own weapon she brought just in case. She knew she was neither lost nor vulnerable. She had important work ahead of her. She had to remind herself of that.

She didn't realize Finhaus was right next to her until he greeted her. She nearly jumped, but the look on his face was almost content, like he was glad for his purpose in this mission.

"Where's Queriven?" Blair asked once she recovered.

He was fixing to answer, but Queriven himself showed right then and interrupted him. "I need you to stick together and wait here in the back. If we succeed, we'll be able to pry the horn from Darkadus. Someone will swing it back to you. I want you to take it and run. Understand?"

Before Blair could say anything, Finhaus agreed. Queriven clasped him on the back and moved by him. The elf carried a new spear, one even shinier than the old one he had. Blair couldn't take it any longer. "Queriven!" she yelled. The elf she held so dear turned his shoulder back. His mixed brown locks flowed out behind him and those eyes were swirling with curiosity. Blair nearly cried when she threw herself at him. He took her and she wrapped her arms tight around him. She brushed her face against his cheek and breathed in his forest scent. "Stay safe," she whispered in his pointed ear. It was more of a spoken prayer than a demand of him. Still, he promised her he'll be all right. Then, before she was ready, he broke away and headed for his post just ahead. She stood where he left her, empty and alone.

Finhaus crept closer to her. To him, he felt like he was intruding and awkward, but he spoke anyway. "I don't know a lot about rokians, but I do know Kielle and Queriven can take care of themselves. Just wait and see."

She didn't look back at him, but what he said comforted her a little.

Queriven crouched in the thick leaves above the elvish watchtower. He knew where every elf hid. There were only a few up with him, but the important ones were more at the bottom. He couldn't see very many of them, but he did see one with a bow. She was sitting in the bushes just outside the entrance. Every now and then, she would look up. She was waiting for his signal and she was nervous.

Queriven turned his head. Dakru was settling in a hiding place somewhere further in the trading post. He caught a glimpse of the end of his blue robe. He nearly laughed aloud at the irony that was Dakru.

He then turned to the road outside the broken wall. Darkadus could be here any second. If he didn't hold complete focus, this whole attempt to trick him would be for nothing.

Queriven inhaled, then slowly let it go. Even with Finhaus right by her side, he worried about Blair. He worried about everyone. This was going to be a battle like no other. Truthfully, none of them really knew what they were getting themselves into with this rokian. His magic was unlike any other in this world. It was unpredictable what he would do with it. Still, Queriven lamented; if Blair was going to be free, there was no other way.

His muscles were beginning to cramp and his legs yearned to stretch out. Queriven bowed his head and lightly turned to the side, trying to find a little bit of relief. He was in that place in the tree for too long — over a short hour at least.

It wasn't in vain for much longer though. Someone was moving ahead. Queriven held his breath. It was none other than Darkadus himself. The girl hiding in the bush looked up again, but Queriven didn't give the signal. He was still too far.

Darkadus' cohorts were behind him, including Captain Yusen Nashōgan. The silver-skinned man turned to look at him as he walked. "Don't wander off!" the rokian accused. "This forest is dangerous. Only those who know how to reach the city should travel."

That brought a spark of rage to Queriven's heart. "Traitor," he whispered to himself.

"Then how can we find the girl?" one unfortunate soul dared to ask.

Surprisingly, the rokian didn't snap. "Keep your heads together, men! We'll find her with our brains and wits." With a lowered tone, he turned back to the road ahead of him. "If she is still in there, that is."

None of the thieves and pirates bothered to ask him what he meant by that. The group was inside the trading post now, and Darkadus hesitated. He knew something was wrong.

It was now or never. Queriven snapped a twig from the branch.

Instantly, the elves in the trading post jumped out, sending arrows and magic bolts flying.

"Darkadus!" a man yelled before an arrow struck him in the

chest.

Then, when the wave closed in, the girl sitting outside the wall jumped out, arrow already drawn. With a steady hand, she aimed and released.

Darkadus was already turning toward her, and it nearly missed him. The rokian growled, sharp teeth showing past his thick lips. He suspected there was something wrong with the image he conjured, but he never thought it would result in an ambush. They tricked him and that made him furious. No one tricks a rokian!

Wide hands went down and pulled a set of daggers from his belt, both carved carefully from old bones. Then he slammed them into the nearest elf. His men were drawing their weapons as well. Queriven dropped from the tree and joined the fray.

The elves closest to Darkadus dared to swarm him as one. Their moves were quick and reckless. It didn't take the rokian too long to see they weren't on the offense but were aiming at the horn he kept on him. They weren't the only people by him though; the pirates were gathering and repelling the army together. The attention split between him and the thieves.

And yet, he always caught a glimpse of a flying weapon whenever he turned his head down at the artifact on his waist. With each elf he pushed down or injured, two more replaced them. There was less space to move around in with each passing second.

The rokian took a step back and allowed a few of the pirates in front. This allowed him to focus on fewer attackers. What the elves had with longer weapons, Darkadus matched with brute force. The daggers weren't much to look at, but it was only a tool he could use to keep himself from harm. Really, most of his attacks came from his throwing punches, speed, and strength.

The girl who shot at him earlier kicked a wounded pirate from her line of sight and took aim again. To her dismay, there was too much chaos surrounding the rokian now. She wanted a better shot at the horn this time, but she was also not willing to shoot at her allies. She just had to hold her position for now and hope something better comes up. Luckily, Darkadus' silver skin made him an easier target to follow. She wouldn't have been able to watch him so well otherwise. In the meantime, she went back to shooting at his men.

Unfortunately, Darkadus was everything he bragged himself to be. He was cunning, powerful, and fast, and was unafraid of the threats swinging at him. Each attack reeked with confidence. His knuckles were already covered with the blood of his attackers. It only spurred him onward faster. No one could get through to him without a plan. He was unstoppable.

Luckily, the elves were also cunning, and Darkadus was much too occupied to know of the elf hidden in the brush just behind him. When the rokian backed up once more, the soldier jumped out and grabbed for the horn. The rokian's reaction was instantaneous, and he spun before it even left his possession. In a single motion, Darkadus turned his dagger over to allow his fingers to reach for the artifact. It was just enough to unbalance it from the elf's hand. Darkadus nearly fell over when trying to take it, but he successfully took it up again. His mind quickly turned to the offense once more.

Before he could regain his bearings though, a sword was already flying his way. Darkadus moved to duck, but he just wasn't fast enough. The tip knocked the horn from his grip yet again and smashed it into the ground, breaking it in a few places.

The soldier flinched, and it cost him his life. Darkadus plunged a dagger into his heart and dropped him low. In the mix of chaos, hardly anyone knew of the smashed horn, even though it was the main target of the elves. One of them realized it though and cried aloud. "The horn! It's been smashed!"

Kielle kicked her foot into a thief's belly and toppled him over. The yell, though she barely heard it at first, alarmed her. Then she remembered an important detail. She swung the dull end of the spear into her opponent's neck and pushed closer to the soldier. "The horn cannot be broken without magic! Keep your eyes open!"

Then magic must have hit it then. In the complete mess unfolding in the field, it would have been impossible to know what happened. Still, the soldier took his leader's advice and took another look. Taking the horn from Darkadus wouldn't be so easy. He must have known they would be after it. The soldier pressed forward, trying to draw closer to the rokian.

It was then when he spotted a few other pouches on him, particularly a leather one in the back just big enough for the real artifact. The elf's jaw dropped upon his discovery, but he knew he wouldn't be able to take it easily. Darkadus would protect it with his life. He needed help.

The soldier decided on a plan quickly and worked his way to the other side. The archer was still over there. All that he had to do was give her an opening. He began pulling and fighting with the pirates between the archer and Darkadus. He then began yelling her name again and again over the cries of battle until he somehow managed to get her attention.

It took her a long while to understand what was going on, but she understood and aimed once more at Darkadus. This time, the arrow hit its target. The pouch went soaring up in the air and disappeared in the fighting crowd.

The pouch fell unexpectedly in front of an astonished elf and thief. Indeed, it was the horn, and it spilled out from the bag. At once, both the fighters swooped for it. The elf was the faster and took off with it. When more enemies swarmed him, he passed it to another elf.

The horn exchanged hands several times, each elf dodging attacks and taking it through the trading post. Finally, it reached the last elf, and the battle cries became more muffled past the brush. Quickly, the young mage passed the horn over to Blair's hands, then he disappeared back into the battlefield.

Finhaus jumped to his feet and took her arm. Blair hesitated, once again looking back at the trading post. With a beckoning from Finhaus though, she let the battle go and followed him back through the forest.

TRICKING THE TRICKSTER

◊ ◊ ◊

Darkadus' every move was from frustration. He already knew there might be a trap somewhere, but he thought it would be further in the forest, not here. He cursed his ignorance. If he knew there would have been an ambush, he wouldn't have bothered with the fake horn and just smashed the real one. It was too late. They had it now, and the girl is probably already setting off with another plan to summon Rocanu. He needed to stop her, but how? He couldn't leave without using too much magic, nor could he send any pirates into the forest. They didn't know their way through.

"I should have smashed that horn when I had the chance," he lamented out loud, ducking under a sword swing. He had to finish this quickly. A quick stab to the belly dropped his opponent and he marched forward. The battle was raging all throughout the field. Already, he could smell the blood spilling on the air.

Another elf threatened him, this one armed with a bow. It was the girl from before, and she was just as nervous as ever, but she drew her string back. Darkadus danced past the arrow as it landed into a human thief behind him. Quickly though, she had another prepared, and let it fly.

He dodged the second, but then came a third. The last thudded high up his arm. He cursed, grabbing the shaft and breaking it apart. The elf's eyes went wide as he approached her and attacked just fine with his bad arm. He slapped her back, the dagger scratching a wide gash on her cheek. But then another elf jumped in front of her.

Darkadus turned, barely missing the spark coming from the staff. He recovered in a second and dove with the dagger. Dakru smacked the weapon with the staff, redirecting it. In came the second dagger, but magic took hold and pushed it away before trying to free it from his grasp.

The tribal man held on and smacked Dakru with the butt of his other weapon. Dakru tumbled to the side, but now the archer was back on her feet. Still, Darkadus was aiming a final strike, and yet Dakru somehow still knocked it away with the staff.

Blood drizzled down the girl's face, but she was more determined than before. She closed in, trading the bow and arrow for two daggers of her own. Darkadus blocked her strike and parried. Dakru released another crackling spark, but Darkadus quickly turned back, placing the girl between himself and the spark.

The girl flinched and began to shake. Darkadus thrust the dagger forward, but the girl slid out of the way and to the side. Dakru was standing with his staff ahead of him.

Darkadus grinned out of thick annoyance.

The city of Sylinna felt emptier than ever before. It was a refreshing warm morning, and the sky was bright blue like normal. As usual as their surroundings were, Blair was not at peace. Every second was potential for disaster. She imagined the fight raging on behind them, Darkadus easily taking out one beloved elf after another. Her heart was racing uncomfortably in her chest, and it wasn't because of her legs racing onward.

"Why are we slowing down?!" Blair demanded of Finhaus.

He threw his head to a deer far ahead. "I've got a plan. Hold on a moment."

She frowned and flicked her hair behind her. She wanted to remind him of the friends left behind and that they should hurry as quickly as possible to break the curse, but she said nothing. She placed her hands on her hips and took a long breath. She was already covered in sweat.

Finhaus crept forward and whistled. The stag lifted its head and Blair could see it twitch an ear. Then, it took a few steps closer, each one quicker than the last. Finhaus reached in a bag at his hip and took a handful of juicy herbs out. "It's so good to see you, friend," he greeted as the animal came close and pressed its mouth over the treats. With his free hand, Finhaus stroked the neck of the fine creature.

He laughed when a younger male, followed by an elegant doe, came up from a different direction. "Of course, you're here too. You never miss out when it comes to snacks." Finhaus turned and gave the newcomer a handful of treats as well. "And who's this?" he asked the young stag as he turned to the female, offering the last of the treats. She was a little shy at first but accepted. "You finally found a girl? That's wonderful! She's beautiful too." After a second, Finhaus went back to the second male, then turned his head to Blair.

"Why don't you come up and say hello?"

Curiosity replaced Blair's anger. What was his purpose for this? She didn't want to meet his friends just yet, not in this circumstance anyway, but something on Finhaus' face told her to go along with it. After all, he knew the importance of their mission. He had to be going somewhere with this.

Blair came forward. The doe suddenly kicked up and retreated a few feet away. She startled the older one too, but he stayed put.

The human was within arm's length now and the male jerked his head back. Finhaus shushed the creature and gave it an encouraging stroke. It resulted to snorting in response. Blair lifted her hand up and brushed against his fur. The sand-colored hair was a little coarse but thick and fluffy. The young stag settled down.

"These two males are going to help us reach Lettir," Finhaus explained as the deer lowered his head and picked at the full grass. "With their help, we should be there quicker. We'll conserve our energy too. We'll then have to climb up the waterfall." Finhaus looked at Blair for a second, and it took her a while to realize he wanted her to do something. Finally, he gestured to the stag. He wanted her to climb on its back.

Suddenly nervous, she carefully grabbed the beast and began pulling up. The stag raised its head and snorted again, but Finhaus kept it from panicking. "Hold on tight, but don't hurt him either. Riding a deer is very different from a horse.

You'll understand that soon enough."

Both intrigue and excitement from sitting on the young stag filled Blair's stomach, and if it wasn't for the stress of the battle, she would have been smiling brightly.

Finhaus easily swung himself up on the other stag's back like he's done it many times before. He looked back at the doe. She was watching them curiously. "I'm sorry we have to leave your girl behind," he lamented to Blair's deer. "You'll have to find her again when we come back."

"Finhaus," Blair called, "how far is Lettir?"

He sighed. She was asking for the sake of rushing back here to join the battle if she needed to, but he knew, whatever the outcome, it would be too late to help their friends. "Far" was his only reply, and he urged his mount forward.

Five thugs loomed in Kielle's space, but she hardly batted an eye. Her strength relied on speed. Hardly anyone of them could dream to keep up. Each step she took was like a graceful waltz, elegant and fair. The sparkle from her spear was like the twinkle of stars as she twirled it around in circles. Most of the thugs hesitated and stepped away from the threat. One who dared to brave it was smacked down to the ground in a heartbeat. The spear came down in a flash, impaling the man. The elf pulled the spear free. The shining blade rejected the blood on its flawless surface, allowing it to shoot free and clean.

No technique was perfect, however, and a pirate snuck behind her. Luckily, help was on the way, and Queriven pushed the man back. Kielle reacted, thinking him an enemy. "Ah!" she cried when she realized it was only her brother. "There you are!" she stopped to swing the butt end of her spear up into a man's chin. "I'm glad to have your help."

Queriven acknowledged her consent without a word. He lunged forward, once, and twice to the other side, taking a thug deep in front of his shoulder.

Kielle and Queriven were now back to back, and although

they were both spear-wielding knights, their practices with their weapon were totally different. Kielle confused her opponents with speed, each move resulting in an amazing blur. Queriven's attacks were quick as well, but not like hers, as he focused on balance and strategy instead. He dodged past flying weapons like liquid, and his spear flashed forward, sometimes tricking his opponents with false attacks. His spear was on the offensive, yet he ducked, jumped, and dodged everything else himself. The long range of the spear kept many enemies at bay.

Queriven looked back as Kielle suddenly laughed. She shook her head, ignoring a previous man's screams. "You know what my younger self would give to have us fight together like this? I've always wanted this chance since you joined the family!"

Kielle pursued a pirate brandishing a longsword, her energy showing in her hops and lunges. Again, Queriven didn't respond, but there was a wide smile on his face.

The two elves were just too slippery. Darkadus clenched his teeth with rage. With every nick and cut, he became even angrier. His attacks were even faster and more unpredictable. He considered how much magic he had left before he would break his own curse he set on Blair. He knew then he was only going to use any as a last resort, even if he felt like he needed it now. "You two are not going to be the end of my magic!" he growled, not even caring if they understood what that meant or not.

He ducked under a flying arrow and charged toward Dakru. The elf didn't hesitate. He slammed the staff into the rokian again. Darkadus took the hit and threw a bone dagger forward, but had to jump back to avoid another arrow. The rokian paused and looked back. Then, he grabbed the shirt of a rookie thief. "Take care of the archer girl!" he yelled, pushing the man toward her. The man looked back in confusion, but he accepted the task and lunged forward.

A spark sent his arm numb, but Darkadus shook it off. Now the mage was all alone. Dakru saw his disadvantage but continued shooting spells anyway. Darkadus dodged past each one, each time coming closer and closer. Finally, Dakru had to use his staff again to keep him away. Darkadus quickly overwhelmed him though. He ducked under the first swing, then swirled around and cut the elf's side. The elf flinched and clenched the bleeding wound. Then came a stab to the chest. Dakru tried to stay upright with his staff but fell over anyway.

Dakru, with his head on the hard, unforgiving dirt, looked to the side. For the first time, he saw how devastating the battle really was. History repeated itself with elf versus human. Already, the ground was tainted with red and littered with bodies, both human and elf. Water bubbled past Dakru's vision. His blood was already spilling beyond his body. Darkness was quickly taking over and he closed his eyes.

Satisfied, Darkadus flicked his dagger around and marched away toward the trees of Aven Forest.

Kielle turned back. Queriven was gone. How long has she been fighting on her own? She didn't really know nor did she know where he was now. She shrugged; she's been handling herself anyway, though she was not completely alone. She could briefly see some members of her unit just ahead, past her attackers. They were stemming the flow of thieves.

She tucked in a low horizontal swing, slicing one man's belly and making him trip into the next. As he fell, the spear caught his jawline. Kielle backed away, finishing them both while they were on the ground. She used them as a barrier so she could reach the men on the other side without them reaching her. The pirate was sick of her attacks and leaped over the bodies. He had to take a beating from the wooden shaft, but he recovered quickly.

Kielle backed up. There was someone approaching behind her. She had to be careful as there were a few thieves behind where her back was now. Suddenly, more and more enemies were surrounding her. Where was her unit?

She distracted the pirate in front of her with her dancing spear, then kicked him in the shin. He bowed over in pain and knocked him over the head. Then she dared to look around. Most of her units that were here a second ago were gone. Now there were only a few left. They were fighting a weathered man with a tall hat, and he was giving them quite a challenge.

There was a sword swinging for her face, and Kielle ducked only a second before the disaster. She came back up with her spear leading and knocked him in return. With the same momentum, she swung the tip into another's waist.

The weathered man with the tall hat was coming closer without her realizing. Each swing and step was in total confidence, and Kielle was his closest target now. Still focused on her attackers, she deflected a sweep from two different swords, then stabbed one in the leg while disarming the other.

Finally, the captain came in. She wasn't even looking. But when he jabbed for her head, she spun and pushed it away. Her gold eyes were on fire. Captain Yusen Nashōgan went low next. Kielle easily parried and pushed him back with the range of her weapon. Now that he was away, she turned to parry another attacker.

Yusen closed in again, but had to jump over a low sweep. He went in from the side and, again, it was blocked. The spear drove away, taking a man in the hip with the same movement.

A swing from a man behind her had her ducking low, and this time, Yusen caught her just barely in the arm. Kielle flinched and did the unthinkable. While still low, she kicked him in the leg and rolled toward him. She was back up on her feet in a heartbeat just in time to parry his attack.

Kielle was no longer alone. Reinforcements were coming and they engaged the attacking thieves who surrounded her. Now she could focus fully on the captain. She twirled her spear around, her parries and strikes falling again in dance. The captain fell in her movements without hesitance.

◊ ◊ ◊

The young stag was breathing hard with each hop. The forest was racing by right before Blair's eyes. Her hair was whipping out behind her and she squinted past the air and the old summer pollen rushing in and making her itch. She had no idea where they were now, but she knew they've been traveling for at least an hour. Were they any closer than they were before? She couldn't tell. She couldn't see what was ahead or back. She only saw trees being sucked quickly behind her. Blair raised her voice. "Do you still know where you're going?!" That came out ruder than she hoped, as she wouldn't have blamed Finhaus if he lost his way. Everything here looked the same at this speed and they couldn't see much of the sky past the thick canopy.

But Finhaus wasn't upset. He turned his head. "Don't worry. We're making good time," he answered. Blair waited for him to give her something better, but he was looking ahead again. His ponytail of deep purple hair was bouncing with each leap of his mount. Blair shrugged. He had the confidence at least, but she was growing tired of the ride. What he said earlier was right. A deer was much different from a horse. A horse galloped much smoother and was more like a slow run than a series of quick hops and kicks. Still, Finhaus looked pretty comfortable.

Low branches threatened to tangle in her hair and Blair laid low, placing her head near the base of the creature's neck. She could hear his racing heart and each one of his powerful breaths. Despite the discomfort, she was quite thankful for the beast. At least she didn't have to walk. Blair allowed herself to take in her senses.

She heard many loud voices of many late summer insects. There were plenty of birds as well. They must be enjoying the generous amount of prey. Blair heard something else as well, but she couldn't tell what it was at first. Then she realized it was Finhaus talking gently to his mount. Blair thought Finhaus to be a lonely sort, but she could see he was fine.

The slipping rays of sunshine were quite warm. She could

feel each one as she passed under them. The morning was waning, and so it was becoming steadily warmer. The hot days were already over and the season of comforting spices was just around the corner. For a second, Blair closed her eyes and teleported back home. She imagined her parents sitting around the table, preparing supper. She could almost smell the fresh juicy goat, crisp vegetables from the garden, and spiced cider. When she opened her eyes again, a wave of homesickness knocked her back. She looked up. The leaves ruffled in the sunlight. Her dear parents were under the same blue sky, probably spending a quiet morning together and praying for their daughter's safety.

A shiver ran down Blair's body and she answered a prayer with one of her own. *Bring me home at least once more, and if it be your will, allow my spirit to leave this world into the world of the ancients. Just look after my parents and keep my friends safe. Kielle, Sirnah, Dakru, and Queriven... They fight selflessly to protect their home and me...*

The stag under her felt her hug him tighter. The creature looked back and saw the human girl low and with her eyes closed. Dark golden hair bounced on her shoulders and spilled down over her face. Her expression was aware and concerned, but it was also at peace. Freckles of different shapes and sizes spattered on her soft and light face. The beast focused ahead again.

Past the ceiling of trees, an approaching mountain blotted out a part of the sky. Finally, they arrived, and just in time too. The stags were growing tired from the journey and needed to rest. Finhaus hoped they will have their strength built up for the trip back.

CHAPTER THIRTY-THREE
TRUE POWER

The forest in front of Blair and Finhaus opened up and revealed a lovely town. It was a much simpler version of Sylinna. The homes were more spread apart, allowing them and the streets to be a little wider. The open space brought in more sun and fresh air, and it cast sparkles on the water of the flowing river nearby.

Blair did not open her eyes until she heard the waterfall in the distance. Her mount was also slowing down. The young stag was at a walk now, and Finhaus was already dismounting. Blair sat up, but the combination of discomfort and the speed she was riding left her rather dizzy. Before she could stop herself, she tumbled right off the deer's back and landed in the grass.

The hard ground brought pain to her back and she heard a light chuckle before seeing Finhaus standing over her. "Are you all right?" he asked and offered his hand.

She took it, the fall leaving her even dizzier than before, and he fought to help her on her feet. Finally back up, Blair brushed herself off and straightened her hair. She inhaled and kept it in her lungs for a while. She admired Lettir's beauty, but the importance of the mission kept her from staring too long.

Finhaus had his back to her and was loving on the two stags

once more. "Thank you, both of you. I don't have any more treats though. I'll have to give you some when I can."

They didn't seem to have a problem with that and began grazing. He gave the younger stag a good pat and turned for the city. Blair could see the river from here, but not the waterfall. "Where do we have to go now?" she asked, racing up to him.

Glancing at her, he answered, "We have to climb up that mountain. It's smooth just on top of the falls. That's where the vayen aray met with the elves of this city."

Curious, she asked him, "Have you ever climbed the mountain before?"

He shook his head and let her down. "I've never climbed it, but I've been here before once or twice. The city takes its history with pride. The town's as wonderful as it looks, really."

Blair looked away. The roar of the falls was growing louder and she thought she could see some spray around the corner. Finhaus suddenly began talking again. "However, I do think the easiest way up is on the other side of the waterfall. If I do remember right..."

Then, Blair flinched. A large set of wings closed in like a blur before it folded and landed on the elf's shoulder. He didn't bat an eye. He looked at the large dark bird with interest. "What are you doing here? Are you crazy enough to follow me all the way out here?" As if on cue, the bird cawed in return. "Are you going to help us find a way up the mountain?" he asked and, again, the bird reacted. It spread its wings and took off.

Blair raised an eyebrow. "You're really good with them," she remarked out loud. "Once, I believed elves could speak with animals, but lately, I've learned that's not the case."

Finhaus laughed like it was ridiculous. "No, that's nothing but a rumor. There are many false things the humans say about us. I never knew why they would say these things, but now I understand." Orbs of vibrant cyan met her face. "There were a lot of things I believed about humans that were ridiculous as well. I see why you're such good friends with Queriven. You're extraordinary. I do hope you see me as a friend as well."

Blair smiled, suddenly feeling at home. "I do see you that

way, Finhaus; you and many others. You and your siblings are like family to me now. Thank you so much for accepting me in your forest."

He smiled joyfully and didn't reply. Blair looked ahead again. The waterfall was in clear view now. The roar and splash were overpowering and water droplets were spraying everywhere over the rocks near the bottom. She could see each one through the sunlight and it even revealed a colorful rainbow near the top. She had to yell to speak to Finhaus. "I hope it'll be dry enough on our way up."

"Yeah, it will be," he agreed. "We'll have to take the bridge over and check the other side away from the water."

On the way to the bridge, they passed a few fields where elves were working. Blair wasn't as uncomfortable as she once was though, and she smiled brightly at them. If Finhaus noticed, he paid them no mind.

The cliffside where the water fell curved in, and it was on that end where it looked the easiest to climb. The rock was thicker with texture, and it sloped the most here. It was still a long way up and Blair squinted against the sun as she tried to locate the top. A second passed before Finhaus was the first to move. He pressed the tip of his foot into the rock and pulled himself up a step.

A slice to the leg brought Kielle down to her knees. Yusen grinned. He finally had her where he wanted her. The sword swung down, but Kielle wasn't going to be caught that easily. In the last second, she rolled out of harm's way and came back up. Blood was spilling from her wound now and her balance was a little shaky, but she held.

She wasn't about to give up and pressed on once more. Her parries and blocks were still quick enough to keep him away, but he could tell by the look on her face that she was growing tired.

This was a matter of life and death now, and adrenaline

kicked in. Her heart was racing, her blood pooling out quicker, and every move she made, she was only slightly aware of. She lured Yusen in with some short spins, then as he came up on the offense, Kielle lunged with the full of the spear. The tip pushed in his side and the length forced him several steps back.

Yusen clenched the gash as the spear withdrew. Upon removal of his hand, he realized the severity of the wound. It must be treated immediately or it could become fatal. The captain was too stubborn to accept any source of weakness though and he rushed ahead with sword swinging.

Darkadus was close to the trees now, and he pressed forward. He's defeated every foe who came to stop him, and now he had his eyes fixed on the forest. He was going to bring the fight to the city, even if no one else came with him. He was sure he would be followed, but at least he would be away from here and closer to the horn.

Suddenly, an elf was standing far to his right. He had an arrow drawn. "Darkadus, stop!" a male voice cried out.

Darkadus turned, but he remained calm. "I figured I would see you at some point in all this," he addressed Queriven, "but I'm busy now."

Of course, Queriven didn't let him go. "You can't win this. You're too late. Blair is already breaking your spell."

Darkadus rolled his eyes. "Come on. You're so predictable. Don't try to convince me of anything. You know it won't work like that."

Queriven was still aiming for him. "Give up now while you have the chance. No more people have to die in this battle."

For just a second, Queriven saw something in his eyes that made him flinch. Was that a spark of fear? Darkadus' next words spat with raw frustration. "I can't! You don't know what it's like over there. It's a dying world and the things that aren't dead are thin and dry." After taking a harsh breath, Darkadus resorted to accusing Queriven outright. "Don't you see how important this is!? My people are suffering and they have been for far too long."

His display had no effect on Queriven. "If your plea is sincere, then ask for assistance. We can help to release both your people and the vayen aray if you're sure the rokians are done with their wickedness. Personally, I don't think they're ready. If the rokians are suffering that far, then why do you commit others to that world in your place? Why do you want Blair to die in that miserable land?"

Darkadus bared his teeth and growled. "You're just like the others! This is why I cursed the girl. I knew no one would help release us willingly, so I had to act by myself." His anger was quickly rising. In the blink of an eye, he threw his bone dagger at the elf.

Queriven ducked under the knife and released the arrow. Darkadus moved away as quick as lightning and was inches from him in a heartbeat. Even Queriven couldn't withdraw his spear in time before Darkadus swung the other dagger in front of him. Queriven tried to lean away, but it sliced him under the arm.

He didn't hesitate further. He took the spear in his hand and stabbed its full length. It missed Darkadus' belly by a hair, and the rokian moved back in from the side. A quick sweep of the spear forced him to back up again, but then he responded by throwing the other dagger. Queriven tucked in the spear and the dagger landed in the shaft.

Queriven held on to the dagger and danced a few steps forward, bringing the spear over in his hands. He made a mistake when he thought Darkadus was unarmed. Darkadus swerved to the side and jumped up inside the spear's range. Somehow, another dagger was inside Darkadus' hand, and the blade nicked a line right under Queriven's chin. The elf staggered back and pressed a hand to the spilling blood. Darkadus was back on him in a second and Queriven blocked further harm with the shaft.

Kielle's stressed body hurt with every breath that came in, but Yusen wasn't doing any better. Blood was still spilling from where she stabbed him. Kielle pushed through the discomfort, though her moves were a little less beautiful than before. Sweat beaded on her face and rolled down in her hair and cheeks.

Though wounded and losing his mind, Yusen was still a formidable foe. The sword in his hand attempted every opening he had. Every second pushed the captain on the offense and Kielle spent more and more time trying to defend herself.

Yusen growled. He was growing weaker. If he didn't strike her now, he'll die shortly. The pirate took a dangerous risk and stepped in closer. His sword stabbed again and again like a thick needle until finally, he hit her. Kielle exclaimed in pain from the deep stab in her upper arm. The sword retracted, thick with her blood.

By some miracle, Kielle allowed her spear to spin with the continuing momentum. Not taking a moment to protect himself, the butt end of the weapon smacked him in the head. His vision quickly blurred and he fell backward. A pool of blood quickly escaped from his body.

Exhaustion nearly overtook the female knight and she clenched a hand firmly on her arm. The ground was making waves under her feet and her lightheadedness didn't help. She was about to faint. "Kielle!" a voice belonging to one of her soldiers cried out. He rushed to her side and took her before she joined the pirate on the hard ground. Other elves closed in, protecting her retreat.

Each step was harder than the last, but Blair pulled herself up one after the other. Finhaus was further way up than she was, though he was struggling a little too.

Still, the top was within reach and Finhaus made it up without stumbling. Now at the top, he bent over for Blair's hand. She groaned, stretching just to take it. He grasped her firmly and pulled. "You need to see this. It's amazing!" he cried out.

Blair was high enough to climb over the top herself now, and he helped her to her feet. Immediately, the brush of wind blew through her hair and nearly buffeted her over. She breathed in until her lungs couldn't hold anymore. Then, she looked in the direction Finhaus was facing and she understood what he meant.

She didn't realize until that moment how far they had climbed. The two were over the top of the entire forest now, and the trees that were taller than the waterfall were only at eye level. The fluffy canopy of Aven Forest was nothing more than a ground full of green bushes. The sight caught Blair breathless. The sky was closer than ever. It was like she could just reach up and touch it. The sound of erupting water was only surpassed by open laughter from her companion. He held his arms out freely, beholding the large world surrounding them. "I can't believe I've never done this before!" he yelled and Blair grinned. "I've been missing out this entire time!"

Blair spun around and her hair whipped in her face. Behind them, the rest of the mountain continued toward the blue sky. The plateau under their feet wasn't perfectly flat. In fact, it was pretty sloped in some places. Rocks and cracks interrupted the thick grass and plants in a few places. Blair closed her eyes. This plateau, while beautiful, wasn't special enough for winged heroes to land, but her spirit stirred and a chill ran down her. She could feel them like she traveled back in time. She could almost hear their voices.

When her eyes opened, Blair was staring down at her wrist. The single wave has faded so far she could barely see any trace of it. Shock took her words for only a moment. "Darkadus is using his magic. The elves are still in danger. We need to call Rocanu now before it's too late."

As strong as Darkadus was, Queriven was giving him quite a

fight. The rokian had to use his dwindling magic just to keep up. Within minutes, both of them were bloodied and tired, and Darkadus became more and more desperate with each spell. His magic enhanced his speed and agility to unnatural limits, and Queriven struggled.

The elf's spear whipped to and fro when Darkadus was near, and Queriven was still hurt. Keeping Darkadus out of range didn't help either because he would throw his daggers. Queriven held onto as many as he could, which was not much. Darkadus was faster than him now, and Queriven had to do everything he could to survive.

Darkadus was several feet away again, and here came another dagger. Queriven sidestepped, allowing it to fly free behind him. Then, he took a bone dagger he picked up from Darkadus earlier and threw it back at him.

With a little luck and surprise, it stuck in his hand. Darkadus grimaced and pulled it out. Unless he used even more magic, that hand was now useless. He flicked a drop of blood from the dagger and rushed in with his good hand.

Even with one hand, Darkadus was too quick. He ducked, jumped, and turned around the swinging staff with ease. Then, Darkadus stepped back on his own and shot out another dagger. Queriven was not quick enough to deflect or dodge this one, and it flew in just below his hip. Queriven fell on his knees.

"You can't win," Darkadus said as the elf groaned in pain. "You know this and you will die if you continue, but you don't have to." Darkadus put his lone dagger away and showed the elf his empty hands. "Let me go, and I'll leave you with your life."

A long time ago, Queriven might have let him. After all, what good will he be to the forest if he was dead? But times have changed. He was protecting something else now, and he wasn't afraid. He was no longer running like a coward.

Darkadus smirked and took a single step to the forest, but a dagger bounced just in front of his foot. He turned again to see the determination on Queriven's face. "I can't let you do that. You'll just have to spend all your magic fighting with me."

Darkadus growled. He wanted to let go easily, but if this is what Queriven wanted, then he would deliver it. "Fine then, elf, but don't say I didn't warn you." He withdrew his dagger again and seemed to leap toward him in a single stride.

Finhaus took the horn gently like it was a newborn baby. Vibrant eyes glanced nervously Blair's way before he brought it slowly to his lips. He sucked in a breath. He wasn't sure how loud or long he could call with his shortened breath, but he gave it all he had.

The music coming from the artifact sent Blair spiraling through the past. She's heard it before, and it was the same long, never-falling wave as before. This time, it was right before her, and it was the sound of freedom. She closed her eyes and a shiver racked her body. It was a powerful tool, especially for being as old as it was.

The sound faded, and she opened her eyes to see Finhaus looking at her. The song of the horn bounced off into the far distance, but besides that, nothing happened. Finhaus was growing visibly uneasy, but Blair was surprisingly calm. She knew the horn did as expected. She knew Rocanu would be there.

The two inspected their surroundings when all of a sudden, Finhaus threw his arm up and pointed at the base of the continuing mountain. "Blair!" he cried out, sounding a little afraid. She followed where he was pointing and saw a thin aura of blue light. The aura shone brighter and brighter with no visible source and Finhaus covered his face. Soon, the light was so bright Blair had to do the same, but it quickly died off and she looked again.

Rocanu was standing in the place of the light, and he looked just as shocked as they did.

He looked just the same as she remembered him; long and angled features, a young simple man for such wise eyes, and giant feathered wings. Only one thing struck Blair as something different. He didn't look at all transparent.

"Am I...?" he began, turning around to grasp his surroundings. He took in the scent of the damp stone and the thick forest. He felt the grass under his feet and quieted under the sound of singing birds. "I'm back home," he whispered in awe. Finally, his gaze landed on Blair. His wings stretched wide open as he addressed her. "You've done well. Thank you so much for bringing me back, even if it's for a short time."

Blair took a step forward. "What do you mean you're back for only a short time?"

Rocanu didn't show any sorrow. "The magic of the horn is powerful enough to bring me back from that dying world, but it doesn't linger enough to let me stay. Soon, I'll fade away again and return to my family, so let's make this quick. Show me the mark of the curse."

She came closer and held her arm out for him to take. He held it gently, seeming content Blair didn't move through him, and he studied the mark. Rocanu was so real than ever before, and Blair seemed to tremble a little under those ancient eyes. He was no longer a vision. He was here, standing just a hair away from her. "Darkadus has nearly worn out this magic," he commented. "It'll be easy to finish off." With his free hand, he brushed over the faded mark like he was rubbing it away. She heard him say a few incantations under his breath and the wavy line disappeared under his fingers.

When it was all cleared, he hovered a thinly striped hand in the air over her heart and listened. She couldn't understand why, but she felt lighter, as if a chain she didn't know was holding on her chipped away. She had the strength to handle anything now. "You're free from the curse," Rocanu stated before he even opened his eyes. He drew his hand back to his side. "Don't you feel it? It's no longer pulling you."

This is what she was waiting for since last autumn almost a year ago. She's been daydreaming for this moment. She thought it would be everything to her if it ever came, but it didn't. Breaking the curse was no longer about her, but about the elves. The land was free from the return of the rokians and she hoped Darkadus could feel the exact moment it broke.

Blair accepted Rocanu's blessing like it was only a step toward saving the world, and she turned to Finhaus. The elf was standing with mouth agape, as if staring into the face of a ghost. When he caught himself, he cleared his voice and bowed politely. "Spoken gratitude doesn't match what you've done for us, but thank you."

Rocanu smiled and bowed his head. Again, he turned to Blair, but he spoke to her with urgency in his voice. "Your friends are in grave peril. They need you to return quickly. I can help you off the waterfall but I'm not strong enough to take you all the way back. Will you allow my help?"

Blair nodded, and Rocanu took a gentle hold of her. The two walked to the edge of the rock. Water was splashing only a few feet away. Then, he spread his gigantic wings and dove. For such a small and slim figure, his grip on her was mighty and she didn't cry out against the forcible wind.

The fall lasted for only a quick second and Rocanu beat his wings. The sound of lashing feathers was deafening, like pounding drums, and the vayen aray lowered her gently to the ground. When she dropped, he quickly soared back up to the top.

Seconds later, he came back down with Finhaus and Rocanu landed on the grass. The elf was somehow even more bewildered than before, and he fell beside Blair. She turned her head back the way through town. She was in a hurry to return to the trading post, but something about the vayen aray held her attention. "So what are you going to do now?" she asked.

Rocanu breathed in, his sharp features were solemn but content. "I'm going to enjoy the time I have left. I think I might fly in the blue sky again and take in the gorgeous scenery. Before long, I'll return to the other world. I have to thank you for this gift of freedom."

For the first time, Blair fell in sorrow by his expression. She didn't know much about him, and she never really wondered. It finally occurred to her fully. Rocanu saved her from his own realm. She understood he must be immortal. He's said things that made her think so before. If that was so, then he's lived in

Lyfíhana before. Maybe he was even in the fight that drove the rokians and the vayen aray into that world in the first place. Rocanu didn't belong there, and he did everything to make sure she didn't have the same fate.

Before she had the chance to say anything else, he took off the ground and flew toward the clouds. Within a second, he was far in the distance, looking like nothing but a large bird. Blair refocused and turned to Finhaus. "Come on!" she cried and dashed past the city.

Queriven was at a clear disadvantage. His leg hindered his movements and he spent most of the time deflecting blows from over his head. The muscles in his arms were on fire. Still, he managed to block each attack, but he knew he wouldn't be able to for long.

Growing desperate, he swung the spear down with all his strength. The wooden shaft smacked Darkadus' shoulder hard and he flinched. Queriven took the opening to stand slowly to his feet. He was beginning to hurt more now and he knew his balance was weak.

Darkadus flashed a dagger ahead of him, but Queriven smacked him a second time with the shaft, then pulled in the spear. Darkadus jumped free before it could cut him and was rushing back in.

This was too tight for the spear, so Queriven took another dagger out. He threw it and the rokian's only chance of blocking it was with his own weapon. He saved himself from the flying bone dagger, but it disarmed him in the process. That was his last one, but that didn't stop him from attacking. He came in with a fist and Queriven grabbed it nearly at the cost of his balance. Darkadus responded with a swift kick. His foot landed in Queriven's still weak rib and sent the elf flying.

Queriven hit his head on the stone wall behind him, and he could only choke for several minutes. His vision was blurring and his head threatened to leave him in the dark. He couldn't let that happen. Darkadus was already flying in to finish him. Queriven rolled over, leaving Darkadus to run into the wall.

The elf struggled to his feet again, but he staggered back and forth. He found his spear was still in hand, and he stabbed forward. There was no way he could win now. Queriven knew Darkadus was right. He was so weak and Darkadus still had so much energy. The rokian easily dodged the wavering attack and closed in. Queriven braced himself for another punch in the gut, but instead, he heard a ripping sound. Something pushed in just under his chest. Forgetting how to breathe, he looked down and saw the hilt of a dagger protruding from his body.

No thoughts ran through his mind. He barely even heard his weapon as it fell. With wide eyes, he looked up at Darkadus' face. The rokian's features were free from evil and pride. It was hard to tell what he felt, but it could have been one of pity. Still holding onto the dagger in Queriven's midsection, Darkadus leaned in and whispered. "I don't do this because I'm cruel. I do it because I have no other choice. I do hope you understand..."

But Queriven couldn't understand the words he said. And when Darkadus withdrew, Queriven could no longer stand without support. Instinct brought his hands to the spilling gash, but his hands were only stained in crimson. He fell on his back and didn't register the hard ground below him. There was no pain and his senses quickly disappeared.

Darkadus backed away. He realized for the first time how exhausted he was. He glanced over at the trading post. There were a few battles still, but the war was finished. Not surprisingly, the elves were winning, though they suffered a great loss. Darkadus suspected a lot of the thieves and pirates already fled. He scoffed and turned back to the trees, but he stopped.

There was no reason to push forward. Blair has broken the curse. He knew because he couldn't feel its ties anymore. His heart skipped a beat in horror. He lost. It was too late.

He had to force his next breath. What can he do now? He couldn't go back to that terrible place, but he couldn't stay here either. Without his magic, he could be easily cornered and killed. Fear took him and he raced out from the trading post and disappeared unnoticed.

By the time Finhaus and Blair arrived on the scene, the evening was falling. The stags have galloped hard yet again to bring them back. Finhaus dismounted, speaking words of praise to his animal friends. Blair didn't wait for him. As soon as she hit the ground, she was running. Her heart was leaping in her throat as she pushed back low branches and bushes.

She needed to make sure her friends survived. They needed to, and she wanted to see Queriven more than ever. After everything they gave, the battle was won. The curse was finally over...

CHAPTER THIRTY-FOUR
ALL FOR NOTHING

The sight that awaited Blair on the other side of the trees left her frozen in place. What remained of the battle was the aftermath. She noted the only elves standing were the healers of the Center Tree. Each one wore robes like Sirnah's, and they examined each body on the ground. Some of the wounded were stirring a little when healers came to their sides, while others were carried away.

She remained where she was until she spotted Sirnah himself. Blair marched his direction, trying not to be sick with the mixing haze of medicine and blood. He was talking with another healer when she called his name. He broke contact with the elf and looked her way. His features were grim and serious, and he said something else in response to the elf. The other healer bowed and walked away.

"Sirnah," Blair said again when she was closer, "what happened to Darkadus? How many elves were lost and where is Queriven?"

He raised his hands to quiet her endless slew of questions. Despite how calm Sirnah looked, she could see he was quite stressed and tired. He sighed and turned his head, not sure where to begin. The casualties were too serious and too many.

Every second ticked like a bomb in Blair's head. She was already on the verge of exploding before he said anything.

"Darkadus and his men were powerful, especially the rokian himself," Sirnah stated. "Reports said he moved at unnatural speeds. I guess that was the infamous rokian magic. Many were injured and many more were killed. Believe me when I say we're doing all we can."

"But where is he?" Blair demanded again, her voice was shaking already.

He sighed again and shook his head. "We don't know. He's gone. No one can find him."

The rim of her eyes filled with tears and a single one dropped when she surveyed the battleground again. "Where are the survivors and Queriven?"

Sirnah hesitated a little too long, but he spoke before Blair went first. "The injured are being treated away from the field. I can't go there right now, but you can follow a healer back there if you wish."

She gave him a brisk nod and took a step away, but he grabbed her shoulder. She stared into his eyes and waited. It seemed like he wanted to tell her something, but couldn't. Finally, after saying nothing at all, he released her and she quickly marched off again.

The healer she followed back into the trees didn't say a word. He veered off the way she came, heading only a little south. It didn't take them long to reach the small clearing, though it was safely away from the trading post.

At once, she took notice of the covered bodies lining to her right. Sirnah was right; it seemed there were more dead than living. The amount shook her to her core. There were a little over three long rows. She turned away. On the other side were the survivors. They were also lying on the ground, but healers had them bundled in cloth and resting their heads on rolls. She took note of the different injuries and she looked at each one while ignoring their moans and coughs.

She also noted that Queriven was not among them...

Finally, there was a face she recognized all the way at the end. Kielle looked just as wounded as the others, but the stubborn girl was away from her wrap and was sitting on a hard rock instead. Her leg was wrapped at the thigh and her arm was in a cast. She looked miserable. She was also dirty and bloody. Blair almost didn't recognize her at first. Her normally beautiful, red flowing hair was dark and limp around her shoulders. The only thing that wasn't affected by the dirt and blood were those bright golden eyes. They seemed brighter than before, though it wasn't because she was doing well. She was being pestered by a concerned healer who wanted her to rest, but she wove him off.

Blair approached her, glad to see she was fine. "Kielle, how are you feeling?"

When the healer saw she had company, he growled and tossed his arms out in frustration. Finally, he left the knight's side. Kielle didn't even give Blair a smile, though she welcomed the human warmly. She looked down at the cast for a moment. "I could be worse, I suppose, though it isn't exactly comfortable," she admitted and then looked around the clearing. "Is Finhaus all right?"

"He's fine," Blair assured her. "I left him to see the aftermath myself. He should be arriving soon."

Kielle breathed a visible sigh of relief. "Good. I'm so thankful the two of you are safe." Just then, another importance crossed her face. She looked back up at Blair. "What about the curse? Was it broken?"

"It's done," she answered and then explained her run in the forest with Finhaus. Kielle seemed amazed by her description of Rocanu, but she didn't say a thing. Blair finished as quickly as she could and glanced over the clearing again. "Kielle, do you know where Queriven is? I haven't seen him anywhere."

Blair's heart sank when Kielle slumped over. She wasn't able to give an answer, but she looked over to the rows of the deceased. Blair internally begged for a better answer and forced the silence until Kielle spoke. "They did everything, Blair." Her voice was lighter and she seemed she was fixing to cry. "They tried to save him, but he..."

For the hundredth time that day, Blair froze. Her breath caught in her chest with nowhere to go and the world darkened around her. She fell numb in an instant. It was like she was in a bad dream. The scenery around her broke into waves, like she was shrinking smaller and insignificant. She shook her head and couldn't hold on to the tears any longer. "No...no," she whimpered. "He couldn't have... He's too strong...he couldn't."

Kielle was unable to comfort her. "A few saw him fighting Darkadus, and that's the last thing we know about the two of them."

Blair wasn't listening anymore. This couldn't happen; not now. They won the battle. This was supposed to be a happy time! Her shoulders began to shake as her world ended before her. "So Darkadus..."

"Blair!" Kielle yelled out, trying to hold onto her friend's sanity.

But it was too late; Blair couldn't take it. Ignoring Kielle's continuing calls, she dashed away from the encampment.

She didn't know where she was going, but she just wanted to keep running. She felt if she kept going, maybe she could escape from this nightmare. But no matter how hard she ran, nothing changed.

Her next breath came out as a loud gasp and her eyes were burning. Finally, she reached her limit and fell into the grass, weeping loudly. She was oblivious to her surroundings and didn't even realize how far she ran from the forest border, nor did she care.

Blair covered her eyes and pressed her head into the grass. Nothing about this was right. She broke the curse! They completed their mission! This was not the time for her to lose her dear friend. *Why did I have to go to Lettir? If I would have waited, maybe he would be alive right now.* The shameful thought made her run a fist into the unforgiving ground. *I told him he needed me! Why wouldn't he listen?!* She yelled her pain into the sky, but there was no comfort or forgiveness. Every minute ate at her heart and she prayed desperately for something to break the discomfort swallowing her. Nothing happened.

She cried her tears into the soil until her head pounded and no more tears fell. The next thing that caught her attention was the call of a wolf in the distance. She lifted her puffy eyes. The sun was already gone from the sky and a serene crescent moon glowed softly instead. The pain was just as fresh as earlier. Would she ever be able to move on without Queriven?

She pushed herself up to a sitting position and turned around. Someone was coming her way. She couldn't see who it was from here, but the figure carried a smooth orb in his hand. It was emitting a blue light that engulfed him. Then she noted the spark of compassionate eyes and realized it was none other than Sirnah. It was at this point that Blair noticed he had almost the same gold shine Kielle had. "There you are," he said when he came by. His voice was loving and calm. "I've looked everywhere for you. I was worried you wouldn't be able to make it back to Sylinna in time."

Blair wiped her eyes and looked away, still upset and more than a little embarrassed. In the corner of her vision, he extended a hand her way. A moment passed and Blair decided to take it. Sirnah pulled her to her feet and extended an arm behind her shoulders as he gently walked with her back to the border.

Blair's mind was a terrible mess, but the world surrounding them was once again at peace. The green grass and emerging nightlife were blissfully unaware of the ugly incident that had taken place just a few hours before. Sirnah was also fighting internal turmoil, but like always, he remained calm and sensible before Blair. Her state of mind came before his own, and he supported her silently for a while before he spoke again. "Blair, I was wondering if you could stay with us for a while longer."

She sniffed one more time and looked at him.

He continued. "I've already talked with Kielle. She said her place is still open to you and Foradue said you are to leave before the start of winter. There's still a good amount of time before then."

Blair pondered the offer for a while before replying. "Why should I stay? There's nothing more to do here. The curse is broken."

Sirnah shrugged. "We all like you. You're one of us, especially after the events today. It might be healthy if we stick together."

A short silence of understanding passed between them and Sirnah spoke again. "We lost many good people in that battle today. That much is true, but... Queriven had a special place in our hearts. He was our chosen brother for nearly a century. He was special to you as well. I want you to know that you're not alone in mourning him. Stay with us and we can comfort one another."

Blair looked away again and considered the options she had. She could stay for a while with the elves or she could return home to Bailiese and be with her parents. Somehow, that last one seemed harder. After all this time, she wanted to free herself of her curse to see her family again, but now she couldn't. They knew nothing of her adventure, and even if she told them, they wouldn't even begin to understand how important Queriven was to her and how he was lost to her forever.

She then remembered something Queriven told her once. He said the past is always moving further and further away no matter how hard you hang on to it. *You either move on or you don't.* A wave of sickness attacked Blair's gut and she chased the memory away. There's no way she could ever be normal again. Turns out she'll be stuck hanging on to the past after all.

Blair looked back and tried to find an answer, but Sirnah interrupted. "Don't worry about making a decision now," he told her. "There's time."

The two fell silent yet again. Neither said another word as they walked through the dark forest.

"This is where we part," Sirnah said as they stopped in front of Kielle's tree. Blair turned to him, wishing he could stay. "I'll see you tomorrow," he promised, as if he read her mind. Then he bowed and turned down the street again. Blair could see the majesty of the Center Tree looming before him even in the dark.

Then, before she could even reach the door, it opened. Though she still didn't smile, Kielle's eyes sparkled after seeing Blair. "I'm so glad to see you!" she cried with genuine joy. "We were so worried when you stayed out so long. Please come inside."

Blair did so and Kielle closed the door. The living room looked just the same as it always has, but it somehow shocked Blair to be back that night. She turned to Kielle. The elf was washed free of dirt and blood and wore clean clothes. The only thing that remained were the nicks, bruises, wraps, and the cast around her arm. "So," Blair piped in. She tried to keep her tone light despite the pain underneath. "They just let you return home, huh?"

Kielle nodded. "Well, I asked them to release me. I told them I was fine and they decided to give me some medicine and clean wraps and let me go. I'm the first knight, so they think I'm pretty tough."

The retort brought a quick smile on Blair's face, but it disappeared almost instantly. "Is there anything you want?" Kielle asked, happy to have Blair back in her home. "Are you hungry?"

Blair shook her head. Despite skipping both lunch and supper, she didn't have the appetite. Kielle didn't press her. "I couldn't eat anything either. I think I'll just be sick." The two exchanged unspoken sadness for a short moment, then Kielle finally broke the lingering void. "Do you just want to go to bed then? You may sleep in the study if you want more room." Blair couldn't dare take the study. That was the room Queriven was in for the duration of their stay. "Actually, I'll like to take my old hammock again if you don't mind."

Kielle didn't hesitate. "Of course."

◊ ◊ ◊

That night was restless and painful. Blair wished so hard for sleep to relieve her aching heart. Eventually, she was able to drift off in a light sleep after a while, but it wasn't long enough. She had to wake up again at some point.

A warm ray of sunshine filtered in through the room and the songs of birds gently stirred her. For a few minutes, she forgot why she was under the hold of so much depression, but she remembered it a second later. The memory bit her hard and she sank back in the swinging fabric. She didn't want to move, press on with the day, or even think. For about an hour, she was still and reluctant. Finally, she decided it would do her no good to stay since it wasn't chasing the memories off any quicker.

Blair slid off the hammock and touched down on the floor. Then she realized with a jolt that Kielle was still asleep in her own bed. Even in her sleep, Kielle looked just as uncomfortable as Blair felt. She wondered how long it took for her to settle, but her wounds and cast must have prolonged the restlessness.

She didn't bother waking her up and slipped downstairs instead. Blair was planning on leaving the tree, but she stopped just one floor down in the kitchen. She still didn't want to eat, but her growling stomach reminded her she needed food to live. Finally, she gave in and prepared a breakfast of fruit and candied nuts and decided to leave some out for Kielle before she traversed into the living room. The tree was so quiet. Too quiet. Queriven was always an early riser and Kielle would always come home from her night shift. It didn't feel right for Blair to be the first one awake.

Memories were creeping in and the silence was even harder than the night before. She needed company, even if that meant strangers passing the street. The urge made her glad she was still in the forest with friends. Perhaps, she should stay for a while after all?

She escaped the lonely room and fled into the pouring light outside. Daily life was already returning to Sylinna, though the few elves who wandered the streets were unusually quiet. The battle from last night hovered over the city like a dark cloud. Blair lingered by the door, not sure what to do next. Would Sirnah or Finhaus be awake right now? Maybe she should visit one of them. She knew Finhaus tended to his field early in the morning and she hasn't seen him since she rushed into the trading post. He didn't know of the terrible aftermath of the battle then.

That was her final decision and she started walking. His home was quite far on the outskirts, but it'll be healthy for her to catch some air anyway. The few elves who worked or passed her by barely looked at her now, and she wasn't in the mood to greet them. The human within Aven Forest was old news. More or less, they accepted her into the city already and the recent events proved to be too heavy to ignore.

She tried hard to focus on her surroundings and forget old memories of Queriven. She wished he was easy to forget. The light dew in the air was cold and all the trees surrounding her were a little less green than she remembered. Blair hoped to have a chance to see them when they changed into stark yellows and reds. At least that was one less thing she had to worry about — the change into autumn. Before she knew what she was doing, she held her wrist up. Nothing remained of the curse. Not even a pale reminder. Her skin was clear and just as freckled as it used to be.

To think this same time last year she was still helping her father with the goats every day. She was oblivious to the forest, the curse, and Queriven. She still wouldn't meet Darkadus under the disguise of Queriven for a few more weeks.

Blair continued to walk, but she balled a fist and bit her lip. It would have been better if none of that ever happened. It would have been better if she just lived her life safe in Bailiese. She should have listened to her parents and never lived up in the clouds. Her stories and heroes in books were way more interesting than her own experience. Her own adventure caused her too much pain. If anything, she wished she could take back the curse if that changed Queriven's fate.

She swallowed the bile rising in her throat and stopped. She was at Finhaus' farm already.

His field was full and ripe and Blair didn't need to study it to know it was of perfect quality. The elves knew their medicine and plants well. As usual, there were a bunch of animals of many different kinds lingering on the property. She knew Finhaus welcomed and cared for them, but she didn't see Finhaus himself.

It was then when a rustle in the field startled her. She turned and watched. Finally, Finhaus emerged over the leaves. His long hair was pulled back like always and he wiped his brow with his sleeve. Physically, she couldn't see any change in him. He was dressed and groomed like normal.

He didn't see her right away and so she called before he fully ducked down under the enormous leaves again. He jumped up and his eyes went wide. He was even more startled than she was. "Blair!" he cried out. "What are you doing out here so early in the morning?"

She moved a step forward, not knowing what to say. His greeting was more surprised than polite, and he didn't even bother to step out of the field. Blair shrugged. "Kielle's still sleeping and I got bored. I wanted to see how you were doing after..."

A grim look crossed his face and he bent down in the leaves again. There was a shuffle and his voice carried out to her. "Oh, yeah. Well..." he grunted, pausing for a second to strain against a tough plant. "I'm doing fine. Thanks for checking up on me."

Blair hesitated. Somehow she doubted he was doing as well as he said he was. "Are you?" she asked gently.

A second later, and Finhaus appeared over the leaves again. This time, he made his way carefully out of the field. He carried a large basket filled with even bigger leaves. He sighed and dropped the basket at his feet when he was near enough to her. He tried to bluff off his hesitance by wiping his brow again. "I think so" came the reply, but it still sounded strange to her.

Blair studied his face and there was a brief awkward silence. "So, can I help you with anything?" he asked, his hands weaving out impatiently before him.

Blair was a little hurt by his question. He was usually more welcoming than this. "No, I..."

Finhaus picked his basket up again and stepped around her. "I'm sorry, but I can't stop my work now. You can come inside if you want."

Her answer failed and she chose to follow him. Finhaus charged past the door with a bang and Blair entered more timidly. The room she stepped into was much different from Kielle's. It wasn't as tidy as hers nor was it very spacious, but it was practical.

There were many growing plants in the room, some of which were coming right out of the floor. Finhaus had his basics, like a table and a few chairs, and even a long bench. With the basket in hand, he passed by the bench in front of the room and dropped the basket on the counter right behind it. The counter was already piled with look-alike baskets, all filled with more plants and crops. Then he took a handful of lush leaves and carried them to the counter to his side, the one against the wall. There was a large bowl of water he was washing them with. It occurred to Blair that all of his baskets were being used and he had to free up space. He dropped the washed ones off on a pile of already clean leaves.

Blair crept closer. She passed by a shelf filled with little things like feathers, shells, broken bits of eggs, and even a full bird's nest on the way. A part of her wouldn't be surprised if he allowed birds inside to use the nest from time to time.

"Sirnah asked me if I would stay for a while," she said, trying to think of something encouraging to say.

Finhaus seemed to ignore her.

"I've decided it would be best. The forest is like a second home to me now and I'm not sure I'm ready to face my parents just yet."

He dropped another leaf and bowed his head. It looked like he wanted to say something in return, but he didn't know what.

"I wish..." he muttered, not even making eye contact with her. "I wish you didn't have to go. I've never met a human before and I've learned so much. Why can't we move on from stupid conflicts of the past? Why must elves and humans continue to live apart?" His voice was rising now and he washed each leaf quicker and quicker. "Our borders are so close to one another. We live on the same continent and yet both people live like the other race is nothing but a myth. It's like we don't exist in your world."

Blair didn't know how to respond. She watched the water dripping off each leaf and grasped once more to something she could say. "Maybe that will change one day, but I can't leave without knowing I'll see you and the elves again."

Finhaus spoke his next answer with little hesitance. "I guess you weren't even supposed to be here in the first place." The basket was now empty again and he pushed by her without waiting for a reply.

Blair followed behind him. "But I was here, regardless of the circumstances." The words flew beyond her mouth without thought and she paused. Did she really wish she never left home? Was none of this really worth it after Queriven's death? She couldn't answer even to herself. "I can't go back and pretend nothing happened."

They were outside again, but Finhaus stopped before he reached the field. Blair wasn't entirely sure why he froze. Did she say something that made him think or was it the view of the field and all the work he still had left? Whatever it was, his hands were trembling and a sob escaped. "Finhaus?" Blair asked.

The cries were louder now and he dropped the basket. Like a child, he covered his spilling eyes with his hands. "It's just too hard!" the muffled voice yelled. Startled, Blair rushed to his side and wrapped an arm around his shoulder. Finhaus remained where he was, head bowed. The gasps in his voice made it hard for her to understand him. "Queriven's gone, my brother is gone! I thought it would be... I thought it would be easier this time since we lost him before, but I can't... I just can't!"

The mutual pain brought tears to Blair's eyes and her grip on him tightened. She buried her face in his shaking shoulder and said nothing.

"We couldn't help him and now you're leaving too. What am I supposed to do?!"

"I'm not going anywhere," Blair replied. "I don't care if I have to meet you, Sirnah, and Kielle at the border. I'll always be here."

He continued weeping for a long time and Blair didn't let go until it settled down. "I don't know how, but we have to continue on. We have to become stronger," she said for both their sakes.

After what seemed like a lifetime, he uncovered his face. His large, reddened eyes turned away from her. "I'm sorry. I don't like it when people see me like this."

Blair smiled and hugged him again. "You're all right." When she pulled away, she had to wipe away her own tears. "How about a quick break? I could really go for some tea."

Finhaus sniffed and looked over the fields. Finally, he kicked the basket out of the way and turned home. Some of the animals were already gathered by the door, looking up at him. If it wasn't for his current mood, Blair knew he would have promised them some treats, but for now, he went right inside.

She didn't stay there very long. It wasn't even noon by the time she left. There was no laughter and very few smiles, but Blair enjoyed Finhaus' company. The two calmed after a while and she even followed him back outside to visit with his animal friends. Finally, he declared it was time to finish his harvesting and he bid her farewell.

Blair pondered over their conversations on her way back to Kielle's tree. The living room was still empty and Blair looked up the stairs. Was Kielle awake? She was just about to call her name, but she heard distant weeping from her room.

Blair hesitated. Kielle would be more difficult to comfort if she didn't try to kill anyone unlucky enough to see such a display. Blair was still upset from seeing Finhaus cry. She wasn't in the mood to see it again. She decided it would be better for both her and Kielle if she just left her alone.

She retreated back outside and moved away from the sobs. Not sure where to go next, Blair sat down in the grass. Queriven's family was now all she had left of him, and she knew she would hold onto them tighter than anything else. Would she dare to think Foradue might change his mind about her leaving before winter? Of course, he wouldn't. There were rules in place. No human has ever stepped foot in the forest in who knows how long. There hasn't been a visitor since the trade was broken; that much she knew for sure. So much has changed since she came to the city though. Sylinna and the elves in it were precious, especially after her loss. She would never do anything to hurt the forest or anyone in it.

Queriven's face tried to appear in her mind, but she tried to chase him away. She didn't want to think of any happy thoughts of him, even that much would hurt. She would prefer if she didn't think about him at all, but the memories came anyway. He was so mysterious and quiet when she first met him. He didn't want to talk at all about his past. After they came to the forest, not only did she learn more about him but he grew past his fears and reunited with his family. In the end, it was better for him to come home. He even danced with her on the night of his favorite festival. Blair's heart felt like it was trying to escape from her chest and her cheeks burned red when she remembered it. She shied away from kissing him then, but she knew she would have tugged him close in a heartbeat if she had another chance. She couldn't deny it. She loved him with her heart and soul.

Tears she thought she already cried were rimming her eyes again. They quickly turned to anger when she remembered something else about last night. How could she forget? Darkadus, the man who murdered Queriven, ran free in Fairdraisha. Where was he now? It was hard to tell. Either he spent all his magic and was now trapped in her world or he still had a little bit left. He wouldn't be able to continue his mission.

She knew he didn't have enough for another curse, but the thought of Darkadus still hovering around sat like a rock in her stomach. It gave her a new purpose. She had to do something about him. Her time of mourning her friends had to be put on hold. She had to react and vanquish the rokian once and for all.

CHAPTER THIRTY-FIVE
THE CURSED OPAL

The sobbing Blair heard earlier in Kielle's room reduced to a few sniffs and cries. Blair took caution as she crept up the stairs. Judging by the sound of clinks and falling footsteps, Kielle was now in the kitchen.

Sure enough, Kielle was setting a plate down on the dining table when she rounded the last step. She was both shocked and embarrassed when she noticed Blair standing there, and she quickly dried her wet eyes with her free hand. "I didn't hear you come in. Where were you?"

Blair entered the room and began helping her set the table. "I didn't want to wake you, so I visited Finhaus this morning." She quickly grabbed a bowl of crisp peas and set it on the table before Kielle had a chance. "I'll serve lunch. Please sit down."

The elf insisted she was fine, but Blair politely repeated her request. Finally, Kielle gave in without a fight and sat down at the table. When Blair finished setting lunch out and filled freshwater into the cups, she sat opposite her.

"So I had some time to think this morning," Blair went ahead with confidence as Kielle filled her plate one item at a time. "It's been bothering me to know Darkadus is still out there somewhere. Do you know if Foradue's looking for him?"

Kielle's gaze flickered up at her. She didn't block the subject, but she didn't seem too happy to hear it either. "He sent a patrol on the perimeter of the forest, but we can't go too far into Fairdraisha with a large team" came the reply.

Blair pressed the matter. "But he can still be dangerous. Someone needs to find him before he does anything else."

Then came a second glance, but this one was more dangerous than the last, bringing out the spark of gold in her gaze. Blair must have scared her. Kielle swallowed a bite of bread and dropped her hand from her plate. "We're doing what we can, but we can't risk the safety of our soldiers either." With a cloth nearby, she wiped her mouth and continued, "And what do you expect to do with him once he's captured? We don't execute people out here and we can't hold onto him forever either."

Blair furrowed her brow in confusion. She hasn't eaten anything yet. "You don't seem very concerned. Don't you think we should do more? He killed Queriven."

Kielle exclaimed in harshness. "See, that's why! You're seeking revenge."

Blair's jaw dropped and she nearly yelled. "I am not! Darkadus is a rokian and a bad one at that. I wouldn't want him around my family, even if he's without magic."

"Blair," Kielle interrupted and went back to her food, "if you're seeking him to protect others and serve him justice, then know we're doing everything we can, but don't let revenge ruin your life. Have you learned nothing about revenge and hatred since you've been here? It ruled over Queriven's life for many years. Please don't repeat his mistakes. He wouldn't want that on you."

"I won't. I promise I'm level on this," Blair replied eagerly.

Kielle gave her a pause, then shrugged. "In that case, I'll be pleased to let you know I'm sending a few elves a little over the border to look for evidence. I can't let them go too far where they might be discovered and questioned though."

Blair looked down at her still clean plate. "Maybe I can help with the search. I can go beyond the border into Fairdraisha easier because of my heritage." Her determination spoke aloud in her favor. She didn't even really think about what she said until it was already out. Blair thought Kielle would add something to that, but she merely nodded and let the subject go. Not willing to push the elf further, Blair finally began eating, though her mind remained on the issue.

◊ ◊ ◊

As Blair predicted, there was no word of Darkadus. The forest stopped talking about him after a little while, like he wasn't really a concern to them anymore. Instead, they mourned their losses and prepared for burial. Soon, Queriven would be laid down to rest with the other fallen...

Blair was sitting outside again, thinking quietly. She was barely holding on to her mental sanity as it was. She didn't want to go to the burial. Blair was afraid she would lose herself completely. She bowed her head. Was Kielle right? Was she really seeking revenge or not? It bothered her she didn't really know. She wanted Darkadus caught, and she worried he might consume her if he wasn't, but she wasn't sure if justice would be enough to give her mind closure. Blair hid her face in her hands.

She wanted to do something, but what? She couldn't go out and look for him on her own. What would happen if she found him? She may be forced to kill him if he attacked, but she didn't want that. She wished she could speak to Foradue about all of it. Perhaps, she could even encourage him to continue searching. She was too scared to. He was powerful and wise, and she was nothing but a little human. He wanted her gone as soon as possible — she knew.

But something stirred in her to try anyway. She came a long way with the elves of the forest and she should speak to Foradue if she wanted to. After all, they wanted Darkadus caught as well, and they helped her when she needed it. It was time for her to return the favor. Blair gathered her courage, rose to her feet, and began making her way through town.

The closer she came to the Center Tree, the more nervous she became. The looming tree was pressing down on her, crushing her senses and killing her with each passing second. The texture of the strong trunk was just as majestic as the forest itself. Even though it was taller than a tower, Blair was sure nothing could shake it loose.

Blair paused for only a moment before the stairs leading up to the platform where they held Queriven's trial. No one was here and it appeared a lot smaller than she remembered it. The foliage around the stairs and grass was the strongest green it's been all year. Blair was different now. She was free from her impending deadline, but that did little to comfort her.

The sun's beams were very warm on the few spots of the ground it was able to reach. That only made the shade much more comfortable. Blair found herself longing for Queriven's presence all the more. She wanted him to experience the full beauty of the summer. The cooling breeze just wasn't the same without him.

Blair shook off the memories for the thousandth time that day and continued rounding the Center Tree for the main door. She should have expected it, but she was still shocked when there was a guard standing by the main entrance. Awkwardly, she began explaining to him why she wanted to meet with Foradue, but the guard opened the door before she finished and eagerly showed her the stairs up. Just as quick as it happened, he left her alone and she stood gaping in amazement. Even without the sudden act, the interior of the Center Tree would still hold her. Queriven was right. It was like a castle, but different. It was big, powerful, and majestic, but it wasn't nearly as stuffy as King Brenmor's castle. No, it was open and just as wonderful as it was comfortable. Unlike Fairdraisha's castle, the Center Tree allowed the abundance of nature inside. Most of the windows were wide open, bringing that sweet summer air in.

Blair then realized she was standing in the middle of the room staring at her surroundings and forgetting her main purpose. She slowly strolled over to the stairs. The various voices from outside kept her rooted in reality, but each step she took was harder than the last, and she began to reconsider her bold action.

But before she could ponder her thoughts, something up ahead gave her pause. Clearly, she lost her mind. Just a few steps above her, there was a sparkle of a little bead. No, it wasn't a bead. It was a mouse with a crystal body. She froze. "Are you really here?" she whispered.

The mouse squeaked and skittered a little closer.

"You're wanting me to speak with Foradue?" Blair asked, guessing it was here to encourage her. It answered again, swinging its rear happily. The long tail swished back and forth with the ease of movement like an animal made of flesh. Then, it scurried down the rest of the stairs and disappeared from view.

Blair smiled and climbed the rest of the long way up with a little more determination. At least she knew now she was on the right track. It was either that or she was growing crazy.

The next floor came into view, and it wasn't long before the tall form of Foradue himself stepped out in front of her. His robed back turned against her, his old hands neat behind his back as he hovered by his collection of precious gems.

Blair wasn't trying to sneak up on him, but she quietly stepped forward. She knew she wanted to say something to announce herself, but she was speechless and afraid. To her astonishment, he said something first. "Ah, the human girl. I've been waiting for you to show up."

Blair tried to respond but stumbled on her own words. He hasn't even turned to face her yet. "Um, you were? I'm sorry, but... I didn't even know I was coming until just a short while ago."

Before she finished, Foradue was turned around. His wrinkled face and posture were the perfect image of relaxed composure. He didn't seem the least bit upset to have Blair here. "To be honest, I didn't know exactly who I was waiting for, but now I know it was you. I had a visitor this morning, see? It was a mythical crystal beast in the form of a little mouse. It was wanting to tell me that something important was about to happen today."

So she wasn't seeing things after all. The crystal mouse she just saw was for Foradue, not her.

Foradue smiled calmly. "They are quite amazing, aren't they? I was fortunate enough to see a few when I was young once. I always wanted to understand them better, maybe even find out where they hide when they're not around anyone. In the end, I never did learn too much about them. Maybe that's for the better. They wouldn't be as magical if we knew their mysteries. Don't you agree?"

Blair was still a little shocked and she merely shrugged.

When she said nothing else, he took a few steps away from her and sat down behind a desk by the far wall. "So now I'm wondering what drove you here at my door," he said in the same tone as he settled comfortably in his seat. "Please have a seat and tell me whatever you wish."

Still a little hesitant, Blair came closer and took the seat opposite him. "I've just been thinking about all that's happened in the last few days and I wanted to offer my help in the search for Darkadus."

Foradue folded his hands together and regarded her. Blair looked down respectfully and took short notice of all the scrolls on the desk. "I know you're already trying your hardest to find him. Please don't misunderstand me. I just thought I could help if you needed me. I can cross into Fairdraisha without them arresting me because of my race."

The elder blinked and Blair worried she did something wrong. But when he answered, he wasn't accusing. "I know I can't help with the city as much as I used to," Foradue said. "When I was an advisor, I wasn't afraid to get my hands dirty. Now that I'm ruler over the forest, I'm often stuck here in the Center Tree, but that doesn't mean I let things go by without my notice." There was a scuffling sound as Foradue took a moment to fold open scrolls and lay them out of the way. He continued, "I'm going to be honest, Blair. When you first came to my city, I was more than a little concerned. It's been a long time since there was any communication with humans, and even longer since one stood within our forest. I can tell you that those visits usually didn't end well." He waited long enough for her to look back up at him. There was a sparkle in those wise eyes. "But you are different. You care deeply for the elves in the forest. Kielle has spoken highly of what you've done for them and she wasn't saying those things when you first arrived. She and her brothers are like family to you now, at least; that's how she describes it."

Blair nodded and twiddled her fingers.

"And the knight who brought you here, Queriven — I do believe you had something stronger between you if you don't mind me saying."

The sound of his name made her heart ache, but she stayed strong. She met Foradue straight in the eyes. "Has that ever happened before? Those feelings between an elf and a human, I mean."

He blinked slowly and wasn't surprised. "It has, but it's been an awfully long time. Those relationships are usually the hardest though. The lifespan between a human and an elf is so different. Still, they say the bond of love is too strong to break, even after a tragedy."

Blair sighed and sank in her seat.

Foradue seemed to do the same and his expression fell solemn. "I am sorry for that loss, but we did what we had to. Queriven paid his debt in full when he sacrificed himself like that. He was truly a remarkable knight in his time before he ran away. Everyone makes mistakes, no matter our efforts to avoid them."

There was a pause of heartbreak. Blair looked away, seemingly lost in daydreams of better times. Foradue allowed the drop of the subject and continued. "As for Darkadus, I worry if we'll ever find him at this point. I can only send a few elves beyond the border and hope they aren't fallen into King Brenmor's hands. Even if I send you out there, that's not much of an investigation team. Unless...you already know where to find him?"

He could see her coming back to reality and she knitted her brows in thought. With just a look, he beckoned her to share her idea. Blair adjusted her seat and sat up. "It's difficult to say if he's there or not, but I do know about an old hideout of his. We couldn't investigate it earlier because we were running out of time, but now I have all the time I need. I could check it out. He may even be there as we speak."

Foradue blinked and turned his head slightly to the side. "Maybe he is. When I scoured for him after he disappeared, I was redirected again. That tells me he's still in this world. He hasn't gone home yet."

Blair's eyes grew wide in response. Foradue nearly laughed out loud as he pushed up off his desk. The elder took a few steps away toward his shelf of gems. "Come here. I want to show you something."

She obeyed and stood up from her seat. Now close to the door leading out to the balcony, Foradue waved his arms over the shelf spanning either side. With pride, he explained to her how the gems came to the elves long ago and were enchanted to accomplish many different things. Finally, he selected an object near the bottom and cradled it in his arms. Dark cloth veiled it. Whatever it was, it looked smooth and slightly oval. "When I learned there was a rokian in our world again, I began studying about them in my own time. I already knew a little about them, but I wanted to know more so I might know how to handle him. Then, I came upon something interesting." Foradue gestured at the object in his arms. "A rokian's curse is nearly impossible to break. It can be difficult even with a vayen aray's help, but if you somehow manage to wipe it off your own skin, did you know you could capture it for yourself?"

Blair only shrugged. She didn't really understand what he was talking about.

Finally, his hand went to the covered object and he carefully removed the cloth. Blair blinked past the thick white of the stone underneath and examined closer. It was a large opal and it shone many dancing colors within the pale surface. She then saw something else within the smooth stone. It was a coherent pattern, and it marked around the body. She knew this pattern. She's seen so much of it. "Is that...?"

Foradue nodded. "It's the mark of the curse. Your curse. After I learned how to collect a rokian's curse, I decided to try it myself. It was very difficult. Not a lot of people knew about this even back then."

Blair's jaw dropped and she marveled at it longer. Finally, she stood up and asked, "So...what do you do with it?"

"It's yours, my dear. You can use it on anyone you wish."

Still confused, she turned her head. Her dark blonde hair fell down the length of her right arm. "So I can use it on Darkadus to send him back home?"

Foradue smiled. "If that's what you choose, but it can do more than that. The properties he assigned it is gone. It doesn't remember its purpose anymore. It is simply an empty curse now. If you wanted, you could place it on Darkadus and have him do anything you wish, just like he had you do when he gave it to you. You see, when you carried it, it was trying to pull you into his world so his people could be free. Because of that, it made you go on this grand adventure to break it. You can now do the same to Darkadus, but you can curse him with anything you want."

If Blair's eyes weren't wide before, they now threatened to pop right out of her skull. This was powerful magic. The thought of it almost scared her too much to touch it. Almost. "What happens if he doesn't do what I ask him to?"

Foradue shrugged. "That I do not know. Redirecting magic has different effects depending on the magic and what's asked of it. However, since this is extraordinary rokian magic, I imagine the consequences are too heavy for Darkadus to ignore."

Foradue waited to see if Blair had any more questions. When she did not, he replaced the cloth over the cursed opal. "If you want to search for him, you may take this with you, but be very careful with it. To use it, you need to shine a ray of light from the opal over him until the curse appears on his skin. I will need the opal back when you're done with it."

Blair took it from him gently, though she still wasn't sure what she wanted to do.

"There was something else too," Foradue said, quickly taking over her attention again. "Rokians are incredibly powerful. A lot of them choose to study in many different areas of magic. There are certain kinds they tend to specialize in, of course, but they are capable of so much more. They can enhance their own skills, manipulate and disguise themselves as others, and some say they can even bring the dead back to life."

Blair suddenly forgot the opal was in her arms. It was lucky she was already holding it close to her body, or it would have fallen to the floor. Immediately, hope came to her mind. Both she and Foradue were thinking of the same thing, but then her heart dropped again. Darkadus may not have any magic left, and even if he still had some, Blair didn't have to know magic to know he wouldn't be strong enough to bring Queriven back.

Still, the sparkle and knowledge in Foradue's eyes gave her hope. She could see him reading her mind. He was supporting her decision to look for him.

Blair remembered the opal and slipped it carefully in a bag on her waist. "Thank you, Sir. I will be careful, and I promise I'll bring the stone back."

Satisfied, Foradue bowed low and Blair chose to do the same. Then, she reached the stairs and descended. Foradue chuckled and returned to his desk.

Blair breathed in the fresh air of the open field. It's been only a day since she spoke with Lord Foradue, and she was much more joyful than before. She was confident she could find Darkadus. Even if Queriven wasn't coming back, it gave her life a new purpose.

The elf standing next to her was a little more worried though. "Just don't let anger take you," Kielle reminded. "Don't do anything you wouldn't have done before the battle."

Blair turned to her. Kielle was feeling better day by day and

Blair had to argue with her to convince her to stay. So instead of coming along, Kielle brought Blair out of the forest. "Don't worry. I know what I have to do," she assured her. It was only the half-truth. Blair knew she needed to send Darkadus away where he won't hurt anyone else, but she wasn't really sure what would happen when she got there, or even if he would be there at all.

"Are you sure you want me to stay here?" Kielle asked for the hundredth time just that morning. "My wounds won't slow us down. I'm moving around just fine and with no pain."

"Thank you, but I want to do this alone," Blair answered. "This is about Darkadus and me, and it's about time I had my turn to deal with him."

Kielle sighed, but she relented. "Fine. When are you coming back?"

Blair had no good answer for that. "It can't be longer than just a few weeks. I'll try to find a horse to carry me there. Give it about two, then watch out for me. You can send Finhaus to bring me back if you'd like."

The elf still seemed a little upset about it, but she didn't argue further. She bowed low and Blair came closer and wrapped her in a gentle hug before departing. The two parted ways without a word, but they parted with assurance.

No matter what happens at Darkadus' watchtower, Blair saw potential and hope. She wasn't afraid of him anymore. If anything, she was more capable of hurting him now than ever before.

CHAPTER THIRTY-SIX
UNCHANGED LANDS

Blair couldn't remember the last time she was in Dunverhart. Was she and Queriven retreating with the stolen horn then? A sense of unfamiliarity fell on her, though she didn't know why. The city looked just the same. Maybe it wasn't even about the city. Maybe it was about her.

She was doing just fine before she reached the town, but now she was a little jumpy. The increased number of soldiers didn't help and she avoided them in fear they may still recognize her. So far, she wasn't bothered by them.

Blair dismounted her dark steed she bartered from a farmer a few days earlier, and she took it to a stable to rest. She tossed a few coins to the owner and walked away from his curious stare. Blair was still dressed in elven clothing, making her look like a foreigner. It wasn't recognized to be elvish, luckily. She was thankful no one appeared to recognize her, though she wasn't sure if it was because she wasn't the priority anymore, or if she was unrecognizable to them. Either way, it helped her a lot. The last thing she needed was a confrontation.

Now back on her feet, she yawned and rubbed her eyes. She's been traveling for quite some time now, but she was so close to the watchtower. Her purpose drove her to continue past exhaustion. She honestly wondered if Darkadus was there or not. Where else could he go? He was stuck in an alien world with nothing to further his goal.

If he was there, Blair wasn't sure what she might do. For her own sake, she prayed she would not take her anger out on him. She's been struggling to sleep at night. A mix of hurtful and beloved dreams disturbed her mind. Deep down, Blair knew she wanted Darkadus to pay for what he did, and those thoughts scared her. Could she be better than that? She didn't want this to become something she would regret.

No matter the anxiety on her heart, she forced herself to calm down and gather supplies. She will need rest and provisions when she faces him...if she faces him.

Blair left the city with her steed before the break of dawn.

A cold wisp made her shiver and cling to her arms. She could see a puff of air with each breath. The mornings and evenings were growing cold again. Blair already recognized the shortening of days. It was hard to remember what it was like this time last year.

It was too early for people to travel just yet. The sun wasn't even lighting the sky. Trees and rocks ahead were nothing but dark silhouettes.

She didn't hesitate or stop until the dark form of the crumbling watchtower came above the thick horizon. Blair didn't blink, though her mind was empty. Her heart held neither acceptance nor hate for whatever was standing in her way. She dismounted and walked forward without emotion. With each step, she was even more convinced he was here. The idea had her creeping to the broken wall quietly.

Darkadus was just on the other side.

Blair took the spear from her back and peered around the corner. She didn't even consider the dark form inside to be someone else. She knew it was him.

The rokian sat on a useless stone against the wall. His limp hands were over his knees and his head was down. He barely moved, but the first ray of sunlight was breaking through and his silver skin was lit up for just a second.

She came closer, no longer trying to hide. Either Darkadus knew she was there and he did nothing, or his mind was far away from here. Blair didn't bother to announce herself. She simply waited.

Finally, the limp form took a deep breath and spoke. "So you found me, Miss Blair. What do you wish to do now? Do you want to run me through for killing Queriven? Or maybe your sense of justice would rather have me locked up for the rest of my days instead. Do what you will. There's nothing left for me anymore."

Blair frowned. The words still refused to fall from her lips. She did nothing. He seemed so somber. Even when she met him under Queriven's disguise, his play on emotion was so different. This time, his sorrow was real, and she's never seen anything like it before. "Why did you do this, Darkadus?"

Finally, he turned his head and looked at her. Those amber eyes seemed to glow in the dark as he regarded her. "You already know why," he answered simply in a plain voice.

"But all this?" she asked again. "Why are you willing to bring so much war and pain?"

Darkadus answered with the same response he always had. "I did it because I had to. I grew up in poverty and pain. I just thought a little more could release my kin from all that."

Blair struggled to keep herself calm, but her voice started to shake. "You didn't have to do any of this. I would have helped you from the start. When you came to me, I was already wanting to help you. All you had to do was ask."

He growled and stood up. Queriven gave him the same lecture and he was tired of being pestered. "I told him too. No one here wants to help a rokian. If I was a vayen aray, all this would have been different, but no one will help me because of my race. Even those who remember the ancient races don't remember mine kindly."

Darkadus was coming a little too close and Blair pointed her spear up to his neck. She realized her attempts at redeeming him was useless. He wasn't going to apologize or regret his actions. "Like I said, do what you want. Run me through!" He spat louder. "I deserve it, don't I?!"

Blair hesitated. Adrenaline poured into her blood and her heart began to pound. A part of her considered it. After everything he did to her and to her friends, he tempted her to take his request. Somehow, she chose not to. There was something better than revenge. "How much magic do you have left?"

For the first time ever, she caught him off guard. The rokian flinched and looked away, but he didn't step back from the spear pointing at his skin. "What does it matter? I can't use it for another curse. I only have enough left to send me back to my old world."

"Is that powerful?" Her eyes were dangerous now and Darkadus relented. There was no point in protecting himself now.

"It's not much in comparison, but I have to use a lot to take me back to my homeland."

Finally satisfied with his answer, Blair swung the spear away. "I was speaking with an elf who studied your kind and he said a lot of rokians can raise the dead."

Darkadus nearly scoffed from disbelief. He already knew what she was getting at. "You should forget it. That falls into the necromantic territory. It's unpredictable and dangerous. Even if I use it, I would be trapped in this world forever. I don't want to be stuck here without it. Everyone here sees me as a monster."

That was all she needed to hear. Blair took the opal from her bag and took the cloth from it. The rays of sunlight were stronger, and it shot off of the stone. The light bounced and landed right on Darkadus, shining brighter than feasibly possible. Startled, Darkadus backed away and shielded his eyes, but the magic already took hold before he was away. The mark of Blair's curse was now imprinted on his forearm where he blocked the ray of light.

Quickly before he realized what happened, Blair covered the now clear opal and dropped it in her bag again. Darkadus rubbed an eye and looked back at Blair. His face said it all. He didn't know what happened until he noticed the curse on his arm. He took a step back and nearly stumbled over the rock he was sitting on a moment ago. "Wh...what did you just do?!" he cried out, running a large silver hand over the mark. Blair noted the beginning of panic before he yelled. The rage in those terrible amber eyes threatened her safety. "You reversed the curse on me?! But how?! No one knows how to do that."

His surprise pleased her. For the first time ever, she had him right where she wanted him, and it was better than harming him. "Do you know the spell to bring someone back?"

Like a wild animal, he bore his teeth at her and hunched over. He was threatening to pounce any second. "How *dare* you treat me like a servant?! I may be different than you, but I am a man all the same. You will not do this to me!"

Blair didn't blink past his attempts to intimidate her. "I do believe, since it's not my magic, hurting me will neither remove nor change the curse. Like it or not, you're tied to me, just like I was to you."

Darkadus sucked in a breath but otherwise didn't move. "He's dead, Girl. We all will die eventually, so why does it matter?"

The retort finally made her angry and she snapped back. "Because you have the magic to return someone yet! I'm going to use the magic you have if I choose for you to use that spell or not. We may as well reverse the mistake you made by attacking us. Now," she cleared her throat and placed her hands on her hips, "do you have that kind of magic or not?"

He growled again at her, but then regained his composure. Unfortunately, she was right. Attacking her now will do nothing. The curse was stuck on him and she had to demand something of him now. "Be careful of what you're asking. Resurrection is a finicky type of magic. There are so many side effects depending on circumstances. To start, the body has to be fresh, and the more wounds there are, the more magic will have to be used. The caster has to know a lot about the wounds and the victim. It works best if the user either saw the death or caused it."

A sick taste lingered in Blair's mouth when he finished, but he provided what she wanted. She has made her decision. "It seems like we're qualified then. We'll leave for Aven Forest at once." She was still a little uncomfortable to turn her back on him, and so she stared at him instead. His amber gaze was like a window. He was covering his fear and uncertainty with animal-like rage. He was remarkable, like a caged cat. A twinge of Blair's soul was a little sorry for him, but still, this is just what he did to her.

"So you choose to let me rot on this planet? It's no better than what I was doing to you. You're just the same and yet you blame me for my actions."

Blair was confident in her choices and she answered him. "That curse is still your own magic. If there's still some left in it after whatever resurrections we choose, then you can use the rest to go home to your dying world."

Darkadus stood straight and pondered. The words hit him hard into curiosity, and he looked like he was about to break into pieces. His eyes glowed brighter and wider. "You're not just wanting Queriven back? You want me to resurrect more of them?" He laughed in disgust. "Even if I can do one, I won't be able to do more than that. That magic is tough on the mind even if you have the ability to control it well. I may be lucky to be alive after trying it."

"Even one is better than none, even if it isn't Queriven..." Blair looked away and tried not to show weakness. "I love him, but I know a lot of other loved men and women died in that battle as well. I'm not alone in my pain."

Without waiting for a response, she came closer with a thick rope in her hands. Then she preceded to tie Darkadus' tattooed arms together. They bulged with heavy muscles. She had to make sure the knot was tight enough. She dared to think he may choose to bite through it later on. "What are you doing?" he asked curiously with a little annoyance. "We already discussed the fact that I can't hurt you. You set the conditions for the curse. I must obey."

She continued until it was as tight as could be. "I don't want to take any chances. How can I expect to sleep at night if you're free and about?"

He didn't answer, and she led him outside the watchtower. Blair stopped again when she came to the dark stallion she had as a mount. She cursed under her breath. She forgot to bring two horses. Darkadus would have laughed at her stupidity if he wasn't in so foul a mood. Blair sighed. "I guess we either have to make one horse work between us or take the road on foot."

Darkadus made a notion to remind her that the fresher the bodies in the forest, the better, but she already knew. "I guess the horse then," she remarked. "But I still don't trust having you at my back." It was her turn to growl as she helped him in the saddle before jumping up in front of him.

The rokian and human barely said a word to each other throughout the next few days. Blair kept him tied up as often as she could without bruising his large wrists. Despite all this, she still struggled to sleep at night. She knew Darkadus was struggling as well. She chuckled to herself when she remembered this was the same man she thought she loved last year. The idea proved to be just as alien to her as the last time she thought of it, though she took it with more humor than disgust. They were once going to flee as lovers. She knew he remembered this as well and she wondered if he was going to use it to manipulate her. No, Darkadus was not stupid. She caught him, and he knew there was no way out of it. She still watched him carefully, but he never manipulated her or tried to break free.

Blair had no idea what will happen once they return to the forest, but no matter what happens, she'll push forward with her head clear from the desire for revenge.

CHAPTER THIRTY-SEVEN
THE ROKIAN'S LAST SPELL

The Aven Forest didn't arrive soon enough between the stress of keeping Darkadus nearby and the ever-growing cold. The leaves were already starting to lose their youthful luster and some were already beginning to change. Blair never imagined Darkadus would be the cursed one by her deadline.

Blair fully expected to see Kielle at the border but was honestly surprised she took her advice and left Finhaus there instead. He was more than happy to see her, though the sight of Darkadus behind her quickly changed him to nervous.

"I see you found him..." Finhaus stated when Blair dismounted. Darkadus, hands still bound, jumped off behind her.

Blair greeted him with a bow. "How long have you been out here? Has Kielle been torturing you?" she joked.

He smiled and shook his head. "We've been taking turns each morning and some of the soldiers of the Center Tree have as well. Lord Foradue's been looking after you."

"Great. Listen, I need to get to the Center Tree as quickly as possible with him."

Finhaus agreed and beckoned toward the forest. "Yes, I know. Kielle told me what you were up to, and Foradue mentioned a few things himself. He's been preparing us for your return."

Blair's anticipation rose the further she walked through Sylinna. She imagined Darkadus felt it as well, maybe more so. The only one who didn't seem to change was Finhaus. He continued talking about trivial topics as they went through. The elves around them were already staring, but it wasn't about Blair this time. Darkadus stuck out like a candle in a dark hallway. Even if rokians were forgotten, one just couldn't forget the large man with silver skin and burning eyes. He didn't utter a word or even growled at the elves but seemed to cower before them.

Blair resisted the urge to run inside the Center Tree; she rather let the soldier by the door lead her instead. The medicine section of the tree where the healers worked and lived was on the ground level, though on the far wall to the east. She didn't know what she was expecting, but she wasn't expecting such a stark contrast to what she's seen so far.

The medicine research hall was moody, but not depressing. There weren't a lot of open windows here, but the darkness was cast off by glowing orbs of light lying about on counters, tables, and some from the ceiling. They glowed in different shades of bright colors, tinting the room in soft purples, blues, pinks, and others. She could see at first glance that this was where the healers worked. Collections of herbs were lying and hanging everywhere. It was hard to tell what a medicinal plant was and what normal ferns and leaves growing in the room were. Flocks of natural leaves covered almost every inch of the ceiling. Between the foliage and the colored lights, the hall reminded Blair a lot of the Aven Forest wilderness.

She turned a nose at the stuffy medicine smells and looked away from an open closet overfilled with supplies like bandages as well as shards and vials of starlight. What Blair saw next was a content Sirnah smiling at her. She bowed in elvish custom and he returned it. "I'm glad you're here," he said and then held out an arm, a smile beaming over his face. "What do you think of the medicine hall?"

Blair smiled and nodded. She remembered this is where Sirnah lived when she took another glance at it. "It's very unique. I'm happy I had the chance to see it."

He answered by smiling bigger, then he saw Darkadus behind her. He didn't look concerned or frightened, but he couldn't take his eyes away. "You have the rokian with you. Did you find out if he could do resurrections or not?"

Blair answered as Darkadus huffed impatiently behind her. "He said he'll try."

"Excellent!" Sirnah exclaimed. "Foradue said if he could, we would prepare one of the fallen for him. Come this way."

Blair obeyed, and Sirnah led her further into the room. As far as she could tell, there wasn't a lot of organization to the rest of the hall. There were many more counters filled with herbs and scrolls, but it was mainly a lot of the same. She did see a rather amazing stairway to her left, but Sirnah continued past it. Now at the far end of the room, they ran into another healer who studied over a scroll on the table. Sirnah explained to him they were going to Foradue's chosen fallen and that they were going to attempt a resurrection. The elf nodded and retreated to the stairs, perhaps spreading the news.

Sirnah stopped in front of a set of curtains and he pulled them far back, revealing a table with a cloth draped over the figure lying on it. "We had to make accommodations for this one," Sirnah explained as he came closer to it. "We couldn't keep it in the room where the injured were, though we didn't have a lot of extra space elsewhere, so the curtain was kind of a last-minute installment."

Now at the head of the fallen, Sirnah gently pulled back the cloth covers, revealing none other than Queriven.

Blair pressed a hand over her mouth and even Sirnah backed away in surprise. This was no coincidence. This was Foradue's doing. He chose to resurrect Queriven in particular. This shouldn't amaze her at all, but the fact that Foradue would choose Queriven after talking with her brought her more respect for the elvish ruler.

Her friend was lying calmly on the table, his face one of quiet peace. His long brown hair was slipping over the ends of the table, revealing his pointed ears. "I never knew it was Queriven," Sirnah stated, trying to recover from his amazement. "I wasn't working with the healers who brought him up." Sirnah lowered the cloth further. Queriven's body was clean of dirt and spare blood from the battle, but he still wore the same clothes. Just under his ribs was a large rip in the tunic, showing the deep red crater of where he was stabbed. The sight frightened Blair and forced her to turn away.

She was looking at Darkadus now and he held up his arms. "Are we going to do this or not?" He continued holding them until Blair finally moved to untie him. She tried not to fumble uselessly, though she was beginning to shake a little. Once he's freed, Darkadus approached his old victim. "I need complete silence so I can focus. I don't know how long it'll take me, but I can't be disturbed." He spread his hands apart and stretched his fingers, then he glanced at the staring faces still around him. "I would advise you to make yourself comfortable. You can continue staring if you like, but try not to move too much."

Blair backed away from the open curtain and almost bumped into Finhaus. Despite staying silent up to this point, he spoke to her now, though he kept his voice low. "I can't believe it's Queriven. A lot of people died in that battle, and with Queriven's past, I wonder how many people will question Foradue's motive. He's taking a risky move."

Blair agreed and focused on her friend, wanting to remove the previous image from her mind. "Yes, he is, but I think he's making the right one. He's offering Queriven another chance."

Deep purple eyebrows knitted together and Finhaus pressed a knuckle to his lips. "Does this mean Queriven's forgiven for his past? If this works, will the Center Tree give him another chance to stay here in the forest?"

Blair never considered that. She didn't have the answer, but Foradue admitted to having different viewpoints of both Blair and Queriven now than when they first came to the city. "I don't know, but I don't think Foradue would revive him just to send him out in exile."

Finhaus said nothing and Blair took two steps to sit down at a circle of benches. Finhaus followed and sat opposite her.

It was so quiet around them. Every minute brought more and more healers. Blair noted most of them came from the stairs. That must be where the living quarters were. If it weren't for the low booming hum and whisper she suspected to come from Darkadus, she would be able to hear the roar of blood in her ears.

She folded her hands in her lap and looked up at Finhaus, but discomfort drove them both to not say another word.

Blair lifted her eyes. She has not said a thing for hours now nor has she slept, but it was long enough she could have. She was kind of rested like she has, but she knew it was because she was just zoning out.

The first thing that grabbed her attention in the quiet, unchanged hall was Finhaus still sitting opposite her. He was sprawled out oddly on the bench. He didn't seem to be sleeping either, but his eyes were shut. She turned to the table past the still open curtains. She couldn't see behind the gathered healers, but she caught a glimpse of Darkadus' dark head. His short, cropped hair was rich black and fluffy at the top but shaved on the sides.

She sighed and leaned back again. She wished she could see what was going on as well, but she didn't want to disturb the crowd. Sirnah was somewhere up there as well, but it was hard to pick which one he was as they were all wearing the same work robes.

Just then, another figure approached, though this was not a healer. Kielle's eyes were wide and concerned when she addressed Blair. "I just now heard you guys were over here. Is he really resurrecting Queriven?"

Her alarmed retort shocked Finhaus to his senses. Turns out he was asleep after all. Blair answered Kielle with a hush. "Be quiet, Darkadus is working on it now. And yes, he's trying to bring Queriven back. We don't know if he has enough or not though because he said resurrection magic tends to be finicky."

Kielle, still hurried, chose to sit down on Finhaus' bench just as he sat straight to make room for her. "Is Sirnah here too?"

Blair nodded toward the healers' direction. Finhaus smacked his lips a little and stretched. "Do you really think the rokian can do this? It's been so long already."

Blair shrugged. "He must be making headway because he hasn't given up yet. He really wasn't wanting to use the last of his magic on this anyway."

Kielle looked so radiant in her perch on the bench. Her back was straight and her hands were on her knees. Blair finally noted the absence of the cast and bandages on her. "It's the last of his magic?" she asked. "I thought he used it all."

"He used all he had available to him," Blair corrected. "He had some set aside to return home with, but I don't think he was really ready to return."

"I don't blame him," Finhaus said. "I wouldn't want to be considered the savior of my kin just to return home and say I couldn't do it."

Seconds passed and Blair turned her head again at the sight of movement. Darkadus was backing away from the table and the healers cleared a hole for him. Kielle stood up. "Is it done?" she asked.

The table itself was still quiet and Blair could see Queriven was still resting on it like before. "I managed to heal the worse of his fatal injuries, but he's going to be weak. Very weak."

Blair studied the elf behind him. There was no movement, not even a rise or fall of the chest. But then, as the stillness fell over everything, even the rokian, Blair thought Queriven twitched a few times. Then, his lungs gasped hungrily for the air it didn't have. The act wrought of pure instinct propelled Queriven up and he breathed in more loud gulps like he was underwater for far too long. The other two on the bench stood up. Blair could see those eyes were wide with alarm. He was scared out of his mind.

The healer closest to him pushed his shoulders back down on the table. "Wh...what's going on?!" Queriven cried, trying to sit up again. The fear in his voice was the loudest Blair's ever heard it.

"Just lie still and try to relax" came the answer. The healer remained remarkably calm and continued to hold a gentle grip on his shoulders.

Queriven's breaths were still coming quickly, but he wasn't fighting the healers anymore. Blair took a few steps forward and the healers allowed her room to see. Queriven's head was turning to either side around him in panic. The stab wound in his chest was completely gone with nothing to show he ever had it. He must have remembered it though because a hand shot up to where the wound was and searched over the skin only to find there was no wound or stitches. He was calming down by each passing minute, but he would remain startled and upset for a while longer.

Blair took a step closer. She was more than a little scared to see him or what his response may be to her. He was quite delirious. "Queriven?" she whispered.

His head snapped over at her call, but his eyes held no recognition. What was going on in his mind right this moment? "What happened to me?" he asked, a pitiful look showing on his face. Blair said nothing, but let him struggle for the answer himself. "There was... a dagger. It was buried below my chest." He traced over the hole in the tunic and looked down. He did see for just a second that there was nothing there before the healer lowered his shoulders down again. Queriven looked back up to her. "There was blood spilling between my fingers. I couldn't breathe."

"Queriven," Blair interrupted him again. Her voice was louder now, like she thought she could catch his attention better. "Do you remember anything else besides the dagger?" When nothing came, Blair sucked in a breath, though the lingering tears burned her eyes. "Do you remember who I am?" she added, a little quieter again.

Queriven breathed out a long exhale and frowned as he searched his confused mind. "Of course, I..." He rested his head on the surface of the table. Blair could tell he was trying really hard to answer her question. His strained eyes scanned the nooks and crannies of the ceiling for his lost memories, but he was on his own. "I sent you and... And..." He blinked and tried again. "Finhaus to..." Now that his breathing was normal, he looked quite exhausted and pained. Finally, the color in his eyes popped and there was the recognition Blair was looking for. He nearly shot back up when he looked at her again. "The curse! Was it broken?"

Blair couldn't contain the tears anymore and a smile grew over her face. She wanted to scream with joy and wrap her arms over him, but she didn't want to startle or hurt him. Instead, she brushed her hand over his arm. "Yes, we did it! We won!" she cried.

The arm moved out of the sheet and he held his hand up. Blair took it with both of her own hands. His skin was already warming up and his complexion was quickly returning as blood was running through his veins again. He seemed happy to have her supportive touch and was much more relaxed now than he has been. Uncontrollable tears were spilling from Blair's eyes, and she slowly let him go as the healers began to close in. Blair backed away from the table to let the elves do their work.

She wiped her wet eyes and saw Darkadus watching her. His face didn't show a hint of joy and Blair saw there was still a piece of the mark on his arm. "I know I made you come here and heal him against your will," she said, sobbing between syllables, "but thank you. This is the best miracle I've ever witnessed in my whole life."

Darkadus showed no change, but she noticed his hands were trembling. Blair wiped her eyes again and focused. Her business wasn't over yet. There was still one more thing she had to do. "I guess it's time to send you home."

The rokian's expression was not of anger; just sadness. "That is not my home. That place is a prison. Can you blame me for wanting freedom?"

Blair didn't back away. "I thought you didn't want to stay here either."

She could tell from the look on his face that he thought she was being ridiculous. "I can't without my magic. I'll be caged up here for the rest of my days, probably being studied by those research freaks. Please, free me of that world, but bring my kind and magic back."

Blair smiled with the knowledge he wasn't nearly as innocent as he sounded. "I'm not convinced that the magic left is strong enough to pull both the vayen aray and rokians from there, and I also don't think you'll behave yourself."

Darkadus wasn't manipulating this time; he was just helpless. "Please, what do I say to them?"

"By the power of what remains of the curse, you will never set another curse on anyone for as long as you live," Blair stated, ignoring him and watching the mark on his arm fade. "And you will go back where you came from, never to set foot on this world ever again."

The mark of the curse was gone now and Darkadus slowly grew transparent like how Rocanu was when Blair first met him. "Blair, no! Don't do this!" he continued calling out until it was more and more muffled with time. "I don't want to die in that world! This is a death sentence!" And finally, he faded out until he was no more.

That was it. Darkadus was finally gone for good. Blair was able to breathe easy now. The ancient power of the rokians vanished from her homeland. Her world was safe.

The healers scattered about in their work again and Blair turned back toward the table. Finhaus and Kielle were now nearby as well. The healers left a soft roll of cloth under Queriven's head. He finally held the composure of his old self. "How do you feel?" Blair asked him.

Queriven groaned. "Not too well, I must admit, but that's hardly important right now, isn't it?" He looked up at the passing healers. "They're all over the place. I don't think they really know what they're doing."

Blair laughed. They probably didn't. After all, how do you treat someone who just came back from the dead? She kept the notion to herself though. Now wasn't time to tell him how he was brought back.

The excitement and stress were gone and now the elf was quiet. Slight perspiration was visible over his skin and he seemed to be shivering a little. Queriven excused his discomfort and weakened state. "I have terrible pain all over, especially in my chest and head. They said it would be best if I rest for a while, so they gave me some medicine."

Blair smiled and wished she could express all of her various thoughts to him, but she held on. There'll be time for that eventually, but not now. "I'm so glad to see you again. I was so worried."

Queriven blinked, a look of confusion falling on his face again. "How long have I been out?"

Blair exchanged a pondering look to Finhaus and Kielle, but neither one of them gave her an answer. "It's been a little while," she finally replied.

"That dagger was pretty deep in if I remember right, though maybe I don't. After all, there's nothing where the dagger was. Did I make that all up in my mind?"

Again, Blair hesitated. She resorted to pulling back a stray hair from his face. "It's hard to say what happened over the last few days, but you're fine now."

His question was not answered, but he accepted it for the moment. He then closed his eyes. He was already growing tired.

Immediately after Queriven's awakening, the city seemed to carry a bit more hope, even though times were still rough. Blair continued staying with Kielle, though she visited Queriven as often as she was able. He was quickly moved to the treatment room in the Center Tree with the rest of the wounded. He was weak for a long time and couldn't be moved much, especially without help, but he kept a positive attitude. As a matter of fact, Blair's never seen him more joyful. The elf smiled and laughed often. It was like he had nothing more to fear in the world. The tense situations of his past were behind him now, and the love from family and friends surrounded him again.

They gave the rest of the fallen a proper burial in the traditions of the Aven Forest. The whole forest shed tears over the loss as they were returned to the earth where they came, but Blair expected more talk over Foradue's choice to resurrect the elf who left the forest twenty years ago. For now, it seemed a few of them questioned his decision.

Shortly after, Blair returned to the Center Tree. This time though, she came to return the opal she remembered she still had.

The guard at the door let her in quickly. Blair hardly raised any concern or suspicion. She climbed the long stair with the wrapped stone in hand and saw Foradue sitting at his desk. He greeted her as she took the stone to its place on the shelf. "There you are. I was wondering when you were bringing that back," he greeted, raising his old eyes from the open scroll on his desk.

"Sorry," Blair answered. "I've been quite distracted in the last few days."

He waved the concern away and stood up. "It's fine, thank you. I heard that Queriven has been recovering pretty well."

Blair nodded. "It'll take him a while, but he can take all the time he needs. It was powerful magic."

Foradue agreed. "Yes, I'm certainly amazed Darkadus had enough to pull it off." He cleared his voice and looked her dead in the eyes. "I was wanting to talk to you about something. Are you thinking about heading home soon?"

Blair wasn't really sure what he was getting at and didn't know how to answer. She was already thinking about returning home for a while to see her parents, but she wasn't really planning on living there again.

"Forgive me. That was a little direct." Foradue placed a hand over his heart and a mysterious twinkle shone in his eyes. "You've been a great inspiration to the elves and the forest, and even to me. For many years, I held a lot of blame over

Fairdraisha because of her king, but you remind me of the good there is in your kin. I was actually wanting to say you may come back anytime. You are a part of the forest now and I'm sure the elves you've befriended would say the same thing. You can stay for as long as you like." He smiled at her blossoming face.

Blair was ecstatic. She nearly hopped up and down with excitement. "I don't have to leave? This is wonderful! I would love to stay!"

He nodded, satisfied with her answer. "Very well then. Welcome to the family." Then, before Blair exploded with joy, he held up a finger. "We must tell your friend Queriven because I'm also letting him stay. Shall we pay him a visit?"

Blair's jaw dropped and Foradue already had his answer. Blair followed him to the stairs. Foradue was slow and in no hurry, but his movements were full of grace. He was old even for an elf, but he was just as sharp physically and emotionally regardless. He talked casually in that smooth forest accent, but Blair was listening only piece by piece. Her heart was racing with the possibilities of an exciting future with the elves. Deep down, she wasn't very surprised Foradue called off both her and Queriven's exile but hearing him say the words was more inspiring than she'd thought it'll be.

Before she knew it, they were at the door to the treatment room, and Foradue pushed it open. There was a line of beds all the way down, and more counters filled with even more herbs and supplies. The injured from the last battle at the trading post alone took almost every single bed, but she already knew which one Queriven was in.

He was actually resting in a bed close to the front and to the right. He was lying on his back, his head slightly propped up on a pillow. At first, Blair thought he was asleep, but his eyes opened at the sound of the door. He seemed even more in shock when he spotted Foradue behind her and he seemed embarrassed that the leader of Aven Forest saw him in his weak condition. Queriven slowly sat up and greeted the two.

Foradue's features didn't change. "Good afternoon. Are you

feeling any better?"

"Uh," Queriven shrugged. "It isn't that terrible, I suppose. All I do now is sleep. They told me I have a pretty bad head injury, so they won't let me do anything. It hurts to breathe a lot of times too." His beautiful voice was uneven with exhaustion and stress.

Foradue smiled. "At least you're here and you'll live."

The sight of Blair moving past him to stand by the side of the bed brought up his change of subject. "I was just telling Blair here that both of you are free from exile. You may stay here as long as you wish."

Just like Blair, Queriven's jaw dropped and he bowed his head. "Thank you, Sir. You have no idea what this means to me."

Foradue folded his hands behind his back and took a step away from the door as a healer came inside. "I was also wanting to give you a job offer. Clearly, you are no longer the coward you used to be. After I heard about your sacrifice at the old trading post, I wondered if you would like to become a soldier under the Center Tree." He chuckled. "Who knows? Maybe you can reach First Knight status again?"

The blunt remark didn't seem to bother Queriven much, but he lifted his head. His face was more solemn now than a second ago. "That's a kind offer, but I don't really know what to say. That was during a difficult time in my life. When I became a knight, revenge was first on my mind. It was very dishonest to those around me. I shouldn't have been so focused on myself. Maybe it'll be best if I start over and pursue something else for my future." Suddenly, he became shy again and wanted to clarify. "I want to thank you for giving me the chance, but I'm not running away this time. I just think it might be better."

Foradue didn't seem disappointed, though he was quite surprised by his answer. "That seems like a wise answer. I'm convinced I made the right choice by letting you stay. Feel free to pursue wherever your heart leads you, but let me know if you ever change your mind." Foradue bowed low and gave them a farewell as he left through the door.

Blair stayed and sat down on the corner of the bed by Queriven's ankles. "You are my second visitor this day," he remarked to her. "Finhaus was here earlier. I haven't seen Kielle yet, but she's probably still sleeping at this time."

Blair was quiet for a short while. She only wanted to listen to him talk. Finally, she studied his shining emerald eyes. "You seem more awake. Are you still a little confused over what happened when you woke up?"

"Ah, it is a lot to take in." Queriven hid his nervousness by running a hand over his arm. "Sirnah told me what really happened at the trading post."

"He did?" Blair asked, surprised he seemed so calm.

"Yes, he told me Darkadus killed me on the field and you reversed the curse on him to bring me back. I never thought you would be so reckless." His eyes dropped from hers and he studied the folds of his blanket. "It's interesting though because I didn't even realize he was in the room when I woke up. I suppose I was just too upset to see him." He looked up at her again. His face shed a piece of that fright he had those few days ago. "I was so scared. That must have been the most frightening thing that ever happened to me. I didn't know where or even who I was. It was like I was in a deep sleep, only different. There were no dreams or thoughts, and even the deepest of sleep carries with it some sort of awareness."

Blair listened carefully, even when he paused and his voice grew quieter. "I was just suddenly there and when I realized it, a wave of agony hit me. My lungs were burning. I was fighting just to remember how to breathe. There were so many people around me."

Blair placed a hand over his. "I was scared too. I don't think you recognized me at first and I was worried you wouldn't."

Queriven exhaled the tension from the memory and gripped her hand gently. "Anyway, I may have heard from my youngest brother that you're leaving. Surely, you won't now that you know you can stay?"

Blair gave him the complete truth. "I'm just visiting my parents. I need to see them and put their worries to rest, but

I'm coming back."

He gave her that suspicious look, like he was silently asking her if she really was coming back. "That hardly seems fair considering my condition. You'll have to help me sneak out if you're planning on this trip soon. I've been healing really slowly, and they told me it'll be a while before I build my strength back." He looked at her with a mischievous glint in his eye. "And don't ask Sirnah what happened when I tried to prove them wrong."

"I'm not asking you to come with me!" Blair retorted. "Just stay here and rest. We have plenty of time for more adventures when you can carry yourself again."

There was a slightly uncomfortable pause and he leaned in toward her. "You know, I didn't think you would go back there after everything we've been through together. What are you going to do now? Go back to raising goats for the rest of your life? Maybe settle down with...what's his name? ...That Hector?"

Blair shot at him, her voice rising a pitch higher. "I promise I'm coming back! And I already told you. I don't love him like that. I love you!"

Queriven didn't say anything and allowed her own words to sink in. Suddenly aware of what she just admitted out loud, her stomach twisted around and she looked at Queriven for help. The outright grin on his face suggested he wasn't bothered. Blair rolled her eyes and blushed. That was probably even the response he was looking for. He chuckled heartily before a coughing fit interrupted him. He groaned and pressed a hand against his chest. "Good," he answered when he was able. "Now, since I'm unable to see you off, I'll just have to make sure I can meet you at the border when you arrive back home. We'll have a lot to teach you, like how to reach the city on your own."

She shook her head at him but smiled. Looks like he still had his old stubbornness of all things. Blair gave his shoulder a gentle shove and stood up from the bed. Once again, he called for her attention. "Remember your promise. If you stay out too long, I'll go seeking for you starting with Bailiese. Trust me, Hector would not be too happy to see me on that day."

Blair returned him a look filled with playful danger and wished him a loving farewell. The watchful elves around her didn't stop her from showing her feelings for Queriven any longer. Because of a miracle, she had him back and she wasn't going to take that for granted even for a moment.

CHAPTER THIRTY-EIGHT
SECOND CHANCES

Inspired after her latest visit with Queriven, Blair packed her things that very night and set off in the morning. The air was fresh with a chilly breeze and full of scents of autumn crisp spices. Somehow, the rolling plains beyond the forest border were colder, like the hug of the trees provided warmth or at least kept the biting wind away.

Blair couldn't be more excited to see her family after she departed Aven Forest at first, but the looming familiarity of her old home sparked a little more hesitance. Everything was so different now and this no longer seemed like the same little village she once lived in. She entered her old streets with hardly a bat of the eye and people around her stared. They were unsure if Blair had returned, or if a stranger like her has taken her place. Those who did recognize her after a while pointed and wove. She returned it but didn't stop moving. She had a particular destination in mind.

It already took her a few days to reach the town after she left the forest, and the trip left her tired and hungry. The memory of home and her mother's cooking came into her mind. She was in for a treat tonight, she assured herself. She could almost taste supper from here.

Finally, her lovely home appeared before her. Smoke was rising from the chimney. Her parents were home and more likely, her father was as well judging by the tint in the sky.

Blair stopped at the door and swallowed the unease rising in her chest. Suddenly, she wished Queriven was beside her, supporting her and encouraging her to go on. Her hands were shaking and she couldn't summon the strength to press forward. What should she say after so long? Could they even believe what has happened to her over the last year? She wasn't ready to see them, but she also knew it was now or never.

She raised a trembling hand and knocked carefully on the door.

There was stillness and Blair's surroundings vanished as she realized someone was coming to the door. There was a click and the frame swung inward just a bit. The woman on the other side saw a peculiar stranger looking at her with bubbling hazel eyes. The girl held strong independence, even if she didn't take note of the peeking spear on her back. The clothes were foreign in design, showcasing the rich colors of the earth. The greens and browns only heightened the aroma of a rich forest. "Mom?" the girl asked.

Isabelle pushed the door away and stepped closer. Her sad eyes held so many questions. She looked the girl up and down. "Blair? Is that you? What happened, Sweetheart?" The woman was already stirring to tears and Blair wrapped her tight.

"I'm so sorry. I should have told you about all this sooner."

Isabelle answered as she sobbed onto Blair's shoulder. "I shouldn't have pushed you so hard. I wish I had encouraged your dreams."

Finally, the woman pulled away and gripped the young spear-wielder's arms. "Please come inside. Your father would be so pleased to see you. You can tell us everything over supper."

Blair followed her inside. Everything was just as she remembered it. Duncan exclaimed upon seeing her and hugged her tightly. "It's been so hard without you. We're so glad you're back." He pushed her back and looked over her again.

He even took another look at the weapon on her back. "And just look at you! You're so grown up! I feel like an old man welcoming my daughter back from battle."

Blair giggled, but tears were lining her eyes. The room was dim, as if she was merely dreaming. Her confusing dance of emotion caught her tongue and spun her breathless. She didn't know what she wanted to say first. "I missed you, Father. I really missed both of you."

Isabelle came forward again and laid a hand on her shoulder. "Where have you been this whole time? We want the full story."

"You know," Duncan added before Blair could answer, "Hector came to us back in the spring in a big panic. He said he saw you right outside town with an elf."

"We're surprised you made it back all right," her mother said. "He told us you trusted him, but we weren't so sure. We thought he might have hurt you."

Finally, Blair broke through and backed away from her smothering parents. "Queriven wouldn't hurt me. If it wasn't for him, I wouldn't be here right now."

Her parents went silent and they looked at each other for support. The evidence was too strong. Queriven was sincere; even they couldn't deny that now. It was Duncan who spoke next. "Perhaps... We were wrong about elves?" Again, he looked to Isabelle, but she merely shrugged and replaced the conflict with a wide smile.

"You must be starving. Have a seat at the table and eat," she said. Blair was happy to oblige and hurried to sit at the table. The warm smells made her stomach growl and she dug in as soon as her mother served her. Duncan laughed in response. The food was rich and tasted just as amazing as it smelled. Once Blair swallowed the first bite, she began her story right from the beginning. Everything went all right and her parents listened without interrupting. It wasn't until she came near the start of the curse when she hesitated. The curious expressions from her mother and father only made her feel more nervous.

"Why didn't you tell us about this?" Duncan asked in a nonjudgmental way. "You didn't have to carry that on your own. We would have helped you."

Blair took fewer bites of her steaming food and she refused their stares. This is what made her hesitant in coming home in the first place. It was time to admit her mistakes. "I guess I was so ashamed of falling for it that I couldn't tell you. Both of you told me to stay far away and I didn't. I felt like it was my fault that I was cursed. You were right, and I was wrong about pursuing him..."

"Well, everything turned right in the end," Isabelle added as she sliced at the meat on her plate. "He wasn't even an elf after all and you did have help. I'm so glad you weren't alone. I can't possibly be mad at you after everything that happened."

Blair breathed the tension from her shoulders. She was finally free of the shame from leaving home alone. She was able to express herself without scold or judgment. Blair continued with her long tale until the sun was gone from the sky hours ago. "I've made an important decision after my experience," she concluded. Both parents leaned over the clean table. "I'm going back to the forest for good." She paused for the message to sink in and looked at her parents on either side of her. They were just as shocked as she imagined they would be. If there was the possibility all this might upset them, this would be the time. Her mother exclaimed aloud and Duncan sat back in his seat, seeming lost in his own mind. Blair didn't wait for them to speak. "Queriven loves me and I feel like I belong with him there."

Another moment of silence. Isabelle folded her arms over the table and slumped, though Blair still couldn't tell what she was thinking. "I never thought it would come to this," she whispered to no one in particular.

Duncan was the first one to speak directly to Blair. "It surprises me too. I would have liked if you were coming home to stay, but I understand," he answered, placing a hand over his wife's arm. "You're so different now. It's easy to see how the forest affected you. If this is what you choose, then I'll accept it happily. I still don't know a lot about the Aven Forest, but I feel you have a better understanding of it now."

That brought another sigh from Isabelle, but she lifted her head. "I can't make those decisions for you anymore. I can't control your dreams; I can only support them." Finally, she reached over and took her daughter's hands in her own. "I wish you the best in the world, but will you do your poor mother a last favor and come back sometime to see us?"

That was something Duncan could agree on. The idea had him on the edge of his chair. "Yes, please do! And bring this Queriven along with you. I would like to thank him personally for his honesty in keeping you safe."

Blair beamed from ear to ear. She wasn't the only one who changed. She never imagined she would see her parents like this before. "I'll see what I can do. I promise."

That answer pleased them and Isabelle stood up. It was hours after bedtime and they were all tired. They showed Blair to her old room shortly after and allowed her to rest.

Blair stayed home with her parents for a few days before missing the forest. She helped her father with the goats like old times and visited with her friends. She spent every moment with the people she loved the most and never took it for granted. And when it was finally time to leave, her parents wished her a farewell and let her go back home easily. The support her family gave her helped her on her way back with no regrets for the past. If it wasn't for Darkadus and his curse, Blair would have never discovered her love for Queriven and the forest. This is what she wanted for her future.

The trees were the rich color of fire and she made it back home with plenty of time before the first snow. She couldn't surpass her wide grin when Queriven was waiting ever patiently at the border for her. Blair broke into a run and didn't stop until she was in his open arms. The elf brushed her hair back gently and Blair tugged him in tight, expressing her love with the kiss they never shared at the Starlight Festival last summer. Then, without a spoken word between the two, they disappeared in the trees of Aven Forest. They were heading home.

Glossary

Aen Vidwal (Ay-in Vid-wal)
A young scholar living in the Limadia Estate. He inherited his ancestors' knowledge on rokian magic, but is content with his estate as is.

Anita (An-eet-ah)
A bard traveling around the land with her family. She's blind, but has a beautiful voice.

Aswren (Ahs-ren)
An elf from Aven Forest, once a good friend of Queriven's.

Aven Forest (Ay-vin)
A large forest taking up the southeastern side of the continent. Home to the elves.

Bailiese (Bale-eese)
A little village of humans in the heart of Fairdraisha. The village has always specialized in raising goats for as long as people could remember.

Barram (Bar-um)
He used to work under King Brenmor to ambush wealthy travelers on the road. He stopped after the king betrayed him.

Blair Tripps (Blare Trips)
The main protagonist. She's a young girl who likes to daydream and read books. She always wanted an adventure though she's happy when she's home as well.

Connell (Con-ul)
A young man traveling with a caravan of bards. Anita and Kain are his parents.

Dakru (Dahk-roo)
An elvish mage living in Sylinna. He used to be a friend of Queriven until his fiancé, Fia, passed away.

Darkadus (Dar-kay-dus)
A rokian seeking to free his people. He's confident in his abilities and he knows he'll do what it takes to help them.

Doulan (Doo-lan)
A stuffy old man in service to the young Aen Vidwal. His master is always trying to break the rules to help him open up a little.

Duncan Tripps (Dun-can Trips)
Blair's father. His family has raised goats in Bailiese for many centuries.

Dunverhart (Dun-ver-hart)
Capital city of Fairdraisha where King Brenmor can be found. It's a bustling city full of guards and soldiers under his rule.

Dyara (Dee-ar-ah)
A little town far on the southwestern coast of the continent. It was destroyed by the rokians over a thousand years ago and was never rebuilt. Also known as the "End of the Road".

Fairdraisha (Fair-dray-sha)
The kingdom of Raek Brenmor. It's on the same continent as the Aven Forest, though the people refuse to mix with the elves.

Raek Brenmor (Ray-ik Bren-mor)
The king of Fairdraisha. He's arrogant and a little too young and inexperienced to rule. Rumor says he jeopardizes his own people by hiring highwaymen to steal from the wealthy.

Fia (Fee-ah)
An elf warrior who was under the rule of the Center Tree. She was also Dakru's lover before she passed away many years ago.

Finhaus (Fin-haws)
A happy-go-lucky elf on the outskirts of Sylinna. He works on an elvish farm though it's often complicated by all the animals who come to see him. Middle brother of Kielle, Sirnah, and Queriven.

Fergus (Fer-gus)
The driver and caretaker of Anita's caravan of bards. He's often seen as the "mother" of the group.

Foradue (For-ah-doo)
The king of Aven Forest. He's an elder of his people and remembers many lines of the Brenmor family.

Gistal (Guy-stal)
The trusted advisor under Raek Brenmor. He comes under a long line of servitude under Fairdraisha's rulers.

Hector (Hek-ter)

Once a blacksmith in training in Dunverhart, he moved to Bailiese to help his master recover from a grave illness. He quickly fell in love with the village and has a crush on Blair.

Isabelle Tripps (Is-ah-bel Trips)

Blair's mother. A simple woman who wants the best for Blair and her safety, though this often leads to her trying to take too much control.

Kain (Kane)

Husband to Anita. He's often seen as the leader of the group even though that more belongs to his wife.

Kerna (Ker-nah)

A child barely in her teen years. Despite the village of Lyfihana being mostly human, Kerna is a selkie from nearby waters. She fears anyone who's either not of her kin or who's not from the island.

Kielle (Kee-el)

The current first knight of Sylinna's Center Tree. She's the older sister of Finhaus and Sirnah, but younger sister to Queriven. She often saw Queriven as a rival growing up and tried to copy him.

Limadia Estate (Lim-ah-dia)

Aen Vidwal's family owns the estate, land, and workers. It's far from any of the towns and relies on merchants traveling down the highly dangerous roads to reach it in Taleena Hills.

Lininea (Lin-in-ee-ah)

The elvish word for Mulicer, a flower that grows in late spring and used for various medicines.

Lyfihana (Lif-ee-on-ah)

The name of the towering mountain on the biggest island south of Fairdraisha. This place used to be the home of the vayen aray, but is now only the home to a small village near the shore.

Lynny (Lin-ee)

Known as the comic relief of Anita's caravan. He sees his group as a big family and is often trying to make them smile, even if that means embarrassing himself in the process.

Medahai (Med-ah-hi)
Medahai is only a young teenager who was recruited on the Sapphire Reef. He was homeless before, so he appreciated the opportunity to work even though the pirates liked to bully him.

Mitmaj (Mit-maj)
A troublesome unseelie fairy. The rogue patrols the forest wilderness in attempts of finding new allies to use against the seelie nation.

Mulicer (Moo-lis-er)
A tall white flower with thin stripes of lavender in the petals. It is often seen as an unremarkable weed, but can be used as medicine for different rashes or soreness of the skin.

Nekene (Neh-keen)
The first mate under Yusen Nashögan. Sometimes he's hard to deal with, but he makes up for it with his open attitude and strict loyalty.

Penacha (Pen-ach-ah)
Often seen as the sister city to Dyara. The towns were close together and often had the same goals or likeness. Unlike Dyara, Penacha is still up and growing in population.

Queriven (Kwer-iv-en)
An elf of mystery. He's lived in Fairdraisha for a very long time because he's avoiding his old homeland. He relates to Blair's struggles.

Rocanu (Raw-can-oo)
One of the oldest vayen aray. His wisdom spans way beyond his looks. He is very open and loves people, even those of different species.

Rokian (Roke-ee-in)
Tribal people now living in another dimension after they were banished along with the vayen aray. They're known for their territorial power and bright silver skin.

Sirnah (Ser-nah)
A young herbalist living and working in the Center Tree. He takes great passion in what he does and is very calm in the presence of danger. Youngest brother to Finhaus, Kielle, and Queriven.

Sylinna (Sil-leen-ah)

The capitol city of Aven Forest. This is where the Center Tree is. Foradue overlooks the state and protection of the entire forest from here.

Taleena Hills (Tal-leen-ah)

The name for the hills surrounding the Limadia Estate. They're very dangerous and is often packed with terrible thieves and highwaymen.

Tallin (Tall-in)

The captain of the Enchantress. He's a good man who worked many decades in the business of Seadrake. Though he works with a rather big company, he dislikes the king and soldiers of Fairdraisha.

Yusen Nashögan (Yoo-sin Nash-oo-gan)

A pirate captain from a far southern land. He's been in piracy since he's been a youngman so he came to value his men and ship.

Vayen aray (Vay-in Ar-ray)

The winged heroes once said to have rescued Fairdraisha by banishing the rokians. They are nothing but a legend now and the only proof they existed is the ruins of their old home on Lyfíhana. Vayen aray are immortal and never look older than young adults.

This page marks the end of this story. If you liked it, share with others! You can leave a review online or tell me you liked it on my social media.

Follow @KristaJainAuthor on Facebook
And @KristaJAuthor on Twitter.

Check out the blog on www.kristajain.com for more content, including short stories.

If people loved this story, I'll add more adventures to the series!

Lightning Source UK Ltd.
Milton Keynes UK
UKHW040929180920
370091UK00001BA/63